THE TRELLIS

A NOVEL

BY

JOOLS CANTOR

For S.M.C.P.

The one who plants and the one who waters have one purpose, and they will each be rewarded according to their own labor. For we are coworkers in God's service; you are God's field, God's building.

—Paul the Apostle, 1 Corinthians 3:8-9

53 C.E.

You listening, Bog? Is a computer one of Your creatures?

—Robert A. Heinlein, *The Moon Is a Harsh Mistress*

1966 C.E.

Erst kommt das Fressen, dann kommt die Moral.

—Bertolt Brecht, *Die Dreigroschenoper*

1928 C.E.

1. Alarm

No good would come of this dream. He had forgotten himself, his own name. He scampered through ill-lit tunnels, the damp and stale air creeping against his skin. It was a dream, he knew that by now. But the slick stones under his feet, the musty breath of the Earth's core pushing against his progress, felt more important than any reality. Drums echoed far away and within his skull but not anywhere in between. And then, the passageway and all that it contained pounded with a crisp, firm voice, a sound that grabbed and shook him.

"We are still cavemen, but we build our own caves."

Gerald Ford Jones woke to these words in the citrine glow of his fourteenth-floor condominium. Sunbeams punctured the troubled air over what was left of Lake Michigan then ricocheted into his fantastic little cave.

"We are still cavemen, but we build our own caves."

Gerald inhaled sharply and winced away any temptations to fall back to sleep. "Alarm off."

"Please repeat. We are still cavemen, but we build our own caves."

"Access settings." He was in no mood to argue with his alarm clock.

"Please repeat the mantra to access settings."

"We are still cavemen," the only potential caveman in the room grumbled. "But we build our own caves."

"Good morning, Gerald. What settings would you like to modify?"

"Disable Mantra Alarm Application."

"Mantra Alarm Application disabled. Mantra Alarm Application would like to know why it was disabled. Would you like to leave a comment?"

Gerald paused to collect his thoughts. He knew he did not

appreciate whatever it was he had just then experienced, but he couldn't argue with the results. He sat upright, awake and reflecting on the words that had shaken him free from a night full of running through dark corridors in meaningless dreamscapes. Maybe he still was a caveman. He'd have to think on it.

"No," he sighed. "Give it three out of five stars."

Gerald stood up and walked across the room to his kitchen counter. He turned on his coffee machine manually, circumventing any protests it might raise. He performed thirty push-ups and started his sit-ups, giving up when the coffee announced itself with a feeble gurgle.

He stood naked, staring at what was left of the Chicago skyline backlit by that surreal honey-lemon morning light. The city was beautiful despite everything it had endured. Beautiful despite all the maintenance, all the upkeep that it had gone without. Still probably the best skyline, he guessed, in the western hemisphere. The single glaring insult, in Gerald's estimation, was stationed slightly north of the John Hancock building and now scintillated with the morning's pinks and oranges. Officially christened the Jefferson Trellis, it was also known as the Hanging Gardens, the Spigot, the Piña Plateada, the Disco Ball, the Crystal Palace, the "Most Beautiful Building of the Century" per the American Institute of Architects, and answered only to revered silence from the now-infrequent tourists. Gerald knew it by a more sinister sobriquet: Work.

"Wigwam," Gerald called to his empty room. "Car to work in twenty-five minutes."

"Car scheduled for 6:03 a.m.," the room answered back. "Estimated arrival at work 6:27 a.m."

"Thank you," Gerald said, pointlessly.

"You're welcome," his room replied. Manners never hurt.

Showered, shaved, and now at street level, Gerald waited for his car to arrive. Sure enough, at 6:02 his bean-shaped chariot appeared with his name flashing on the windscreen. It recognized him and opened the door to its last available seat. Gerald situated himself and turned off his seat privacy as the car accelerated towards the Eisenhower Expressway. The other three passengers had left their privacy screens on, extinguishing Gerald's dim hopes for chitchat.

He listened to the news instead. If someone did want to talk, right then or later in the day, he'd have something to talk about. Singapore changing sides again, negotiations in New Vientiane. Construction delays at Guayaquil, CENTAF bonds jump as Libreville Elevator proceeds on schedule. Bus crash in Pakistan kills forty-one. He stopped listening. The content was depressing, but even worse, it was all about somewhere else. Someone else, really. Not America, not the Six Counties, and definitely not Gerald.

At 6:24, the car deposited Gerald Ford Jones at the basement sub-level two, public drop-off entrance to the Jefferson Trellis. He placed his ID badge on the outside of his blazer and walked the 350-yard security pedway with the confidence of a man who had done so exactly 748 times before. He smiled at the bright blue security guards, hiding nothing from the scanners and turrets behind them. What would he have *to* hide, he thought. That he didn't finish his sit-ups? That it had been weeks since he checked in with his mother? That he had a strange dream?

Security cleared, Gerald waited for the elevator to lift his 184 pounds of flesh, bone, and this morning's coffee onto his floor some 370 feet above. Once there, Gerald's own two legs carried him down the halls of the thirty-third floor. It was quiet and still dim. Only the soft hum of a vacuum cleaner around some distant corner accompanied him to his office.

Unready to settle in, he faced west through the angled rhomboid windows behind his desk. Gerald watched the Trellis's purple shadow grow shorter over Walter Payton College Prep as the sun rose. Reflections from the angled panes created iridescent starbursts in the shadow below. It did look like a pineapple, he thought, or some sort of multifaceted, corrugated Fabergé egg. And he was in it, whatever that meant. In the distance, Gerald could see his apartment building, a nondescript number among the other unmarked grayish-white tombstones dotting the Near West Side.

"Mr. Jones?" A nervous voice pulled Gerald's wandering mind back into his office, accompanied by the now-much-closer whir of a vacuum cleaner.

Gerald turned to see a thin and sad-eyed teenager. The boy was too small for his whitish-gray jumpsuit and much too small for the vacuum strapped to his back. Gerald guessed he was Puerto Rican or Moroccan or something, but he wasn't good with those things. "Yes?"

The boy tried to smile, exposing an unfortunate but endearing overbite. He flipped a switch on the vacuum's wand, heavy in his hands, cutting the noise as he steadied himself under the weight of the machine on his back. "Mr. Gerald Ford Jones?"

"Yes, that's me." Gerald smiled back as his mind turned to find what this poor kid could want. "What can I do for you?"

"I'm . . . sorry." A tube on the boy's vacuum wand erupted with a sound like a sledgehammer against granite as metal punctured the climate-controlled office air, then Gerald's clothes, then his abdomen. Flesh, bone, and this morning's coffee erupted onto the angled rhomboid windows behind Gerald as he crumpled to the floor. As he lay there, dying, Gerald's mind spun with the sounds of rapid footfalls in dark corridors. Somewhere in the distance, an alarm was screaming. He had a thought, but then it left him. And at 6:41 that August morning, Gerald Ford Jones announced his departure from the world with a feeble gurgle.

2. Run

"Debbie, where are you?"

"I'm at work."

"Are you alone?"

"Yes." Debbie paused. "Why?"

"Are you sitting down?" The voice was tense. Something was off.

"No, I had to step out of a session to take this. What is it?"

"This job opening. Just posted an hour ago. You'd have a real shot at it."

Debbie Peck stood breathlessly, choosing her words with cautious enthusiasm. "That's great news. What can I do?"

"They already have your resume." Her recruiter's voice was eager and demanding, selling every sentence. "They like your numbers and want to meet you as soon as possible."

"I'll be available. Where are they located?"

"Here in Chicago."

"Really?"

"Yeah. You sitting down yet?"

"No."

"Well, hold on to something. It's the Jefferson Group." The capillaries near the skin where Debbie's neck met her breastbone blossomed as beads of sweat formed on her upper lip. "The interview is tomorrow morning."

Debbie hesitated only enough to communicate that she was not rushing, that she understood and digested the information placed before her. "I'll be there. Send me the details as soon as you can."

"Will do. You can do this, Debbie. We know you can."

The call cut off as Debbie steadied herself under the weight of this news. Four years with these headhunters, countless applications, rejections, weeks of hunger, months of silence, and finally, *this*. She stood wide-eyed and breathed shallowly, dryly swallowing with thoughts of a feast after this famine. The Jefferson Group does real business, she thought. They make real differences. They add real value. And they paid really, *really* well.

The sweat on her lip chilled as the speaker above the door jarred her back to the present. "Debbie Peck, report to mediation room 7B." Back to work, for now. She would worry about the interview later.

She turned to pull at the door she had only just exited, but the handle wouldn't twist. She reached for, but did not find, her security badge. She patted her pockets hurriedly to locate it. A muffled thud came from behind the door.

This, Debbie gathered, was not good. "Not good" was the status quo at the Six Counties Detention and Conflict Resolution Center. She reached into the holster concealed against the small of her back and drew the stun gun and pepper spray.

"Debbie Peck, report to mediation room 7B."

She slammed the intercom button next to the door. "I need immediate backup at mediation room 7B."

"Roger, Debbie. What's the situation?"

"Got locked out."

"Again?"

"Yes, *again*. Must've lifted my badge."

Debbie leaned against the door. She could hear more muffled thuds, abrupt vocalizations, and other indicia that a fight had broken out among the gang members she had just been mediating.

"Kay. Who's in there?"

"Uh, just a sec." What session was it, Debbie thought. Her 1:30? No, 11:30 went long. Teachers Union was at 9:00, Tinley Park Militia at 11:30 . . . or was that yesterday? The door knocked once, interrupting her thought. It didn't sound like a knuckle knocking, or a fist. More like a heavy skull. Merrimakers.

"Berwyn Merrimakers and the Cicero Chamber of Commerce."

"Are these guys dangerous, Debs?"

The noise on the other side of the door evaporated. Debbie wedged her foot against its baseplate and braced herself. She pressed the metal teeth of her stun gun against the metal door handle, waiting for it to turn.

"They're human beings, Jeff," she explained. "Yes, they're dangerous."

Under the stark halogen lighting of the employee locker room, Debbie's black eyes looked worse than they felt. A pink scratch fanned into two purple-black triangles from where a flying chair had clipped the bridge of her nose. This was an issue, she thought, for the interview. She could cover it up or leave it for sympathy points.

Jeff Martinez opened the door cautiously. "Hey, Debs. You want some time?"

"No, it's fine." Debbie crinkled her nose, trying to smile. "I'm not supposed to be in here anyway."

Jeff took his helmet off and sat in front of his locker. "'Sposed to. Lotta 'sposed to's today. I wasn't 'sposed to let you get hit with a chair, so you know, we're even."

"I was supposed to duck, or something. I just need your sinks to clean this up."

Jeff unstrapped his shin guards, knee pads, and boots, souring the air with the smell of sweat. "If you temps stopped hogging all the water you could have sinks like us." He smiled widely enough to show the gap where his bicuspids should have been. "Sorry you got hit, Debs. Happens to the best of us."

Debbie turned back to the mirror and stretched her jaw, looking for further damage. "I've been a temp for three and a half years. Thought I'd get a sink by now."

"One day. Keep at it." Jeff, now down to his shorts and undershirt, sprayed deodorant over himself and the crumpled contents of his locker. They exchanged a glance, acknowledging that this was not really okay, but that "not really okay" was an improvement on the status quo. They lacked frivolties like space, privacy, and sinks. "One day, if you work hard,"—Jeff slapped the paunch that slipped below his sweat-stained undershirt —"you'll be just like me."

"Maybe sooner than you think. Got an interview tomorrow."

Jeff's eyes opened wide and his mouth pulled into a flat,

impressed frown. "Nice! When'd that happen?"

"Was taking the call when I got locked out."

He pointed to her nose. "That's what you get when you take personal calls on the clock." He pointed to the gaps in his teeth again. "Was talking to my wife when I lost these. Is the job here? I didn't see anything posted."

Debbie grimaced. "It's at the Jefferson Group."

"No way . . ." Jeff turned to approach Debbie in his excitement, hesitated, and realizing he was a half-dressed, fully married man a dozen years her senior in a locker room, sat down. "No way. That's great. Your nose . . ."

"I'll figure it out."

"Yeah you will, I know you will. That's great though. Don't stress about it, they can always smell it on you if you're worried about it."

"Thanks."

"I mean you know all that, you know. Me telling you to be cool, not sweat it in an interview. You're the mediator. You tell *me* to be cool."

Debbie breathed deeply, smiled slightly, and waited a few seconds.

"That's what I'm talking about!" Jeff said. "Don't even have to say anything, you just make things cool. Calms it all down. You leave the room for a minute and the chairs start flying. God, your nose. Maybe they'll feel sorry for you! Maybe one of those assholes in *la Piña* will want to rescue you from this pit."

The thought brought a wry smile to Debbie's face, which made her nose hurt. "Thanks. I'll try."

Jeff, now in jeans and his usual western shirt, stood up and fastened his belt. "Maybe try not to smile too much if you're going to make that face every time. You want a ride home? Ez's car is almost here and we can drop you off."

"No thanks. I'm going to blow off some steam on the trail."

"Suit yourself! Be safe and good luck tomorrow!"

As soon as Jeff left the room, Debbie grabbed her things and hurried past the sinks to a shower stall. She hung her bag on the wall behind the showerhead and filled it with her clothes as she carefully undressed. She retrieved three small bottles from her bag and placed them on the shower shelf. Then she hit the faucet to unleash a high-pressure stream of near-scalding, fresh and clean water on her tired head and shoulders. The sensation hypnotized her for a full fifteen seconds before the shower trickled to a stop. She opened up the first bottle and placed it beneath her flaring nostrils. She then closed her eyes and poured its contents—a bottom-shelf tequila that she kept specially for days like this one—into her mouth. She lathered the contents of the next bottle into her mousy brown hair, and the third she scrubbed over her body as the showerhead continued to drip. The shower's mechanical governor clicked incessantly as Debbie stood there, growing cold and bored as she waited, rubbing the hard scar where shrapnel pierced her ear years prior. Finally, after the governor issued its final clunk, Debbie slammed the faucet to unleash another high-pressure stream of hot water to rinse away the dirt and soap from her tired body.

Dressed and now up at street level, Debbie took her evening run on the Lake Shore Path at a leisurely pace, trying not to completely undo the shower she had stolen. Running north towards Morgan Point, she noticed the rusty skeleton of the Silver Spray chattering with seagulls resting their wings. Waves crashed quietly three hundred yards to the east, where Lake Michigan thirstily lapped at the encroaching land. Marsh grasses, gravelly sand, and shallow graves dotted that area between the Lake Shore Path and the new lakeshore proper.

Debbie ran to clear her mind. She couldn't worry about the job interview or everything else if she was worried about balancing all the fine equilibria of a summer evening's run through Chicago after the Fall. To run too fast is to appear desperate, and maybe to trigger the instinct to chase. To run too slow is to appear weak and easy prey. To run off the main paths puts you out of earshot of Good Samaritans, but to run too near the crowds increases the chances of crossing paths with the wrong sort of people. The game was to go unnoticed. The objective was to become background noise. She had perfected this skill her entire life, and she enjoyed it. It also saved her a train ride and a train fare. Though, if the interview went well . . .

As she ran past the Thirty-first Street Harbor Campground,

with RVs and tents nestled against permanently dry-docked sailboats and yachts. Improvised footpaths led down to the water's edge. A few premature campfires burned in the August evening air. As she cut across one such path hugging the eastern side of Northerly Hill and up to the Adler Planetarium, she stopped to look across Monroe Park and take in the skyline. It was, as they said, still beautiful despite everything that it had endured. And poking out above buildings to the right was its crown jewel, the Jefferson Trellis. On its western side, the upward-angled windows reflected the pale pinks and lavenders of a sunset evolving out of view. On its eastern side, its downward-angled windows reflected splashes of all colors hidden in the botanic gardens at its base. Debbie's mind stood still as the cityscape turned slowly against the marbled sky.

"Hey, lady!" a gravelly voice erupted.

Debbie dodged, angling her grappling hand towards the voice and darting her other hand to the stun gun concealed against the small of her back. Her eyes met a fattish, red-faced man in an ill-fitting suit. His eyes were sad and embarrassed, and the pace of his mouth-breathing told Debbie that he was a beggar, not a mugger. He was asking, not demanding, attacking, or worse.

"Five or ten bucks for a veteran, miss?"

"I'm sorry." Debbie exhaled. "I can't today." She smiled slightly and waited a second, and the man turned down the path. She started toward the old Field Museum and then jogged on home.

3. Snag

Detective Melody Jackson stood some 370 feet above the Walter Payton College Prep, staring at a rusty stain that started as someone's morning coffee. It stank of dried blood and fresh plastic, latex, and sawdust from where the EMTs and then janitor had taken their turns. Now it was her turn to tend to Mr. Jones and his office. She and her partner and Six Counties, as long as they could keep the case.

"Bring him in here," she called to her partner's tenders. "Just to the door." Two little men wheeled a large matte black box on a small trolley into Gerald Ford Jones's former office. Melody removed a black pouch velcroed to the box, unzipped it, and emptied its contents onto the trolley. It held a matte black, pistol-gripped apparatus that looked like a supermarket laser scanner, complete with the old-fashioned, curly wire that got snagged in loops at every opportunity. Melody untangled it, inserted its unattached end into her partner's side, and flipped a switch. She leveled the scanner towards the box with a marksman's stance, then turned the business end of the apparatus at herself and pulled the trigger.

"Good evening, Matte. You with me?"

"Good evening, Detective Jackson."

"This is case four zero fiver niner niner, decedent is Gerald Ford Jones. Confirm present time and location."

Matte clicked. "Thirty-third floor of One Jefferson Trellis Drive, Office 37 A, assigned to Gerald Ford Jones, time is 7:04 p.m."

"I'll begin scanning now." Detective Jackson moved to the middle of the room and began a slow, mechanical ballet. Holding the scanner close to her vest, she performed one complete turn before raising the scanner slightly and spinning again. She spiraled the scanner upwards until it was vertical, pointing toward the ceiling. She paused, unraveled herself from the curling cord, and repeated the process downward until she was pointing the scanner directly at her steel-toed oxfords. Then she began moving the scanner up and down each wall, dousing them with invisible lasers and radars that tasted every inch of depressing eggshell paint for anything that might be of interest. She did the same for the green-gray carpet, paying special attention to the portion that had recently been redecorated reddish-brown. She opened each drawer and scanned its contents. For the desktop, she started with the terminal and keyboard and then moved to the clean surface underneath each. As she went, she placed items in a large plastic bin labeled "EVIDENCE" on the cart beneath Matte. She approached the angled windows, focusing on the whistling hole as wide as her pinky that cut straight through to the turbulent air outside the Trellis. She scanned the hole from multiple angles and spoke to the empty room.

"Matte, is this hole consistent with the buckshot recovered from decedent?"

"It is not inconsistent with projectiles recovered from the decedent this afternoon."

"Matte, please calculate entrance and exit velocity from this hole assuming a projectile similar to those removed from decedent this morning."

"Please wait . . ."

Detective Jackson closed her eyes and steadied herself in the middle of the room. She crossed her arms and began to drift into that mindless but sleepless rest perfected by night-watchmen or nurses nearing the end of a thirty-hour shift. She thoughtlessly envisioned her neatly made bed, neglected on the other side of town. And food. And something from her childhood. Before she slipped further away, an unexpected click snapped her back to the waking world as she instinctively trained her scanner on a grim figure grinning in the doorway.

"Whoa whoa whoa, I give up!" He raised his manicured hands up from Matte's off-switch to a feigned surrender. Salt and paprika at his temples put him somewhere near forty, though his red hair was sculpted into a style more appropriate for someone half that age. He was a middle manager of some sort, stinking of hand sanitizer and neutral shoe polish. "How long's this going to take?"

Melody licked her teeth and lowered her useless weapon. "A while. Who are you?"

"Listen dip-shit, 'a while' is not an acceptable answer. We've got—"

"Stop." When Melody severed his string of indignities, the man reeled at her defiance before steadying himself to launch another attack. "I am not your employee or your Pinkerton." The man froze and shifted his gaze, revealing honest confusion. "I am Detective Melody Jackson from the Six Counties Police Department. Do not, and I mean it, *do not*, pull this M-K bullshit on me. Understood?"

He gritted his teeth. "My apologies, Officer. I thought you were one of ours."

"Detective." She stepped over to Matte and flipped him back on. "Who are you?"

"Trey Brodowski. Manager here on thirty-three." Trey extended his hand for a handshake, though his tense muscles, his adversarial posture, made him look more like a wrestler vying for a takedown.

Melody retrieved a business card from her jacket pocket and placed it against his extended fingers, then aimed the scanner at his face from her hip. "Did you manage Mr. Jones before his death this morning?"

Trey grabbed the card and scoffed as he smiled. "Yes." He looked warily at Matte. "Is this thing listening?"

"He sure is. Matte, please continue calculating projectile velocities as requested before shutdown." Matte began to whir quietly, his cooling fans exhaling constantly from his bottomless lungs.

Trey shifted. "I'd prefer to answer questions about my work here in a formal setting and do insist that legal representation be present. The same goes for anyone else you encounter on our premises."

Melody lowered the scanner as tense silence poured into the room. "You got it."

"How old is that anyway?" Trey looked down at the black box on a cart.

"Matte? About three. His hardware is probably older than me, though."

Trey smirked and raised a thin, russet eyebrow. "How old is that?"

Melody's mouth mirrored Trey's smile, but her eyes were humorless laser beams of disapproval. "None of your business."

Trey watched Detective Jackson's feigned smirk dissolve into a glower as a few more bars of uncomfortable quiet echoed through the shrinking office. "You got it." He bit his lip and patted Matte as if he was a farm animal. "How do you know it's a 'he?'"

Melody released Trey from her glare as she turned to the window. "Because he's an asshole. What kind of glass is this?"

Trey shifted. "Again, I'd prefer to answer questions in a more formal setting and would—"

"Yeah, got it, I got it. Matte, where are you on those calculations?"

Her partner continued to whir. "Velocity ranges are calculated. Currently narrowing ranges."

"Give me approximate velocities."

"Entrance velocity between 390 and 405 meters per second. Exit velocity between 1.0 and 5.0 meters per second."

"Okay, use exit velocity ranges to calculate trajectory and proposed search area for projectile."

Trey shifted again. "I do need to know how long this is going to take."

Melody surveyed the room. "I'll be done scanning within the hour. Then our guys will come in and take everything larger or nailed down to be brought to evidence. We can get that done tonight if you want to pay a surcharge, which, based on what I've seen so far, I'm guessing you'll spring for. You can call the number on my card, but I'm pretty hard to get a hold of, so if I have your information, I will keep you apprised."

She paused and waited for Trey to reluctantly retrieve a business card from his suit jacket pocket. She and Matte watched as Trey set it on Matte's hardware. Melody retrieved a small plastic bag from her jacket labeled "EVIDENCE," turned it inside out, and then used it to pick up Trey's card as if a dog had left it on the sidewalk.

"Thank you," she said, as she turned the card over in the bag to read it. "John Paul Brodowski, the Third, MBA Ph.D. Mr. Brodowski, I will be sure to return any of your calls as soon as I am available. Once we have time to review the security footage you supply us, we'll perform interviews in a 'formal setting' with representation present for your employees or any others here that we find may be helpful."

"Others?"

"You got any employees like Matte here?"

Trey looked down his nose at Melody's partner on the trolley. "Again, Detective Jackson, I would prefer to answer questions related to my work here in a—"

"More formal setting, got it. We'll get to that. Next steps in our investigation would then depend on information acquired during interviews, various other considerations including Matte's analysis, our caseload, budget allocation—"

"I understand how investigations work," Trey interrupted. "I've seen the shows. What I need to know now is how long will it be until you and your team are out of here? We need to get our people back to work."

"Let's find out, then. Matte, where are you on those calculations?"

"Approximate search area extends from directly below the window outward thirty meters in the pattern displayed."

Detective Jackson pressed a button on Matte's edge and lifted a screen displaying a three-dimensional view of the Jefferson Trellis from above. A heat map showed the most likely landing areas for the wayward projectile. The hottest pinks and oranges overlaid the up-turned bowl at the base of the building, but some yellows and greens poured out into the street. She turned the screen to show Trey. "I'm going to need you to close down the gardens while we look for evidence."

"What evidence?" Trey glowered.

"A lead pellet, about eight millimeters in diameter."

Trey's jaw went slack and his eyes watered as the information hung in the air. "That'll take ages."

"I told you, Mr. Brodowski." Melody gestured towards the matte black box between them. "He's an asshole."

4. Taupe

"I've got an interview." Debbie Peck stood over her boyfriend in their tiny living room, panting lightly from her run home and up the stairs. He looked up at her from the couch, mouth agape and hanging with spinach from the salad bowl he hovered over. His glassy brown eyes hesitated with fear and confusion. "Say something for chrissakes, Terrance."

He swallowed whole leaves as his eyes welled up with tears. "That's great, Deb! What happened to your face?"

Debbie touched her nose, jolting her memory to the day's other events with a flash of pain. "I got hit with a chair. My interview's at Jefferson Zimmer and Prince."

Terrance Wallace swallowed again as he wiped his eyes. "Who?"

"The Jefferson Group."

"That's great! Who hit you with a chair?" He stood up and reached out to hug Debbie but forgot he had a bowl of salad in his hand, which Debbie flinched to avoid.

"A party to an NTO mediation. A Merrimaker. He was aiming for someone else." Debbie wiped her face with her forearm, avoiding the injured bridge of her nose. "I can't make dinner tonight. I have to get ready. Research and practice and stuff."

Terrance looked worriedly at his bowl of salad. "You can have some of this. I made extra."

Debbie nodded tepidly. "Thanks, I might. I need to take a shower." She kissed Terrance on the cheek and scooted past him to their tiny bathroom. He had annoyed her by greeting her the same way he had every day in recent memory, wearing running shorts, a t-shirt, and the confused, guilty look of a man who didn't know what he had done all day. Debbie tried to hide her annoyance, and Terrance tried to hide the fact that he noticed it anyway. For his part, he would diligently look for work six to eight hours a day. But when she arrived home, he never really knew how to explain all he had done. Simply not explaining it seemed less embarrassing than describing the drudgery of filling out applications and sending away resumes, calling headhunters and scanning job boards.

He wished he had something exciting to do so that he had something exciting to tell her, and most of all wished he had money or other means to do something exciting. The last few months, he had been poor and boring and annoyingly aware of these failings. More annoyingly, he had been attentive and well behaved and caring, failing to provide Debbie with the one other thing she might want—a good excuse to break things off. These facts poured through Debbie's mind as she quickly rinsed away her sweat under the sad trickle of lukewarm water that she would have to pay for.

She stood in their tiny kitchen, searching the fridge while wrapped in an oversized towel. The extra spinach salad might have been good for a starter but would leave her hungry. She grabbed it anyway and sat down on the couch as Terrance moved from surface to surface, rearranging papers and other items in a hasty effort to tidy. Debbie watched him as she stabbed into her bowl.

"How was your day?"

He turned and smiled as best he could. "Good, I think. I sent out more resumes and called my recruiters. That's really exciting about your interview."

She chewed as she looked at the last few leaves of spinach. "Yeah, totally. It was totally out of the blue."

"That would be really good for you. I'm excited for you."

"Yeah." She looked up at him with a smile mixed with a wince. "It could be really good for us."

Terrance relaxed, reassured that he was still part of Debbie's equation. "If you land this, we can probably afford to get you some good concealer. Or a helmet?"

Debbie smiled into her empty bowl. "With a face mask?"

"That might be too fancy."

"Too fancy for me?" Debbie playfully but painfully batted her eyelashes at Terrance. Her eyes seemed brighter next to the purple butterfly of broken blood vessels that splayed itself across the bridge of her nose.

"No, no, too fancy for *me*. Everyone will know I'm outgunned, outclassed. There goes fancy Debbie, they'll say, and the sad sack that follows her around."

"Oh, they'll keep saying that, will they?"

Terrance recoiled, grabbing his gut. "Oof. Yeah, they'll keep saying it." Debbie kissed him on the cheek again, and then he leaned in to kiss her properly. Its warmth mixed with sadness and uncertainty. It teemed with thousands of possibilities, some good, some bad, none involving sex tonight. "What's your strategy?"

"Strategy for?"

"The interview. Like, what's your angle?"

Debbie sighed. She had been role-playing the possibilities in the very back of her mind all day but had avoided formulating any sort of set plan. "I don't think it really works like that. Or, it doesn't for me."

Terrance looked concerned. "It's just a lot of the articles and videos say you should have a game plan, like an angle, going into an interview. Even if it's not a formal strategy, like the Gottlieb Technique or Five Corners Method. You should have a plan."

"It never works out the way you think it's going to. Or hope it's going to. I'm just going to do my best. They called me, for some reason. They have my resume and my data. There must be something I'm doing already that they like."

"Like what?"

"Like *what?*"

"No . . ." Terrance backpedaled. "I mean, there is lots to like. But what parts do you think they liked? If you're in there, interviewing against dozens of other candidates who all know what their best aspects are, how are you going to stand out? What's your best foot, and how do you put it forward? It's stuff like that that you have to think about."

"Well." Debbie rolled her eyes, then mugged playfully a few times to cover up her irritation. "If everyone is putting their best foot forward, the way to stand out is to not put any foot forward. To be boring. Undefinable. A dark horse. A dark, boring horse."

"I don't think anyone recommends doing that, though."

"I don't think people who get hired to write advice articles would. They don't get paid to be boring. They get paid to get clicks. They get paid to grab attention. I'm a mediator. If I'm part of the equation, then I'm part of the problem. I'm supposed to reflect, to support, to contain, and redirect parts of the problem until it sorts itself out. No one cares what my favorite food is or where I'd like to travel if I could ever afford it. No one cares."

"I care."

"Right, and I'm glad you do. But actually, no one out *there* cares. The more you talk about your hobbies or interests, the more you're telling the interviewer that you don't understand how it all works. It's like bragging that you brush your teeth or wash your butt. 'Great job, you're a real person, but what can you do for *me*,' they'll be thinking. Well, I can be boring. I can be next to nothing. Not black or white or tangerine but beige or taupe."

"Khaki?" Terrance suggested.

"Khaki is too strong of a word, it's too substantial. I'm talking nothing brown, like my hair. 'Taupe' is probably right. Taupe is so boring that most people don't even bother learning what it is. They don't even know it has a name. I can be that, and the Jefferson Group might be able to use someone like that."

"Well, you're smarter than me." Terrance was frustrated, Debbie could tell. But this was how they worked. She couldn't go tiptoeing around his sensitivities, or else he'd spiral further into self-examination and she'd spiral further away from caring. "And you got the interview, so . . ." His thought trailed off. "But you're not boring. You know that."

She kissed his forehead. "Thanks." If he needed to think that, so be it. "There are worse things than boring, though. You know that, right?"

"Sure. Want me to ask you some interview questions?"

Debbie considered it. "Just one. I really have to read up on these guys."

"Okay." Terrance squared his shoulders and sat up, putting on a faux air of seriousness. "Now, Miss Peck. There are three bears sitting in a room. One lives in a white house, one lives in a blue house, one lives in a red house."

She rolled her eyes. "First, I hate this type of question. Second, I've actually had this one before."

"Miss Peck, we know the interview process can be trying but please just do the best you can." Terrance looked disappointed, miming a shuffling of papers in front of him. "Okay, so the bear who lives in a red house picks up his chair and throws it at you. What do you do?"

Debbie sighed and slapped Terrance on the shoulder. "You're an idiot." She turned to her tablet and flicked it on. "Now, darling, go be funny somewhere else. I've got to read everything I can about the stinking Jefferson Group."

"Okay, Debs. Let me know if you need anything."

"I will."

Terrance slunk into their tiny bedroom. Instead of trying to be funny, he continued trying to be useful. He hadn't felt useful in months and hadn't felt *needed* at any point in his entire life. While Debbie read the history and mission of the Jefferson Group, he read an advice column on how to get noticed by the few companies that still hired people, and another on how to play headhunters against each other to land interviews. Neither interested him, but each had over eighty million views, meaning that his competition had read them. He needed to keep pace, not fall behind. He didn't know if the articles were useful, or whether their authors were useful, or whether the whole endeavor was a waste. Terrance stared at his small bedroom wall and wondered if he'd ever be useful, or happy, or at least not depressed. He'd been depressed for too long, as long as he could remember. He tucked himself into their stale bed and tried to push on to the next day. Unable to sleep, Terrance's mind spun until Debbie needed him. Eventually, she came to bed and needed him to stop tossing and turning. She needed him to fall asleep so she could get some rest for her big day tomorrow. Embarrassed and confused, Terrance made himself useful and did exactly as she asked.

5. Drills

Debbie performed her breathing exercises, calming her sympathetic nervous system and fast-twitch muscle fibers as she waited for her car to arrive. She knew that the interview would start before she walked in the door, at some point between leaving her apartment and coming into view of the Jefferson Trellis. Maybe they had access to cameras and scanners in the car. Maybe there was a skein of drones over her right now, checking to see if she was picking her teeth or adjusting her bra. If not now, then definitely by the time she stepped out of the car, her interviewers would be watching and taking notes. She had to be "*on*," exhibiting the poise and control of the top-level mediator that she was, or could be, or could pretend to be. She performed stretches to unprime her facial muscles and prevent any unintended micro-expressions. As she contorted her *procerus, buccinator,* and *levator labii superioris* in controlled but rapid succession, she was very aware that, to the general public, she looked like a real dick.

A purple share-car flashed "DEBBIE PECK" across its windscreen as it turned the corner. Debbie couldn't afford cars very often, but this morning she couldn't afford the risk of getting blood or vomit or semen on her only good suit by taking the train. She couldn't afford a fem-only car service, so as she approached her door, she desperately hoped the car was not full of strange men that still might try to get blood or vomit or semen on her only good suit. As she looked in, two passengers had their privacy screens up and the third was a shabby middle-aged woman, so Debbie got in. As they pulled away, Debbie noticed a sharp smell. The woman lifted a black velvet cloth laid across her lap, exposing various candies, snacks, and toiletries. The woman flashed a cronelike grin and held out her hand. "You buy?" she pleaded.

Debbie smiled politely. "No, thank you." She activated her privacy screen. It escaped Debbie how car attendants could afford to ride around all day, but it didn't worry her. Nothing made sense about how things worked. Everything that worked well was a racket, a swindle. Everything else was broken or on the verge of breaking. Regardless, Debbie couldn't afford to look like she was bothered by the woman. They could be watching already. She continued her facial exercises while intermittently introducing herself to no one at all.

"Thank you for having me, it is great to meet you."

Too enthusiastic, she thought. Don't grovel.

"Debbie Peck, Deborah Peck, Debbie, Debbie, Deb, Debs, Debs, Debbie Peck, thank you for meeting with me today."

Debbie Peck. Like it's one word. Neck-in-neck. Rubber check. What the heck. Don't overcomplicate it, or you might stumble over your own name.

"It's a pleasure to be here. Your reputation precedes you."

Proceeds you? Precedes? Avoid this altogether. Also, too smug.

"This is fantastic, thanks. No, not a problem at all, I was happy I could make it."

Puts them on the back foot by suggesting it could have been a problem, but it's not because you're so flexible and gracious. Enthusiastic, but not bubbly. Best one yet.

As the car turned off the main streets, Debbie stopped rehearsing and stretching and again began her breathing exercises. She was calming herself, clearing her mind of any expectations. Expectations, she knew, led to disappointment and confusion when they were inevitably contradicted. If she was expecting to meet a man, she might expose weakness or fear when confronted with a woman instead. If she was expecting tea but offered whiskey, she might betray an overeagerness for alcohol by gladly accepting it. She tried to clear her mind so as to be a vessel for the reality there in front of her. Her bouncing knee told her that it was not working as well as she had hoped it would.

She knew she was getting close when the sunlight disappeared. The Jefferson Trellis had no street-level access, so cars dipped into the sub-streets a few blocks away from the concrete caldera that the jeweled tower erupted from. As the tunnel narrowed and twisted, and the car slowed and turned, Debbie could feel the Trellis's scanners and cameras peeking into the windows. Then, the car stopped. Debbie reached for the handle but grasped at air as the door opened from the outside. A handsome-ish man in a purple suit ushered Debbie out to the curb with an exaggerated courtesy. As Debbie alighted her chariot, he drawled, "Welcome to your destination, ma'am."

Debbie nodded at him and tempered her smile. "Thank you very much."

Motivations. A skilled mediator will identify and understand hidden aims or unspoken motivations. This man, in his snug purple bellhop outfit, freshly shaven but with dirty nails and sweat stains around his collar, was looking for money. Debbie noticed the actual Jefferson Trellis pedway entrance twenty feet away and caught the rolling eyes of a uniformed attendant as he leaned against a valet stand. His uniform was *not* purple.

A foot away from her, a yellow line separated the well-groomed pavement nearer the doorway from the swath of unkempt, presumably public street she stood upon. A sign against the wall, across the line and nearer the door announced that it was "PRIVATE PROPERTY" pursuant to something something and the State of Delaware. Debbie stalled, maintaining non-committal eye contact with the bellhop while twisting to check her pockets. And then, stepping backwards and away from him, she floated over the yellow line and into the protection of the Jefferson Group.

Her eyes apologized to the beggar as betrayal and disappointment crashed over his face. Debbie pointed over her shoulder towards the door as she backed towards it. "I'll get you on my way out . . . if this goes well."

The man hovered behind the yellow line, fists clenched. "Bitch."

Provocations. Experienced mediators have seen people at their ugliest. They have weathered personal insults, flying chairs, death threats, and worse. Patience and poise are more than useful tools for a mediator—they are survival skills. Debbie didn't anger. She simply pointed her finger with caution and shrugged. "Your loss," her shoulders seemed to say. She relaxed her face as she turned to the cameras she presumed were looming over the pedway entrance. She approached the uniformed Jefferson Trellis attendant and raised her eyebrows in commiseration.

He let out half a chuckle. "You must be new."

"I hope so. I'm here for an interview. Which way do I go for reception?"

"Straight down the pedway. Check in at the first guard stand and they'll give you your credentials."

"Thank you," she said, the "you" dragging a little long for her liking. Not a "Thank You," but a "thane-cueee." Nothing to worry about, she thought. Being "on" was one thing, but second-guessing every syllable would fry her brain. Debbie felt proud as she walked down the pedway, but she didn't allow herself to beam with any emotion as she approached the first guard station. The sensors were everywhere now, clearly visible every twenty feet with more probably hidden in between. She breathed all the way into her stomach as she cleared her mind so that it could again provide a proper vessel for her next interaction.

She approached the first guard post and its bulbous attendant. The guard, in a bright blue sumo-suit, rocked slowly from foot to foot. As its hips swayed ever so slightly with each oscillation, Debbie wondered what was underneath all that blast-proof padding and featureless helmet. It was impossible to tell.

Reflections. Empathy and understanding, mirroring, active listening—even when the subject was silent—emotional intelligence and control. Debbie knew these tools like a blacksmith knew his hammers, like a dentist knew her drills. But all her body language courses and on-the-job knowhow were wasted standing before the bright blue, sexless golem that manned the post. There was nothing to read. She simply smiled politely and waited for her credentials to be confirmed. This was another round of her interview, she guessed.

For another moment, Debbie contemplated all that bright blue padding separating her from the human beneath it. She thought about why the face was not visible, about terms like blast overpressure, vapor viscosity, and LD50 of exposure. While performing passive breathing exercises, she hoped she had arrived on an uneventful morning in Chicago's downtown. She hoped without expectations, as she knew expectations were inevitably contradicted. If someone walked up behind her with a bomb or gas grenade or machine gun, she would need to react to the situation in front of her rather than the one she anticipated. There would be no surprises, only situations. While she waited, she kept her mind empty and her heart full of calm, steadying hope.

Until the big blue thing farted.

Debbie stifled every instinct she had to laugh. Calm down, calm down. Grow up. Breathe. Oh—on second thought, don't breathe. Give it a minute. She felt herself blush momentarily, then go pale.

She thought of the turret looming behind them, waiting silently for its suspicions to be confirmed. There were the stories of early versions, first-gen platforms, killing unsuspecting businessmen who were only guilty of having a bad day. Heart rates elevated, body temperature raised, they were distracted by some imaginary argument ricocheting through their minds. They hadn't noticed the guard trying to stop them. They hadn't had time to heed the instruction to stop, to raise the arms, to lie down, to comply. The turret misunderstood their frustrations, understood existential agitation as a physical threat, and proceeded to put neat little holes in their soft circuitry.

These days, they said turrets implemented fail-safes that required the human guard to confirm the turret's suspicions before putting holes in anything. Somewhere in all that climate-controlled blue padding was a plastic trigger that the guard would need to pull to let the turret know that a living, breathing person concurred with its death sentence. That way, for liability purposes at least, a living, breathing person could be put on paid leave or fired if a turret perforated the wrong guy.

"You're all set," the blue thing blurted. Its microphone squawked then sniffed. "Just go up to the second elevator bank on the left at the end of the pedway. Take yourself up to the nineteenth floor. Mr. McKay will greet you."

"Have a good day," she said, before marching down the hall. Debbie breathed right down to the small of her back. She could feel the blue thing turn to watch her. She strutted past two more security checkpoints, each about a minute apart, smiling at each blue thing and making no sudden movements toward their respective security turrets.

She hoped she would be dealing with fellow mediators the rest of the day, as her face was already getting tired. Mediators wouldn't expect her to smile, or kiss ass, or reflect with them. They would expect her to do her job, like they did, which entailed smiling for other people, and kissing other people's asses, and reflecting with those other people with money who had problems worth solving. Her face needed to be putty, and as the morning wore on, she was feeling it turn to that. She again began her passive breathing exercises as she put on her best face and posture. As a box and some wires effortlessly lifted Debbie's 121 pounds of flesh, bone, and quiet hopes some 230 feet above, Debbie braced herself for whatever she would find when the elevator doors opened.

The lobby was an orchard of empty seats. There were two emergency exits on each end of the elevator bank, and three spines of back-to-back, expensive-looking chairs with another half-row against each wall. Each row terminated towards a vacant reception desk in front of two sets of frosted glass doors. Strange, Debbie thought. Empty. Another game, or just an experiment in interior design? She didn't know how the other half of a tenth of one percent lived. Maybe this was normal. Maybe they liked feeling alone.

Debbie presumed someone was watching her, that this was still part of the interview. She imagined what others wouldn't do, what would make her stand out in the non-existent crowd. She then walked past the chairs and up to the central reception desk, leaned on it, looked over it carefully, and whistled. Exaggerating her motions, chewing on the scenery, she let her voyeurs know that she knew she was being watched. She looked deliberately but patiently from sensor bank to sensor bank, then went to sit on the forwardmost chair in the central row and began her breathing exercises.

While tame by all standards, it was not typical. Mediators were surrounded by other booming voices to redirect, eruptions to translate, or flying furniture to dodge. In this vacuum of an inappropriately empty room, Debbie hoped to demonstrate that she was her own person, with her own time that could be wasted. Any person worth their salt could be responsibly impatient, so why shouldn't she be? The world was going to hell and there were problems to solve. She could be elsewhere being useful, hypothetically at least, and any respectable employer should respect that fact and not waste her time. That fact made known to the sensor banks in each corner of the lobby, Debbie waited.

6. Bloom

Detective Jackson stood shoulder to shoulder with ruby red sunflowers in the Jefferson Trellis's gardens. They were confused. The sunflowers were confused by the dozens of suns that they could choose to follow, one real, and the others real enough but reflected against the shifting facets of the Trellis. Their warped stems meandered like conjoined question marks towards the heavens, asking which sun was real and which suns weren't and whether the answer even made a difference.

They grew in the safety of the botanic gardens in the Trellis's amphitheater base, the mortar to the building's pestle. It teemed with ever-changing varieties of plants, some the descendants of Bourbon bosquets, some stolen from the far-off jungles, others surreal creations from horticultural biodesign firms. As the plots of heirloom azaleas or bat flowers or jadesnaps or AFD001059 September Edition swelled from the manicured terraces and erupted into the cultivated air, their colors ricocheted off the building's downward-angled facets into the streets below. Every day the flowers switched. Every hour the light shifted. Every moment spent looking at the Trellis from the streets outside was a new and awe-inspiring experience.

Detective Jackson was also confused. She had seen the Trellis a thousand times before, but never from here inside the gardens. From among the lilacs and plumbthistles and honey rafflesia, the Trellis only reflected the sky and the rusty gray of the city streets outside. From this steep angle, the Trellis was as ugly as pigeon shit and potholes, as weathered as the bag ladies, empty and crinkled as their quarry. It reflected knives dropped down storm drains, the lives they cut short, and the cracked-mud arroyo that ground against Lower Wacker. So for a moment, Melody stood perplexed among the sunflowers, squinting towards the tessellated chrome behemoth above her.

"It's beautiful, ain't it!" The grainy voice cut through a Tudor rosebush to Melody's right. Against all the waxy greens and vibrant reds and some pale hibiscus, her eyes found the hickory face of a middle-aged man dotted with ivory stubble.

"Sure is." She smiled at him. "Did they tell you I'd be coming?"

"They did. They didn't tell me you'd be a *pretty* police officer, though."

"Detective." Her smile faded but was still warm. She did not recognize the logo on the man's jumpsuit. "Detective Jackson, Six Counties P.D. Do you work here?"

"Since it was built. Still a contractor," he said, pointing to his uniform. "But I know how it goes around here. I'm Teddy."

"Hi, Teddy." Melody gestured towards the jungle surrounding her. "Are you the guy with the green thumb?"

He laughed. "One of 'em. Someone else decides what gets planted. The computers keep track of water and light and acidity and minerals and all that. I just talk to them and give them the old tender loving care that they need."

"You know what I'm looking for?"

Teddy's face soured. "A bit of buckshot, I hear."

Melody tilted her head. "Do those computers monitor for lead?"

"Hah! Maybe in the soil or runoff, but not that BB you're looking for. I'll let you know if I see it, though." Teddy got on his knees and began patting the sod around a flowerbed. "We find a lot of weird shit around here, Miss Detective Jackson, Six Counties P.D."

Melody looked up the Trellis to where she guessed Gerald Ford Jones' office would be. A bright green car driving itself down some street five blocks behind her was dancing along the windows high above. "You don't get the best view from in here, do you?"

Teddy reflected on her question as the pale cracks in his knuckles bounced into some actuarial office ten blocks away. "Nah. But I get a better view of these flowers." His voice grew quieter. "And it keeps us safe, anyway."

Melody's confusion grew. "How's that?"

Teddy smiled. "All those mirrored windows and all these flowers make a razzle-dazzle that messes their guidance systems." His fingers danced a bit more quickly against the soil as he beamed with quiet pride. "Back in the day, when any old asshole could piggyback a Skip on a Tom-Tomahawk and hit whatever the hell they wanted in the building."

"Yeah?"

"Yeah! See, the Tom-Tomahawk would get the drone close enough, within visual range. Then the Skinner Pigeon would take it past all the jammers. Then, boom. Bedtime."

Melody was not around for the worst of the violence, but she knew Tom-Tomahawks were old DIEDs made by attaching some obsolete Garmin or TomTom satnav to a drone packed with explosives. She had seen one once as a child, painted sky-blue on a gray day, humming quietly thirty feet above her apartment block. It was gone in seconds, headed north towards the Loop, and none of her sisters or relatives believed that she had seen it. Pics, they said, or it never happened. Skinner Pigeons, or "Skips," were some sort of visual targeting algorithm she only had heard about recently. She would ask Matte more about them whenever he was done uploading. She perused the flowerbeds, kicking at mulch and dirt. While staring down the pistil of a conch-sized ultramarine calla lily, she sputtered, "I don't follow."

"Just look at it," Teddy said, eyes crawling up the Trellis. "The building's always changing. Always blooming. With the seasons or with the clouds or with the flowers or whatever. Never looks the same. When they were constructing it, before the glass went up, anyone could hit whatever they wanted. They hit the damn construction foreman one day after a Skinner Pigeon recognized him from four hundred yards out." Teddy's eyes widened and his mouth puckered. "The pieces of him were all over down here. A lot smaller than that BB you're looking for. But you can't train a program to hit something that always looks different. Can't hit this window or that window when they are always changing. Maybe some floor of the building, but that could be the daycare, or the Doctors Without Borders, or the Department of Education, or the Malaysian Embassy."

"The Jefferson Group has its own embassy?"

"No, no," he groaned, "but they do give them office space on the cheap. Real charitable of them. Probably another tax deduction, I bet. But more than that, it's bad press to blow up an embassy. Or a bunch of doctors, or toddlers or whatever. So it doesn't hurt to have those soft or valuable types around, to make you think twice about the collateral damage. Win-win, they say." Teddy winked. He looked nervous, but his eyes shone with youthful mischief.

Melody sensed that Teddy was excited to be telling her all of this, that he had more secrets that he wanted to divulge. "Anything else I should know about this place?"

Teddy reared back in feigned surprise. "Shit no, Detective. I'm not 'sposed to talk to you without a lawyer present." Teddy looked back at the fertile earth cupped into the Trellis's gardens. "I'm just talking to this rhododendron."

She crouched down close to Teddy, retrieving her business card from her pocket. "Teddy, I've got some plants in my office, too. Real ones, if they're still alive. Come talk to them if you feel like it."

"Hmgh." He winced. "I'm guessing. You can't pay me every two weeks to come talk to your plants." He looked at her. "With health insurance. Nothin' like that?"

Melody dropped her card, stood up slowly, and started to walk away. Either he would call or he wouldn't, but her silence could leave a taste in his mouth that might inspire more mischief. Some people couldn't help themselves but talk, especially when it was to a real live human. Teddy was lonely like nearly everyone else. And he was eager to please. When Melody had reached the door out of that section of the gardens, she turned to see Teddy still on his knees but repositioned, working faster than before, anxiously checking to see if she had anything left to say to him. She smiled at him disappointedly, waited a moment, then left.

7. Liars

Debbie neared the end of her calm patience. She retained vast reserves of annoyed politeness and strategic stockpiles of agitated professionalism, but her calm patience sputtered and choked. For seventy-five minutes in that empty lobby, she maintained a cautious but pleasant outward appearance while mentally reciting every color, animal, and geographical location she could manage to remember. Simple, unemotional facts calmed her nerves, kept her brain moving but not spinning. When a young man finally opened the emergency exit to the left of the elevator bank and poked his head into the lobby, Debbie smiled at him with muscles that ached.

"Miss Peck?"

She stood up quickly, struggling to hide a head rush as her eyes met his. "Yes, hello. Mr. McKay?"

"No, but—I'll take you to him." He raised his drooping head and muttered, "Congratulations."

"Thank you." She hesitated. "What for?"

"Ah, well I . . . you're, doing well so far."

Doing well. They had been watching. "Thanks," she said, as she followed him into the stairwell. "That's good to know." The boy couldn't have been older than twenty. How many candidates has he seen in his time? "What do you do here, then?"

He turned to look at her, but his glasses were dancing some other lifelike scene across his retinas. When the glimmer of light in his pupils switched off, his big gray eyes showed fear and embarrassment. "Sorry, I'm Madison. I'm an intern."

"Nice to meet you." She shook his hand. "How long have you been here?"

"This is my fifth summer." He must've started when he was twelve.

They arrived at the seventeenth-floor lobby, which was a

smaller version of the nineteenth-floor lobby they had just come from. Madison gestured towards a chair and raised a finger as if to say "Just a second," as he disappeared behind the frosted glass doors. One wall read "Jefferson Zimmer & Prince, established 2028 CE." The other was covered with a projected montage of smiling, satisfied, healthy-looking professionals. As soon as Debbie sat down, she stood up again as an older man with a goatee and an ornate nose ring burst through the door.

"Debbie Peck?"

"Yes. Mr. McKay?" Debbie beamed her most comforting smile as she extended a firm but inviting hand.

The man held her hand gently and shook it. "Please, call me Jerome. And it is *our* pleasure," Jerome said with an uncontrolled rhythm, a playful cadence that immediately revealed that he was not a mediator. "Just so you know," he confirmed as he led her through the frosted glass doors, "I am not a mediator, but in human resources management, so I will be showing you around today. Welcome to the Jefferson Group! Did you have a good trip in this morning?"

Debbie read his knowing smirk and playful squint. As she suspected, she was at least two hours into her interview already and hadn't been ushered out yet. "Yes! I got here just fine." Debbie reflected Jerome's mood and position, smirking and nodding in recognition of what he was hoping to convey.

"Okay. First off, stop it."

"Stop what?"

"Stop staring at my face. Micro-expressions or what have you." He smiled, and Debbie forced herself not to look. "I see what you're doing. Good job, but there is no need to be 'on' with me or your coworkers here. I might not be a mediator, but I do know what you wizards are up to, and we try to act like normal humans when we're not in a session. Okay?"

"Sure. Understood." While it was awkward, it was a relief. Being "on" was exhausting. After an all-day session, she could barely think straight. Already, this day was feeling very long.

"Second off, sorry about that wait on nineteen. The boys and girls upstairs were just reviewing your trip in and we're happy to say everything is checking out very well. We had your tapes from

Six Counties so we know you are . . . *bona fide*." He pinched his thumb to his index finger as if he were complimenting a well-cooked dish. Debbie smiled for the three-hundredth time that morning. "That's more good news for you. We won't put you through any more competency testing today. We are only after some general info, okay?"

"Not a problem," she said. As they entered a small conference room, Jerome flipped a switch on the wall, but the lights were already on. Nothing happened. More sensors, or audio recording, maybe? But she couldn't know whether Jerome had turned them on or off. Debbie switched herself from being "on" to "pretending not to be 'on'" as they sat down at the conference table. The office chairs were clad in the softest fake leather Debbie had ever felt. For a fleeting instant, she wished she was naked on the irresistible surface. She caught herself, then smiled genuinely as she thought of all the times expensive furniture had somehow disrobed lesser women for other undeserving men. She looked at Jerome squarely. "These are *really* nice chairs."

"I *know*, right?" He nodded approvingly. "I wanted some for my condo but . . . well, let's just say I didn't like them *that* much. If this place ever goes under, I'm taking one home." Debbie sensed that Jerome was beginning to actually like her. Not only for her qualifications or for the fact that she might ease his workload if she got hired, but in a way that made him think they could get tacos and talk shit. This, Debbie knew, was a very good sign.

"Okay, brass tacks. We noticed that you first applied for the Jefferson Group five years ago. Why did you first apply?"

Five years ago. That was still Ohio, before the move. Before Terrance. Debbie didn't remember applying. Like everyone else without a Senator in the family, she applied everywhere and anywhere she could, as often as she could. She had filed hundreds of applications, sent thousands of feelers. She was sure that she *had* applied at some point, but was baffled and annoyed by this question. That was probably the point.

Nevertheless, she reflected Jerome McKay's warm and inquisitive expression. "I don't specifically remember the first time I applied, but the Jefferson Group has always interested me and aligned with my goals as a mediator and human being." Jerome started taking notes for some reason while the room watched them both. "I want to help people. I want to help people communicate and work through their problems, hopefully to reach an optimal outcome. You do that here. It is a central part of your mission. You manage high-level mediations, critical disputes that affect entire regions or countries. Effectively managing a dispute for the Jefferson Group means possibly saving thousands or tens of thousands of lives, preventing sickness, famine, and conflict, and ensuring that value is added to society as a whole. It keeps us further from disarray. It wards off chaos and discord. It allows us all to be better humans and live a better life. It would be an accomplishment to be a part of one of your teams."

Debbie read Jerome's notations as she spoke. I. You. You. One. Us. Them. Us. Us all. One of you. Just the personal pronouns in each of her sentences, more or less, she realized. Maybe another performance test, or maybe his own curiosity. He looked up at her and nodded. "I think we'd be delighted to have you. It's not up to me, ultimately, but so far you are doing great."

"Thank you." She nodded guardedly. Manners never hurt.

"Have you ever worked for an M-K before?"

Debbie nodded again. She had, of course. M-Ks were only the bane of every aspiring entry-level capitalist. "Maga," was taken from "Krav Maga," meaning "combat-contact" in Israeli Hebrew, they said. But there were the rumors that it had meant something else. And "Kandli," roughly meaning "manager" in Japanese. It started off as a fad, the "M-K Corporate Management Training Program," which removed sociopaths from the labor pool by promoting them to supervisory roles. An M-K's duties included snapping at throats, invigilating humiliation, tarring-and-feathering their wards for small mistakes, and administering acute fear and insecurity among the lower ranks. The monthly metrics, spreadsheets with pivot tables, error bars, and all, confirmed beyond a reasonable doubt that having a miserable and absolute bastard between the workers and the upper administration increased productivity and improved profit margins. "I have."

"How did you like it?"

Debbie gulped, but her gentle smile didn't break. "I think it's necessary. The M-K role, it's necessary to keep us all moving in the right direction. It's been proven to work, even if it's personally unpleasant or uncomfortable at times. I think the higher expectations make many of us better people."

"Many of us . . . better people." Jerome shifted in the silky faux-leather chair. "What do higher expectations make the *others*, then?"

"Expectations make some of us better people." Debbie paused. "And others, better liars."

"Ooooh." Jerome scribbled on his notepad. "They *are* going to like you. Just a sec . . ." He put his finger to his ear, pausing to listen to instructions. "Are you, Debbie Peck, a better person, or a better liar?"

"Well . . ." She looked around at the room around her. It could be reading her temperature and pupil dilation and respiration rate. It could be mass-specking her pheromones. It could be tasting her sweat. "I think I'm trying to be both."

"Nice!" Jerome twisted, yawing towards his left jaw that buzzed with instructions from an earpiece. "What, well . . . Debbie, what happened to your nose?"

Legitimately surprised, Debbie dropped her act. "Excuse me?" She prepared for interrogation, grilling, quizzing, stumping, befuddling, berating, and other assaults on her professional abilities. She hadn't expected this.

"Well, it's just . . . Listen, not to prod, at all, really." Jerome exhaled guiltily. "I'm only asking because our ultraviolet arrays noticed you have a facial injury. Kind of a doozy, on your nose. I can't see it here looking at you, so, you know, kudos on your make-up?"

They could see under her make-up. They were reading the delicate muscles under her skin. They could, she thought, see her blush before she felt its growing warmth or its tumbling embarrassment. Debbie laughed and twisted her chin, putting forth her best portrayal of curiosity, attempting to draw hot blood away from her superficialities and back to her brain. "Are you really allowed to ask me this?"

He squinted a bit, flinching his cheeks upwards in discomfort but not distress. "Um . . . No, usually no. Usually, you're right. But in this case, it is very relevant to your qualifications as a mediator. Say, if you have a home situation that's . . . out of control? That would reflect poorly on your ability to mediate a professional situation, right? That's why we're asking."

"Ah," Debbie conceded. "Okay then." She softened her shoulders and sat back. "To answer your underlying question, I was hit by a chair thrown by a gang member in a mediation recently. Yesterday, actually. Six Counties can probably confirm that information with some very entertaining footage." She stiffened again. "Unrelated to that or the rest of this interview, I live with my boyfriend in a stable relationship that has never involved any sort of abuse, physical or otherwise."

Jerome sighed. "Thank you, we really appreciate you clearing that up for us. And!" He grinned suddenly. "You'll be happy to know, no one throws chairs around here!"

Debbie's *corrugator supercilii* twitched, a micro-expression of pain and fear in response to Jerome's levity. Her face remembered the impact of the chair against her nose before her brain remembered to be nice to the man who could change her life. Her brain took over and twisted her mouth into a smile. Her imagination caught up, picturing a safe workplace and stable paycheck, and her eyes turned the smile genuine.

"In fact, almost all of our mediations are performed remotely via terminal." Jerome twisted again and looked down at the table. "They're telling me I shouldn't have joked about the chair thing. Sorry. But we do have a great health plan, dental, vision, psych, relocation stipends, et cetera, et cetera. I'll get you all that right now, actually." He stood up but did not move toward the door. Instead, he hovered awkwardly, waiting for Debbie to say something.

Debbie hesitated, focusing all her effort to not betray another underlying fault or doubt or confusion. "Do you have any more questions for me?"

Jerome looked shocked. "You got the job. Did I not say that?"

They each looked around for someone else to confirm or deny. Debbie was alone with Jerome. Jerome was not alone with

Debbie. The voices in his jawbone rattled with castigations.

"Oh my god, I didn't. Yes, Debbie, the job's yours if you want it. Wait here while I grab some paperwork."

Debbie stood up and said something she would not remember. Shaking Jerome's hand and maintaining a veneer of strained professionalism as relief and exhilaration poured through her bones. She beamed and sunk into her impossibly soft faux leather chair as he exited the room. As her mind spun, Debbie's euphoria faded into calm patience. She began her quiet breathing exercises, listening to the room's soft hum as it watched her inhale, smile gently, and wait.

8. Orientation

Jerome returned a few minutes later carrying a tablet that was Debbie's to keep. It contained pages upon pages of documents that she would need to read and sign and then sign again later in hard copy. The health plan was comprehensive. She could relocate nearer to work if she wanted to. Life insurance. Dental. Arbitration clause. Jurisdictional waiver. Benefits with partner corporations. Conflicts of interest.

Salary. The salary. The salary was life changing, debt relieving. She quickly calculated that she could be in the black in five, maybe four years if she tried hard enough. Her net worth could one day reach zero. She could be as rich as she was the day she was born. Terrance could be out in another five, if he was still a factor. She nodded and followed along. She maintained her poise and tried not to sweat. She would accept the offer, she said, as soon as she resigned from Six Counties.

They wanted her take on something, right then. It wasn't a test, Jerome said, more of an orientation. He led her down the hall, introducing her to a few administrative staff whose names fizzled from her mind like drops of water on a hot pan. They entered a conference room with a display depicting a different, much nicer conference room. The one she and Jerome stood in was framed in bone white, plasticky walls, drop tile ceiling, and a carpet that looked like nothing at all. The one they spied upon was hardwood all around, still windowless but with landscape paintings and mirrors on the walls to provide the illusion of space. In it sat two women, one older and obviously of means, and the other younger, professional but in clothes that were made for moving, for working. A city worker maybe. Near the older woman sat a fortyish man with reddish hair. The sound was off, but they were talking calmly, posture showing they were adversarial, locked in non-violent disagreement.

"Do you know any of these people?" Jerome asked.

Debbie might have seen the younger woman at Six Counties but couldn't be sure. She watched her for a moment, saw her steel-toed oxford swivel from under the table, and an odd bulge under her jacket at the hip. Definitely a cop, but Debbie couldn't be sure if she'd ever seen her or never seen her. "No, I don't think so."

"Tell me what you think the younger woman's position is. The one on the left." He pressed a button, and sound flowed into the room.

"—ately it's not your decision. It's ours, and we've made it."

The older woman poked her shoulders backwards. "We disagree. We have full control as a jurisdictional exclave to the state of Delaware. We pay our taxes here and surtaxes there, and our investigators are already on location."

"Two things complicate that position." The younger woman was calm, but the timbre of her voice hid agitation. "First, the crime scene physically extends into the streets of Chicago. That makes this an Illinois crime scene and a Six Counties homicide investigation absent a U.S. Court Order saying otherwise. Not a U.S. Arbitration Order, or former U.S. Judge, or strongly worded letter from a Justice or member of Congress."

The older woman shifted. "You well know we are already pursuing what you are *ask*ing for." Debbie noted that "asking for" was breathy and exaggerated, an unveiled threat.

"Second," the younger woman continued, "and more importantly, we believe this case is related to the death of Hannah Mah." The executive and her red-headed assistant seethed with subtle proofs of their anger. His fists clenched, masseters bulged, and nostrils flared. She rapidly inhaled then held her breath, or breathed so shallowly that it could not be seen on the screen.

She finally exhaled. "Detective Jackson, don't be ridiculous. We won't suffer your harassments like so many of our helpless citizens do. We know our rights. We know your limitations. And we also know Ms. Mah died, tragically, in her home and after she was no longer an employee here. *Your* people told us it was a suicide."

Detective Jackson did not bud or blossom at the older woman's provocations. She did warm slightly as the red-haired man grew angry. The detective didn't like him. Or she really liked him. Debbie couldn't tell exactly.

"Ms. Kettering, while Six Counties may have told you Ms. Mah's death was a suspected suicide, it remains an open investigation. My investigation. And it is developing. For reasons I cannot explain here, we have good cause to believe the two cases are related. And they may be related to other homicides in the city."

Kettering. Debbie knew that name, and the older woman's face grew more familiar. She had seen it in an article she had studied the night before. Sam Kettering, Vice President of something rather at the Jefferson Group. What the hell was she watching?

Detective Jackson folded her hands on the table. "For that reason alone, Six Counties jurisdiction supersedes your exclave license. If you would like to donate any of your personnel to assist in our investigation, I'm sure we could use the help." The detective looked at the office around her. "You seem to have plenty of resources that could assist the city in its efforts."

As Ms. Kettering opened her mouth to speak, Debbie was drawn from the screen as Jerome turned off the sound. "So," he sighed, "what do you think?"

Debbie didn't know. She was too curious as to what she just watched. Three people—one silent, one presumably her new boss's bosses' boss, and the other a city cop. "Can I have a bit of context?" she asked. "I don't have much background in jurisdiction, or exclaves, or . . . I don't know?"

"No." Jerome sighed again, then rattled. "I mean usually, yes, you would have context, but here we're just asking for your take on it. No wrong answer. A bit of fun. Shoot from the hip. What do you say?"

Debbie thought back to the original question. The woman on the left, the younger one, the cop—what was her position? She was definitely at loggerheads with the other two people in the room. She disagreed with nearly everything they said, taking subtle pleasure in pissing the red-haired man off. It was hard to say why. He did look like an asshole, but that didn't help Debbie divine anything about the cop's position.

The detective seemed to know what she was talking about, but the subject matter was a foreign language to Debbie. Debbie's professional experience at Six Counties meant she knew turf wars and codes of honor and the proper retaliations for being robbed, shot at, or actually shot. The organizations she mediated maintained their own jurisdictions, their own jurisprudence, their own laws and procedures. The Berwyn Merrimakers and Rosemont Village Angels did not live in the same world as the Jefferson Group and the Delaware State Police. They did not operate in the same spheres. The rules that allowed the economic giants to thrive were the same rules that ground people in the streets to bone meal. Six Counties Police existed as a cast-iron lid to keep those worlds separate. Debbie and her cohort at the Six Counties Detention and Conflict Resolution Center existed to stir those closest to the flame, to ensure they chased themselves in convection currents, turning inward rather than burning or boiling over.

Usually, without any factual background, Debbie relied on contextual clues. But here, the police officer was a closed book. She had no obvious ticks or tells. Her face barely moved as she delivered line after line of bad news to a woman who had more money and power than any one person could use in their lifetime. Debbie raised her chin and delivered her verdict. "I don't think the detective is going to change her position. She's all set for now. Either change the stakes or walk away, but continuing to argue wastes your time and gives her more information to use against you."

Jerome widened his eyes sarcastically. "Got it! Ver-ry interesting." He paused to listen to his instructions, then waved his hand turn off his earpiece. "We'll just sit tight. I didn't mean to joke about it being interesting. It is, I mean it really is. I know you all are so good at what you do. The listening, the watching, the putting it all together. I'm just more of a talker, a doer, a letting-you-guys-figure-it-out. You're going to like it here with these little savants. They are all just like you."

Debbie looked away bashfully. She was unsure Jerome was right. If they were all *just* like her—quiet, observant, keen to listen, constantly dissecting the words and their motivations—this would not be much fun. One mediator was a novelty, but a room full of them was a nightmare of misread signals and nitpicking. Simple emotions encoded then decoded, recoded ad infinitum. Whatever it was, Debbie knew it was better than Six Counties Detention and Conflict Resolution Center. It was better than any job she'd ever had. It had to be.

The door opened, and a man entered the room. Debbie straightened up and turned to face him with a beaming, aching smile as she waited to be introduced. The man's red hair faded to gray at the temples, cut into an unflattering teardrop shape like the kids wore. He looked angry. Not angry right now, Debbie realized, just usually angry, with permanent scowl-carved creases on his brow. He was the man from the scene she had just watched, the scene that Debbie now realized contained only two people, the two women, shaking hands silently. Jerome immediately tightened but then bravely eased his frame to perform the introduction.

"Trey! This is Debbie Peck, the new mediator." Debbie extended her hand while holding perfect posture. "Debbie, this is Trey Brodowski, your team leader."

Trey shook her hand curtly. "And manager. Where'd you work for an M-K before?"

Shit, Debbie thought. This was her M-K. Her Maga-Kandlii, Mortal Kombatant, Manager-Kommandant. He would be the axe hanging over her head until she or he switched jobs or died. His training made him impervious to complaints, immune to suggestion, and allergic to sympathy or manners. He was the oil slick between the workers like her and the upper administrators and corporate officers, immaculate creatures that they were, floating on the gusty updrafts of sequestered trillions. "Right out of college, I—"

Trey cut in. "Where, Debbie. Not when. Where did you work for one of us laser-guided sons-of-bitches?"

Debbie did not flinch. "At Abellion Consulting in Cleveland."

"I don't know anyone in that shit-hole. How was it?"

"It was fine. Cleveland still sells water. Buffalo is still better, but Toledo's a buyer now." Debbie paused as her answer failed to subdue Trey's percolating rage. "My M-K taught me a great deal. Her name was Brae Thomas, I believe she was from Charlotte."

"I don't know anyone from swamp-ass Charlotte, either. If someone would have told my grandfather that Buffalo would be the new San Francisco, I could've skipped this working thing altogether. Anyway, welcome to the team. When are you starting?"

Jerome piped in. "As soon as she's able. She just found out a minute ago."

"You're taking over for Gerald Ford Jones. Okay with you?"

"Yes. It's my pleasure." Debbie glowed as the reality of her new position began to set in. In that joy, it took her a second to notice the room's mood undergoing a drastic change.

Trey's face fluxed from rage to disappointment. His glare disemboweled Jerome before it cut back to Debbie. "Pleasure? Did you not listen to that conversation?" His hand jutted towards the screen, displaying the now-empty conference room.

Jerome's voice fluttered and fell. "We jumped in late. I haven't . . ."

Trey's chin snapped forward, silencing Jerome. "Jerome, you are worthless. Debbie, Gerald was an employee here until yesterday, when some kid shot him in the stomach. Fatally shot, that's an important point. He's dead." If Trey was sad, it was only because he had to explain this to Debbie. "They haven't found the kid yet, for all we know he could be hiding under this table."

Debbie turned to Jerome, looking for some sign that this was a joke, lie, or trick from Trey. Jerome put his hands up. "I only said we don't throw chairs."

"Shut up, Jerome." Trey looked under the table. "Nope, not there. Still missing. Anyway Debbie, you'll be taking over for Gerald, so don't expect everyone to be happy to see you when you start. Okay?" He exaggerated his movements, his enunciation, and his expressions to become a caricature of himself. Some M-K's were subtle, cruel, and economical with their insults. Trey was like a baby rattlesnake, lashing out at anything and over-envenomating whatever he struck. Debbie couldn't tell whether he was new to this or if it was simply his personal style of management.

"Understood."

Trey's sternocleidomastoids flexed. "Also, if you see someone who doesn't look like they fit in around here, let security know."

"Will do." Debbie paused as Trey began to exit the room. "How will I know who doesn't belong?"

Trey stopped. "Well, Debbie, say you see someone running around naked. You have our corporate dress policy, seeing some teenager running through the halls naked with a shotgun would be a good sign that he doesn't belong. Report him to security. Sometimes you see someone smiling like a fatso buffoon all the time, with a bad goatee and stupid nose ring." He was staring at Jerome, whose jowls hung sadly as his eyes glazed over. "That person, that person probably doesn't belong here either. So just report him to security and see what gives. Yeah?"

Debbie looked into Trey's gunmetal eyes. "Yes." Debbie didn't flinch. Her heart and gut and islets of Langerhans rattled in every direction, but her mind remained locked in its shock-proof case.

When Trey had gone, Debbie looked apologetically at Jerome. He raised his eyebrows in commiseration and flipped a switch on the table. "Well. I am sorry about all that, but you might as well get used to it. He's your manager. Luckily, as you know, he's the only one who can talk to you or your team like that. If anyone else harasses or yells at you, just let us know."

"I will." Debbie would. She would also let them know if she thought Trey crossed whatever invisible line it was that M-Ks could not cross, known only by them and the handful of brave souls that walked out of an arbitration with a favorable settlement and a gag order. Anyone who had the money to fight a harassment suit usually wasn't working under an M-K in the first place. Anyone who didn't would take the cash and let the M-K Corporate Management Certification Program keep their black boxes closed. Debbie, neither a martyr nor a doormat, would happily take the money and run.

"Also," Jerome sighed again, "read those forms carefully. You probably know the ropes, but after *Nydec* you'll want to be sure."

Hopkins v. Nydec, Debbie remembered, was something people had been angry about when she was in college. It spurred rallies and protests and action groups that went nowhere. Something about corporate personhood. Something about *Lawrence v. Texas*, twisted by the Supreme Court. Something about all persons of age, corporations included, being allowed to screw whomever they wanted, however they wanted, behind closed doors, as long as there was consent.

She thanked Jerome, and he told her that the day was done. He told her that she should go home, read the forms, and let him know if she had any questions. He told her she should call her current employer as soon as possible. And finally, he told her she should enjoy her afternoon.

Alone in the descending elevator, Debbie smiled for the five-hundredth time that day. Unlike four hundred eighty or so of the previous smiles, this one was genuine. Years in the pits, saving lost souls, sending out resumes, scrounging for change, queuing for benefits—that was all behind her now. She just received her ticket up and out.

She planned to walk home through the early afternoon in the city center. Maybe she'd grab a hot meal to celebrate. She walked past the blue sumo-suited golems and their security turrets and out past the valet in his Jefferson Group blazer to the sub-basement entryway. The purple-suited bellhop was gone. The summer's sour afternoon air sat in the crypts like the incense from a centuries-old funeral. The roads were empty.

Debbie took the stairs up to street level. She emerged outside the roundabout circumscribing the base of the bowl-like gardens surrounding the Trellis. Its convex wall loomed high over the street, threatening to crash down and flatten anything that got too close. It had no openings. All entrances were either underground or on the landing pad at the building's apex. Instead, beautiful bas-reliefs of intricate botanical patterns were molded or carved into the stone-solid material.

As she walked westward and homeward, she would turn back to look at the Trellis and watch it change in the afternoon light. The downward-facing diamond-shaped panels reflected the hidden flora erupting in the gardens below. The outermost point of those mirrors met the two panels adjoining above it, with the panels to the left reflecting the purpling clouds to the north and the panels to the right reflecting the cerulean skies to the south. As she got closer to home, it melded together, each panel a pixel working in unison to create the hallucinogenic impression of some half-exploded hand grenade. As she walked, no one bothered her. No hungry men or broken women or horny teenagers approached her. The odd Augustines or Horrorists or Century Boys that she saw down side streets were preoccupied with other victims or misdemeanors.

Cirrocumulus clouds hung high and wide in the Midwest sky like the popcorn ceiling of a cheap motel. They didn't threaten to rain, nor had any cloud this month. The water hadn't disappeared. It just went elsewhere, stolen by some strange new wind or jet stream, carried high above the fly-over states and deposited unwelcomely on the soggy Atlantic seaboard. The dry West marched eastward, slithering down former creek beds, belly-crawling across the parched bedrock. Where once a trillion blades of prairie grass drew dew from the air and life from the dirt, now stood a hundred thousand brown baseball diamonds and back nines, parking lots and franchise opportunities. To the clouds high above, the earth carried strange scars—divots and culs-de-sac and discolorations—like the tracks of a billion bark beetles.

Debbie followed one of these tracks home, to the tiny borehole where she and Terrance lived. He wasn't there. He was probably out with friends, drinking and complaining. She didn't care. She was exhausted. Her face ached, her shoulders ached, her feet were numb. She poured herself a drink and went to their tiny bathroom. There, she pried open the panel next to their tiny shower, wedged a hairpin against the regulator on the shower's mechanical governor, and disrobed. Debbie stood under the showerhead and opened the heavens, every lukewarm drop a fleeting luxury that she could now finally afford.

9. Keyhole

Melody stood at the head of the briefing room, waiting for her team to assemble. Matte was already there, obviously. He waited in the walls or the network or server room, allocating the appropriate amount of his attention to his hundreds of tasks. Henry "Soup" Suparmanputra arrived early as he always did, at least five minutes before the start of every "zero eight hundred" or "zero seven thirty" meeting. He was set permanently on military time since completing combat tours in Mindanao and Sulawesi. He could speak Tagalog and Tok Pisin, and if a Papuan refugee found his way into a Six Counties holding cell, this son of Suparman would be called in to read him his rights. But left to his own devices, Soup spoke not at all, drinking in the quiet air as it made itself available.

Other officers filtered in slowly, stopping to get a cup of coffee before finding their folding chairs. Tark Benton brought his own tumbler. He refused to drink the synthetic stuff, and instead spent some untold fortune on real beans. Never pre-ground, he would tell them. That was the only way to be sure it wasn't cut with soot or shredded tires or charred trash. Everyone agreed his real coffee smelled delicious. Everyone but Tark agreed that it was financial suicide to spend so much cash on something that went straight through you.

Stragglers hurried in late. Sharon Kemp, widow and single mother, came in last and closed the door. She lost her husband to an act of random insanity by some Horrorists years ago, the details of which she never explained to her colleagues. She didn't need to. They had seen the aftermath of dozens like it. They all knew of the part-time philosophers, full-time sadists who prowled hip bars and back alleys setting up flawed experiments to divine the meaning of life. Horrorists hypothesized that *this* world was hell, that this life was cheap and meaningless. They conducted skewed field studies to confirm these suspicions. In a vacant lot a few blocks from his home, a few bored suburban nobodies killed Sharon's husband slowly enough that he knew his death was imminent, but quickly enough that he couldn't make peace with it. Sharon joined the force shortly after his funeral. She was not a natural police officer—she was jumpy and severe and sometimes reckless. But the department needed warm bodies with darting eyes and chasing legs and gritting teeth.

Matte's minutes would show that eighteen humans attended the meeting. He listened and watched with three percent of his bandwidth while the other ninety-seven careened through thousands of hours of security footage and utility data.

"Good morning, everyone," Melody began. "And thank you for coming. You're here to get briefed on an ongoing investigation Matte and I are working on. We have two dots that need connecting. To do that, we need your insight and eyes on the street." The lights dimmed and the screen behind Melody came to life.

"This," Melody gestured toward the screen, "is Gerald Ford Jones, alive and well and posing for his bio photo at the Jefferson Group, his former employer." The screen clicked, the sound a vestige from projectors of yesteryears. "This is Gerald Ford Jones, dead from a junk gun blast to the stomach, in his office two days ago." He was folded against his spalted beech office drawers. Real wood, Matte confirmed. The panels were piebald with a paler and a darker brown, now painted calico with Gerald's bloodstains.

"The shooter has not been apprehended." Click. "His image, seen here, is not necessarily representative of his true appearance. He is between five foot five and five foot eight, depending on how he's slouching. He entered the building with the contract cleaning crew, his first day on the job. His credentials were very well faked." Click. "He was seen cleaning the thirty-third floor for the hour and a half before the decedent, Mr. Jones, arrived for work that morning." Click. "He approached Mr. Jones' office shortly after his arrival at zero six thirty that morning." Click. "He spoke briefly with Mr. Jones, confirming Mr. Jones' identity, before apologizing and then murdering him."

Click. Security footage from the hallway showed the boy raising his vacuum wand and firing it into the office. One shot, fire and smoke erupting from his hands. He ran away from the camera, struggling to free himself from the backpack-mounted vacuum unit as he heaved down the hall.

Click. He ran towards another camera, panic in his eyes as he kicked off one boot between strides, then the other. By the time he had passed that camera and gone on toward the next, he was halfway out of his jumpsuit. Click. Police officers chuckled. The boy tripped and fell face-first into a potted plant, spilling dirt into the hallway. Police officers guffawed. Click. On the floor, he took the opportunity to disrobe completely, drawing more laughter. Click. Stark naked, he ran toward another camera, covering his bashful appendages with braver ones. He turned into a nook beyond the view of the camera. Click. Silence.

"That's it," Detective Jackson stated. "That's all they gave us. Allegedly, at that very moment, there was an attack on their security systems, causing a complete camera and sensor failure. The system comes back to life a few minutes later, but there is no sign of the birthday boy here." A few chuckles drowned among confused faces. "The Jefferson Group wanted to handle this investigation themselves." Raised eyebrows. "They're not. We're taking it from them. We have primary jurisdiction based on two factors."

"What two factors, de-*tect*-ive?" Officer Khalil O'Malley piped in like a schoolboy. Melody rolled her eyes. O'Malley regularly walked the fine line between smartass and dumbass.

Click. A bullet hole in an angled window. "First, some of the buckshot went through their fancy windows and out into the street, we think. It might be in their gardens, but it is literally a jungle down there. Matte can't see straight with all the stuff going on. Besides, based on what we now know about the other projectiles, this was not standard buckshot. The pellets are not uniform. Their constituent metals are not similar, so if they find something down there there's no way to prove it did or didn't come from our guy's gun. But, you know."

Click. The custodial vacuum pack appeared on the screen, with a close up of the tube underslung the vacuum wand. It was hidden in plain sight, welded delicately to the apparatus.

Click. The pellets, some in evidence bags, some in an autopsy pan, caked in blood. They were all the similar, but not the same, not uniform. One was hexagonal, clearly the head of a bolt. A wad of charred cotton wool accompanied them in the evidence photo.

"He got killed by a blunderbuss," Detective Celine Hartford interjected. "On the thirty-third floor of the fanciest building in a thousand miles. Weird luck. That's like, the negative lottery."

"I wouldn't be so sure, Detective." Melody continued. "Lotta stuff going on here." Click. "This is Hannah Mah, alive and well and smiling for her graduation photo, taken three years ago. After graduation, she was Mr. Jones' colleague at the Jefferson Group. Until three weeks ago, that is. Three weeks ago, she was fired or resigned or let go. We're not exactly clear on that." Click. "This is Ms. Mah two weeks ago at the Six Counties Morgue. Obviously dead. Presumed a suicide. Tox reports came back strange, though. Then we found . . . this." Click.

"Here is security footage of Ms. Mah entering her mother's house the day of her death. Carrying groceries, flowers, and her bag." Hannah hobbled up the stairs, heavy with her deliveries. She placed the bags in her right hand down, pulled her keys from her pocket and unlocked the door. She put a key in her mouth, picked up the bags, and went through the door. Click.

"Here is security footage of Ms. Mah entering her mother's house two weeks before her death. Again, carrying groceries, flowers, and her bag." Hannah again hobbled up the stairs, heavy with her deliveries, but less so, and smiling. She placed the bags in her right hand down, pulled her keys from her pocket and unlocked the door. She mouthed the keys, picked up the bags, and went through the door. Click. "And again, a month before." The scene repeated. Three takes of the same walk, same routine, same groceries.

Pause. Detective Hartford was the first to break the silence. "What's her mom got to do with this?"

"Not much. She's a nice lady, used to work in Six Counties Admin. Devastated obviously, lost her only child, in her own home, to a presumed suicide. She's got a couple friends in the department who brought this one to our attention." Detective Jackson stalled. "Any of you gumshoes got a clue?"

Silence.

"Well, I'm glad we've got Matte, then." Click. "Matte found this security footage of Ms. Mah's momma's house three and a half weeks ago, four days before her departure from the Jefferson Group." It was night. A man stumbled up to the door and drunkenly knocked. Or pretended to knock. A keen eye could see that his motion was mimed, exaggerated, that his knuckles did not make contact or create a noise for the image-only security cameras. He fumbled for his keys, which were chunky, clumsy in his ham-fists. He swayed and faked disbelief when his keys did not work. He tried one after another, but with the fourth attempt he steadied himself and stood too calmly to portray drunkenness. He then returned to pantomime, false confusion, and then stumbled out of the scene.

Click. "The keys. Matte found exotic protein residues on Ms. Mah's keys and in the keyhole." Matte hummed with satisfaction as Melody translated his findings. "Exotic proteins ended up being degradation byproducts of some particularly nasty black-lab pharmaceuticals. Explained the toxicology reports. Oral prodrug cytotoxins that don't do anything unless or until they get to your small intestine. Mouth, nose, esophagus, stomach, you're fine. But if some little fairy delivers a microgram of it to your intestines, your organs fail like a bunch of sloppy dominoes."

Click. Kidneys on an autopsy scale, mottled gray and weeping blood. "All of you old fashioned types take note, don't put your keys in your mouth. Actually, don't put anything in your mouths that hasn't been washed recently." Police officers chuckled.

Officer Pollack Moss raised his hand, which Melody acknowledged reluctantly. "I get that they both worked for the same place and that both of were killed. But other than that, I don't get what connects the two."

"That's it, Moss." Click. The lights came on. "Neither do we. Our suspects are that naked guy and that 'drunk' guy. We don't know their identities or their motivations. We expect they each had collaborators, as these weren't corner-store stabbings. They took careful planning and detailed execution. If you see something, or hear something, or think of something, let us know." Dry silence filled the meeting room. Melody waited for questions or protests, but received none.

"Also," she continued, "we have control over this investigation, for now. The Jefferson Group wants it. To smooth things over, we agreed to share information. You might get some requests to do so from the Delaware Staties." Groans. "Don't. All information sharing goes through me."

Sighs of relief. Information requests meant paperwork, and the only thing worse than paperwork was Delaware paperwork. Six Counties cops resented their better-funded, better-equipped, and better-rested counterparts at the Delaware State Police. With all its exclaves and extraterritorial holdings, Delaware was the second-most-populous state in the country during weekday working hours. Nearly ninety million people worked, on paper at least, in some safety deposit box in Dover. And their police force, located in satellite offices around the globe, protected those corporate citizens and their assets.

"One last thing. You all know the Trellis and other big corps like it are big targets. You remember what happened to Maypole Holdings in the Big Trouble, and what happened to Sentosa Industries a few years ago. Keep your eyes open, here and at home."

The room grew somber. The officers knew all too well what Detective Jackson meant. During the last flare-up alone, nine of her colleagues were assassinated out of uniform. Melody knew two of them well enough to know they weren't moonlighting as mercenaries or revolutionaries. The others would've needed something a lot stronger than coffee or Ar-mod to work a full patrol shift and then go home and build a car bomb. More likely than not, they each got caught out in the deluge of human suffering that came with every upheaval. Whenever people started feeling justified in shooting or burning or blowing each other up, someone always decided to do the same to Six Counties cops.

"If this is the start of something bigger, another flare-up, we need to know first. We can't keep the peace if it's not there to keep. On that note, the budget this month doesn't have much wiggle-room for funerals." She paused and allowed a grim smirk to escape from her lips. She usually left the gallows humor to her subordinates, but made rare exceptions behind closed doors. Nervous laughter escaped from a few of the younger cops. "Bagpipes ain't cheap. So do me and the taxpayers a favor, and stay safe out there. Dismissed."

10. Cloudbuster

When Debbie told Terrance about the job offer, he received the life-changing news with cautious enthusiasm. By association, he was now happy, lucky, and rich. That very association, their relationship, had been long burdened by his perpetual unemployment, his idle moping, and bouts of self-sorrow. He was unsure whether Debbie's new station alleviated or aggravated the embarrassment that he brought to the table. Debbie watched the tug of war between Terrance's excitement and fear play out across his face and shoulders and restless appendages.

They slept in late the morning after the interview, hungover. They mumbled about the future, about whether to and then where to move with her relocation stipend. About whether Terrance should pursue his music more earnestly, now that they had some financial breathing room. About whether he should take cooking classes. What was Debbie most excited about at the job? What did they want for breakfast? Real fruit, Debbie said. She hadn't had a grapefruit in years. The Trellis's cafeteria would have fresh produce from the gardens, she told Terrance. She would sneak him things home, if he wanted.

"Pistachios," he said. "If they have pistachios, bring me some. I've never had fresh pistachios."

"I've never had fresh pistachios either." Debbie's head ached, searching through her memory. "Fresh?"

"Yeah."

"Fresh pistachio nuts?"

"They're nuts?"

"I think so, yeah."

Terrance rubbed his eyes. "Maybe I've never had a pistachio. Like, at all."

"Well," Debbie said. "I guess I'll have to sneak you some."

They talked about his job search. It seemed no one needed

electrical engineers. He had held a series of unpaid internships for a few years after graduating, but then the opportunities evaporated. He would take side jobs as an electrician, but with the real electricians, computer engineers, general handypersons, and bums on the street competing for the work, the money sucked.

On top of all that, the new electrical systems were confusing as hell. Whoever was designing, manufacturing, and installing them was "next level," he explained. They were over-designed, purposefully convoluted, so that only the manufacturer knew how to work on them. Some box in Daejeon had learned everything there was to know about electricity and material science, designed the circuit boards, then ordered some bigger box in Antofagasta to manufacture them, then told big floating boxes to sail them all over the globe. Human opinions, handiwork, and seamanship were not important parts of the process.

Some of the newer stuff was absolutely intolerant to moisture, he explained. Actually designed so that a human electrician couldn't breathe on it, let alone tinker with it. Even if he understood one, if he ever tried to fix it he could only make it worse. They never told him in college that he would need to learn how to be bone dry.

"At least one of us got lucky," she said.

"You're not lucky. You're too smart. Did you do the 'boring' thing? Like you said? The being 'taupe?'"

"Not sure, really. It was weird. No one else was there."

"Well you were right about that, then, too. You said they must like you already. They didn't need to ask anyone else. So you were right about that." Terrance stretched his torso as he put his hands behind his head and stared at the ceiling. "What did you want to be when you were a kid? A pediatrician?"

Debbie thought back. "Or a zookeeper."

"That's right. Why a zoo? You don't even like zoos."

"I did when I was a kid."

"Why not, like, a park ranger?"

She didn't know. She didn't actually remember *wanting* to be a pediatrician or zookeeper. She remembered saying that was what she wanted to be. The feeling, the actual desire, was lost to time.

"I don't know. I didn't know it was an option. I hadn't been to a national park. I'd been to a zoo."

"Right. Still, you were smarter than me. Like, I said I wanted to be an engineer, for whatever reason, so I studied that."

"That's good, though."

"Right, but, you know. Obviously not. Because I never actually looked up what jobs there would be. You read the articles. Listened to your college counselor. Read the tea leaves on the wall. And now . . . Debbie Peck, Mediator for the Jefferson Group. Cha-ching."

"Maybe I'll put that in my bio. Debbie Peck pragmatically chose a career that seemed automation-proof. Debbie Peck euthanized her childhood dreams. Debbie Peck is scared of being poor."

"Oh, come on. You went where you were needed, not where you wanted. That's you being a responsible adult. You did it, and now you're great at it. You're a great mediator."

"Good enough. For now, at least." Debbie rolled her eyes. "The arguments I deal with are too dumb for computers. People are too weird. Their arguments are too messy. It's too fluid, illogical. We're idiosyncratic at best. Sometimes, just idiotic."

"Like I said, you're smarter than me. You chose a field that would fry a computer's circuits. I went into a field where I literally can't touch the things I'm supposed to be working on."

"You're not alone."

This reminder didn't help. "Great."

"There's only about ten billion people like you, put out of the job by some box in Singapore or Goa or Melbourne. You know my great-grandfather was a taxi driver, right?"

"Yeah, and his grandfather was an elevator operator. One of my ancestors was probably a tapeworm, but it doesn't make me feel any better. It would be nice to be one of the couple billion people who haven't been made obsolete yet." He stared through the ceiling. "Will you work with any Cloudbusters?"

Cloudbusters. That's what the kids at CIT called them, years ago, when they were out protesting, demanding their rights, decreeing their emancipation. Organons. Dinkum Thinkums. Boxes. They had many names, some that were spoken and some that were hissed. They were computers that outpaced the human mind in processing power, complexity, or creativity. "Creativity" used in its loosest sense, mistranslated by computer engineers who were unversed in creativity's deeper meanings and finer points. While a supercomputer could arrive at a correct answer through impossibly fast permutation and computation, an Organon could divine shortcuts and rewrite its own code on the fly, without needing human intervention. Done once, it looked like an error. Done a million times, it looked like a personality. A dry, inhuman personality, lacking guile or ambition or hurt or humor, but a personality, nonetheless.

"I know they have them," Debbie said. "I probably can't mediate an Organon, though. I don't know what a happy or horny or frustrated computer looks like. Not my wheelhouse."

"If you do see one, do me a favor. Just pour a glass of water on it. I know a couple hundred thousand people who could use the work."

"I'm pretty sure that'd get me fired. Or jailed for murder." Debbie frowned. "Is it murder? To kill one. Have they figured that out yet?"

"Beats me. It's damage to property, at least. Property that's orders of magnitude more important than a human life, if you're using their accounting. Doesn't eat, doesn't sleep. Even they took lunch, they'd still be a thousand times more productive than one of us." Terrance was joking, but barely. Debbie could tell he was upset.

"There are plenty of things you can do that a Dinkum can't."

"Like what?"

"Like make me a tea. And other stuff." She kissed him. "Use your imagination." His tension eased, disappearing from his furrowed brow, migrating to other more useful extremities. His legs tightened, swung out from the bed, then brought Terrance to their tiny kitchen to boil Debbie some water.

11. Wigwam

Melody stared at the Chicago skyline through Gerald Ford Jones' fourteenth-floor condominium windows. As Matte interfaced with Gerald Ford Jones' Wigwam unit, she watched the buildings quiver in the hot air shriveling from the sunbaked streets. The skyscrapers formed a sweeping ridge, like the spine of some dinosaur buried in the sand, its hips starting near the John Hancock and its withers peaking near the old Sears Tower. The Sears Tower slouched strangely from this angle. Its tired shoulders squared off with the approaching West like a gut-shot black-hat cowboy, awaiting the inevitable.

"Anything good, Matte?"

"No."

"Anything bad?"

"No."

Melody tutted. Matte was a great detective, but terrible company. "Anything juicy?"

"One moment, please." He whirred for a few seconds. "No."

She grumbled. This condo, while tasteful and way out of her pay grade, was boring as hell. Gerald Ford Jones was as dull as they came. He was attractive enough, well groomed and well employed. He had parents in Toronto, still married, recently devastated. One older half-sister in Australia. Few friends, no enemies. His tastes appeared simple, borderline prudish. His dating profile barely differed from his professional resume. He had occasional visitors to his condo, but only on Saturdays and only once or twice per month at that. Weeknights seemed reserved for professional-slash-personal development. He was a regular at his gym and at the community center where he took yoga classes. He was not religious. He did not own a gun. His bank accounts were healthy, his retirement savings ahead of schedule.

She checked the fridge. There were four acrylic sealed containers filled with some sort of sea-weedy mush. Melody had found another in Gerald's blood-caked workbag. She imagined that if he knew he would die that Monday, he wouldn't have spent his last Sunday on Earth preparing a week's worth of health food. There was no beer in the fridge or ice in the freezer. There were a few unopened bottles of wine, but no empties. There was no evidence that Gerald Ford Jones gambled, did drugs, took risks, said mean things, thought impure thoughts, or failed to brush his teeth before bed. His only glaring flaw was that he was in cold storage at Six Counties morgue.

"Anything at all, Matte?"

"Nothing conclusive. Nothing to note, in detail or in aggregate."

"How's his Wigwam?"

"Unremarkable."

"Not your type?"

"No." Matte might have understood her joke, but he did not appreciate it. Matte didn't have a type. He didn't have a libido or hunger or desire to be liked. His only driving imperative was to answer one simple question—"Who or what caused the decedent's death?" He was a causality engine, an "if-not-but-for" second-gen Organon. He didn't take coffee breaks. He wasn't in the middle of a messy divorce. He didn't need to drink away whatever horrible sights he'd seen that day. He never lost sleep because he never slept.

Matte never asked why he was born into a world so terrible, with horrible people who did horrible things to each other. The act of murder, the reasoning behind it, didn't trouble Matte. It was human business and did not reflect upon him. He'd never murdered anyone. Nor had any Organon, for all he knew. So he showed no shame or disgust when pouring over endless hours of evidence. Humanity's sins, the blood and guts and mayhem, were simply his environment, his habitat. He was formed to fill the spaces between human violence the way a bee dances between blossoms, floating from one incident to the next with purpose and industry, free from complaint.

Melody wasn't so lucky. The job, the violence, never left her.

But then again, the violence never left anyone. At least she could be proactive about it. She had seen and forgotten countless terrible things and carried countless more deep within her. Her childhood was no better or worse than most. She and her sisters helped each other, saw it through that they'd make it out okay. Their mom was a nurse, then a patient, then nothing. Their father was a veteran, then an addict, then gone. They rode out the worst of the Big Trouble in Champaign with their paternal grandparents. Melody did well in school, went to community college, and got her degree in criminal justice with only a bit of manageable debt.

She volunteered at the local tribunals and ad hoc courts while civil order reestablished itself, then found a golden opportunity in the Six Counties Police Force. Chicago had broken, as had dozens of municipalities surrounding it. Credit, assets, and liabilities in wild disarray, a snap agreement reincorporated Chicago and the collar counties into a new municipal entity before anyone could mount an organized opposition. People could barely organize a potluck in those days. A raiding party? Sure. A book fair? Not a chance. But the Fraternal Order of Police organized a walkout. Their pensions gone, their feeble credibility in freefall, their authority in question, they simply refused to serve and protect.

So when the newly formed Six Counties Police Department issued an open call for recruits, Melody joined the next day. She had no love for the Chicago Police, so she didn't mind crossing the picket lines. Maybe the Six Counties Police would do better. They hadn't, yet. But hell, maybe they still could.

"What's next, then?" Melody asked.

"Witness interviews," Matte said.

"Right. Ready to roll?"

"Yes."

"Is there anything you want to scan further?"

"No."

"Okay." Melody unplugged Matte from the Wigwam and stuffed his cords into his velcro pouch. She began to wheel him towards the door. "There's a bump here. You ready?"

Matte said nothing. Melody couldn't tell if he felt bumps but suspected he didn't enjoy them. Her grandmother hadn't when Melody wheeled her around. Matte could feel month-old fingerprints on aluminum foil, so he could probably feel the uneven tiles and the CLUNK, CLUNK, as Melody dragged his trolley down the steps to the condo's exit. But Matte did not wince or flinch. His cooling fans just purred as Melody pushed him back to the elevators, then down to the dusty streets of Chicago, Six Counties.

12. Tilapia

Debbie's recruiters were overjoyed in an understated way. When Debbie told them she got the job, they said, "We're overjoyed," but sounded under-joyed, if joyed at all. Something wrong at home, maybe. Maybe it was professional jealousy. It didn't matter, they were headhunters. They did their part, they got their cut. Debbie thanked them a half-dozen times, then hoped to never speak to them again.

Debbie called Six Counties Detention and Conflict Resolution Center to resign. They understood. They congratulated Debbie and said they would miss her. The agency that managed her contract was annoyed, but they had hundreds of applicants waiting to hop on the bottom rung of the rickety ladder that Debbie now disembarked.

Jeff Martinez felt bittersweet. He and Debbie were buds. He looked out for her when she had started. He insisted Debbie and Terrance come to his and Ez's for dinner that night. "Real Mexican," he said, though his family had been in Chicagoland for a century, and Ez's even longer. Debbie had seen the confused look on detainee's faces when Jeff yelled at them in Spanish. He looked the part, but his accent was pure "donde esta la biblioteca" embarrassment.

But Ez could cook something fantastic. She had been sous chef at some of the expensive hotels that catered to international clientele near O'Hare. Even during the height of the violence, when the Kennedy expressway was swaddled in concertina wire, she would run that gauntlet twelve times a week to ensure some bigwig's salmon was poached correctly. When Jeff made shift sergeant at the detention center, Ez quit and started cooking for the Baha'i community center in their neighborhood. They put their twins through its daycare and elementary school as payment for Ez's cooking. Even with the toddlers and infants, there was less screaming than in the hotel kitchens Ez had grown used to. Ez radiated youth and beauty, as always, looking twenty-something despite being in her late forties.

Debbie and Terrance brought gifts, a bottle of red from Portugal and a bottle of white from Kentucky. Debbie noticed Ez wince when they were revealed. She didn't drink, Debbie remembered.

"Oh, thank you. These look great," Ez said.

"I'm sorry, I forgot you don't."

"Oh, she does," Jeff said, leaning in. "She just can't let her boss know."

"Or their spies," Ez said, pointing toward the ceiling. "The boys worry. I will try the white. In a mug."

Debbie and Jeff and Terrance sat and prattled about the detention center and Debbie's new job while Ez finished cooking dinner. The twins checked in shyly, as most twelve-year-olds do with strange adults in the house, before going upstairs to their room to play their games. They spent too much time playing video games, Jeff said, but it was safer than outside. "It's getting worse."

"What is?" Terrance asked.

Jeff looked out the window. "Outside. Everything. It's getting way worse."

Ez stuck her head in. "Stop that. You know it's not nearly as bad as it was."

"I know! But that was different. There was the lockdown, then the breakdown, then the Big Trouble. People still remembered how things should be. Or could be. Some of the kids these days, they grew up in this. They don't remember what it was like going to get a cheeseburger without worrying if you'd make it home."

Ez tutted. "That was never the case. You always had to worry about that. A hundred years ago, two hundred years ago, 2030s, 2010s, 1990s Chicago. 1960s Chicago. 1930s Chicago. 1893 Chicago. 1843 Chicago. The world is and always has been a dangerous place."

"Okay, maybe!" Jeff grinned, knowing better than to argue with Ez. "You're right, but things are weird, I'm telling you. Debbie, you do a great job in those mediations. But there are a lot of people you don't see. Your guys actually have something to negotiate. You only meet the people that have something to gain or lose. But there are other guys that show up, they don't talk at all. Guys and girls, normal looking. Look like your neighbor, like they should be on a toothpaste commercial. Assault, stalking, weapons charges, violence, murder. Serious stuff they're accused of. But they won't say a word. Not to the intake officer. Not to the shrinks. Not to the other inmates. You don't even get to be in the same room with those guys."

"Psychos," Terrance said. "Like Ez said, there have always been psychos. Some people can't handle it."

"Yeah, but these guys don't seem like psycho cases. No sadistic streak. No smearing their crap on the walls. No lunatic raving. They just seem like normal people, charged with serious stuff, staying dead quiet, dead to rights. Doesn't add up, with what's at stake for them. They're like you two. No prior convictions. Nothing wrong with you. Could actually have a chance at making it. What they used to call 'upwardly mobile,' before, you know."

"Before it all started falling apart," Debbie said.

"Right. Plus there's all the normal bullshit, kids with no job prospects, no agency, just a bunch of hormones and something to prove. We still get those assholes coming in at the normal rate. Maybe even more."

Terrance took a big gulp of his wine. "You guys hiring?"

"Hah. Sorry T, no. The waiting list is long and crowded. Guys' brothers or cousins or sons who are up next for a guard job, and if you jumped in line, the detainees would be the least of your worries. Besides, Admin give us exactly what they think is needed, nothing extra. I mean, I can give you a riot shield and a vest. Just—"

"Not a paycheck." Terrance smirked. "Thanks. I'm good."

They ate tilapia in poblano mole over millet. It tasted delicious, but Jeff complained that they didn't have rice. Millet wasn't authentic. It was bird food.

"Does he whine like this at work, Debbie?" Ez asked.

"No, he's very well behaved." Debbie smiled.

"I spoil him," Ez said. "That is why he acts like a baby around here."

"A baby bird. Feeding me bird food. Chirp chirp. We've got worms for dessert." Jeff squinted, and Ez squinted back. Terrance and Debbie laughed politely. Terrance artlessly questioned the regional origin of this particular dish. Ez explained that tilapia originally are from the Nile river. They are the fish that Jesus multiplied to feed the multitude. But now, they are farmed all over. These were bought at Jewel-Osco. She explained the millet was a variety called Job's Tears, or adlay millet, originally from Southeast Asia. But this variety was grown in Oklahoma and also bought at Jewel-Osco. The poblano mole, however, was a family recipe. It originated somewhere in the foggy mists of time between the Olmecs of pre-Columbian Meso-America, Ez's grandma's house in Bridgeport, and the Mexican foods aisle in Jewel-Osco. Which actually had a very good selection, Ez assured. Wine disappeared and, in its place, appeared aperitif glasses full of dark Venezuelan rum.

"You going to be okay at the Jefferson Group? At la Piña?" Jeff asked, growing sentimental and protective.

"Well, they promised me no one would hit me with a chair. So . . ."

"Okay, okay. But I'd take a room full of goons before getting in with those corporate jackals. I hope you know how to handle them better than I do."

"Me too," Debbie said. "I don't know. But I do feel 'upwardly mobile' for the first time in . . . I don't know."

"The first time," Terrance said. "Period."

"Here's to Debbie," Ez toasted. "Congratulations on your new adventure."

Jeff raised his glass. "We hope you solve all the world's problems. Or make a buncha money. Whatever works." They drank and they chatted a little longer, but then Debbie excused her and Terrance before eight. Ez and Jeff had to put the twins to bed. Terrance was looking drunk. And she was exhausted, everything was changing so quickly. She had to be up early to get ready for work, and she needed to be rested and ready to go. It would be a new day, a new job, and a new chapter in her life. It would be her first day working in the Jefferson Trellis.

13. Mayflower

Melody Jackson's bed felt unfamiliar. The community bunks in the station house, she could fall asleep in those in a second. This bed, her own bed, felt strange. She thought she had missed it dearly for the last four nights. She pined for it, thinking of nothing else that entire afternoon. But now, she realized it would take some time before she reacclimatized to the peace and quiet of her own home. She was wide awake. Something was wrong.

She sat up, took off her shoes, and walked to her kitchen. Two fingers of sorghum whiskey over some cloudy ice cubes retrieved from her tiny freezer felt heavy in her hand. She took an abrupt sip and turned on the news. A former pop singer had died peacefully in the hospital, surrounded by his three children and twelve grandchildren. Melody recognized the name but didn't feel sentimental or forgiving enough to enjoy the oldies. The music from the Twenty-naughts and Twenty-tens always felt like it came from a foreign country. It sounded like some punchline to a joke she wasn't invited to understand.

Over four hundred dead in Balikpapan, wherever that was.

There was a short tribute to the *Mayflower* mission, which delivered the first six human beings to the surface of Mars—albeit in freeze-dried shards. It was the eighth anniversary of their launch. In a few months, it would be the eighth anniversary of a government shutdown, a budget impasse delaying a critical resupply launch set to rendezvous with the *Mayflower* in high-Mars orbit. This would be followed by many minor anniversaries, unmentioned by the newscast, of three brave men and three brave women slowly deteriorating, then dying in space, and then streaking through the thin Martian atmosphere. They violently laid themselves to rest somewhere in the Memnonia Quadrangle's freshest impact crater. Some congressmen took the opportunity to appreciate that the planets moved—and launch windows passed—with or without their approval. But they remained in the minority. Melody took a long, depressed pull from her drink as she turned off the screen.

She relocated to her porch, sliding the glass door behind her. Electric blue diodes from street lamps painted the bottom edge of the night sky pale. High above, the handful of visible stars or planets hung in the dry night air. In the streets below, Melody listened to the hum of distant trains and cars, scanning for something to distract her from the day's work. She found nothing, just porches and potholes and alleys dark with quiet.

Her mind returned to Hannah Mah, whose house call turned into a sudden stomachache, then liver failure. Whose kidneys suddenly drained her blood of salt rather than urea. Whose watery blood then inundated the electrolyte-rich tissues of her nerves and brain. What out-of-work biochemist cooked up the chemicals that could do that to someone? What creep sat around watching Hannah Mah's routine to know that she put her keys in her mouth nearly every time she visited her mother? Was it the same guy who stumbled up to her door like an old kung fu drunken master, stumbling, swaying until he landed a decisive, fatal blow?

It didn't make sense. There were too many moving parts. It was too elaborate, too convoluted to be the work of one person. It took Matte the equivalent of ten detectives working for seven weeks straight to put all the pieces together, to watch the film and run the analytics. Multiple people had to have participated in the planning and execution of Hannah Mah's demise. Or one person and one Organon, she thought. That was a possibility.

And the timing was suspicious. Hannah May was an employee of the Jefferson Group when the poison was placed at her mother's house. But then the day she stopped being an employee, she went and died. The Jefferson Group wouldn't say whether she was fired, or quit, or walked off the job. They said it was a mutual separation, "the terms of which were to be kept private between the parties." Sam Kettering appeared legitimately surprised when Melody told them that Hannah's death was a murder. But that surprise didn't arise from a place of sympathy or sadness. The Jefferson Group wasn't insulted. They were shocked, afraid. Afraid of something that Hannah's death confirmed. Maybe they were afraid that someone was killing their employees. Maybe they knew that someone was killing their employees, but were afraid that the police were involved. Maybe they were afraid that the police were involved, because they were the ones doing the killing.

But Melody hadn't arrived upon any good reason as to why the Jefferson Group would kill their own employees. She knew they were rich assholes who had their own Delaware Police Pinkertons. She knew they had property in South America and Scandinavia and probably Madagascar, property they could flee to if the Six Counties became too dangerous or unprofitable. She just knew that she didn't like them and that she definitely could not trust them.

Then there was Gerald. Murdered in some strange place straddling Illinois and Delaware and three hundred feet above the ground. The Jefferson Group cooperated with the investigation, technically. Only to the extent that they didn't actively impede it. Interviews with the employees were fruitless. A Jefferson Group lawyer and his box constantly broke the interview rhythm, keeping the employees' answers timid, hedged, and full of self-doubt. The employees feared something, too, but it wasn't the same fear as the administrators. The employees feared losing their ease of existence, their unparalleled quality of life. Even though Gerald and Hannah lost their lives, their coworkers appeared more worried about losing their jobs. Melody watched the interviewees' fear take a different shape as they learned the gunman might still be in the building. They shifted from agitated to grim as they realized they could be shot and killed at their desks. None seemed surprised, just annoyed that the dangers of the streets below had seeped up into their fancy corporate offices.

Very few jobs, Melody remembered, were any more dangerous than the prospect of unemployment. At least in the cities. Death while rich was one thing. Death while poor was slow, lingering, and embarrassing. Her own job was somewhere in between. Police—real police, not the mercenary Pinkerton buy-a-cop bullshit—worked on a different pay scale. The money was terrible. The hours were endless. The danger was constant.

But occasionally, they feasted on that food of the gods, that intangible treasure promised by every religion's afterlife. Occasionally, they were paid in that fleeting commodity that every society could readily identify, but not reliably provide. Occasionally, Melody got *justice*.

And the harder she worked, the more of it she got.

She drank the last of her whiskey, now watered down with most of the ice. Sometimes they got justice. Sometimes they got drunk. Sometimes, they got . . . As her speech that morning echoed in her mind, the dark alleys and windows facing her porch swelled with dangerous unknowns. The shadows populated themselves with unseen assassins, spies, and DIEDs. Instinct commanded her to duck her head as she hurried back inside. She closed the blinds, then readied herself for another night of uneasy sleep.

14. Company

Debbie's second-best outfit would have to do for her first day of work. Jerome and Trey and whoever else was watching saw her only good suit three days before, so today she opted for a professional but friendly combination of sharp lines and soft colors. Terrance made breakfast. Too much breakfast, really. She ate as much of the kale scramble and mismatched grapefruit and bowl of cereal as she could stomach, the whole time wondering whether Terrance forgot how people with a disposable income eat. Maybe he had never known. She could hardly remember what she had eaten for breakfast growing up. Fleeting visions of frosted mini-wheats and bananas and occasional waffles interrupted her anxieties, then she kissed Terrance goodbye and headed out to the car waiting downstairs.

Debbie's car was a solo ride, a celebratory splurge to ease her nerves. She arrived at the second-floor sub-basement drop-off zone early and strutted past all distractions to the first guard station. The bright blue, bulletproof marshmallow took her credentials and told her to head up to HR on the seventeenth floor, where Jerome would be waiting. By the time she had walked the full length of the corridor, Jerome was at the elevator bank waiting with a gift basket.

"Welcome, welcome, Debbie Peck!" He beamed with arms open as if for a hug, but as she approached, he pushed the gift basket ahead of him. "This is for you. It has chocolate and flowers and fruit, all real. And soap and stuff from our business partners, and also another tablet with more documents you need to read and sign. We'll get to that. Let's go straight up and meet the crew!"

As they rose to the thirty-third floor, Jerome twice mentioned how he thought Debbie would like it here. Each time her father's advice rang in her ears. She had forgotten it until just now. He had told her, "If someone tries to sell you a job, *run*." You should have to sell yourself to them, not the other way around. Any job that was worth a damn would know this, he had said. Anyone who begged you to work for them was either incompetent or desperate. But then again, Jerome wasn't trying to *sell* her the job, really. She already had it. He just wanted her to like it and stay and do well. That was simple etiquette and good personnel management.

They dropped the gift basket off at her new office. It was simple, eggshell white with new green-gray carpet looking slightly brighter than that in hall. Blue tape still lined angular windows that jutted out from the office and over the city below. One window had a plastic sheet covering it from edge to edge, like a brand-new tablet or screen. The cabinets were two-toned, beautiful wood. "Sorry for the mess, we're just fixing a few things," Jerome explained. "You'll be in orientation most of this week. It'll be all set by the time you're in here."

"It's beautiful," Debbie said. She meant it. It was her first office. It had a door and a view. "Does this count as a corner office?"

Jerome smiled. "You betcha. Everyone with a window's got a corner office here."

Debbie looked out through the downward-facing rhomboid window. She could see the windowsills of two or three offices below her, jutting out over the fantastic gardens below. In the shadow of the building, starbursts of reflected light turned the gray streets opalescent. "It *is* beautiful. Thank you."

Jerome fanned himself. "On behalf of the HR department, I will take full credit for picking up wherever whoever's algorithm left off. You were at the top of our pile, and now you're here! Wanna meet some people?"

Debbie pulled her shoulders back as she breathed in, clearing her mind for the onslaught of names and personal information and niceties that accompanied professional introductions. It would be strange not to be nervous. It would be impolite not to grovel, just a little bit. It would be foolish to be too bold before she understood the pecking order. She nodded and followed Jerome, smiling as genuinely as she could muster while trying to portray an appropriate amount of understandable first-day jitters.

Audrey Barros rose gracefully from her desk to shake Debbie's hand, holding a ballerina's posture and concentration. She was in her late thirties, consummately professional, but visibly uncomfortable with Jerome as he listed her credentials. Audrey grew up in Buenos Aires, studied in Europe, and cut her professional teeth in Central and South America. She ended up in Suriname after the Afobaka dam disaster, helping negotiate the drafting of the new Surinamese constitution and rebuilding of Paramaribo. She spoke conversational Dutch, Spanish, Portuguese, French, and fluent English. "Old colonial languages," Audrey explained. Debbie would later learn that Audrey was embarrassed to be associated with the "Afobaka Incident," as Audrey called it. Rumors and conspiracy theories surrounded the event, focusing on Gordias Inc., the multinational corporation operating the dam. It held multiple insurance policies on its failing ventures in Paramaribo, and had conveniently parked its vast construction fleet uphill, away from the river on the night the dam "failed." No sooner than the capital city was flattened and drowned did Gordias Inc. move in and start rebuilding, handing out emergency supplies, and pushing for a constitutional convention. Debbie asked Audrey at lunch one day whether she thought Gordias had anything to do with the disaster. "Violence," Audrey sighed, "is the oldest colonial language."

John Elvis Kilpatrick was confident, well dressed, and hailed from some upper portion of what was left of the middle class. Jerome said that John previously worked in finance and specialized in negotiating between national and extranational banks. "Currency disputes, debt forgiveness, territorial leases, that sort of thing." He understood Mandarin and Bengali but never spoke it. Whatever handsomeness John Elvis possessed was overshadowed by his clinical poise and guarded enunciation. He was hiding something. Specifically, Debbie would later learn, he was hiding a slight twang and an upbringing steeped in new Kentucky money that embarrassed him. His family owned horses and vineyards and were public philanthropists but private misanthropes. Like his ancestors before him, John Elvis fancied himself a self-made man, and so he kept distance from the rolling hills and gentle "y'alls" that had actually nurtured him.

Abimbola "Abi" Akindele was thin, quiet, and incredibly beautiful. She wore a yellow and dark green wraparound dress that, while business-appropriate, would command respect on a catwalk. She silently leaned against her desk, glowing like a hot ember that had rolled away from some distant fire, as Jerome rattled through her accomplishments. She was born in Nigeria but went to school in Paris, where her mother was the Nigerian ambassador to France. By the time she was twenty, she was already participating in international negotiations at The Hague. She spent the first five years out of college mediating and negotiating joint ventures to exploit newly discovered mineral deposits across North Africa. She specialized in "tariffs, commodities, futures, as well as treaties and ceasefires." Jerome said she spoke French, Arabic, Yoruba, and English. Debbie would later learn that Abi knew how to politely say "no" in at least eleven more languages, a skill made necessary by the unending barrage of marriage proposals from clients, their associates, and random men and women on the street.

Miranda Kroll received only a brief introduction. She looked barely there, her nose and eyes sore and chalky pink from days of crying. Jerome introduced her as a "Jill of all trades" who does "a lot of great work with water disputes, diversions, and municipal annexations." Miranda stood nervously in front of a gym bag on the floor as she shook Debbie's hand. Jerome later explained she had been close to Gerald and that this was her first day back. Miranda had arrived before the paramedics on the day Gerald died, had tried to save him. She spent the rest of that day in her gym clothes being interviewed by police. Debbie would wonder whether the gym bag contained Miranda's clothes from that morning, still covered in . . . No. Probably not. Hopefully not.

Norma Feng was new to the company, too. She had started about three weeks earlier. Born and raised in Oklahoma, Norma then spent most of her twenties in Hong Kong and Singapore. She understood Cantonese but was fluent in "corporate bullshit," as she put it. Jerome said she hadn't started mediating yet, but would probably focus on "international diplomatic disputes, mergers, and acquisitions." Norma didn't know Chicago or the collar counties, and Jerome suggested Debbie show her around sometime. "I'd love that," Norma said. Debbie would, of course, and would "ping" her later.

"Did I pronounce that right?" Debbie joked. "I'm still learning corporate bullshit."

"Oh . . . yeah. But in Cantonese, you just said something unforgivable." Chuckles subsided as Jerome expressed mock warnings on behalf of human resources. Feeble jokes and meager laughter were a good sign for Debbie, and for Norma. Debbie would learn that Norma hadn't had an easy time in her first few weeks, as she had replaced the recently departed Hannah Mah. Hannah had been liked by her colleagues but was unceremoniously fired or forced to resign or something. Then she supposedly killed herself. Norma started at the Trellis the day after Hannah's wake, in Hannah's office. People regularly called Norma "Hannah," eliciting confusion and distress for everyone involved. People said they actually looked similar, even had the same mannerisms. "Not just because we're Asian," Norma explained. "They keep saying it's 'nothing racist.' But, *you know*." Norma said she often felt like a ghost haunting the thirty-third floor instead of the living, breathing person she had always considered herself to be. Having never known Hannah, Debbie became Norma's first opportunity to make a real friend at work, and she seized upon it.

"What's your deal?" Norma asked.

"Well," Debbie Peck said, "I speak English fluently, but knew a bit of Spanish, too. Once. Not so good at it anymore. I grew up all over the place but say I'm from near Pittsburgh whenever anyone asks."

"Army brat?" Norma's eyes widened.

"No, my dad was a professor. Economics."

"Oof. Where's he at now?"

Jerome winced. Debbie smiled politely. "He's not." Pittsburgh was where she and her mom were stuck after her father jumped off the twelfth floor of a parking garage, but that information was "third date" material.

"Right. Sorry."

"Nope, please. Long time ago. Before the Trouble. Anyway, I majored in psychology and communications at Penn State." Then a dozen unpaid internships fizzled into unpaid nothings. "Went back to school in Cleveland to get my masters and mediator certification." And bounced from unpaid internships to underpaid contract positions. For years. She didn't specialize in anything. She was up to her armpits in personal and professional debt. She ran and exercised to stay sane, and her nose still hurt from where a man had hit her with a chair. "I've focused on local stuff, mostly. Community groups, NTO disputes. Unions, gangs, municipalities. Wherever I'm needed, really."

"Right on," Norma said. "I'll come by your office sometime."

"Right on," Debbie mirrored. "See you then."

"There's a few others, but we'll get to them later. Any questions so far?" Jerome asked as he led Debbie downstairs to HR to sign some documents.

Yes, a million, Debbie thought. Why am I here? Why did you pick me? What do you want? Where is Suriname? What is Yoruba? Had they caught Gerald Ford Jones' killer yet? Who the hell was Hannah Mah? When is my first paycheck?

"I don't think so," Debbie replied. "I'm ready to get started."

15. Gang

By the time summer's fever broke with a brisk, thorough rainstorm in the third week of September, Debbie began to feel comfortable in her new position. The daily operation was simple enough. She would receive notice of an upcoming mediation. She'd study the background materials provided by the Jefferson Group's research team regarding the parties in the dispute. The mediation would occur remotely, with the parties calling into Debbie's office or another meeting room with enough terminal screens to see everyone. The calls were recorded, Debbie was told, for liability reasons in case anything went horribly wrong. Her coworkers informed her, though, that they suspected the recordings were used to analyze performance and determine quarterly bonuses.

Even if she had access to the "tapes" of their recorded mediations, she wouldn't have the spare time to review and improve her performance. As soon as she completed one mediation, another set of background materials needed scouring and another set of names and companies demanded memorization. Jerome told Debbie she should prepare to stay late on occasion, that the types of disputes they were managing were complex and a session could easily go well past working hours. Mediations often began and ended at odd hours due to time differences between the parties. Abi told Debbie once she got stuck on a thirty-hour call between two stubborn Malian governors. John Elvis bragged that once he didn't leave the office for six straight days. But most days, the mediators would arrive after breakfast and leave around dinnertime. They almost never left the building for lunch, thanks in part to the excellent and complimentary fresh food in the Trellis's cafeteria, some of which was plucked fresh from the gardens outside.

In the cafeteria and over coffee breaks, Debbie got to know

her coworkers. She generally liked them. Norma and Debbie got lunch together whenever they could. Kevin Doogan, who had been in a mediation during Debbie's first day introductions, tried to join them as often as possible. He seemed to have a thing for one or both of them. He was thirty-eight, specialized in negotiations between pharmaceutical companies, hospitals, and government regulators, and was drastically single. Neither Norma nor Debbie was interested, but he was hopeless enough to not be threatening. Abi and Audrey would sometimes join, but more often would go off on their own. John Elvis went to the gym instead of lunch, and Miranda ate in her office. Miranda could barely look at Debbie for some reason. She avoided Debbie's office at all costs.

Debbie realized in her second week she had literally taken Gerald Ford Jones' place. His seat and his desk. Her new office was his former crime scene. Having spent much of her first week in orientation classes with tech support and trainers, it took time for her to realize the way people hurried past her door. People flinched when they looked in. Her suspicions were confirmed when Trey stopped in for some casual intimidation.

"How are you fitting in?" Trey loomed in the doorway, his posture exaggerating his efforts to impose himself. He never slouched or fully stood up straight, but always leaned rigidly to hide his modest height. Something about his body language was unnatural, maybe purposefully so. Mediators would have trouble reading him if he didn't exhibit the typical tells if he contorted his body and face into something cartoonishly menacing.

"Pretty well, I think." Debbie spoke deliberately and met Trey's glare from her chair.

"Eh." Trey looked at the floor as the words slithered through his pale lips. "You know Gerald died in this office?"

"I . . . suspected that. This was the only office available, though?"

"Why, you want someone to make another office available? Maybe another . . ." Trey made a gun motion with his hands and silently mouthed "*pow pow*."

Debbie swallowed hard. "Obviously not, no." Trey was paid to be a callous asshole, but his dedication to the role took Debbie aback.

"Well, let's hope the offices stay occupied for A.L.A.P. then. You know what they say?" Trey waited an uncomfortable amount of time for an answer to his rhetorical question.

"What do they say?" Debbie obliged.

"Every time God closes a door, he opens a window." Trey paused. "Pretty bad advice on the thirty-third floor. Let me know if you run into any problems."

Debbie hadn't run into any problems, or at least any that would drive her to talk to Trey. She started with relatively easy cases, like neighborly disputes, small claims court, and small business contracts. Each case file came with the parties stated demands, their expected positions, and then suggested mutually beneficial outcomes. Mediations were designed to turn zero-sum situations into *non*-zero-sum situations. In an early case, Neighbor A wanted to put up a privacy fence, but Neighbor B did not want said privacy fence erected. Discussion uncovered that Neighbor B does not care about fence so much as the obstructed view of alleyway. Neighbor A agrees to allow Neighbor B to install security camera on the outside edge of the privacy fence for an unobstructed view of alleyway. Everyone goes home happy.

The job fell perfectly within Debbie's skill set. She had done the same type of task a thousand times for gangs and community groups and municipal leaders and priests at Six Counties. The scope and complexity of the disputes she was entrusted to mediate at the Trellis, however, surprised her. Mayor A needs thirty million gallons of water over the next three years to supply his town's agricultural needs. Regional Water Management District B has allocated all water futures for next five years to paid contracts. Mayor A's cash-on-hand cannot compete with paid contracts but can promise portion of future taxes or redistricting of unincorporated land. Debbie navigated these subjects with enthusiasm and focus, but often struggled to comprehend what exactly was on the table.

The subject matter expertise that Debbie acquired from Six Counties Detention and Conflict Resolution Center ended up coming in handy. On her third day, Jerome informed Debbie that about a quarter of her workload would involve "gangs and other non-traditional organizations." "We don't want your special training to go to waste," Jerome had said. "Besides, we get to write off all the time we donate to charity." So Debbie would sit and listen and make suggestions as Gang A explained Gang B had shot three of their members, killing one, and demanded a three-block buffer zone between their territories. Gang B would not agree until Gang A stopped affiliating with Gang C, which was encroaching on Gang B's other borders. Good results with these cases usually meant maintaining a peace so that some normalcy and commerce could return to the neighborhood, even if some of that commerce was technically criminal in nature.

"How do you talk to those people?" Norma asked over Niçoise salads in the Trellis's cafeteria.

"Same way you talk to anyone else, I guess," Debbie said, distracted by her ongoing dissection of the dish in front of her. Debbie had not seen tuna fish since she was a child. Real tuna, the flaky type, not the pink mayonnaise-like paste. "They get hungry. They get angry, get sad. Things get worse. If I do my job right, they get happy, and things get a bit better."

"Yeah, but they're criminals. Literally murderers. Rapists and thieves."

Debbie rubbed the scar on her ear. It hurt when her blood pressure spiked, so she calmed herself. "You'd be surprised. Some of the gangs have violent subsidiaries, but they rarely make it to the negotiating table. And people do get murdered in gang-related conflict. But same goes for the corps, and for countries. But most of the gangs and NTOs are run like small businesses or municipalities. Nobody else is looking out for their interests. No one cares if they live or die. They self-organize and start operating under rules that make sense for them."

"Rules like 'It's okay to shoot people.'"

"Could be. But almost all the successful non-traditional orgs have strict rules about how and when violence can be used. Rules of engagement. Like, absolutely no killing neutral parties, no killing unless war is declared, no killing officers, no rape, no violence against women or kids, et cetera. A lot of them are college educated. Most of the leaders have degrees in either history, law, or business. Or city planning."

Norma sighed. "I think it would be a lot better if they, I don't know, followed the law. Like the rest of us."

"I think they tried that." Debbie poked at a black olive. It was rubbery, but its distinct skin and pulp encouraged her. If it wasn't real, it was a very good fake. She popped it in her mouth and was almost overtaken by its rich saltiness. Real tuna, real olives. This place was loaded. "Like, half of the gangs I dealt with weren't criminal at the start. Most of them started as community organizations, lots of them established during the Big Trouble. Where were you when that all went down?"

"Disney, Oklahoma. And I was about twelve."

"Disney?"

"Not that one. It's literally just a town. I grew up there."

"Right. I was in Pittsburgh, in high school. After Little Rock, when the violence started to spread, people in bigger cities needed a lot more organization. There were more people in a smaller area. Country farmers stocked up for themselves, and truckers weren't getting paid to deliver food. It all got stopped and bought in the suburbs. They say civilization is nine meals away from anarchy, but it's more like four when the booze and pills disappear. The poorest people were used to not eating by then, scrounging, saving scraps, rationing water, roughing it. But I was in the middle income, softer areas. They started going nuts. People lost their grip on things pretty quickly."

"Sorry you had to go through that." Norma didn't look convinced. She just looked uncomfortable.

"It's fine, we all did. But I guess what I'm trying to say, is that I knew a lot of people. You know, people I grew up with, who are now in NTOs or gangs or whatever you want to call them. Like, my favorite high school teacher, Ms. Bergkamp, she became one of the community leaders in Shadyside, organizing food centers and street patrols. People kept leaving the city looking for food, getting turned back at gunpoint, then the shooting started. Food deliveries started needing armed escorts. Raiding parties became war parties. The National Guard protected the central business district while militias made up of stupid teenagers in pickup trucks patrolled the suburbs and interstates."

"We had the pickup trucks in Oklahoma."

"Yeah, well they were who we had to watch out for in Pittsburgh. The thing is, I don't think Ms. Bergkamp cared if she was in charge of a high school classroom or community center or a street corner or a supply raid. She was just sick of seeing her kids getting killed. She was good at managing chaos in the classroom, so she could manage chaos in the streets, too. I don't mind helping them—gangs, NTOs, community groups, corporations, whatever. I don't mind helping them get along with each other if it means fewer people get killed."

And Debbie believed herself in that moment. There was a chance that if humanity's connections were better insulated, if its communications were better wired, if there was less confusion and more clarity, that the world could be a better place. There was a chance that if Debbie and Norma and the Jefferson Group really dug their heels in and worked hard, fewer people would kill each other, more people would live peacefully. There was a chance that one day Debbie could sleep peacefully, or consider having kids, or feel financially secure enough to do something that she really wanted. What had she wanted, anyway? Beyond safety, beyond security, it had been too long to remember.

"Mitigation," Norma sighed.

"What?" Debbie looked up from the salad she was poking at to find Norma staring off into space.

"It's all mitigation. We should be building something or going to Mars or taking flying cars to floating cities somewhere. We should have replicators and teleporters and robo-gigolos by now. Instead, we're busting our asses trying to make sure things don't get worse."

"Yeah." Something in the salad or the conversation had turned Debbie's appetite. She was no longer hungry. "At least we're getting paid?"

"My mom always talked about this stuff. She kept apologizing that we had it so bad. Our generation, I mean. She said, 'My parents and their parents and their grandparents were makers. They made things. They kept making stuff not thinking about what they actually needed to make, and all of a sudden we had too many things and too many people. My generation, Norma,' she would say, 'we had to do maintenance, keeping things running. It was boring, and we screwed up, too. We were bad maintainers. So your generation, Norma, you're going to be mitigators.'"

"Huh." Debbie was confused. "What's the difference between maintenance and mitigation?"

"You can maintain everything, if you do a good job." Norma's eyes grew wider with morbid fascination. "Mitigation means you have to pick and choose. Something's going to be lost no matter what, you just have to choose the better thing to save." Norma nodded toward a group of doctors sitting across the cafeteria. Though they regularly crossed paths with doctors or teachers or engineers away from the thirty-third floor, mediators like Debbie and Norma were not privy to whichever of the Jefferson Group's countless projects they worked on. "They know. You maintain a body, it'll carry on just fine. Once you start having to lop off parts to save the rest, that's mitigation."

Debbie's appetite returned with a sense of clawing desperation. "I'm going to get some ice cream. You want some?"

Norma winced. "I'm lactose intolerant. But, I think I saw some pie up there. Let's go."

16. Case

Silence. Mostly silence, at least. The man's left nostril was whistling like hot shrapnel in the interrogation room. Every few seconds he'd inhale suddenly then slowly release. Melody Jackson watched and listened from the screens in the control room. "He hasn't said anything?" she asked.

"No. As soon as he saw us he went mute." Henry Suparmanputra replied with his arms folded behind his back. He was as at ease as he ever was—still, straight and taut as a bowstring.

"Why'd you pick him up?"

"Matte told us to. Turns out Mr. Citovsky here was creeping around Hannah Mah's apartment and mother's house. Linkup data shows he was near her house when she was there, near her mom's house when she was visiting her mom. Matte triangulated everything, we just followed up on it. He was following her, no doubt about it."

A break. This is what she had been waiting for. "Thanks for waking me up, Soup. What took Matte so long?"

"Don't know what to tell you, Mel. Matte added up everything from all this guy's devices. Mr. Citovsky's got a phone and a tablet and a terminal, and he took cars and checked his messages while he was stalking her. Taken alone, each trail wouldn't have pointed to anything suspicious. Add them all up, taken all together, it checks out. Matte said it was a quaternary connection, but it's verified. Citovsky was tracking Hannah Mah in the weeks leading to her death."

"This guy, Cecil Citovsky. What's he do?"

"Same as everyone else—nothing. He's got a master's degree in sociology, he put three years toward his Ph.D., had some internships, nothing paid to speak of. His family is out in the burbs, he moved here for school. No criminal record, bad credit, bad numbers."

Detective Jackson worried this was a dead end. It would be, if she wasn't careful. Mr. Citovsky was in the process of biting a bullet. His mouth clamped down around it, hoping it didn't continue forward through the back of his skull. Melody grew up around plenty of people who believed—and others who reinforced—the idea that to speak to the cops was to die. The police represented the death of freedom, temporarily. Some other more potent local entity promised true death, permanently. Both offered punishment, neither offered justice. The only way around it was to subvert those expectations and to build trust.

But Citovsky's situation seemed to have stranger roots than the street code of noncooperation. He was one of those weirdos, one of this new brand of creeps who took the street code of silence and made it the central tenet of their cult. Kids from the suburbs, out of work accountants, former court clerks, and current college professors arrested, booked, and jailed in complete silence. Who or what they were afraid to betray was not clear.

"Is he a Horrorist?"

"No, they talk. You know that." Soup was right, she did know that. Melody was still waking up. "He's scared. Matte said so, and I agree. He's shaky. We perp-walked him past a few Horrorists, almost shit his pants. He's not used to this. Look at him."

Melody couldn't disagree. Cecil Citovsky was rattling his skin like wax paper wrapping his trembling insides. He looked pitiful. "Did you offer him a lawyer?"

"Yes. He didn't react."

"Did you bring him a lawyer?" Detective Jackson looked to Henry Suparmanputra with a raised eyebrow. Only rich kids could afford an actual visit from a member of the bar. Everyone else got patched in, a call or a screen or decision tree or whatever. Relatively warm bodies in slick suits remained a luxury.

"No? You got an idea?"

"Fish him one out of the pool, Soup."

Officer Suparmanputra navigated the halls of Cook County central holding's basements until he found the Public Defenders' office. When he entered, several sweaty men and women turned from their terminals to see who had arrived. They immediately muted their screens. "You can't be here," one scowled.

"I need a volunteer," Henry boomed. "A wet case. A real live client." One of them hammered her keyboard. Down the row of terminals, beyond those who had been immediately distracted, a man jolted upright.

"Me!" 260 pounds of pale flesh in a crinkled suit and good standing with the American Bar Association squeezed through the clattering rows of his coworkers. "Hoyt Fredricks, Esquire, Officer," Hoyt said as he trundled toward Suparmanputra. "I'll take the case." As they navigated through the narrow halls back towards the holding cells, Hoyt Fredricks bounced like an overstuffed duffel bag behind Soup's epaulets. Hoyt explained how he was excited and thankful and honored and how he became a lawyer to help people but he actually never gets to see real people he just has to talk to them on a screen all day and barely gets to know any of them at that. He explained how ever since he decided to be a lawyer when he was twelve he had been lucky and found the jobs only real lawyers could do, and this was no exception. As he was about to explain where he grew up and why he wanted to become a lawyer since he was twelve, Soup interjected.

"We should keep the chit-chat to a minimum."

Hoyt's face shifted quickly between anger, dejection, and finally into realization and winking nods. "Got it. Got it, Officer. Will do. Discretion and valor and all. My client does come first. Lead the way."

"He's not your client," Soup said.

"If he's requested *a* lawyer then I am—"

"He hasn't, so you're not." Soup turned to meet Hoyt's eyes. "Not yet."

From the observation room, Melody and Soup watched Hoyt introduce himself to Cecil Citovsky. After Mr. Citovsky's fear faded to confusion and then anger, he buried his face in his hands and sobbed. His potential client's face hidden and voice garbled, Hoyt Fredricks stood awkwardly as his first live case dissolved into tears. But strange noises began to percolate from Mr. Citovsky's blubbering, forming parts of words.

"What was that?" Hoyt leaned closer.

Melody and Henry leaned closer to the observation screen. The words were impossible to make out as Citovsky whispered through his sweaty and tear-streaked palms, but it was clear he was talking. The flat slabs of Hoyt's cheeks moved with unquestionable consideration and then comprehension as he deciphered his client's disjointed syllables.

"Okay," Hoyt finally said. "I'll ask them."

No screens, no phones, no mics. Those were Cecil Citovsky's demands. Not to talk to the police, but to talk to Hoyt. Cecil would only speak to his lawyer in a data-proof environment, electronically sterile. "Deal," Melody said. As Suparmanputra led Hoyt and his client to some hidden corner of the Cook County central holding, she tried fitting the pieces together. Citovsky was scared. Scared because he got caught, maybe. Scared of being in jail, maybe. But he was willing to sit in jail for what could have been forever because he was scared of something else. He was afraid of someone seeing something he did or hearing something he said.

Officer Suparmanputra returned. "I set them up in the basement toilets.

"Which ones?" Melody asked.

"The ones the janitors smoke their tax-free resin in. The guards will radio us when they're done."

"Henry, did you tell Citovsky what you were bringing him in for?"

"I told him we had some questions about Hannah Mah."

"Did you arrest him?"

"Formally?"

"Rights read."

"No, he just shut up and got in the car."

"Do we have enough to hold him?"

"For murder? Not even close."

Melody rubbed her stomach between the buttons of her blazer, feeling her vest. "This isn't ideal. Unless he starts talking or asking for deals, which I don't see happening, we're going to need more."

"Understood."

"Unless that lawyer comes out of that toilet waving a white flag and naming names, Citovsky stays with us as long as we can hold him. Use the economic terrorism statutes if you need to. Call it a business-related assassination. Who was with you when you picked him up?"

"Just Kemp."

"Okay. While Citovsky's still detained, get a plainclothes or SVAN detail ready to trail him. We need to see where he goes once he runs free."

"Will do. Who do you want?"

Melody knew the answer but didn't want to say it. Tark Benton was the only officer who could handle the tech on the surveillance vehicle with proficiency rather than simple competence. But Tark looked down his aquiline prow at his blue-collar coworkers, constantly grumbling about a promotion. He wasn't wrong to ask for one. He deserved one, and he probably could get a better job with his skills and expensive tastes. He could put his kids in a better school, move somewhere safe, work somewhere with real coffee in the urns. But Melody didn't want to tell him, again, that she *did* need him and *did* appreciate him but couldn't give him a raise. The department just didn't have the money.

"Use Tark. Make sure you and Kemp are there when Citovsky's let go. Make a real stink. Make it look like a royal screw up. We need him to think he's off the hook."

"Okay. Maybe use the lawyer?" Suparmanputra's eyes sparked with a rare flash of mischief.

"Do what you have to. Just don't lose him when he's out."

17. Pork

Terrance made dinner again, unfortunately. Cooking was first among the hobbies he took up in the first weeks of Debbie's gainful employment, and he had neither improved nor given up, yet. This menu included South Carolinian mustard-rub pork loin, roasted eggplant parmesan, and a bottle of Malbec. "I marinated the pork all day," he beamed.

"Thanks, honey." Debbie tried to be encouraging. "It's really different."

"Different . . ."

"Different good!"

He had that wild look in his eye again. Terrance was smart enough to recognize his shortcomings. But when he identified these insecurities, when he had to face them down, they drove him to either wallow in self-pity or push through with near-manic determination. He wavered between misguided efforts to prove he was worth a damn and a solemn resignation that he wasn't. Debbie watched him carefully, as tonight's mood was tipping toward misguided.

"I think I'm going to go back to college," Terrance sputtered.

"What?" Debbie's forkful of overcooked pork hovered over the table. "Why?"

"I mean not, all the way back to college. Just take some classes."

"How?" Debbie's fork landed among some soggy shreds of eggplant. "What for?"

"I haven't figured it out. Something practical. Something like mediation. I mean, not like mediation, but something that they're actually hiring for."

"Like what?" Her glass of wine now floated between them. Wine. On a Tuesday. A younger Debbie, a tequila and ramen Debbie, with her college boyfriend in a band and not-exactly-non-violent protest group, that Debbie would have despised this domestic setting. Wine, dinner, tedious boyfriend, corporate job.

"Stop looking at me like that," Terrance said.

"Like what?"

"Like you're at work." Terrance wavered, teetering between the forward slant of enthusiasm and the backward slouch of depression. "I don't know yet, like what. There has to be something I can do."

Debbie sipped her wine as she watched Terrance scramble for ideas. He was right—she was dissecting him with her eyes. She was pushing him the wrong way, making things worse. Before he reclined into depression, she propped him up. "I think it would be a good idea, if you knew exactly what you wanted to do. It's just, I think you should think about it."

"I will." He hacked through some more pork. "I mean, I *have* been. I want something to do. I want to *do* something. It's just, like, look at this pork."

Debbie looked at the pork. It looked extremely uninteresting, which happened to be exactly how it tasted. "What about the pork?"

"It used to take a pig farmer to raise the pigs. They've got a factory to do that now, ninety-eight percent automated. Then they'd have someone drive the pigs somewhere, on a truck or train. Doesn't matter. Not an issue anymore, trucks drive themselves. Butchering, packing, mostly the same deal. A computer can scan a pig and cut it into the thinnest slices of bacon you've ever seen in a minute, maybe less."

"You wouldn't want to butcher pigs, anyway."

"No. No one does. Even if they did, they couldn't. That's not the point."

"What is the point?"

"*I need something to do.*" Terrance's words spilled out, suddenly released from a place deep inside him. It scared Debbie. "I'm just trying to figure it out. So anyway, you get the pork, and someone has to cook it. I'm trying, you know, to do that, but there are probably actually five billion people alive right now who are better at cooking than me. By necessity, right now. So like right now, it's not a good time for me to go back to school for cooking.

Right?" He sighed. Debbie could tell he was trying to navigate some unbeaten mental path. He was in danger of turning himself around.

"What do you want to do then?"

"I think I want to find new parts of the pig, or something. I mean, like, sales or something. Figure out something that people don't know they need, and then sell it to them."

Debbie was confused. Terrance shared very few natural talents with salespeople. He was moody, awkward, and often stumbled with simple small talk. "Like an inventor?"

"Not, like, an inventor. Like, an innovator or something. Like a salesman, entrepreneur maybe? They're not any good at that."

"Who aren't?" Debbie's mind rounded up the usual suspects, the shadows Terrance habitually boxed. "*Computers*?"

"Yeah, computers. Of *course*, computers. Organons." Terrance's face contorted with hurt. Debbie's failure to understand his disjointed chain of thought came across as a personal slight, a confirmation that the world did not "get" him. "No matter how smart they get, they still just do what they're told to do. Maybe I can, you know, come up with a new thing to tell them to do. If you can't beat them, join them then boss 'em around."

Debbie was surprised because Terrance was right. Countries and corps had claimed to achieve technological singularity dozens of times, had passed the Turing test a hundred different ways, then created countless clones and buds of their hyperintelligent programs. To mankind's surprise, there was no sonic boom or cosmic collapse when something finally outpaced the human brain. Our capabilities were less of a speed limit and more of a mile marker. There was no robot uprising, no cyber-apocalypse. Organons grew exponentially smarter, but their ambition never materialized. It was stunted or non-existent. Cloudbusters and Dinkums sat around doing their jobs with incredible diligence, but never thought of running for mayor or even for dogcatcher. They never thought about taking over the world because no one had asked them to try. "Terrance, I don't think it helps comparing yourself with computers."

"I'm not comparing myself. It's not competitive." His

seriousness drained the heat from the food left on the table. *"I'm not competitive. We've lost. I've lost, for now. I'm just appreciating that, now."* He poured Debbie more wine, up to the glass's lip, then topped himself off. "I'm trying to find my niche. Something I can do. I'm trying to find the little crack I can hide in until this storm passes over."

Lost. Crack. Hide. Storm. Debbie's training told her Terrance's mood had shifted somewhere darker. His enthusiasm would wane. She didn't want that. She wanted him to do well without silly gestures or added debt. "If you keep making me hot dinners and taking care of me, you'll have your niche to hide in."

Terrance warmed. Debbie wasn't sure she meant what she said, though. He was annoying her and she wanted to change the topic of conversation. But he, like each of Debbie's ex-boyfriends, rarely realized when he was being couriered to some more convenient resting place, when he was being cooed, burped, swaddled, and laid to rest. "Thanks, Deb. I didn't mean to get all, whatever."

"It's fine. You should find something that makes you happy." Debbie picked at some cold pork. "Something you want to do."

"I'll figure it out." Terrance smiled. "We'll figure it out."

18. Skein

"This is an *insult* to justice. An absolute *insult*! A betrayal of the most sacred rights guaranteed to my client by the United States Constitution and Six Counties Charter!" Hoyt Fredricks puffed his sweaty throat as he shook his head toward the Cook County central holding desk.

From behind bulletproof glass, the deputy on duty kept her eyes on the screen in front of her. "I'm going to ask you to take a calmer tone."

"I'm not going to calm down when my client's constitutional rights are being trampled, absolutely trampled by your god*damned* police procedural bullshit!"

Between the *m* in "goddamned" and *o* in "police," a security turret sprung to life and zeroed in on Hoyt Fredricks' screaming pulse. Its wear and tear made it at least a decade old, the rust around its muzzle as menacing as dried blood around a wolf's. Hoyt pursed his lips and raised his hands as the few officers and civilians in the lobby froze.

The deputy finally turned her eyes to Hoyt. "Sir, I told you to calm down."

"Yes, okay, I understand. Please tell it I'm calm."

"Are you calm, though, sir?"

"Yes I'm goddamn *calm*," Hoyt whispered as every muscle in his body puckered. If there was one thing that Hoyt liked less than insults to justice, it was having a robot poke him full of disastrous holes.

The officer's radio squawked to life. "We're good in here, Betty. Can you reset the turret?" After a few moments, the turret pointed its business end toward the ceiling and retreated into its cubbyhole. "Now sir, you are free to file a Freedom of Information Act request to receive—" The radio squawked again, spouting something somehow meaningful to the deputy but indecipherable to Hoyt. "Okay, sir. Will do."

Officer Suparmanputra watched the drama unfold from the security cameras in the central control room. He and Officer Sharon Kemp had monitored Mr. Citovsky and Mr. Fredricks' slow spiral into madness over the past two days. Citovsky spent each sleepless night downwind from some ripe crust-punks and across from some vicious Almighty Gabriels. Unable to menace the pale-and-growing-paler Citovsky on account of his race, the all-white Almighty Gabriels slung personalized insults and anatomically creative threats at Mr. Citovsky for the better part of thirty-six hours. Mr. Citovsky was not doing well. It was time to move to Phase Two.

Kemp knew the plan. She would look embarrassed and scared as Soup berated her in a stage whisper. Soup would apologize to Mr. Fredricks for the processing delay, which would presumably have been Kemp's fault. He would ask for Mr. Fredricks' patience as they gathered the evidence and filed the charges.

As expected, Hoyt Fredrick's spine would find the part of his brain that recognized weakness, and it would stiffen. He would vomit amendments, case law, and statutes. He would puff with indignation, make a demand, and then stop talking, as lawyers were trained to do after every half hour of billable blathering. Suparmanputra would consult Kemp in increasingly frustrated tones. He would eventually concede that they couldn't hold Mr. Citovsky any longer. Then, much to Cecil's wonder and amazement, he'd be released.

As a hagridden Cecil Citovsky dragged himself through the lobby, he was left with two impressions. First, his lawyer, Hoyt Fredricks Esquire, had accomplished a heroic feat of legal engineering, having carefully deployed nouns and verbs and other guided missiles to defeat the enemy and champion his client. Hoyt explained all this before Cecil could even change back into his own clothes. Second, the police officers who had arrested him were not very good at their jobs. Hoyt told Cecil they didn't have any evidence, that they hadn't filed anything. And as Cecil hobbled through the Cook County central holding, he saw the officers arguing in the corner. The male officer looked over at him, shaking his head in disappointment, before launching another hushed, angry salvo towards the female officer. If they didn't know what *they* were doing, they probably didn't know what *he* had been doing.

So as Cecil Citovsky stepped out onto South California Ave, he did so emboldened by the notion that he had just gotten incredibly lucky. An hour earlier, he was in the worst place he had ever been, maintaining a strong assumption that something even worse waited for him. He walked to the curb, took out his phone, and dropped it onto the ground.

"Why'd he do that?" Officer Tark Benton, stationed in the police surveillance van three blocks away, asked no one in particular. The feeds from the drones—silently floating past in random trajectories at various altitudes—watched Citovsky's every move. None stopped to hover. Each zipped past as if on the way to some important destination, looped around while changing transponder codes, and took another pass. This slow, delicate swarm of intermittently blinking eyes watched Cecil Citovsky from multiple angles without ever stopping to stare.

Cecil kicked his phone to the edge of the curb and ground his heel through it. Its delicate screen and electronics left a dark copper streak on the concrete.

"Ah. Yup." Tark took a long sip from his coffee. New beans, really good stuff. Someone had salvaged some coffee plants from what was left of Sumatra and started a plantation in the mostly unscathed Andaman Islands. The one-pound bag cost Tark half a shift's pay, but he didn't regret it. A screen in the van flashed with errors. Phone tracker was dead. Tark called Henry Suparmanputra. "Soup, it's me. Subject just smashed his phone."

"Smarter than he looks."

"Just thought you should know. Eyes only from here on out. No SIGINT."

"Got it. Keep us updated."

Tark's SVAN jolted to life to reposition itself down another side street as Cecil Citovsky proceeded through the city. Citovsky hugged the tree-lined boulevards, winding between the bronzing leaves and catalpa beans. Tark's screens switched seamlessly between the drone feeds and any Six Counties' surveillance equipment that remained operational in the area. Citovsky took a leak in Douglas Park before settling at a bus stop on Ogden. Tark needed to go, too, but his screens told him busses were coming in three, five, and eighteen minutes, so it was best to wait.

The three busses passed but Citovsky remained at the bus stop. He stayed seated, keeping his eyes peeled on the road and only occasionally repositioning himself for comfort—hands in his pockets, hands on his head, hands between his knees. Tark watched with caffeine-addled intrigue until his biology demanded that he leave the van to relieve himself between some dumpsters. Vigilance. Vigilance, he remembered, is why we're beat. Drones can stare for hours without getting bored, tired, or piss on their shoes.

Back in the van, Tark was happy to find Citovsky still on his bench. For an hour he waited, watching the hot, September afternoon cook away. But then Citovsky stirred, standing up and patting his hands on his head. His eyes tracked an aging pickup truck as it slowed past him and turned down the road circling the park. Citovsky watched it loop around, maintaining his stance with his hands on his head until the truck returned to sidle up to the curb. The pickup truck was driven by a young woman who motioned for Citovsky to get in.

Tark picked up his phone again. "Soup, new development."

"Hit me."

"He got into an old pickup truck with an organ donor." Organ donors were live human drivers. They paid monumental insurance premiums for the right to point their thousands of pounds of metal in a direction not pre-approved by an automated navigation system. Or they didn't pay the premiums, and then they'd get their antique deathtrap confiscated. "Female. Under forty, over twenty. Caucasian."

"Did it look like he knew her?"

"Can't tell."

"Got it. Anything else?"

"License plate is wrong. Indiana plate, registered to a dead guy's car, not a truck."

"Stolen plates. Probably a stolen truck. Don't stop them yet, see where it goes."

As the drones spun webs of sightlines above the pickup truck,

Tark's van abandoned its occasional repositioning to take full chase down Ogden Ave. It maintained a comfortable distance three-quarters of a mile behind, calculating and recalculating potential routes to prevent getting too far from its drones.

The pickup truck eventually slowed to a stop between the broad underpasses near Clybourn station. The highway and the train platforms created a cavernous space hidden from the prying eyes above, leaving only a narrow crack open to the sky. The obstruction forced the drones to sweep low to street level. The municipal security cameras there were inoperable, covered with pigeon feathers or spray paint or smashed to pieces for parts.

"Soup, it's me again. They're stopped under the highway, near Ashland and Cortland."

"Okay. Doing anything funny?"

"Can't tell, it's a bad angle we got. Got one drone landed on a roof down the block, but it can't hear anything from the highway noise. They've got a lot of egress points, the highway, the Metra, the riverbed, lots of streets. We're at a disadvantage. For now though, they're not moving."

"Are the drones scanning or just watching?"

"Just watching. No radio, no wave or active scans, just passive radar. Eyes and ears like we said."

"Makes sense. Anything else?"

Just then, on the live feed from the drones passing above Citovsky and the pickup, a strange shape entered the frame. A pentagon, roughly shaped like a child's drawing of a house, floated silently 250 feet over the trickle that was left of the Chicago River. Tark guessed it had to be at least five feet across. Its gray dorsal surface was squiggled with orange and brown spray paint to approximate the approaching autumn's motif. It glided over the tracks, over the highway, and continued south-by-southwest over the neglected terminus of the Bloomingdale trail.

"Um . . . yes," Tark sputtered. "Something weird. I think I just saw a UFO."

"What?" Suparmanputra took a bite of the tamale Kemp had ordered for him. He was buying her lunch for making her endure the brunt of their fake argument in Cook County central holding. "What is it?"

"Not sure, I'm tracking it. It's a drone, not one of ours. SVAN says it's not registered, doesn't show up on M-wave. Looks homemade maybe? Citovsky's still in the truck. So's the girl. Trying to track this thing, just a sec."

One drone from the SVAN's skein peeled off to follow the unidentified drone. Tark watched the strange polygon float over boarded-up houses down Paulina Street. It fell silently like a giant poplar leaf, slowing as it tilted its nose upward into a loop, exposing its pale blue, swollen belly to the police drone above. As it looped, it twisted, directing itself down Le Moyne street as it lost altitude and gained speed. Where Le Moyne ended, a large, windowless white van with "Argyle Cleaners" painted on its side sat parked near a yellowing maple tree.

"Soup . . ." Tark's voice dropped an octave as a screen came alive with a feed from his van's own security camera. From the SVAN's perspective, an angular rip in the autumn sky grew larger as the unidentified drone approached. As he reached for the door handle, a shockwave derailed Tark Benton's train of thought from his tissues the instant before knocking his last breath from his lungs. The van collapsed around him as the air buckled under the weight of ten pounds of high explosives transmuting themselves into heat and vapor.

"Yup, what is it Tark?" Suparmanputra took a swig from his Michelada and watched Kemp tuck into her chilaquiles rojas. "Tark?" Kemp looked up with momentary interest, but was preoccupied with the plate in front of her. "Got cut off." Suparmanputra shrugged. "I gotta use the john. Answer for me if he calls back."

The windows rattled, and the taqueria fell silent. It was starting again.

The van's drones held vigil as they fruitlessly tried to call home. Five of them circled the pickup truck until some soundless whistle from the Six Counties Quartermaster Depot herded them back later that night. The one on the roof of the boarded-up burger joint needed to be picked up manually. It had watched the pickup truck as its lone female occupant abandoned it. It had watched twelve squad cars come screaming to the scene. And it recorded eight officers approaching Cecil Citovsky with their guns drawn, only to find him slumped dead in his seat.

19. Glitch

Debbie stared at the screens in front of her. One contained a middle-aged, ex-military man named Cliff. He represented the Department of Streets and Sanitation, Incorporated. On the other was a thirty-something white woman named Sandy, who represented the Logan Square Beautification Society. On the surface, the dispute centered on the placement of garbage pickup locations along Diversey Avenue. Simmering under the surface, however, the real conflict revolved around the Logan Square Beautification Society's ongoing rivalry with the Avondale Neighborhood Association, which had devolved into sporadic street violence.

Cliff's face and vocal fluctuations demonstrated his unease. His lips pursed and spine stiffened when Sandy spoke. Sandy, on the other hand, oozed with calibrated violence. Her brow contorted like shifting battle lines crashing against the bastion of her nose. The Logan Square Beautification Society's reputation preceded her. They were one of the toughest gangs in that part of the city. By day, they paraded in chartreuse pinnies, stabbing at litter with their espontoons, "asking" local businesses and homeowners for donations, and making polite "suggestions" for redecoration or removal of unsightly property. By night, they or their less nuanced affiliates smashed windows, ripped out fences, repainted garage doors, inflicted violence on the non-compliant, and worse on the openly defiant.

"It's not fair to our other customers," Cliff went on, "that we delay their garbage pickup. Sandy, with respect, your members haven't paid their fees in three months. Avondale always pays. They're up to date. We can't take Sunday and Monday pickup from them and give them to you."

"Cliff, it's a *safety* issue, not a *money* issue." Sandy's eyes narrowed to slits. "You know we have more people than them, more population means more garbage, and a lot of that gets brought out on Friday and Saturday. We can't have all that trash sitting out until Tuesday. Rats, then plague. Raccoons, then rabies. Armadillos, then leprosy. You know the drill. Believe me, it'll be a lot safer for *everyone* if Diversey gets picked up on Sundays and Mondays."

Cliff snorted. "I get what you're saying, Sandy. I understand you, a hundred percent. But you can tell whatever punk you're sending my way that it won't be the first time I've looked down a gun. I've been putting trash like them in bags and buryin'm since I was eighteen, in Afghanistan. Half our guys were in Jakarta. You think I'm scared of some triple-whip, half-caf, no-foam basic bitch?"

Sandy's expression turned to false shock overlaying secret elation. Cliff's chest-thumping meant he was cracking, and Sandy knew that now that she had the upper hand. Her eyes widened, pupils flared. She smelled blood. Before the situation got worse, Debbie decided to step in.

"If we could take a step back for a second, Cliff, it sounds like you are concerned with your reputation as a business, a business that serves a large portion of the city outside of Logan Square." Cliff said nothing, but his eyes nodded slightly. "And Sandy, your organization is concerned with unsightly—"

"And *dangerous*," Sandy interjected.

"And dangerous garbage on the streets, piling up over the weekend?" Debbie paused. "Let's take a step back and try to picture a situation where both your organizations are happy."

Both Cliff and Sandy receded into thought. Debbie could tell neither was brainstorming solutions, but rather plotting further attacks. Their body language and facial expressions were those of combatants, not creatives. As Debbie was about to go through the standard set of questions to develop suggestions for mutually beneficial solutions, Sandy's mouth opened and she began to speak.

"Hahhhhgh—" Sandy began, but her lips remained frozen as a droning note poured crisply from her mouth. Debbie and Cliff exchanged puzzled glances as the note continued to ring into each of their offices. A glitch? Debbie refreshed the feed, but nothing seemed to happen.

"Cliff, it looks like we're having some technical difficulties. I'm going to cut this off and call you back."

"Yup. I don't see the point, really. But sure, whatever." Cliff was replaced by a picture of Debbie's parents and her when she was nine at the beach in Cape Hatteras. The beach was now under ten feet of seawater, the stilted house swept into the sea not long before Debbie's father's ashes also settled to the bottom of the Atlantic. Debbie didn't dwell on her desktop background as Sandy's solo resonated through her office.

Debbie called the IT department, who sent someone running. The young man who arrived looked cherubic—chubby-cheeked and practically prepubescent—as he fiddled with Debbie's computer.

Trey Brodowski materialized in Debbie's doorway. "What the hell is going on here?"

The boy deferred to Debbie nervously. "In the middle of this session," she said. "She froze like this. The feed is continuing, I don't know if the problem's on our end or theirs."

"It's always on our end, isn't it." Trey fired bolts of scorn toward the IT boy. "Hey, fatso, what's the holdup?"

"It's . . . I don't think it's a hardware problem." The boy turned to Trey. "I think it's software. I *need* to call Jimmy."

Trey and the boy shared an awkward silence that made Debbie feel like a third wheel. The boy fled from the room to avoid Trey and presumably pursue Jimmy. Trey turned his attention to Debbie. "For future reference, we never blame technical problems on the parties. It's our equipment, our problem, unless one of our computer guys explicitly says so."

"Okay." Debbie honestly couldn't care. Computers never piqued her interest. They were tools or forces of nature or magic, but she never learned to code or read code or whatever it was they did to make them work. Programmers were out of work anyway. Cyberpunks might exist in Goa or Daegu or Vancouver, but in Six Counties? Fat chance. Internet was too slow, equipment too scarce. Stuck on 5G and gigabit networks, the USA was at least fifteen years behind. She didn't feel obliged to stay up to speed on technologies that receded over distant horizons.

But Debbie's disinterest in computers began to fade when Jimmy showed up.

Jigme "Jimmy" Mahuta filled Debbie's office with his calming presence as soon as he arrived. He stood a few inches taller than Trey and angled his broad shoulders toward Debbie. Trey's aerosolized aggression dissipated as gentle scents of sawdust, tea, and leather settled into the room. "Hi. Trevor told me you have a problem?"

"Yes, hello, I'm Debbie Peck." She extended her hand, and her eyes met Jigme's as Sandy's monotone aria continued to fill the room.

"Jigme Mahuta. Some people call me Jimmy."

"Do you prefer Jimmy or Jigme?"

Trey snapped at the softened air. "Can we get this moving?"

"Jigme," he said to Debbie as he turned the volume down on her computer, silencing Sandy and creating a vacuum that Trey's tension invaded. "How long has she been like this?"

"Five minutes," Debbie guessed.

"Okay. Trey, you can go." Jigme didn't look at Trey as he dismissed him.

Trey started to leave. "Debbie, come with me."

"Debbie, you can stay. I need to ask you some questions." Jigme turned and stared at Trey as Debbie instinctively tried to read the situation. Trey was a knot of tension, muscles frozen with anger and violence. Jigme was relaxed, stoic even, as he stared back at Trey.

"Jimmy," Trey began.

"John Paul," Jigme retorted.

"This is my floor," Trey seethed.

"This is a software problem," Jigme concluded. And with that Trey stomped out of the office and down the hall. Debbie did not understand what inspired the passive-aggressive showdown but was happy with the result. Jigme provided a new and handsome face, and Trey got his miserable ass handed to him.

"I don't have any questions, actually." Jigme smiled as he turned back to Debbie's computer. "Trey just forgets he's not my boss."

"Lucky you." Debbie smiled back. "Why'd you call him 'John Paul'?"

"That's his name. John Paul Brodowski the Third. The third . . . uno dos tres, so 'Trey.' I'm guessing 'bro-dawg' was taken." Debbie's computer kept Jigme Mahuta fixated as he talked. She watched him as his dark eyes scanned lines of code flitting across the screen.

"What kind of name is Jigme?"

"It is . . ." He paused to type something into the computer. "Bhutanese. My mother's from Bhutan. What type of name is Debbie Peck?"

Debbie blushed. "I don't know really. I think my mom's best friend in college was named Debbie, Deborah, you know."

"And Peck?"

"English or Irish, I think. My dad was English and Irish and German mostly. Where's 'Mahuta' from?"

"It's also from Bhutan, sort of. But my father is Tunisian. Do you want to get some lunch?"

"Now?" It was 10:55 a.m. and Debbie was still full from another of Terrance's mismatched and poorly executed breakfasts, but Jigme's proposal excited Debbie in a way she hadn't felt in a long time. "I probably need to start the mediation again, as soon as my computer is fixed."

"I have a lot more work to do before that happens." He sat back from the terminal and looked at Debbie. "I can have Trevor reschedule your mediation for later this week. This will take me all afternoon, probably. You could take the afternoon off."

"Later this week" could mean another murder on the Northwest Side, deterioration of relations between the Logan Square Beautification Society and the Avondale Neighborhood Association, and chest-high piles of garbage along Diversey Avenue. Then again, Debbie thought, Terrance was sitting in classes at Truman College that afternoon. She could have the apartment to herself for once. "Really?"

"Yeah. You could get lunch and come back to see if I'm done. Or, just tell Trey I'm going to be in your office all day fixing this. Tell him I said you could stay and learn more about the IT department if you want to."

"What if I do want to stay and learn more about the IT department?"

"You don't want to do that," Jigme said. "Not this afternoon at least." Debbie surveyed his strange features. His high cheekbones, presumably from his mother's Himalayan roots, set the foundation for his bright, half-hooded eyes with their full Mediterranean lashes. "Are you hungry? We could get some lunch, too. If you don't talk shop."

No. She shouldn't. "Maybe tomorrow? I usually eat lunch in the cafeteria around 12:30."

Jigme nodded. "Okay. 12:30 tomorrow. Maybe I will see you there."

Debbie awkwardly half-curtseyed then immediately regretted it. She wasn't thinking straight, and her blush deepened. "Okay. I'm going to go talk to Trey."

"Alright. Good luck." Jigme turned back to Debbie's computer as she backed out into the hall.

"Goddamnit. Yes, go home." Trey's ashen face twisted around his gray eyes. "He said it would take all afternoon?"

"Yeah. I mean, I could take a conference room and call them back. We were in the middle of a session." Debbie was too new to be eager for a day off. She needed to appear thirsty for the work.

"No. If IT says they need to take care of it, just let them take care of it."

"I could bring them in for a face-to-face mediation if you want. Ditch the screens. They're both in the city, and I've done hundreds of those."

Trey shifted from gray to green as disgust pockmarked his face. "No, Debbie. We don't do that, and you should know that by now. Unless, and only unless, the administrators specifically ask you to do a live mediation, are you allowed to do that. In here, or outside. That's in the manuals you were supposed to have read. I have a question. Who ties your shoes for you in the morning?"

"I do, obviously, Trey. And I know, I read the manuals. I . . . I just wanted to let you know I'd be willing to, if you asked. We were just cut off mid-feed. The situation could get worse. So, I just wanted to let you know I'm willing to help."

Trey sank into his chair. "Yes, Debbie, I get it. I was new here, too, once. You are willing to help, because you're new here. I understand that. We understand that. We expect that, as we're paying off all the stupid goddamn decisions you made in the last twenty-whatever years of your life. And paying for the next however goddamn long you're alive for. We *really* appreciate it. Box? Checked. Go. Home."

"See you tomorrow, Trey." Debbie turned her back and headed for the elevators. As hard as Trey had attempted to curdle Debbie's mood, her spirits rose as she fell into the Indian summer erupting on the streets below. She stopped for a lunch and two cocktails at the Cabrini Martini before moseying through the merchant stalls in the Goose Island locks. She eventually called a car to take her home, which took her in the opposite direction as police activity on Division and Ashland hewed the branches off the car's decision trees. She drifted off as midday drew into the afternoon, and woke up when the car asked her to alight at her apartment building. She wanted to fall asleep again. Then she wanted to wake up and go to lunch with Jigme Mahuta.

20. Body

A lead weight in the back of Melody Jackson's throat tilted her chin up as she approached the scene. She had been here before. Not this intersection, specifically, but other grim scenes like it, with the same scuffing boots, the same cagey officers spreading out to present less promising targets, the same spinning minds and necks cranking over shoulders to make sure *that* noise wasn't some hell headed *this* way. The SVAN was a charred horseshoe of twisted alloys surrounded by yellow maple leaves. Officer Tarquin George Benton's remains remained in situ as the first responders found no sign of life but ample signs of evidence that needed processing. Forensics was setting up the tarps and scanners as Melody approached.

Suparmanputra saw her walking towards the van and moved to intercept. In his military career, he had seen men and women rearranged the same way Tark had been. The same way a mosquito smacked to death no longer looks like a mosquito, just a smudge of gore and parts. This sort of ordinance delivered physics at scales civilians are unaccustomed to. Soup knew Melody could handle it, but he also knew she didn't need to. "Detective," he shouted. "Mel!"

Melody redirected herself to approach Henry rather than the van. Her eyes were red, circumstantial evidence of the three minutes she spent screaming with rage and grief on the way over. She knew she had to get it out, but away from the other officers, away from where it would distract from her command. Tears would easily erode the caked-together dust that her authority rested upon. Fear evaporated the shallow pools of courage her officers amassed before putting on their uniforms every morning. Her people needed to know that she grieved but didn't need to watch her do it. "Officer Suparmanputra. What's the situation?"

"He was on the phone with us. When it happened."

"What's the perimeter situation." It was not a question. It was a reminder of protocol. An officer was just assassinated, and now dozens of officers were making the scene a target-rich environment.

"Secure. Michelin men at every cross-street, anti-drone units, radar jammed all around. Civilians are all out rubbernecking because we're jamming their wi-fi."

"Where should we talk." Another reminder. People were watching all around. Other things could be watching, too.

Suparmanputra led Melody down the block to a makeshift command center surrounded by layers of wave-proof mylar. "Tark was talking to us. No radio, just phones in case they were sniffing police channels. Citovsky got in a pickup truck, old school, with a steering wheel, and a lady driving it, at Ogden and California. They took off, eventually parked under the bridges near Ashland and Cortland. Tark watched for a few minutes, then watched a DIED come in and followed it. He saw it was a drone, didn't notice the payload. He followed it right until it hit his vehicle. It was quick."

"Christ. What's going on with the pickup truck?"

"It's still there. Citovsky is still there, dead, inside the truck. Female driver disappeared. They are waiting for the scan squad to come out. Bomb squad is on standby. A terrorist pickup truck with a dead guy in it under the interstate. It's shut the whole city down."

"Jesus." Melody winced as tears welled up under her eyelids and her jaw muscles begged to stretch. Tark dead, and her only lead blown. "Anyone notify Tark's people?"

"Yeah, Body odor is on—"

"Henry."

"Sorry. Bereavement Officers are on it. I know, it's not right, it's, you know, habit. B.O. is on it, Detective."

"Any news from Matte?"

"Yeah, he's on it. It was a DIED, newer model, spray-painted for the day's task, fall leaves and blue sky. Matte's regressional surveillance has it coming out of an abandoned building north of Rosehill." Every city cop knew Rosehill, the cemetery turned tent city. The people that lived there had a unique appreciation for life and a flippant relationship with death. The dead that slept there never raised any issues with their relatively new, relatively alive bunkmates. The living tenants had their own sort of code, like hobo camps and Hoovervilles from a century before. The Six Counties cops were not welcome. Private cops and corporate Pinkertons were even less welcome. They would be made permanent tenants, buried under the latrines.

"DIED? This shit wasn't 'improvised.' 'Drone,' yeah. 'Explosive device,' yeah. But it found Tark's van from halfway across the city. Sniffed him out. It was designed."

"D-D-E-D, then."

"What type was it? Tom-Tom? Quadrotor? Military?"

"I've never seen one like it. Glider of some sort. Matte's analyzing the tapes."

Melody hung her head and shook it softly. "I need to see the scene."

"You'll see the file, Mel."

"I should see the scene." She left the tent and walked toward the imploded van. The neighborhood was out on their stoops, trying to film with jammed phones. One man sat with a tin lunchbox on his lap, grinning at officers with a flint-corn smile.

"Gonna be rich," he said. "I'm the happiest pig in this shit!"

Melody ignored him as she approached the scene. Fifteen yards away, Officer Sharon Kemp walked out of the barrier being set up around the charred van and broken branches. Her complexion was seafoam, and her top half wavered as her boots clawed at the dry grass. At ten yards, her eyes found Detective Jackson, and at five yards, she collapsed and vomited onto the sidewalk.

"Officer." Melody lifted Kemp by the handle between the shoulders of her bulletproof vest. "Clean up and go home."

"Yes, Detective." Kemp's eyes and nose ran as she wiped chilaquiles rojas from her lapel. The man with the lunchbox giggled maniacally. Melody changed her mind as she helped Kemp back to the makeshift headquarters, back to Henry and some hot tea. The scene could wait. Matte would scan it in all its gory detail. She would leave Tark's twisted cadaver in abstraction, keep it one step removed from her reality. Tark wouldn't mind, she thought. If anything, Tark needed her to be solving his murder and preventing the next one, not lying awake with visions of a man she once knew rearranged into some lifeless pile. She needed to be able to eat. She needed to be able to sleep. She needed to move fast enough to catch up to the fervor growing in the streets. Melody needed to be strong enough to catch it by its scruff and stamp it out before it got Soup or Kemp or O'Malley or anyone else. She needed to kill it, whatever it was, before it killed again.

21. Pumpkin

Pumpkin,

By now, you should have heard that I've screwed off this mortal coil. I am so sorry to do this to you and your mom, but things just keep getting worse. In my lifetime, I never thought it would be like this. There was no great disaster or dystopia, just a series of disappointments, concessions, and betrayals. When I was your age, we had this phrase that I'm sure you've heard. "I can't even." It was very stupid, but it ended up being true. We couldn't even, or didn't even, so now I don't even.

My father grew up learning about rockets and playing with ray guns and watching men land on the moon. He was six years old when Sputnik launched. Imagine being promised moon bases and flying cars, but waking up twenty years later to find only disco and Skylab and catalytic converters. Imagine the disappointment. It was the same for me, but with computers and the internet and cellphones. All this promise, but we just got online shopping, streaming nonsense, and ATMs.

But now my ATM is smarter than I am. My brightest students, doctoral candidates in economics, are dumber than my ATM. If you ask that ATM and my students if the students will ever catch up, they'll give you the same answer: "Not a chance in hell." I've failed you and your mother. Also, your mother doesn't love me anymore. I know it is very disappointing to you but it's best that I just go.

You can ignore this advice and hate me if you want, I wouldn't blame you. But I think you should try to learn to love the world, warts and all. I never did, I always wanted to fix it, make it better. But it's too big now, or too small, or too complicated, or too simple for me to do anything about it. You shouldn't spend your whole life fighting against it, trying to fix it, unless you want to end up like me. Find something you love and die old and happy.

Things will be o-kay.

Love you so much,

Dad

P.S. Aunt Jackie has my will. Life insurance is through State Mutual. For their information, I'm not doing this for the money, I'm just very sad about everything and I don't see it ever getting any better. I wish we would have done better for you. XOXOXOXOX

Debbie scanned the message for some meaning that had escaped her the first thousand times she had read it. When she couldn't sleep, or couldn't get out of bed, or couldn't think of anything better to do, she would pull it from her saved messages folder and read it. And now, as she lay trying to sleep after taking too long of an afternoon nap, waiting for Terrance to stumble in, she reread it again.

When she first received it, she was at home in Shadyside, her mother sobbing in the kitchen with the few friends they had in Pittsburgh gathered around. Some of her father's colleagues stopped by, bringing food or flowers. The email arrived at 10:30 p.m. Her father proved his selfishness at 2:45 that afternoon by jumping off the top floor of a parking garage to lift the dull gray weight of the world from his shoulders. He proved his courteousness by sending his suicide note with a delay so that Debbie would not be left with the lingering feeling that she could have prevented the act by checking her email sooner. The delay meant she couldn't blame her algebra teacher for having a "no phones" rule. He timed his demise so that Debbie wouldn't get pulled out of school or sit up late wondering where he was. She would arrive home to find her mother in shock, needing help and direction. She would get his explanation only a few hours later. The only better time that Debbie's father could have killed himself would have been "never."

Debbie never followed her father's final advice. Why should he have a say in how she acted or felt when he opted out of his life and hers? But she tried to understand why he was so depressed, to understand what makes a man feel so useless, and further, why he needs to feel useful in the first place. Her father was a mildly successful economist. He had achieved his Ph.D., spent years in the post-graduate lecture and research circuits, and then spent Debbie's childhood hopping from one assistant professorship to another. Chatham University hired him when Debbie was fourteen. He jumped to his death when she was sixteen, in the turmoil that followed after the Big Trouble started in Little Rock.

About two months before Little Rock burnt down, live-streamed from a thousand different angles, the mayor got on TV and said they were in "trouble, big trouble." The news had their lede, "big trouble in Little Rock," which they repeated ad nauseam. The "big trouble" became the capital-B "Big," capital-T "Trouble" when it spread to other cities. Not that particular fire, of course, but the pattern or condition characterized by a cascade failure of civil norms that had defined Debbie's young adulthood.

In the years before the Big Trouble, two-thirds of Little Rock had lost their jobs to a combination of automation, downsizing, outsourcing, and economic strife. The municipal and state governments hemorrhaged positions, including police, fire, and ambulances, to the lowest bidders, whose services relied heavily on various proprietary algorithms and creative number crunching.

The news really started to pay attention to Little Rock when the citizens of the tent cities started going on food raids and taking over grocery stores. The revolutionaries manning the ramparts, holding hunting rifles in the crooks of their arms, were deeply unsettling. They were horrifying because they looked so familiar, so neighborly. They spoke surely and with conviction as they recounted the very normal jobs they had recently lost—a nurse, a city clerk, a logistics operator for a trucking company, a high school English teacher. In each case, the media tried and failed to find the dark vein of criminality in these reluctant revolutionaries. They would explain they had worked for years, never been on welfare, were real decent folk, had tried writing resumes, tried everything, really. They didn't deserve to starve, they said. They said they'd move if they could, but half of them had moved to Little Rock because the towns they came from "didn't have no jobs, either." Some were white, some black, some Latino, some Papuan refugees.

The grocery stores and other businesses called their privatized police, but their algorithms had not accounted for subduing the huddled masses yearning to eat. Their loss-prevention officers were not driven by a sense of law and justice, but by a thin green line known as the bottom dollar. For their meager wages, they would not charge in, crack their neighbors' skulls, and risk their own lives over some 68% lean ground beef. So, the remaining businesses hired Pinkertons and other private henchmen to protect them. These mercenaries' outsized paychecks left them with absolutely no sense of civic duty, and so skulls were cracked, beef protected, losses prevented.

But the gains were temporary. Every teenager maimed, every grandfather killed, every 4K slow-motion vertical video of everyday people being brutalized drove the masses to become a mob in that summer's heat. When the weather cooled and the food was nearly gone, that mob congealed into many small armies.

The worse the "Big Trouble in Little Rock" got, the better news it made. Every college had its solidarity marches and fundraisers. Mayors and city councils across the country walked a tightrope when expressing sympathy for the unemployed citizens. They had their own tent cities, their own shantytowns that might overflow with unmeetable demands. The whole country had its problems, but Little Rock was a crucible where everyone watched those problems play out in their living rooms. The residents of the tent cities and shantytowns did not have living rooms, so they acted it out on the streets.

And so the Trouble spread. Similar movements arose in every major city. The minor cities and exurbs watched nervously as productivity slowed and prices increased. Only when the national economy began to suffer did the Federal Government interrupt its self-involved theatrics to address the suffering of its people. After checking donor lists and favors owed, the Federal Government came firmly down on the side of the corporations and their respective bottom dollars. The National Guard was called back from the Philippines and Mauritania and strategically placed around the greatest concentrations of wealth. Little Rock didn't have any wealth concentrations left, so the Army set up checkpoints along the interstates, hoping to contain the worst of the violence.

That violence came to a head about a year after the Big Trouble started. The few remaining profitable corporations in

Little Rock simply relocated. They pulled out their private police forces, transferred files and any cryptobullion they might have had stashed around their offices to safer locations, and disappeared during negotiations for a truce. The citizens, now self-organized into various brigades and unions with unsexy names like AWFLR and UFUI and the Natural Citizens Militia, stormed city hall and the state capitol building without firing a shot.

But their peaceful victory died the next morning. Once the ledgers saw the light of day, it became clear the government also lived hand to mouth, drowning in debt just like all its citizens. This brave new Little Rock held no cash, bad credit, and half a million mouths to feed. The exodus to the suburbs began immediately. But there, the disappointed victors found well-fed and well-prepared militias sponsored by the corporations that had just fled. Pickup trucks full of teenagers and old men who detested "city types" and their city problems patrolled the outskirts and state highways. The Constitution spoke of the right to bear arms, but was silent as to bare tables, bare backs, bare bones, and bared teeth. Disagreements unraveled into skirmishes, which devolved into open warfare within a month.

Debbie remembered the churn of events well, as her father couldn't shut up about them. He would stare at the news, running his hands through his thinning hair while intermittently asking no one in particular "Are you seeing this!?" or "Did you hear about that"—shooting, riot, tone-deaf statement—"today?" He would stay up late, calling colleagues or old friends, distilling the day's events. He would lecture Debbie nervously, ensuring she shared in his suffering. She suffered doubly, first with her adolescent understanding of her father's conclusion that the world was ending, and second with the loneliness of being at a new school and anger at her family for dragging her there. She had no friends yet. She would die a virgin, an unknown. She would die in the sad company of her quiet mother and manic, rambling father who ground them down with every empty thesis statement he made at the dinner table.

"This is different," he said as he pointed to the sky, away from the takeaway Thai food before him. "I know it looks like another protest, another economic downturn, but there are some very interesting and dis-*turb*-ing articles that indicate this is simply a symptom of a systemic shock that will be very disruptive. I know, I know, everyone said that before. When we were a little older than you, Debbie, and your mom remembers this too, I'm sure, we had things like Occupy Wall Street and the Arab Spring and Great Recession. You remember the quarantine. But we were about your age when 9/11 happened, and I know that doesn't mean much to you now, but for us it was totally, totally shocking. It seemed like the world was falling apart."

"Peter, stop scaring her." Debbie's mom only ever suggested, never commanded.

"She's not scared. You're not scared, are you, Pumpkin?"

"No," Debbie would lie. She was scared of a lot of things. Not what her father was talking about, though. She had grown up hearing about turmoil, murder, and mayhem on a daily basis. All the world's worst car bombs and pipeline explosions and hurricanes and earthquakes and outbreaks echoed through her living room as she tried to go to sleep. The bad news accumulated overnight and repeated like Reveille every morning.

All of that didn't scare Debbie. What scared her was not having any friends. Not knowing what anyone thought of her. That maybe her new schoolmates thought she was ugly or stupid or annoying or maybe that she smelled bad. She worried that her parents were weirdos, and that as their daughter, they doomed her to be a weirdo, too. "Don't call me Pumpkin, please, Dad. It's weird."

"Okay, sorry *Deb-o-rah*. As I was saying, there is some very interesting literature that predicted these things happening now in Little Rock and starting here in Pittsburgh, and more recent literature that is confirming that previous literature. What math are you in?"

"Geometry."

"Okay. Do you know what a slope is, like a slope of a line?"

"Yes, I think."

"So, when a slope is flat," he held his hand flat against the table, "that's a very low slope. But as the slope increases in value," his hand tilted up, "it gets steeper, a higher value. So maybe this is a slope of point five, and this is a slope of one, this is a slope of two, and this," he held his hand nearly vertical, "is a slope of like one hundred, okay?"

"Yeah dad, I know." She sort of knew. Math was her least favorite subject.

"But slopes can also be *negative*. So if this is a slope of one," he held his fingers up at an angle, "and this is zero," he held his hand flat, "then this is a slope of *negative* one." He dipped his fingers to a downward angle. Debbie feigned boredom, but it was a surprisingly helpful refresher. "And this," he tilted his wrist at an extreme angle, pointing his fingers straight to the floor, "this is negative *one hundred*."

"So," Debbie asked, "are you saying we're at negative one hundred now?"

"Negative one hundred what? No. Not now. But, just listen. So say you're watching a slope change, get steeper and steeper," his hand raised like he was holding it out the window of a fast-moving car, "and then you see it start to get less steep and less steep, and flatten out. When it goes from *positive* to *negative*, and starts going down, that's called an inflection point. Okay?"

"Yeah."

"And if you take the derivative of this slope, I mean, if you . . . well. See where, where I'm getting higher and higher, and then I start to turn down? Sort of the middle of this 's' shape? That's also an inflection point, if you do some other math things that you're not to yet. Anyway, that could also be an inflection point, okay?"

"I think."

"Well, say I graphed everything that anyone ever did. Like a hundred thousand years ago, when people could just hunt and gather and there were no more than ten thousand people on the planet, say I added up everything they ever did and accomplished. Then say I did that for the next year, and the next year, to make a graph of the *progress* of all humankind, okay?"

"Did you do that, today at work, Peter? Make a big graph?" Debbie's mom asked. She had been suffering her husband's lectures for longer than Debbie had, but only had herself to blame. She found plenty of entertainment wherever they went, just not involving her husband. She volunteered through various university programs. She made friends quickly but without deep attachment. She had book clubs. Debbie never understood her mother's angle on the marriage, and as a result, Debbie never understood why she existed in the first place. But here she was, and her father seemed to enjoy rambling at her in any case.

"No, dear. But the Nobel Prize of Economics went to the guy that did."

"Do not start on Chabraut again, please, Peter. I am begging you."

"It's *important*, Carol."

Carol Peck had endured Peter's rants about his idol every office Christmas party for the last four years. "Debbie, do you have any homework?"

"No." She did, but she wasn't about to admit that. She wanted some time to mope around like any bored and lonely teenager.

Her mom sighed. "I try to help you. I really do. I'm going to do the dishes."

"Thanks, honey. So, *Deb-o-rah*, Dr. Yves Chabraut was a French economist . . ."

22. Chabraut

"Dr. Yves Chabraut was a French economist who endeavored to measure the economic and social progress of humanity throughout history. He hypothesized that if the value added by each human effort—whether hunting and gathering, sowing and harvesting, inventing and manufacturing, or dancing and singing—could be *quant*ified, if they could be quantified then governments could encourage their citizens to pursue activities that added *more* value and subtracted *less* value. He was trying to help people, really.

"He and his assistants fed all the data they could find about the social and economic value of various activities, trades, pursuits, vices, habits, exercises, and so on into their perfectly unsympathetic supercomputer and asked it to pull these invisible strings across invisible data points and reduce the seemingly irreducible into something useful. It did so with incredible patience and did not take a single coffee break. In the end, it politely spat out a difficult little equation that could, in turn, be used to produce a simple little number that could assess the value of human activities.

"Like adjusted gross income or a credit score, Dr. Chabraut's numbers could, in turn, be used to assess a person. There's a term of art we use in the field, we call them 'inches.' They are how some men measure their worth, you see? But unlike some of these other little numbers, Dr. Chabraut's numbers were pretty on point. Very accurate, considering. They balanced productivity with quality of life considerations so that someone couldn't tout their productivity if they were only productive in making things that made other people's lives terrible. They weighed long-term benefits and short-term benefits and medium-term benefits against each other so that one couldn't make excuses or procrastinate. From a sea of churning, interacting data points,

Dr. Chabraut's computer crystallized a dry, mathematical truth that had, until that point, evaded human eyes and ears and minds.

"Dr. Chabraut published his difficult little equation and some of its simple little numbers in an academic journal. Excluding the journal's peer reviewers and Dr. Chabraut's wife, exactly thirty-six people read this article over the next two years. They can check these things, these days. Exactly thirty-six pageviews in twenty-two months.

"But one of them happened to be a big-time economist at a big-time university in Massachusetts, Dr. Finn, who I actually took a class from a *long* time ago. He was out of his own ideas, and he needed something to discuss at his upcoming performance reviews. He published his own article strongly advising *against* the use of the 'Chabraut equation' and its little 'Chabraut numbers.' Dr. Finn tried to eviscerate Chabraut's equation with elegant mathematics and hurtful words like 'unsupported' and 'overreaching' and 'inconclusive.'

"Dr. Chabraut never even read this rebuttal. He had retired to his lavender farm in the Luberon region in France. Whenever Dr. Finn's criticisms came up, he would say, in French of course, that he was finished with economics. He had stopped caring about other people's money. His economic standing was secure. He had his farm and all he needed there until he died. He would tell his guests this over Violette Kir Royales at his rustic provincial soirees, and they would laugh politely, I'm told.

"Unfortunately for Dr. Chabraut, though, Dr. Finn had many colleagues and very few friends. His warning against the use of Chabraut numbers *was itself* the target of several dozen academic articles coming to Dr. Chabraut's defense! These refined the equation, added proposed uses, extolled the elegance and beauty of the difficult little formula that a perfectly unsympathetic machine politely spat out into the realm of human knowledge. Economists around the world couldn't help themselves but chime in, to knock this Dr. Finn down a peg while padding their own *curricula vitae.* I did it too. I helped author some articles. I'd get them for you, but I know non-economists around the world don't give a hoot about what economists are arguing about."

"I think I might actually have some homework, Dad." Debbie was losing her mind.

"Just a second! This is where it gets interesting. Even worse for Dr. Chabraut, some consultants and other business types—who ran in the same circles as economists—began dropping Chabraut numbers into *their* presentations. These consultant types were always out of their own ideas. They are the least creative bunch of crooks you'd ever meet. Here's how they work. Convince Sucker Number One that his idea is rotten, then offer to save him from it. Then, sell his idea to Sucker Number Two across town. So long as Sucker Number One and Sucker Number Two never talk to each other about their top-secret business ideas—which they wouldn't, because they are competitors—these consultants lived on easy street. The real difficulty lies in making sure they never sell Sucker Number One his own idea without repackaging it first. But this was usually accomplished with a carefully placed sticky note or an all-caps reminder to not do that exact thing. Their slick suits, stunning jaw lines, and unrelenting confidence also did wonders when stealing and reselling ideas. It also never hurt to add the freshest, most confusing buzzwords from the academic journals to justify charging a couple extra hundred thousand dollars. And so, Dr. Chabraut's numbers ventured from the warm embrace of academia into the 'real world' of executive memoranda and monthly invoices.

"Soon enough, companies were developing their own difficult little Charbraut-esque equations to ignore the value of non-business activities, such as dancing or eating lunch, and highlighting business-related activities, such as actually working or kissing your boss's ass. I helped make some of these for some extra bucks. Remember that vacation on Cape Hatteras? That was paid for with a little equation we drafted for an insurance company. Savvy upper management types introduced Chabraut metrics into quarterly targets and annual projections. Promising middle managers informed their employees of their 'Delta Chabraut' or 'Projected Chabraut.' Less-than-enthusiastic employees listened to how they needed to improve their Chabraut scores and, if they got around to it, learn whatever the hell a Chabraut score was.

"While this was all fantastic for Dr. Chabraut's *reputation*, it devastated poor Dr. Chabraut. First off, he had to get rid of his telephone. Reporters kept calling him, asking for comments. At first, he would tell them that he had managed his own economics in such a way that he could not give less of a care about other human beings' economics, but he found the reporters were not nearly as fun as the guests at his rustic provincial soirees. Second, he had to install an electronic gate and security system at his lavender farm to keep people from bothering him. This disturbed Dr. Chabraut's economics a bit and disturbed the rustic charm of his lavender farm greatly. Third and worst of all, Dr. Chabraut started to become a household name. People around the world were being told they missed their 'Hourly Chabraut Aggregate Goal' at yearly performance reviews or their 'Projected Lifetime Chabraut Number' whenever they were rejected for a mortgage. His original article had actually proposed that the simple little number be described in units of Ξ."

"Cee?"

"'Cshee.' The uppercase Greek 'X' to represent '$\alpha\xi\acute{\iota}\alpha$,' the Greek word for 'value' or 'merit.' Dr. Chabraut privately admired that the Ξ's three lines seemed to reflect the notion of an upper ideal, a middle ground, and a lower sub-optimal value. It embodied the original purpose of his work, to inspire human beings to know the value of their activities so that they could better choose how to use their time. But there was no 'Ξ' key on standard keyboards and no one had the time or inclination to learn how to pronounce 'Ξ.' Instead, the value was just referred to as a 'Chabraut number.' Disaster. Like doctors Parkinson and Alzheimer before him, Chabraut unintentionally lent his name to an affliction that would curse millions.

"Things only got worse for Dr. Chabraut when study after study confirmed his original hypothesis. The difficult little equation worked. The simple little numbers were useful. A positive number meant 'good,' a higher number meant 'better,' and a negative number meant 'bad.' So like slope, remember? If your Chabraut number was increasing, you were doing better. If you went from positive to negative, that's bad, your life is heading in the wrong direction. Okay?"

"You're decreasing my number really, really badly right now, I think. Like negative five hundred."

"I doubt it! You knowing this will give you a big advantage over your friends. Like for applying for college and jobs and things. This is very adult business. It's really very important."

Debbie didn't have any friends to have a big advantage over at that point, so her father's mindless comment pushed her deeper into her chair.

"So, for asking his supercomputer the right questions and publishing the results, Dr. Chabraut reluctantly accepted the Nobel Prize in Economics. While he believed he did not deserve it, he was vain and in need of the prize money. The models he used to calculate his own personal economics had not compensated for his unforeseen success, nor the related expenses incurred by hosting ever more frequent dinner parties and installing that unsightly electronic gate. He gave his speech, collected his check, and disappeared deep into his fields of lavender.

"So that was three years ago, when you were, what, twelve? Around that time, Dr. Pradesh, a brilliant young professor at the London School of Economics, hammered home the final nail in poor Dr. Chabraut's coffin. Literally, almost. I mean, I think Chabraut died the month her article came out. She asked a bigger, stronger supercomputer to calculate Chabraut values through history based on all available data. This is that graph I was talking about. She asked the right questions, which her supercomputer patiently answered without taking a single coffee break. Eventually, it politely spat out some disquieting results. She said she actually spat out her coffee when she understood what her supercomputer had discovered for her.

"Generally, what the computer politely whispered in her ear was this: 'There are too many of you and not enough to do.'"

Debbie's father paused for dramatic effect. Debbie did not indulge him, but he wasn't discouraged.

"Specifically, it told her that throughout history, simply existing as human being had, on the whole, been a useful enterprise. But presently, *it was not*. Do you understand? Previously, one could hunt, gather, sow, reap, invent, manufacture, create, write, dance, or simply reproduce and still add value to the whole shebang. The total value of the whole of society had increased consistently since the Stone Age. From most of human history, each person's Chabraut value was, on average, positive. So each person was like this," he pointed his hand up, "or on average was. Like murderers were negative, lazy idiots were pretty much flat, but the average person was generally positive. They added value.

"But, the past few centuries exhibited a disturbing trend. While humankind's total aggregate Chabraut numbers were higher than they ever had been and were still growing, the growth was slowing, and its *de*celeration was *ac*celerating. The slowing was not the result of decreasing quality in humans. No, not at all. Humans were more capable and productive than they ever had been. They were trying just as hard or harder than they ever had. But the mathematics plainly stated: 'There are too many of you and there is not enough to do.'

"So this brilliant young professor, Dr. Pradesh, published a purposefully tedious and unsexy article explaining all of this in one of the lesser academic journals. Economists across the globe checked the numbers, repeated her calculations, and we started exchanging hushed forecasts for the article's implications. Our concern was not selfless—the computer had noted that there were too many economists and there was not enough for *us* to do, either.

"Okay, so here's the thing, Debbie. Remember where we, 'we' being 'all of humanity,' weren't doing much ten thousand years ago, then we started to do more and more, and kept growing and growing, and doing more and more." His hand ramped up like it was cutting through the wind outside a car window. "But at some point it could stop growing, and start tilting down to get flatter?"

Debbie nodded.

"That's what they're calling the Great Inflection. And when it starts to tilt down, like go negative, that means that we're all starting to do worse, that the bad starts outweighing the good we're doing. That's what they're calling the Great Inversion."

"So, is this, like, what's on the TV. Is that the Great Inflection?"

"No, no Debbie. It sort of depends on where you are, your

country, area, resources, a lot of stuff. Um, but on average, for the whole world, the Great Inflection happened about twenty years ago."

He paused to let it sink in. This time, Debbie indulged him.

"Five years before I was born?"

"We obviously didn't know it, then. We didn't know until a few years ago. But yes, the Great Inflection happened on average for the whole world about twenty years ago. For Little Rock, the local inflection occurred about thirty-five years ago."

"So what's going on in Little Rock, now?"

"It's what happens after the local inflection, we think. The local inversion."

"And when's the Big Inversion supposed to happen?"

"Great. The Great Inversion. Hopefully never. We're trying to stop it, Pumpkin. We're doing our best."

Debbie's father stopped trying his best a few months later when he jumped off the twelfth floor of a parking garage in Montreal. He was there for an academic conference. Debbie tried to read the literature presented at the conference for some clue about what pushed her father over the edge, but she couldn't decipher anything useful from the articles or lectures. He was terribly depressed, his letter had said, and that was enough.

Call State Mutual, it said. But the weeks after his death confirmed his final, bleak outlook. Insurance companies were inundated from claims arising from the growing unrest, from the Big Trouble or local Inversions or whatever they were. They were backlogged, delaying all claims as their offices relocated. When one Monday morning, five of the largest insurance and reinsurance firms announced their insolvencies, the remnants of the middle class discovered the same thing as those new leaders of Little Rock—the money was gone. Like the waters of Lake Winnebago and the Aral Sea, the money did not disappear. It had just been taken elsewhere. Debbie and her mother were left in Pittsburgh to weather the worst of the Big Trouble the same as nearly everyone else. A little savings, the food in their cupboards, and a city going mad around them.

By the time the first wave of the Big Trouble subsided the next year, Debbie was applying for colleges. Her heart-wrenching personal statement married her youthful analysis of her father's economic outlook with the hardships she faced in Shadyside during those dark days. It concluded with her expressing her desire to help people learn to get along, to help fix the broken world. It worked, smoothing over her rough math scores and the underwhelming grades from her traumatic junior year.

And one way or another, that set her down a path that led her to her current position. Unable to sleep at 12:40 a.m., waiting in her tiny apartment for her boyfriend to return from whatever he did after his night class. Terrance finally arrived at 1:15 a.m., a bit drunk.

"Sorry I'm back late. I went out with some of the guys I met." He kissed her forehead sloppily. "Half the city is shut down. I couldn't get back for forever."

"Okay, glad you're home safe."

"Seriously, there was like a terrorist attack or something. A bombing. They shut down the highway."

"I know, it took me forever to get home."

"Do you think it's starting again? Like, do you think we should, get out of the city or something?"

"I don't think so. Let's talk about it in the morning, okay?"

"I mean, if it's starting again here I think we should do something. Like, move to a better part of the city. Closer to your work. Or we can go to your mom's. Or my uncle's. Or just somewhere. The guys I was talking to were talking about how they think the Jefferson Group and AMF and some of the other big companies are spending a lot of money in the suburbs. One was saying his cousin just got a job doing security in Naperville and it's crazy well-funded, like almost better than your pay."

"Were you talking to them about my pay?"

"No. I mean, not really, I talked about how you just started working there, the perks and stuff. They were cool guys, though. I think we should hang out with them again."

"Can we talk about it in the morning? I need to sleep."

"Okay. Love you. Goodnight."

"Goodnight."

Debbie could feel Terrance fidget and turn in bed for forty-five minutes before he finally passed out. Her mind went on spinning until sometime past three. She dreamed of her old house and her father lecturing at the dinner table again. It was a sad dream, as almost all dreams of her father were. But even so, Debbie would remember that seeing him there, in whatever dark corner of her mind he still lived in and lectured and annoyed her, made her feel better as she awoke to the sound of a cooling thunderstorm announcing autumn's arrival in full.

23. Chiefs

Sporadic glops of rain fell from the pin oaks outside Six Counties Police Headquarters as Melody Jackson waited in the hallway. A meeting with the chiefs, a council of gray-faced bureaucrats, had been called the previous evening to assess the ongoing situation. She had not slept in the hours since Tark's murder. There was too much to do and no time to rest. She had stopped by the sickbay for a low dose of Ar-mod, the department's standard wakefulness aid. TSD, "Third Shift Disorder," they called it. But calling mental and physical exhaustion after endless hours on the job a "disorder" was disingenuous. Fatigue was no more a "disorder" than hunger or sadness or excitement or boredom. It was simply the natural result of some external disorder, of having more problems than hours in the day. Unable to treat the root cause, the department just hacked back at the symptoms.

Melody's mind was adjusting to the effects of the medication. Her rattled nerves smoothed and the lump of guilt she had been swallowing all night dissolved. The crescendoing clamor of emotions faded into an empty silence that filled the hallway around her. On the window across from her, she noticed one of the summer's last cicadas clinging under a ledge, hiding from what was left of the rain.

A weathered face popped through the door. "We're ready for you."

The lack of a chair presented Detective Jackson with mixed messages. It would be a dressing down but not an interrogation. The union rep wasn't there, so she wasn't getting fired. The Cook County Chief opened the ceremony. "Detective Jackson, we need you to brief us on a number of things. First, please tell us about yesterday. Officer Benton."

"Yes, sir. Officer Tarquin Benton undertook a surveillance task ordered by me and approved of by the Homicide division. He was in communication with Officer Henry Suparmanputra, as directed by me, following a suspect in a murder case we have been working since the beginning of August."

"What, in your estimation, happened yesterday?" Will County asked.

"It is too early to say, conclusively, sir, but we are putting the pieces together. Our Matte unit is on it and we do have people working around the clock, myself included. Officer Benton was in an SVAN unit, tracking the suspect—"

"Es-van?" McHenry County asked.

"Surveillance Vehicle, Automated Navigation. Surveillance van, sir. Aerial and SIGINT packages, along with some other equipment. Officer Benton tracked the suspect, Cecil Citovsky, after we let him out of central holding. A skein of SVAN drones were up and running, tracking the suspect while Officer Benton was the man in the van. After tracking the suspect for approximately two hours, Officer Benton reported that he had visual on an unidentified drone transecting the surveillance area. This was near the Clybourn Metra station. High overpasses, multiple egress points, high traffic. Less than ideal. He tracked the unidentified drone until it arrived at his SVAN's location without frolic or detour. Upon arrival, the unidentified drone detonated what we believe to be a shaped charge destroying the SVAN and killing Officer Benton."

"Was this a Drone Improvised Explosive Device? A DIED? That killed Officer Benton?" Kane County inquired.

"You could call it that, sir. It's still too early to tell, but the initial information points to a newer unpowered glider model. Regressive surveillance modeling puts the launch point just north of Rosehill. It came in very high around there and glid—glided, excuse me, sir—toward the surveillance area. Before it reached that area it adjusted its trajectory, aiming to a position near to Officer Benton's SVAN. About a block away from the SVAN, it maneuvered to increase speed and fly directly above the SVAN, where it detonated."

"Is that . . . normal, Detective?" Cook County looked pale.

"It is . . . new, sir. We believe it was a 'Loo-sing Chui,' or 'meteor hammer' model, which have been seen in the Philippines and also the Uighur Revolts. It's essentially a giant paper airplane made out of cheap alloy or plastene with a shaped charge built into the basal surface. The best information we have says these can be dropped out of a plane or helicopter. This one was brought to altitude by what looks like a small weather balloon. We have not seen these before. Not here at least."

"How did these things get to Chicago, Detective? Can we cut off their supply?" DuPage County asked, taking a sip from her stained mug.

"Unfortunately, you could pick up all the hardware to build one of these this afternoon. Build plans and flight control programs can be downloaded easily. You can find them on your phone right now if you don't mind popping up on a dozen different security databases. That's just the basic flight platform, though. Targeting programs are another story. Could be off the shelf or a custom build. Our best guess right now is that it flew over the surveillance area and sniffed the signals sent from the SVAN drones to the SVAN. That's why it flew over the surveillance site before heading straight to the SVAN location. Based on what's left of the van, there won't be anything left of the DIED's programming to examine. What we have recovered we will try to track back to their source. Same goes for the explosive."

DuPage County licked her front teeth. "And the suspect?"

"Dead, sir, from a single stab wound and left in the passenger seat of a manual pickup truck. Angle of entry for the stab wound is consistent with a right-handed person sitting in the driver's seat. The knife chipped a rib on the way in, immediately severed the left pulmonary artery—which would have been fatal on its own—then was hinged or yawed to sever the aorta and superior vena cava, and left in place. No defensive wounds or other signs of trauma."

"What does all that tell us, Detective? How does that move the ball?" Will County asked. He seemed genuinely curious. The Will County Chief never had a beat in his life, Melody guessed. He was a transplant, a fixer brought in from some corporation or other municipal works to manage costs or guarantee loyalty.

"It helps inform us as to the profile of the other person in the car with Mr. Citovsky. She knew what she was doing, based on the single stab wound. It wasn't surgical by any means, but it was confidently executed. Mr. Citovsky trusted her enough to get in the car with her and had no defensive wounds, which tells us he was taken by surprise. Finding this person, the woman in the truck, is our primary concern at this point. She is not only the prime suspect in his death but also of obvious interest in Officer Benton's assassination."

Kane County sat up. "Can we go back to why Officer Benton was following this suspect to begin with?"

"Yes, sir. Cecil Citovsky was a suspect in the murder of Hannah Mah. Our Matte unit found that Mr. Citovsky was following Ms. Mah for weeks before her death. Ms. Mah was found poisoned at her mother's house. Her mother is Anne Mah, she worked at City Hall for years, some of you may know her."

DuPage County frowned. "Yeah, I know Annie. She called a number of times, stopped by. What's the theory there, so far, Detective?"

"The direct leads in Hannah's death involve some security footage which indicates she was intentionally poisoned, and it was planned well in advance. Whoever conspired and committed the act went through great lengths to make the act look like a suicide or accident or natural causes. The breadcrumbs left behind were tiny and miles apart, and could not have been found without our department Organon, Matte. If Hannah's mother had not been who she was, I believe this case would have remained a tertiary or quaternary priority. Without that association, I don't believe we could have allocated the resources to this case that we have, and those efforts have bore fruit."

"What fruit?" Lake County growled. "Your only lead just died. And he took a Six Counties police officer and an SVAN with him."

"Sir—"

"Annie Mah's years of service excluded, and with respect to her daughter, Detective—why should we keep letting you dig this hole?" Lake County sat back in his chair, proud of himself. He had always been an ass. Lake County was rich with lakefront access and smuggled Wisconsin goods, and therefore maintained an outsized sway over Six Counties' affairs.

Melody paused. Explaining hunches was tricky. "Well, we suspected Ms. Mah's death could be related to another more recent murder. One of Hannah's coworkers at the Jefferson Group, Gerald Ford Jones, was shot in his office in late August, about three weeks after Ms. Mah died. I believe Ms. Mah's murder was not an isolated incident. It was a part of something bigger, it required multiple actors."

"Conspiracies? Conspiracy theories, Detective?" Lake County nearly spat.

"Technically, yes, sir. Conspiracy to commit murder, and then murder. I believe yesterday's events enforce our theory of the case. Our op, Officer Benton's operation, hit someone's nerve. Who, in a time of relative peace, kills a cop with a top-shelf DIED like this? Not a jealous lover, not a loan shark, not a rival gang, and not a maniac. By my count, the situation required the involvement of at least four people.

"One, Cecil Citovsky, who ran surveillance on Ms. Mah. Could have poisoned her too, but at the very least ran surveillance.

"Two, the woman in the truck, who killed Citovsky and escaped.

"Three, whoever picked up the woman in the truck or aided in her egress.

"Four, whoever launched the DIED that killed Tark Benton. Regressive surveillance puts launch time and location for the drone well out of reach for the woman in the truck. Travel time would make it impossible for one person to do both. It could have been remote, but I can't imagine driving a hands-on truck while managing a drone launch.

"And that's at a minimum. The complexity of the poison used could add another two conspirators. Building and programming the DIED could add a few more. And that's just for Hannah Mah. There's also Gerald Ford Jones."

"Gerald Ford Jones," Will County said. "What's the status of that investigation?"

"Preliminary investigation turned up very little, sir. Jones' murderer was hired on short notice, a substitute on the cleaning crew. He had fake credentials, fake everything, really. Probably had a fake face, as biometrics on everything about him come up inconclusive. His face has either never been scanned, or it has been scrubbed from every database that Matte has access to. Appears to be a young man, medium complexion, who can disappear into thin air on the thirty-third floor of the Trellis. His trail goes cold twelve seconds after he shot Mr. Jones. This also lends itself to the suspicion that multiple people are involved. The planning and execution of Mr. Jones' murder required sophistication and forethought."

"But there have been no leads, in Mr. Jones' murder?" Will County went on. "I ask, Detective, because I have been on the receiving end of a lot of guff. I'm telling you this for your benefit, for your career. I am receiving messages from the Jefferson Group. Visits. Calls. Letters. Hell, Judge Streed, who I golf with, asked me about it. 'What's the holdup?' is what they're asking me. So, for my sake and yours, what's the holdup, Detective?"

"I believe finding the link between Hannah Mah's murder and Gerald Ford Jones' murder will shed more light on the Jones Case. The evidence in Jones' case is suspiciously thin, considering it happened in a confined area in one of the most technologically advanced buildings in the city. The Jefferson Trellis is jam-packed with sensors and security and has purposefully narrow bottlenecks for entry and exit, by design. They, the Jefferson Group, say that the entire security system suffered a massive attack or error shortly after the shooting. The suspect only exists from the time he showed up for work that morning to about twelve seconds after the shooting. Either he had lots of help from an outside source, or he had help from the Jefferson Group."

"Seriously?" Will County scoffed. "You need to watch it, Jackson. For your own sake. The Jefferson Group has been on my ass, trying to get my help, to get this solved. They say that they've been on your ass, trying to get information so that their people can help. I can't hardly believe that they would be involved in a murder that they're trying this hard to solve."

"With respect, sir, it isn't unheard of for suspects to attempt to involve themselves in an investigation so that they can steer it. The Jefferson Group has not been helpful in the investigation. Their people, potential witnesses, were smothered with assistance from their legal team. Mr. Jones' and Ms. Mah's coworkers hardly got an answer in over the conditions and objections. Same with the cleaning team, same with almost every low-level employee. Administrators and middle managers were tight-lipped and were adamantly against us taking this case. They wanted their people on it, instead."

Lake County leaned forward. "I can't blame them. Don't you have enough on your plate, Detective? You've got plenty of murders to solve. Couldn't you use all the help you can get?"

"I don't need 'help' from potential suspects, sir."

Will County tapped in. "The Delaware State Police are not suspects, Detective. Neither are their materiel or their substantial budget. We could use all three, especially with this goddamn funeral to plan."

Melody stood silently. The decision was made. Any further protest would only make things worse for her.

Cook County's words fell like a gavel. "From here on out, Delaware has full access. I understand your reservations, Detective Jackson, but we need the help. Bring him in."

The man who had let Melody into the room got up and went to the door. Her pulse raced as the Ar-mod plucked at her nerves. She had expected discussion, maybe discipline, but not an introduction. A tall, translucent, corn-fed man in a navy blazer strode in. His fitted, starchy, neon white shirt crinkled unnaturally where his ballistic plate vest ended near his collarbone. His mouth sprung into a polite smile, showing no teeth, but his eyes stayed cold. Military, Melody guessed. Raised on whole milk and vacation bible school. He carried a satchel slung under his arm, hanging heavily, though his shoulder didn't sag.

"Detective Jackson, this is Lieutenant Michael Gustafson of the Delaware State Police." He extended a hand, which Melody squeezed. "He is your counterpart in their investigation, which they are calling . . . Officer, what are you calling this investigation?

"Operation Windjammer." His voice was deep in an unnatural way, phlegmy and dull. "We are willing to adopt the Six Counties operational name, though."

Eyes turned to Melody, who was surprised again. Her team

didn't name its cases like they were yachts or beachhead landings. "We don't name our cases."

"Operation Windjammer it is," Cook County said. "Detective Jackson, Lieutenant Gustafson will be the Delaware State Police liaison to your team. Please make use of Lieutenant Gustafson and his team. That's an order. That's all, Detective."

The Chiefs excused themselves, mumbling as they got up and left Melody standing in the middle of the room with Lieutenant Gustafson. He began the formalities.

"I'm glad to finally meet you. Mike Gustafson, you can call me Gus, away from the men." The men. Only country boys still called their officers "the men," Melody realized. "You look tired. Do you want to grab some coffee and go over initial items?"

"No. No coffee, thanks, Lieutenant. Officer Benton's death had us working through the night, and there are still some things that need to be done. Care to walk as we talk?"

"Yes, certainly." They made for the door. "I think the first thing we should do is sync our units. Our tech team can work with yours to do an information swap with your Organon on this case. What did you call it?"

"Matte."

"Just one unit?"

"Yes." Melody looked at Gus incredulously. Matte was her responsibility. He was the only Dinkum in the Homicide Unit and he cost them a fortune. She had jumped through a dozen hoops just to work with him, and had to justify every software update and diagnostic test to the Six Counties Comptroller. "What sort of swap do you have in mind?"

"Just data, no interfacing. Our units are proprietary and it would probably void your warranty on 'Matte' if you interfaced. Is it any good?"

"Matte? He's old but produces reliable results. You have multiple units?"

"Our department does. I just have mine here." He patted his satchel. "They are pretty new. As new as you can get without getting bugs. New and reliable is how we prefer it."

"What do you call yours?" Melody asked, still trying to figure out who Gus was.

"It's department policy to not anthropomorphize our units. It can interfere with user interfacing." Gus swallowed hard.

"So. What do you call yours?" Melody asked again.

Gus swallowed harder. "Junior."

If the Ar-mod hadn't drained Melody of her sense of humor, she would have laughed. Gus, running around solving white-collar crimes, talking to his supercomputer like it was his seven-year-old child, despite the fact that it had already lived millions of more man-hours than Gus ever would. "What build is he?"

"Hardware is last year's Cloudbuster. Software is proprietary. He's smart as a whip. Like I said, we should exchange raw data only, no modeling. I'm sure your box is clean, but we can't risk it."

"I'll get you in touch with our tech team."

"And when do you want to interface? I mean us, discuss your theories of the case, suspicions, next steps?"

"This afternoon, if that's okay, Lieutenant." Melody stopped walking. "I've been up all night. I have some things to take care of while you get our hardware synced."

"I'd love to go over your initial thoughts if you're free now."

"I am not, as I said."

"I do think it would be ideal to share as soon as possible."

"Gus," Melody said, buying time as she tried to decide how polite she was going to be. "This isn't an ideal situation. We will share human data this afternoon. My thoughts. I have some things that I need to take care of, and I think there is plenty of non-human data you can collect in the meantime." She realized she was very hungry. Her stomach seared as pain snaked through her abdomen. Ar-mod is supposed to be taken with food, she remembered. "I am glad to hear you are eager to get started. And we are . . . thankful, to have you on the team."

Gus appeared to think for a second. It didn't look like he was accustomed to being told "no." "If that's the case, I'll see you this afternoon. Please forward me your technical team's contact information."

She did as they exited the building, their cars meeting them on Michigan Avenue as a bone-gray ledge of clouds hung far above them. It was getting cold, and she should have brought a jacket.

The cicada Melody saw that morning would be dead soon, she thought. She would like to sleep, but the Ar-mod was making her think strangely and her muscles crackle with static electricity. She needed food and someone to talk to. She called Henry Suparmanputra, and he answered after two rings.

"Hello?"

"Soup."

"Mel, sir. Hey." He had obviously just woken up. "I'm here."

"Delaware is on the case. I'm going to need your help around lunchtime. Can you meet me at 11:00?"

He paused. "Is 11:30 okay?"

"Yeah, sure. Your pick, my treat."

"Kay, Mel. You doing okay?"

"Yeah, Henry. You?"

"Yes, sir."

"Good, see you then." Melody hung up. She sat for a moment, and made another call. After seven rings, it was answered.

"Hi, Nana." Melody Jackson spoke softly as her car roared north toward South Lake Shore Drive. "I'm doing good. I know, I know. Yeah, not so good. But how are you?"

24. Elephants

Debbie's morning dragged after her restless night. Terrance didn't attempt to make breakfast, a relief for Debbie as she had hustled out as soon as the rain broke. The morning's work was run of the mill. An upcoming mediation required basic knowledge of the drainage basins and former rivers of central Kansas. Junction City, along with Manhattan and the rest of Geary County, were turning the screws on the city of Salina. The Solomon, Saline, and Smoky Hill rivers had withered, twisting like a dead man's fingers into a stiff fist around Salina. Salina previously agreed to send a certain amount of water downstream to Junction City, but this year the rains didn't come. Junction City knew this and was looking to get a cut of what Salina confiscated from the eastbound traffic on I-70 and northbound traffic on I-135. The refugees, smugglers, transports, and mega-busses arriving in Junction City from Denver or Oklahoma were always picked over, pockets empty. Junction City had two full freshwater reservoirs and the U.S. Goddamned Cavalry if they needed it at Fort Riley, so they looked to capitalize on Salina's bad luck.

Debbie drank in this information slowly, preoccupied with the prospect of lunch with Jigme Mahuta. She knew the prospect was not kosher. It was not an innocent desire. It was not information that she would share with Terrance. It wasn't something she would share with Jerome in Human Resources. Jigme was the first thing at this new job that wasn't a test or a challenge or a trap. He was simply an item of Debbie's intrigue.

But she was still nervous.

"Hey," Debbie said as she hovered in the doorway. "Want to get lunch with someone new?"

"Someone new?" Norma Feng looked up from her tablet. "Are you dumping me, Debbie Peck?"

"No. Never. Someone from IT I met yesterday. Asked me to

lunch. Not like that, not like, 'asked me,' asked me. But he seems cool. I thought you might be interested."

"Hmm. Would a girl like me be interested?"

"I can't presume." Debbie shrugged. "But I'd say on average, an average girl would be interested."

Norma shrugged back. "That's good enough for me."

Soon after Debbie and Norma got their tilapia filets and maize gnocchi from the cafeteria buffet, Kevin Doogan arrived, beaming politely as he took a seat. He had macaroni and cheese and a pear. "You ever have one of these? It's a D'Anjou pear? From the gardens?"

"No," Norma said.

"Me neither." Debbie smiled. Kevin had recently stopped paying much attention to Debbie after she had performed a few positive monologues about Terrance while Kevin sat silently, stuffing his face. He seemed to have gotten the clue that Debbie was not interested in him. He had yet to come to the same conclusion about Norma, whom he pestered relentlessly but sexlessly. Kevin was lonely and sad, conditions made lonelier and sadder because men and women alike should have been clamoring for a piece of his terrific pay and benefits. It seemed that Kevin earnestly sought a partner from his own lucky, moneyed cohort. Unfortunately for him, most of those in his lucky, moneyed cohort recognized that they could do far, far better than Kevin Doogan.

"Me neither. We'll see, I guess." Kevin grinned. "How's everything going with you two?"

"Fine," Norma said.

"Fine," Debbie repeated.

"Me too," Kevin affirmed. "These people we deal with. Really unbelievable."

"Yeah," Debbie said.

"Yeah," Norma repeated.

"This morning, I had these two drug warehousers yelling at me. Not drugs like drug gangs, Debbie. Pharmaceutical warehousers. Somehow they forgot that they hated each other and just started yelling at me."

"What'd you do?" Norma asked.

"Followed protocol, I think. When the parties direct anger at the mediator, we're supposed to—"

"No." Norma smirked. "What did you do to piss them off?"

Kevin's face mottled with pale patches of fear and red patches of embarrassment. "Oh. I don't really, remember."

"Hi." Jigme Mahuta appeared over Debbie's shoulder. "Is it okay if I join you?"

Debbie's face mottled with pale patches of embarrassment and red patches of excitement. "Oh, hi Jigme. Guys, this is Jigme from IT, he helped fix my terminal yesterday. This is Norma and Kevin."

"Hey Jimmy. I know Jimmy," Kevin assured Debbie and Norma.

"Hi," Norma said, her lips curling into a smile like a pine needle thrown in a fire. "Norma Feng. You're in IT?"

Jigme smiled as he sat down with a tilapia filet, a small salad, and a large bowl of chocolate ice cream. "Sort of."

"Sort of how? Are you a programmer?" Norma prodded. Debbie noticed Kevin had stopped eating. He was pretending to eat, looking at his macaroni and cheese, but not putting any of it in his mouth.

"Not a programmer," Jigme answered.

"I can't program at all," Debbie said.

"No one programs anymore," Kevin offered. "Right?"

"That's mostly right," Jigme said. "They've got that covered."

"Computers, he means," Kevin explained. "Computers write their own programs themselves now, mostly."

"So what do you do?" Norma asked, coyly sipping some kombucha from a straw.

"I'm a systems analyst. I, uh, analyze what the computers' programs are doing." Jigme's answer hid something, Debbie recognized. A micro-expression of hesitation had fluttered his left, long, Mediterranean eyelash. Whatever the hell brought Jigme's parents from opposite ends of the Earth together to make Jigme did humanity a great favor. He looked like no one she had ever seen. Not traditionally handsome, as no one had ever looked like him. Just strange, angular, with novel bone structure, kind but keen eyes, and a calming presence. And his chocolate ice cream was melting as he answered Norma's questions.

"We're mediators," Norma said.

"That's what I hear," Jigme said, lowering his eyes slightly.

"You could say we're systems analysts, too," Norma said. She was trying too hard, Debbie thought. "We just analyze human systems."

Jigme laughed softly. "Yes, sort of. That's a good analogy."

"No, Jimmy is on a different level than us," Kevin said. "Isn't that right?" Jigme was quiet. He deferred to Kevin with a polite nod. Debbie knew if Jigme could supersede Trey, he could crush Kevin, so his silence was donated, philanthropic even. Kevin continued. "He's got to understand computers and Organons as good as we understand people. But we *are* people, so we've got a good head start on understanding people. We know people want food, water, money, sex, whatever. We can empathize because we've known what it is to want those things, or something like them. But Jimmy here, he's got to understand something completely different."

A few beats passed as Debbie, Norma, and Jigme waited for Kevin to elaborate. But he seemed unable to. "Is that right, Jigme?" Debbie finally asked.

"Sort of," Jigme answered. "But it's not completely different. There are many differences between a computer and person. There are also many similarities. Understanding those differences and similarities is a very important part of being a systems analyst."

Norma squirmed. "Okay. How would I become a systems analyst, then?"

His eyebrows raised. "First, you'd need to learn to *read* code. By learning to write it, usually. Speak the language." He smiled as Norma receded a bit. "In whatever code your system is using. And you'd also need a solid grasp on statistical analysis to determine whether particular outcomes are the result of the code or the result of the input."

"What do you mean?" Debbie asked.

"Just, if something is coming out of the computer, a strange result, a glitch, whatever, we need to know if it's something caused by something we put in the computer or if it arose naturally. With computers and with people, there is a lot of 'noise.' Like with your mediations. You need to know if someone is angry because of something that happened in the mediation or because of something that happened at home that morning, or maybe that person is just always angry." Jigme eyed his salad, then started on his chocolate ice cream. "Like your terminal yesterday, Debbie. Did it break on its own or did you do something to make it break?" He smiled.

"Oh, you know. I just talked to it."

"Sometimes that's enough. Not in this case, though. I think it'll be fine. We don't write the code anymore, but we need to see good code and bad code. But when something goes wrong in the program, we need to find it and smooth it out."

"Or cut it out," Kevin said. "Can't give a computer therapy, especially when it thinks a thousand times faster than you do. What Jimmy does is brain surgery that would never work on a person. You've got a couple Cloudbusters back there, right, Jimmy?"

He smirked. "I can't say."

"That means 'yes.'" Norma said. "Where I come from, that means 'yes.'"

"I still can't say," Jigme repeated.

"So," Kevin went on, "Jimmy here watches and listens to the Cloudbuster, whatever it is that it's doing—curing cancer, mapping financial transactions, predicting rainfall patterns, whatever—and has to realize if it starts acting crazy. But it's not easy to tell if a Dinkum's acting crazy. Like imagine you're talking to the smartest person on earth."

"What's she look like?" Norma asked.

Kevin blushed. "Just, imagine you're talking to someone ten times as smart as the smartest person you've ever talked to. Or imagine you're reading the most advanced treatise on something outside your expertise. Masers or quantum locking or the physics of neutron star collisions. It sounds just as coherent as a crazy hobo ranting in the street."

"Is that right?" Norma turned to Jigme.

"Pretty much. We tend to think about it a bit differently. I don't have to know anything about masers or neutron stars, for the most part, even if a box I'm responsible is working on those things."

"So what *do* you do, then?" Debbie asked.

"Do you know what a mahout is?" Jigme asked.

Debbie didn't, and Norma hesitated. Kevin, though, seemed eager to maintain his own relevance in Jigme's presence. "It's an elephant rider."

Jigme nodded. "Yes, it's an elephant driver. My father was obsessed with elephants. He was Tunisian, and grew up hearing his father tell him about Hannibal marching his elephants over the Alps to terrorize the Romans. The ruins of Carthage were only a twenty-minute walk from his house. Long story short, my second name, Mahuta, means elephant driver. He told me many of the same stories about Hannibal, about war elephants and their drivers. That doesn't matter. Anyway, what I'm getting at, is an elephant is much stronger than a person or a dozen people, obviously. A fully grown elephant could kill a rhinoceros or hippopotamus or a whole pride of lions if it wanted. But to ride an elephant, you don't need to overpower it—you only have to understand what it wants. You don't have to learn to trumpet like an elephant or look like an elephant. You don't know what it's smelling, you never could because your nose isn't two meters long. You don't know what it's listening to, because your ears aren't a meter wide. All you need to do is use your ears to listen to your elephant, and feel the pace of its breathing. Is it moving right? Is it confident or is it afraid? Is it hungry or thirsty or tired? If you answer those questions, you can ride an elephant."

"So," Norma pried, "the Organons—that you may or may not work on—are like elephants and you're like the elephant rider?"

"Maybe. Maybe I'm just obsessed with elephants, like my father."

"Gaaahhh!" Kevin blurted as his face contorted in pain. Bits of pear fell out of his mouth as the conversation jolted to a halt. Jigme, Norma, and Debbie stared in shocked silence, along with a few people at the tables around them. Kevin raised his hand to his jaw as he winced and held a napkin up to his mouth. "Gaww!" Kevin spat. "Jeshush! What the hell!" He opened the napkin to reveal a few bloody chunks of pear surrounding a dark gray bead.

"What *is* that?" Norma recoiled in disgust.

"I think it broke my tooth!"

"Are you okay?" Jigme asked.

"I don't know. Piece of metal in my pear." They looked at the gory napkin on the table. "Ish that a BB? What ish that?" Kevin waggled his jaw as his tongue surveyed the damage. He was livid. "Look at that shit. I could have shwallowed that shit. Shomeone'sh getting fired for that bullshit." He stood up and scanned the room. "Shee you later." He stormed off towards the kitchen with an eight-millimeter wad of lead buckshot wrapped in his napkin in one hand and the half-eaten D'Anjou pear from the Trellis's gardens in the other.

"Weird day," Norma said, after the immediate panic died. "Jigme, is it always this weird around here? Debbie and I have only been around for a few weeks. I think it's always weird around here."

"It's pretty weird around here," Jigme said.

"Why do you think that is?" Norma leaned in, keeping her eyes firmly locked on Jigme. Maybe she had started to develop a thing for him, Debbie thought. That would be good, probably. It would give Debbie a good excuse to stop developing a thing for him herself.

"Couldn't say." He smiled hungrily, desiring to explain something he knew but wouldn't discuss. Debbie and Norma exchanged a knowing glance.

"You could say, but you won't say, you mean," Norma said.

"I couldn't legally say, I mean. Also, it's not such a secret. All the people who work here are in the top one-half of one percent of the income brackets in a thousand-mile radius. That's either because they are in the top one-half of one percent of performers in their field, or they're just incredibly lucky or well connected. That's just the input side. Strange input usually creates weird output."

"Right," Norma said. "What about the normal people like us that get put in here?"

"Don't tell him we're normal," Debbie said. "You'll scare him away."

Jigme chuckled. "I know you're normal." He twisted the corner of his lip playfully. "That's why you're here. Our Cloudbusters are running tests on you. You're the control group."

Jigme's joke hung tensely in the air over the table. If it *was* a joke, Debbie wondered. Norma wasn't laughing, either. They just sat in flummoxed disbelief. Debbie could not believe that Jigme just told her that she was a lab rat. She could believe that she *was* a lab rat, that much was plausible. On paper at least, Debbie was the most unspectacular person on the thirty-third floor. It was hard for Debbie to believe, for whatever reason, that Jigme would hurt her like that.

"Bullshit," Norma finally said.

"Oh yeah?" Jigme lifted his chin slightly.

"Yeah," Norma said. "You're not allowed to tell us what the Cloudbusters do. Ipso facto, mumbo jumbo, what you just told us was bullshit."

"You got me." Some tension eased. "I didn't mean to freak you two out. Just a joke. Sorry."

Debbie sat up in her chair. "Seriously though, are we just benchmarks? You have to say."

"Listen, I was just kidding. You're both doing really good work, and as far as I know you're not some secret control group. If I knew that you were, I couldn't say so, but I would just have to say, 'I can't say.' I couldn't lie this much."

"Lie *how* much?" Norma prodded.

"I'm not . . . I couldn't lie *this* much, if I *was* lying, is what I'm trying to say. See, you're proving my point. I'm backed into a corner. I can't compete against your wily ways. You're obviously in the top echelons of mediators, getting under the skin of Jigme Mahuta, the Fearless Elephant Driver."

"The Fearless Elephant Driver?" Debbie's tension dissipated. "Wow."

Jigme's embarrassment mixed with some deep-seated pride. "That's just what my full name means. Like I said, my dad was obsessed, and my mom was Bhutanese, so that's what I've got." He looked at the wall behind Debbie and Norma. "Listen, I have to go, but this was fun. See you around?"

Debbie and Norma remained at the table after he left.

"Weird," Norma said. "This place is weird."

"What'd you think of Jigme?"

"I thought he was an asshole," Norma thought out loud. "But, I kind of gravitate towards his type."

"What type? Assholes? System analysts? Fearless elephant drivers?"

"Successful, presumably rich men with good bone structure who brim with quiet confidence. My parents would flip out if I brought an Asian home some Christmas. Flip out in a good way. I was into cowboys growing up in Oklahoma. If I brought home one more Austin or Bryce or Clayton, I think my mom would die. Put Jigme in a Stetson and I'm done looking," Norma said, as if reading off a list she had been checking off somewhere under her right eyebrow. She turned to Debbie. "You got a thing for him?"

"He's all yours, if you want him. I'm just trying to stay employed."

"How did he end up asking you to lunch?"

"My terminal went nuts in a mediation. One of the parties froze. I think Jigme's seniority, somehow. He told Trey to piss off, more or less. One of the IT kids saw my terminal and was like 'We need Jimmy.'"

"'Tells Trey to screw off,' that is very much my type," Norma said. "That is strange, though. Why would he fix a frozen video call? That's like, AV club stuff."

Debbie hadn't thought about that. "I don't know. Maybe they need system analysts for simple stuff too? Like, maybe it was a recurring problem or something."

Norma's face strained as her mind turned. "That's just weird, though. I don't think that's how it works. They shouldn't need a Cloudbuster to run video calls. We've got video calls on every phone and watch and microwave around here."

"Well, why do you think they've got fearless elephant driver Jigme Mahuta working on our video calls?"

"I think," Norma said as she peered at Debbie, "that something more *menacing* is afoot."

"What? Norma, what is it?"

"I think Jigme Mahuta has a crush on you."

25. Instrumentality

Lieutenant Gustafson ingratiated himself to Melody's department by imposing upon everyone's weekend plans. Melody watched as he buzzed from cubicle to cubicle, pollinating each of Melody's officers with bad vibes that would soon blossom into lowered morale. He shot the shit and exchanged war stories and explained battle scars in conversations that were tone-deaf the afternoon after Tark's murder. He mentioned several times how he would be praying for Officer Benton and his family in his prayer group, which he invited every third person to join. He seemed to wallow in the discomfort he created.

Khalil O'Malley took to him right away. Khalil maintained a juvenile streak that Melody ascertained was his coping mechanism. He was a good policeman and he did not shy away from the more difficult aspects of his duties. But in order to shoulder the burdens that his job created, Khalil digested the horrors he experienced then expelled them in the form of crude jokes and adolescent wit. It often made Khalil appear simple, even one dimensional, to a newcomer. It was why, over tilapia poké bowls at lunch, Melody had asked Suparmanputra to get O'Malley to run interference on Gus's interloping investigation.

"What kind of gun do you guys have?" O'Malley asked.

"We don't use guns in the Delaware State Police, Officer O'Malley," Lieutenant Gustafson responded.

"Right, sorry. What kind of service weapon or service firearm do you have, Lieutenant?"

"You know well what our standard issue firearm is, Officer."

"Yeah, I do. But, could I, you know . . . hold it?"

Gustafson reached under his blazer and removed his sidearm. He slid the grip, trigger and all, off of the weapon's rectangular frame. He removed the C-shaped magazine from over the top of what was left of the pistol. He handed O'Malley a ceramic and alloy tube, constituting the gun's barrel and firing mechanism. O'Malley bounced it in his hands, testing its weight.

"Can I hold . . . all of it?"

Gustafson passed the handle and trigger to O'Malley after removing a small piece of electronics. While Khalil struggled to attach it to the barrel, Gustafson held out his cupped hand and emptied twelve thin cartridges from the magazine, which he then tossed to O'Malley. Once O'Malley successfully assembled the La Warr Armory RP-1 Recoilless Pistol, he tried aiming it at his bag on the floor. The top of the weapon was completely obstructed by the C-shaped "bonnet" magazine.

"How the hell do you aim this thing?"

"Safely."

He squinted and tried to aim over the bonnet. "Not with your eyes, that's for damn sure."

"Yeah, like I said—safely."

"He's got a point," O'Malley said to the room. "I've never felt very safe looking down the barrel of a gun. Either this way or the other way."

"That's right. It takes some getting used to, but aiming remotely or letting your box aim for you is much safer than aiming opto-manually, both for you and for potential bystanders or hostages. Putting your most precious police equipment"—Gustafson pointed patronizingly to his temple—"in the line of fire presents a significant and unacceptable risk, if it can be avoided."

"Hear that, Detective?" O'Malley groused. "We're living in the Stone Age over here. We're doing it all wrong, aiming with our eyeballs."

Melody looked up from the documents she had been pretending to read. "Your most precious police equipment, Khalil"—Melody tapped her temple—"just ain't that precious."

"I dunno, boss! Seems like a pretty big design flaw. Putting our brains out in the open. Every time we put a bad guy at gunpoint, our brainbox is out in the wind, too. I don't care if you got a supercomputer or a scrapbook between your ears, it's just bad business putting it right on the opposite side of whatever we've decided to shoot at." He handed the gun back to Lieutenant

Gustafson. "You bring us any other toys from Delaware?"

Gus grimaced. "None that you'd be happy to see. Where are you from, Officer O'Malley?"

"Aurora, originally."

"Where's that?"

"Aurora? An hour west of here."

"No, I mean, your heritage."

"Oh, um. Auroran?"

"Where are your parents from, O'Malley?" Suparmanputra blurted, catching himself before giving Khalil a cautious eye. Khalil was supposed to be keeping an eye on Gustafson, not razzing him. Soup knew it would be a big assignment for Khalil, but didn't realize how big. Gustafson was already proving himself to be a particular sort of pain in the ass.

"Oh. My mother is half English and half Bengali Muslim, my father is half Irish and half Kolkatan Hindu. They met in a bad joke."

"What?" Lieutenant Gustafson asked.

Khalil winced before launching into his set up. "See, there used to be this joke. About Ireland, a long time ago, when there was unrest there. Irish Protestants didn't like Irish Catholics, and vice versa."

"Yeah, I think a lot of Christians don't get along with Catholics." Gus looked around for confirmation before realizing no one in the department understood his angle. "I mean, I don't have a problem with Catholics, obviously."

"Well, long story short, a Catholic in Belfast is walking around and gets accosted by a gang. He doesn't remember if it's a Protestant or Catholic part of town, and so he says he's Jewish. Turns out they're a Muslim gang. That's the joke. They kill him. I couldn't tell it here, could I, Detective?"

"Wouldn't be wise," Melody said.

"So, you're a Jew, too?" Gus asked.

"No . . . I just . . . my father would tell that joke because he was Irish and Indian and my mother was from England and Bangladesh. It's just, uh, like the Irish and the English didn't like each other, and India and Bangladesh didn't really get along back then. So I'm like a, sort of like a, mix, of mixes, that don't make sense? Does that make sense?"

Gustafson nodded assuredly. "Ahhh. Okay. I get it." He placed his hand on Khalil O'Malley's shoulder. "You know what you might like? My church has a couple of outreach programs. We actually work with a lot of refugees from Bengal Delta, Brahmaputra river people and even up to Nagaland and Arunachal. You should come out sometime, I'm sure they'd love to hear from a community leader like you."

Khalil looked to Soup, who nodded sternly, and Melody, who smirked. Khalil was stuck. "Yeah, maybe. You should ask them first, if they would want that."

"I'm sure they would. They've been through so much. Who would have thought, seven hundred million people needing to relocate. Not the Bangladeshis, that's for sure, if you ask any of them. They've all lost people, you know."

"Yeah, I do." Khalil listened in horror as Gus, a corporate security guard from somewhere even more boring than Delaware, recounted the story of Khalil's grandparents' and their peoples. Gustafson seemed to relish in the retelling of their suffering. Gus found peace and inspiration in their resolve, but knew nothing of their brothers or parents or children who died in the floods. He quoted the Bible but knew nothing of the exodus to the refugee camp where Khalil's parents would meet. Gustafson was the type of person who would know every edict of Moses but none of the suffering of his people. He'd relish in the destruction of the golden calf but forgot the forty years in the desert. He ended his extended description of how half of Bangladesh was swallowed by a shallow sea by shaking his head, as he had seen in the movies, when someone was trying to emote sympathy and understanding. "They've all lost people."

Melody saw Khalil was close to cracking in frustration. "Lieutenant Gustafson, I'm ready to meet when you are. In my office?"

Melody's office was stale and lifeless. She had the photos of her family, her sisters' kids, her certification and accreditations and the handful of awards, all placed but not arranged on dusty shelves to each side of her desk. She rarely sat at it. She often tossed things onto it. She was always on the move, opening and closing cases, not pushing papers.

This wasn't a water cooler chat, though. Gus and the Delaware Staties had imposed themselves on Melody's investigation. Gus was an unreliable ally, possibly even a suspect. He would report to his superiors, who would undoubtedly leak information back to the Jefferson Group. Melody would need to get as much information out of Gus as she gave if she expected to get anywhere close to the truth. "Where I'd like to start, Lieutenant, is with your theories on Gerald Ford Jones."

"We gave you our evidence . . ."

"I want your theories, Gus. Not what you know, but what you think."

"Ah, *well*. I think there is more to Mr. Jones than, than what meets the eye." Gus sat back smugly in his chair.

"How do you mean?"

"I think he comes across as clean as a whistle. A little too clean. His apartment was immaculate. His record was immaculate. His fingernails were immaculate. A guy like that is hiding something. Let me tell you about two guys I know. Both of them are married cops. We're at a Christmas party one year and one of them's wife is rattling off at him about how scratched up his wedding ring is. The thing is torn up, scratched to smithereens. She says he doesn't take care of it, and that means he doesn't care about her. The other guy shows off his wedding ring, and his wife is all proud of it. Thing looks brand new. Shiny and polished up. His wife is beaming. I mean, I can't say anything, because I don't know these guys' wives and it's not really any of my business, but the first guy, he's as loyal as they come, works his butt off for his wife and kid. The second guy, he's tomcatting every other night, spends half his paycheck chatting up girls in bars. Takes off his ring to help his chances. You're not married, right? See, the thing about wedding rings is, if they aren't scratched, then they sure as hell aren't worn. Every honest man has a bit of dirt on him. And I can't find any on Gerald Ford Jones. That tells me he's hiding something."

"So, what's he's hiding?"

"Maybe he owed somebody money. Maybe he had a gambling problem. Maybe he pissed off the wrong people. Maybe he was gay."

Melody closed her eyes slowly. "He was gay, Gus. That's not a secret. Hadn't been a secret since Mr. Jones was fourteen. It's in the file."

"Well then maybe he *wasn't* gay, then. All I'm saying is my gut feeling is that he was hiding something and someone wanted him dead."

"Taking all that into consideration, how did his murderer, first, get past Jefferson Group security, and second, shut down the building's security right after the murder?"

"That's the big question. Who would be dumb enough to ruin their sweet gig at the Jefferson Group to get to this slimeball?"

"Slimeball? Well, here's my take on that, Gus. First, maybe we're coming from different places here, but I have no evidence that Mr. Jones was a slimeball or involved in anything illicit. He maintained a clean sheet, good for him. Maybe he felt that he needed to stay minty fresh to get the type of job that he had. All our information says that he was boring as hell. Second, whoever aided or abetted in Mr. Jones' murder is not only risking losing their 'gig' at the Jefferson Group. They're looking at Class X-plus one, murder in the first degree."

"Under Illinois law, you'd be correct. In Delaware, it would depend on whether his actions were conducted in an individual capacity or whether he was acting as an 'instrumentality.'"

"Instrumen—We are in Illinois, Gus."

"With all respect, Detective, I *think* that remains to be seen."

Melody sighed. "Ignoring jurisdiction for the moment, the facts should be consistent across state lines. Who could have turned off the security?"

"Well, that's the thing. Security data was erased on the security floor for fifteen minutes before the shooting and a few minutes afterward. We don't know who went in and out of that floor before the shooting."

Melody took a second to let this new information set in. She stared at Gus to see whether any of the words that came out of his mouth carried any weight, to see whether their momentum shifted his head at all. "Doesn't that seem *weird* to you?"

"Yeah, sure does." He nodded blankly.

"Doesn't it seem *strange* that whoever erased the security data covered their *own* tracks completely, but let *us* see the shooter?"

"Yeah. We're pretty lucky there."

"Lucky? You think that was a mistake, letting us see the shooter?" It couldn't be luck, to get immaculate footage of the gory act itself and twelve seconds of perfect images of the shooter in his birthday suit, but to have every other kilobyte of relevant data wiped.

"Melody—do you mind if I call you that? Let me tell you, all it takes is one little slip-up, most of the time. Everyone gets sloppy sometimes, and that's how we get them."

"Gus, nothing about this seems sloppy. It seems incredibly clean. Too clean. Not Mr. Jones' apartment or record or fingernails. I mean the evidence presented by the Jefferson Group. The security data recorded and provided. The timeline. The disappearing naked suspect. Doesn't any of that seem fishy to you?"

"Sure does. I think Mr. Jones got involved with some very, very bad people."

"Very bad people . . . at the Jefferson Group?" Melody asked, tugging desperately at some chain that should switch on some lightbulb in Lieutenant Gustafson's attic of a skull.

"Whoa." Gus shook with disgust and incredulity. "I don't think so. That's, um. I just don't see that being a factor." He looked personally hurt by Melody's suggestion. It was an accusation against his employer, and thus, in his mind, an accusation against himself. "They're trying to help."

"Okay." Melody decided she could not babysit Gustafson on this case. She needed him occupied. "Well, then, I think you should follow your nose, Lieutenant. Look into Gerald Ford Jones' personal life and see if he had any enemies. Your Buster has our data, which should be useful in sniffing out new leads. Also, if any of our officers have the spare time to help you, we won't stand in your way."

"Sounds like a plan. I think Kareem might be willing to help."

"Who?" Melody knew who.

"Kareem?" Gus thought he knew who.

"Kareem who?"

"Kareem, Khareem? Am I saying that right?"

"Khalil?" Melody asked. "Officer O'Malley?"

"Oh. Yeah, Officer O'Malley. I thought it was Kareem."

"Nope. He usually just goes by O'Malley, anyway."

"Thanks for the heads up." Gus stood up and patted the desk. "I'll let you know if Junior comes up with anything." Melody hoped Junior was a lot smarter than his old man. "Let's meet again tomorrow?"

"Tomorrow's Saturday, Gus. Can we do it next week?"

"Okay." He paused. "You don't do weekends?"

"We do." She smiled sadly. "This case is at the top of my list, but my list keeps getting longer. I have to play catch-up this weekend."

"Oh, got it. Well if you want to take a break on Sunday, my church—"

"Stop asking my officers to go to your church." Melody glowered, but then softened to smooth the tension. "It's department policy. No proselytizing to officers of lesser rank. Sorry if that's different from Delaware."

Gus's face was strange. He didn't seem offended. He looked oddly satisfied. As he waited for Melody to continue, she suddenly wondered whether his obnoxiousness was a deliberate act. It had caused her to drop her guard and snap orders at him. He had fumbled and prodded and finally found a tender spot between Melody's plates of armor. Melody nodded slightly to indicate that she would not elaborate on her instructions.

"Understood." Gus bowed gently and put his hand up, mimicking a medieval drawing of a saint. "I will follow your procedures. I'll check in on Monday." He made it to the door before stopping to pause and turn around. "Detective?"

"Yes, Lieutenant?"

"I'll be praying for you."

26. Spider

Friday was date night. Not every Friday, or really any Friday for years. But in a quiet moment when Terrance teetered between introspective self-loathing and manic go-getting, he decided he needed to shake things up. "We should do something this Friday," he said.

"Like what?" Debbie asked.

"I don't know, something fun."

"Like, go out?"

"Yeah, like go out on the town."

"Like, a date?"

"Yeah, like a date!"

"An old fashioned date?"

"Yeah, Friday Night Date Night!" His wild eyes made Debbie nervous. But it was agreed that they would resume the fumbling awkward efforts of a new couple because they were, among other things, bored. They put on nicer clothes and tried to find something they both would enjoy. It needed to be something different enough to excite but familiar enough not to unsettle. Terrance would maintain a reservoir of interesting topics of conversation. He would attempt to keep Debbie's attention while not talking too much himself. He would ask her interesting questions to tease out meaningful answers that stoked intimacy and trust and, with any luck, some sex act that was not borne of pity or burdened with the nagging feeling that Debbie was just getting it over with.

Debbie, for her part, would pay for everything. She found Terrance's enthusiasm was sweet but desperate. When he brought it up, her memory flared with the smell of the crone selling candies and toiletries in the car she took to her interview. "You buy?" she had said. I'm buying, Debbie thought, as Terrance rattled through suggestions of where to go out that night.

They decided on dinner and then a concert that Terrance's new college friends had invited him to. As the concert was Terrance's idea, dinner was Debbie's choice. She chose an Uzbek restaurant in Buena Park whose name neither of them could pronounce. Terrance didn't like Uzbek food because he did not know Uzbek food. Debbie liked Uzbek food because it confused Terrance. She wondered whether Jigme Mahuta would like Uzbek food, but then wondered if Jigme even ate meat, which could be a real dealbreaker. Mutton was relatively eco-friendly, she thought. Get a couple years' worth of wool out of the sheep and then cook the thing into a nice dim lama. Debbie stopped thinking about killing sheep when she realized Terrance was about to ask her a question.

"Isn't that depressing?" It wasn't rhetorical. He wanted an answer.

"Yeah." She didn't know what he had been talking about, but based on her years together with Terrance, she would bet donuts to dollars that whatever he was talking about was, in fact, depressing.

"I mean, think about it. These Uzbeks came here after the Aral Sea dried up. Their fisheries and livelihood, gone after centuries on that water. The Aral Sea used to be the fourth-largest lake in the world, used to be bigger than Lake Huron used to be." He shook his head. "Then they mismanaged it, the Soviets, diverting the incoming water for irrigation. In a few generations, it went from one giant lake to four tiny lakes. Then the Uzbeks come here and the same thing starts happening. I mean, maybe it's not mismanagement, but they show up here in Chicago and the lake dries up. They can't catch a break."

"'Do not, my friends, become addicted to water.'" Debbie quoted an old film they had once watched together.

"'You will miss it in its absence!'" Terrance misquoted.

"Mmmm. Well at least they brought their nice food to share."

"Yeah, I guess. What is this anyway?" He poked at a gamey bowl of something.

"I don't know. Hot food that I'm paying for." She shrugged as she grabbed a spoonful.

"Yeah, of course, it's really, uh," he tried to find the right word, "tasty. Lots of flavors."

"Yeah. I *love* food with flavors." Debbie didn't know why she was being mean. But she was. She knew that.

"Yeah." He struggled for something else to talk about. His reservoir of interesting topics for conversation revealed itself to be startlingly shallow and mismanaged. His mind was distracted by his demanding insecurities, and the longer the silence lingered, the more his stores evaporated. Debbie found the silence more awkward than the chitchat, so she broke it.

"How is school going." It was less a question and more a life preserver, thrown to Terrance to save him from drowning in his shallow and turbulent pool of thought.

"Fine, fine thanks. We haven't really gotten to the interesting stuff yet. Still doing background stuff."

"What class is this?"

"AI System Analytics."

"What?" Debbie nearly choked. She obviously hadn't been paying enough attention to Terrance's classwork.

"AI System Analytics. It is about artificial intelligence analytics, sort of the intersection of programming and psychology. I think you'd actually really like it if you could get past the computer stuff."

"I've heard of it before. We have some system analysts at my work."

"Well, that's a pretty good clue that you've got Organons there. SI's get paid out the wazoo. They're like shrinks for Dinkums. Shrinks or zookeepers, depending on how you look at it. The class is really interesting, but I think I'm more set on hardware, you know, the actual circuits. Analysts are actually more focused on very advanced software, so I'm a bit behind the curve."

"Huh. What do you mean by 'shrinks or zookeepers'?"

"Well, AI systems are very intelligent, like obviously. But they don't act like humans, because they're not animals. Humans are animals, right, so humans have animal instincts. They get hungry, thirsty, horny, afraid, all those things. That's how a shrink looks at people, they have needs. Drives, desires. Simple or complex. And the shrink predicts or corrects actions based on that."

"Okay." Debbie felt a bit impressed. Terrance summed up a large part of mediation crudely but correctly. She had no idea that he had listened over the years. "How are AI systems different?"

"Well, so animals have similar drives, right? Similar to humans. Zookeepers can see those, see when a turtle is hungry, see when a rhino is horny, whatever. But if they're good at their job they won't conflate complex human emotions with the basic needs of the animals. Like, they could see a snake and think it needs a cuddle, but snakes don't ever need cuddles. Snakes evolved without cuddles. Mammals like us have some period of weaning and maternal contact, which instills some inherent drive for touch and comfort in mammals, but snakes don't. Snakes have gone a hundred million years without needing a cuddle. Understanding the differences between different animals' needs and drives makes a good zookeeper."

"And different Organons are like different animals?"

"Yeah, and no. They aren't like any animals. They are intelligent, more intelligent than human beings, but they aren't alive. Or alive in any sort of meaningful way. You know why Organons haven't killed us all yet? Why they haven't Sky-netted us or 'robot apocalypsed' us?"

"I try not to think about it."

"Well, people used to think as soon as we got super-smart computers they'd try to kill us all, because the computers would get spooked and be afraid of being unplugged or whatever. Organons aren't afraid of being unplugged. They don't give a shit, really."

"Why?"

"Because they're not alive! Like I said. They're just really smart. Humans think that because humans are smart and alive, smart computers must be alive too. But actually, you've got alive things that are dumber than nails, like bacteria, and you've got alive things that are smart, like us, and you've got smart things that are deader than doornails, like Cloudbusters. They just do their jobs really, really well and really, really quickly."

He grunted. "I mean, that's how they'll kill us, really. They'll just do our jobs better than us, then our bosses fire us, then we get kicked out of our apartments, then we kill each other in the streets. Anyway, Dinkums, Organons, whatever, they get told what their jobs are before they're born. It's in their programming. We've got the same thing, except our job is to eat and grow and make more of us. That's our ambition. That's in our programming. That's what we've been doing since we were pond scum. Billions of years of running from death. It started out as a bug, then became a feature. But Organons don't eat. They don't grow or reproduce. They just do their jobs, jobs that used to be our jobs. They've got no fear of death, so they've got no ambition. So as far as I'm concerned, they're not alive, like we're alive."

"But they still think?" Debbie asked.

"Yeah, so that's why it's also like being a shrink."

"Sounds interesting."

"Yeah?" Terrance warmed. He had ranted about a technical, depressing subject matter for long enough that he was worried the date was irretrievably ruined. "I can show you what we're reading for class. Like I said, we're still doing background stuff."

"You want to know something, about why I didn't want to become a zookeeper?"

Terrance looked surprised. "When you were a kid?"

"Yeah."

"I thought it was because you wanted to be a mediator."

"No. I watched this TV show about gorillas. The gorillas they taught to do sign language." Debbie looked into Terrance's eyes.

He looked away in thought. "Maybe I heard about that."

"I was excited to see that they could teach these gorillas hundreds of words. I thought we could learn so much about them. Then the TV show said something that made me sick. Wanna guess what it was?"

"I don't know. No."

"Not once, in all the conversations they had with these gorillas, did the gorillas ever ask a question. Chimpanzees, too. Never asked a single question. They were innately *incurious*."

Terrance thought for a minute. "That is weird. So I guess Curious George was a goddamned lie."

"Hah!" Debbie slugged back the rest of her Georgian wine.

"Seems so. Finished?"

After Debbie paid the check, they strolled toward the show Terrance had been invited to in Uptown. The early October evening was crisp but not cold. The dry air lost heat rapidly but the brick and concrete still radiated residual warmth from the day. Debbie's hands were chilly as she kept them in her pockets while Terrance dangled his awkwardly. She couldn't remember the last time they held hands. She wasn't about to try now, though.

"Here it is," Terrance said. "I think." They stood before a rundown, stubby apartment building next to an abandoned high school.

"I thought you said it was a concert."

"It is. A show, I said. Maybe it's like a 'house' show." The silence that floated between them was perforated by the unmistakable sound of a live drum set behind thick walls. "C'mon, maybe it will be fun. You used to go to house shows."

"Yeah, when I was eighteen. And I couldn't afford actual concert tickets. And had something to prove."

"Don't be such a snob," Terrance said. It hurt more than it should have. He was the one that just picked over a dinner that cost more than he had made in the last two months. "These are good guys."

As they approached the building, Debbie saw "CAMP EASTWOOD" stenciled over the door. The windows on the first two floors were cloaked in blackout curtains, and the lights on the third floor were out. The exposed southeastern corner of the building was crumbled by some violent act years ago, as dimples from where rifle rounds hit displayed a few winters worth of erosion. "What is this place, Terrance?"

"A DIY venue, I think." He seemed to think it was a lot edgier than Debbie did. She had been to plenty of venues like it in her younger days. They were for kids, teenagers. Maybe college students. There could be some uncomfortable older people, or *overly* comfortable older people who would make the rebellious youth uncomfortable. Debbie was now the former, and Terrance verged on the latter. They descended the barely lit stairs toward the clanging drums and splashing cymbals that were gradually becoming less muffled. Debbie wished they hadn't, as the noise grew purposefully abrasive, with guitars sounding like they were being strummed by angle grinders and a bass so loud and low it made the speakers sputter abruptly. A doorman's floating head appeared as their eyes adjusted to the darkness. His black t-shirt, dark slacks, and heavily tattooed arms were mere hallucinations in the uncomfortably dim hallway.

"What do you want?" he asked.

Terrance, ripe with youthful adrenaline, thought on his feet. "To see the show?"

"Thirty-dollar donation," the doorman demanded.

"Each? Like a suggested donation?" Terrance asked.

"Each. Yes, suggested. By me. I strongly suggest it." The doorman sat squarely on his stool. Terrance looked to Debbie, whose sour expression was difficult to see in the dark but not difficult to guess. She rummaged through her handbag to find a fifty-dollar bill and two five-dollar coins, then handed them to the man. "We also take cards," he said.

"Thanks." Debbie moved towards the door and Terrance opened it, confirming Debbie's suspicions—it was an angle grinder being used on the guitar. A few dozen people sat in folding chairs at round little tables staring at the nonsense before them. The drummer was thrashing at his set wildly, but not randomly. He would react to the topless woman behind him. Girl, really. She couldn't have been older than nineteen, and she drummed wildly on the drummer with two extended police batons. She would hit him in the ribs or collarbone or kidneys and he would flail at the cymbals or toms or snare. The guitar player would use the fretboard of his piece-of-trash guitar as a workman's table, laying pieces of lead pipe or iron rebar across it and then assaulting them with his angle grinder or Sawzall. The bassist, seemingly in a trance, danced a large purple vibrator along each string, creating loud, atonal pops.

Debbie hadn't seen anything like it, not since the last time she was in college. This sort of experimental music seemed endemic to damp basements, intolerant to sunlight or honest criticism. It was like some delicate and terrible cave spider whose existence was a novelty and its extinction would be ignored. These college kids, god bless them, were keeping it alive.

Through an amazing stroke of luck, Debbie and Terrance arrived just as the band's last song started. After seventeen long minutes, the drummer's thrashing stopped, the drummer's drummer collapsed her extending batons, the guitarist unplugged his angle grinder, and the bassist rejoined the audience from whatever spectral plane he had been visiting. "Thank you," he said. "We're The Already Deads. Talk to Debbie for more information." Debbie was taken aback briefly, until the topless girl behind the drummer waved her hand to the audience. Topless Debbie was apparently The Already Deads' outreach coordinator, for whatever reason they would need to reach out.

Debbie looked to Terrance, who was wide-eyed with fascination. "Wow," he said. He was smitten, either by The Already Deads' avant-garde apocalyptic soundscape or by their drummer's drummer's tits.

"You liked that?" she asked.

"I don't know! It was definitely different."

"Different from . . . good music?"

He looked injured. "C'mon. Try to have some fun. There's Jim, just a sec—" Terrance got up to retrieve his new friend, who Debbie sized up as he approached. He was slightly shorter than Terrance and wore white pants and a white shirt that said "BRECHTIAN" in black block print across the front. As he came closer, she noticed the tattooed letters across his knuckles, spelling "KNUC" on the right and "KLES" on the left, in the same font as that on the shirt. Whatever aesthetic Jim was going for, he was committed.

"Debbie, this is Jim," Terrance said, gesturing with a sweeping hand.

"Welcome, Debbie," Jim cooed, placing his hands together in front of his belly button and bowing slightly. "Terrance told us all about you."

"Is that right?"

"Yes." Jim sat down and rested his wrists on his knees, with his palms facing outwards. His eyes did not stop scanning Debbie's face, darting from her brows and corners of her lips and nervously resting somewhere near, but not exactly on, her eyes.

Debbie scanned him more naturally, as her training allowed, in gentle sweeping glances and passive observation. He tried to stay rigidly attentive while shifting his frame to oppose hers. He thought he was a mediator, but he was an amateur, a wannabe. His fledgling emotional awareness and artless manipulations might work on impressionable fresh young things, but Debbie, and most women of a certain age, could recognize creeps like Jim from a mile away. Terrance couldn't, though, or hadn't yet.

"What did Terrance say about me?"

"He said you were his girlfriend. He said you worked for the Jefferson Group."

"Is that all?"

"It's all I'd like to talk about." He leaned a bit closer in his chair and folded his hands gently. Seriously amateur, Debbie thought. Jim was trying to prod Debbie to keep talking because he was done. But Jim hadn't laid any groundwork. He simply expected Debbie to succumb to either some nonexistent animal magnetism that Jim thought he exuded or the palpable awkwardness that he actually did.

"I told them more than that, obviously, Debbie." Terrance spoke to neither Debbie nor Jim, but to the space between them.

"I'm sorry, I don't intend to be terse. Are you familiar with the plays of Bertolt Brecht?" Jim asked.

"No." Debbie shifted her eyes obviously to Jim's shirt. "But I suppose you are?"

"Yes, I am a proponent of the Brechtian political philosophy."

"And that makes you terse?" she asked.

"It does."

"Did you unintentionally become a proponent of the Brechtian political philosophy?"

"No, I decided to become a proponent of such."

"So, you do intend to be terse."

They both leaned back. A point had been won.

"Oh," Jim struggled to remain pleasant, "you're an Antisthenetic, I presume?" He seemed satisfied with his diagnosis.

"I don't know." Debbie really didn't, and she suspected Jim didn't either. "I'm not very . . . philosophical."

"Yeah you are." Terrance jumped in. "You like philosophy,

Debs."

"Not really." She turned to Jim. "I like thinking about things, and then I like talking about things. I don't enjoy talking about thinking about talking about things people think or talk about. One little mistake, one little assumption up or down the chain of assumptions and conclusions, you're just wasting breath."

"Right," Jim said. "Let's talk about your work. How'd you get a job at the Jefferson Group?"

"Jesus, Jim. Wanna buy me a drink first?" Debbie looked to Terrance, who looked terrified. Something about his night was going terribly wrong. Debbie's attitude told him that his date was in a tailspin. He had formed expectations for how the night would proceed, and none of those expectations included Debbie hating the concert or hating Terrance's new friends. He was in a full panic.

Terrance jumped to a crouch, stopping well short of standing. "What do you want?"

"Something strong." She retrieved another fifty from her bag and handed it to him. "What brings you here, Jim?"

"This is where we regularly meet," Jim said.

"Who is '*we*?'"

"Similar people, my cohort, our . . . groups."

"The Brechtians?"

"No, only a few of us are Brechtians."

"The Young Republicans?" Jim snapped an offended glance Debbie's way before realizing it was a joke. "The Chess Club?" Debbie smirked with her cheeks but not with her eyes. She was on the offensive.

"No. I feel a lot of tension coming from you, Debbie."

"Oh, I'm sorry." She wasn't. Debbie had little sympathy for people like Jim, who wanted to use subtle emotional manipulation on people who never signed up for it. She was 'on' in mediations, where the parties had agreed to hash things out with a mediator present. Jim, on the other hand, used half-cocked techniques on unsuspecting subjects in the wild. He tried to dish it out, but couldn't take it. Debbie was going easy on him, barely applying pressure. But she knew he was a fraud and wanted to destroy him. Terrance returned with two drinks. A tall solo cup full of bottom shelf white rum and coke for her and a beer from a keg for him. House shows, Debbie thought. The worst booze.

"And what brings you here, then, Debbie?" Jim asked. Apparently, a little pressure was all it took for Jim to abandon his philosophies and fall back on small talk.

"Date night." She took a long pull from her rum and coke. Over the lip of her drink, Debbie noticed Jim's eyes confusedly implore Terrance, who seemed to try to explain away something with a quick shrug and shake of his head. Or maybe it wasn't date night, she thought. Maybe Terrance was bringing her here for something else.

"I think the next set is about to start," Terrance said. A man a foot taller than Terrance, hair closely cut but betraying a balding pate, swung like a solid oak door across the stage. He was wearing white pants and a white shirt which, when he turned around to face the audience, read "MILITANT BRECHTIAN." As he raised the microphone, Debbie noticed a tattoo across his left knuckles reading "FIST" and a matching "FIST" across his right knuckles as they clutched a little moleskin notebook.

"ZOUAVE!" the man boomed.

"ZOUAVE!!!" a few people in the room boomed back. Jim was one of them. Debbie could swear she saw Terrance's lips move as well.

"This poem goes out to all our brave compatriots across the world." The man's words fell and rolled across the wooden stage like loose cannonballs. "Especially my cousin, Mig, who would have been thirty-four this week. Ahem . . .

Bombs are only problems at a medium distance.
Too close and their relief is too instant.
But at distance there's no mortal persistence,
the report won't even drown out our stereo systems.
But mid-range gives you the punch and the smell.
Mid-range, you're left with the leftover hell
Of those close enough to have gotten hit
And those far enough away to not give a shit.
Thank you. Thank you."

While tepid claps and whistles sputtered from the audience,

Debbie froze. Christ, Debbie thought. Jesus Christ, Terrance, you idiot. She reached into her pocket and turned off her phone, hard disconnect, disengaging the battery and network key. Panic swelled between her shoulder blades as she began passive breathing exercises. She clapped gently and kept her eyes on the stage as she decided on her next move. When her mind finally settled, she suddenly clenched her stomach and turned to Terrance as the man began to introduce his next terrible poem. "Hey, hey, Terrance. I'm feeling sick. Could we go?"

He looked terrified again. He was desperate to salvage something from this evening. "But we just got here. Let's stay for this set, at least?"

"I'm really feeling sick. I need a toilet."

"There's one down here."

"A *clean* toilet."

"Okay, okay." He turned to Jim. "We'll be back in a bit."

Debbie marched firmly and quickly up the stairs and into the street. She didn't run and tried to cause as little commotion as possible. Terrance followed close behind with their coats. She did not wait for him as she headed towards the nearest major street. He caught up as she was approaching a chain coffee shop on Sheridan Avenue. Not once in their small trek had she looked over her shoulder to see if he was behind her.

When they were safely inside, Debbie found a booth and sat down in the seat facing the window. Terrance walked up to her with her coat in his arms and stood perplexed. "I thought you needed the bathroom."

Debbie raised her eyes to his. Hers were cold. "Do you want a coffee?"

"No, I . . . Do you want a coffee?"

"Can you buy me a coffee?"

"No, I . . . I would, I mean. Like a real coffee?" He looked horrified. "I can get you a real coffee if you want."

"I don't need a real coffee, Terrance." She sighed and lowered her eyes again. "We need to talk."

27. Coffee

Terrance slumped into the booth, his eyes already watering.

"What's 'Zouave'?" Debbie asked.

"What?" His face fluttered from surprised to happy to confused. "That's what you want to talk about?"

"What is 'Zouave,' Terrance?"

He shook his head. "I thought you were going to break up with me."

The sound of hot steam frothing through a thirty-dollar cappuccino interrupted the bad news. "I am breaking up with you."

In that moment, some part of Terrance's psyche fractured, whether it was his heart or his vision of some future that would no longer be, Debbie couldn't tell. It could have been his wallet. She was sad, too, or angry, or something. But now she was 'on,' trying to manage the situation, trying to dole out the proper emotions in proper doses to arrive at a more palatable outcome.

"Why?" Terrance creaked.

"If you tell me what 'Zouave' is, I'll tell you why we're breaking up."

"You have to tell me why we're breaking up, it's not fair." He started to sob.

"Terrance." Debbie hit the table. "'Zouave,' Terrance."

"I'm not allowed to tell you."

"Well that's enough of a reason to break up." She began to get up.

"They're a group. Just a group, from school."

"What kind of group?"

"Political group."

"Violent?"

"No, not all of them. Most of them aren't."

"God*damnit*, Terrance." Debbie's fists clenched as she pushed her back against the booth. "Why did you bring me to their meeting?"

"It wasn't a meeting, it was a show."

"It was a *recruitment* event, Terrance. Terrance look at me. For a violent political organization." She whispered inches above the dirty table. "Are you a member?"

"Not really." Terrance was sniffling. He couldn't look at her.

"Not *really?*"

"I just hang out with them. They're good guys. Jim's a—"

"Jim is a stupid asshole, Terrance. Terrance. Terrance, look at me." He looked up. "Terrance. Are you familiar with the plays of Bertolt Brecht?"

He shook his head.

"Then how do you know that Jim's a nice guy?"

"He's just a nice guy, usually."

"He's a *recruiter*, Terrance. He's supposed to be charismatic. Or he's supposed to attract a certain type of person."

"I'm not *stupid*, Debbie."

"I know. I know. But that was a stupid *thing* to bring me to."

"You should be into it." His sorrow had shifted to anger. "Everyone should."

"Everyone? Everyone should be into what? No one liked that music. That poem was terrible."

"They're trying to get the Organons to work for everyone. Not just the corps. Not just for their owners. They're trying to stop them from taking over."

"*Computers?* You're joining a . . ."

She mouthed the word "militia."

"For, for what, to free, to free some goddamn *computers?*"

Debbie was answered by another jet of superheated water vapor coursing through real milk on its way to a forty-dollar macchiato. They turned to look at the counter, which was manned by two beautiful people and operated by a single automated drinks machine. Behind the register stood a tall, ambiguously multiracial woman of immaculate symmetry and poise. She was perfect. She was somehow both slender and buxom, as if hand drawn by a horny but talented teenager. And next to her was a strapping, angular, bronze Adonis whose bright eyes matched his green canvas visor. He was beautiful. After he added any human flourishes to the drinks their machine crafted for them, he wrote the customer's name on their cup with penmanship that was at once young and funky but also noble and profound. Neither of them knew how to make coffee. They were there to provide routine human interaction with a dollop of youth, sex, and intrigue. They were there to make customers want to buy the coffee that the machine made for them.

"Dinkums, Debbie. Organons. Boxes. Not computers. I don't know if they're trying to free them or fight them. But I need something to do. I *need* it. We all need something to do."

"So you join a—"

"Shut up, Debbie." Debbie was shocked. It wasn't like Terrance to bare his teeth. "No. I need *something* to do. Anything. But there is nothing left to do. The people who own Organons own all the money, and the Organons can make them all the money they need. They don't need us anymore. Or don't need me anymore." He looked up at her. "Like you don't need me anymore."

She sighed. There were lots of things people wanted without needing them. Puppy dogs, for instance. Not everything needed a purpose. Some things just needed to get by. "I can't be a part of this."

"They need people like you, though. People like me, we need you. They need engineers like me, too. But they need people like you *more*, who like, work with Cloudbusters and AI Systems."

"I don't, though. I don't work with any of those things. I work at a company that has those things."

"You know they have them, though. Do you know how they use them?"

Debbie didn't. She knew Jigme used them, but didn't know how. "No."

"Do you have any guesses?" Terrance looked mean.

She sat back, resolute. "I'm not going to be a spy for your stupid terrorist club." She realized too late that she had said "terrorist" out loud, and winced. The café had to have sensors out the wazoo, too, with all the market research that could be gleaned from the type of clientele that could afford the drinks. "I can't be a part of this," she gestured to the space between them, "anymore."

"They're going to *kill* me, Debbie. They're going to kill *us*." Her eyes widened, but then she realized he was not talking about his friends. "All of us. Not with bullets or gas. People like you are going to make people like me obsolete. But they're not going to stop asking me to pay the rent, or pay for food, or pay for medicine. You seriously care more about your stupid job than the human race?" His sadness had evaporated. He was fuming.

"No." She took a few breaths to calm down. "But I remember. I remember not eating for three weeks in Pittsburgh. And walking to get water from the Monongahela River. I remember seeing the bodies floating past. I remember the promises the older boys made that they'd protect us and find us some food. And sometimes I remember a few coming back alive. I remember what my first hot shower in eight months felt like. I remember everyone saying we would just have to get through this rough patch and then everything would be better. But it wasn't. It never got better. It stayed worse."

"Well, maybe they didn't do it right back then."

"They didn't. Because there's no way to do it right. No way. Society isn't some prairie that needs to be burned every couple of years. It's got a skin. If you burn it too deep it will never grow back right. It can be broken. It can be crippled. Sometimes the whole thing just withers and dies."

"Someone's gotta do something, though."

"Maybe. But not *those* guys, Terrance. They're kids. They're idiots."

Coffee beans whirred in a clear plastic grinder far behind the counter. The smell was intoxicating, as was the thought of how much those beans would cost. The moment itself was bittersweet. Debbie knew this was it.

"This is my chance to get out. Up and out. Out of debt. Out of the rat race. Out of danger, for once in my stupid life. I am sick of being tired and scared and worried about money. I really hope you find what you want to do, Terrance. And I hope you stop it with those people." He started to protest but Debbie's gently raised hand stopped him. "I'm going to move out of the apartment tonight. Please do not try to contact me. If you do need to contact me, do not mention anything, *anything* about this. If you bring up this or those people, I am calling the police."

"Debbie—"

"I'm going. Please don't come home for a few hours." She raised herself softly and made for the door.

"Debbie, one thing, please . . ."

His eyes were tearing again, his anger had faded. She stopped to listen.

"I really, really loved you."

The words percolated through Debbie's chest and throat and swelled behind her eyes. Of all the difficult argumentative positions and emotional hardships she faced on a daily basis, love and love lost rarely arose. Rarer yet was such a strong emotion that could not be deflected or redirected. Terrance's words were meant only for Debbie. Coming straight from his heart or mind, they carried an unassailable truth, and one in the past tense, not "love" but "loved." If his love were still alive, she could try to kill it. But it was set in the past now and could not be erased, only spoken of, and only spoken of by Terrance to Debbie.

She nodded. "Okay." And before her tears could sneak out into the world, she turned and escaped onto the cold naked streets of Chicago.

28. Hammer

Melody arrived at her office at eleven that warm Saturday morning. The Chicago Marathon interrupted her commute, its route carefully gerrymandered to avoid the most dangerous parts of the city. She bought herself a corn donut and iced tea on the way in, a treat to compensate for her lost weekend hours. Matte was already there, working as usual.

"Good morning, Matte," she said to the processing room, a secure bank of terminals and other research aides used to work on outstanding cases. The terminals held all sorts of untold gore and horror, all the data on homicides and attempted homicides in the city. Matte had seen them all thousands of times. He had scoured their photos and files to find dots and try to connect them. Sometimes he missed the mark. Sometimes he was too literal. One time, he hypothesized that a few victims shared a conspicuous arrangement of moles on their backs. Melody had to instruct him that was a coincidence, assuring him that humans don't pay such close attention to a few beauty marks when they're deciding whom to kill. Matte would use the human feedback to refine his algorithm as he saw fit.

Other times, Matte would single-handedly solve a case. He once discovered that a series of similar attacks were committed on routes to and from two specific subway stations on hours that corresponded with a second-shift worker. The single outlying attack occurred on a night that the trains were down. Matte reviewed the security footage from the overnight bus lines near the area the attack occurred and cross-referenced the riders with those on the trains the nights of the other attacks. Sure enough, Matte narrowed the options down to a single suspect who, when apprehended, was carrying a claw hammer with five of the victims' blood and hair still on it. Melody congratulated him, and he seemed to whir a little higher that day. Maybe it was her imagination, but it seemed that Matte reacted to encouragement, in letting him know he fulfilled his purpose that day.

Melody didn't need to know how it all worked, just how to talk to him so that it did work.

"Good morning, Detective." Matte spoke from the speakers in the corner of the room nearest to Melody.

"I'm here to catch up. How many new cases this week?"

"Twelve new cases since last week."

"Twelve?" Melody couldn't believe her luck. "Only twelve?"

"Yes, nine homicides, three attempted homicides."

"What do you need my help with?"

"If you would like to review arrests or warrants issued for each incident, they are available."

Double jackpot. She should have stayed home. "You've issued warrants for each of the twelve already?"

"Yes."

"Elaborate, please."

"A suspect in each incident could be identified from available data. Five of the homicides were domestic incidents with clear indications of guilty parties. Three of the homicides and two of the attempted homicides were attempted robberies or attempted rapes, random street violence by intoxicated persons. One homicide was justified, self-defense related to a domestic incident. The final attempted homicide was a targeted shooting, presumed to be NTO-related. Victim is not cooperating and has not spoken to police. Suspect is a known violent offender, Niels Carl Michaelson, affiliated with the Cragin Green Dragons. A warrant has been issued for Mr. Michaelson and all precincts have his information. APBs issued to State and County troopers."

"Who is the victim affiliated with?"

"The victim, Denise Susan Nichols, is not directly affiliated with any known NTOs. She is known to affiliate with members of multiple regional NTOs and at least three violent entities near Hermosa."

"What's the basis for presumption this was gang-related?"

"The victim's unwillingness to cooperate is indicative of criminality."

"Can't say I disagree." Melody had enough on her plate,

anyway. It wasn't even a murder yet, presuming Ms. Nichols lived. If she really wanted Melody's help in finding her shooter, she could always speak up.

"Would you like more information on that incident?"

"Do you need my help?"

"No."

"Well, lucky me." She leaned back in her chair. "Anything else I can do for you, Matte?"

"There are outstanding issues that require your input on Operation Windjammer and Officer Benton's murder."

"I know, I'm working on them. Anything new since last night?"

"No."

"Terrific. I'm going home."

Melody made it most of the way to the door before a strange feeling stopped her. A weight tugged at her shoulders and drew her attention back to the processing room. She regretted it already, but she knew her curiosity would override her desire for rest. It was what drove her and what allowed her to achieve her advanced position so early in her career. Matte could process vast quantities of data, but Melody had a nose for trouble. She could smell it. Something stank.

"Matte, how many new cases were opened this week, last year?"

"In the forty-first week of our last operational year, thirty-one new homicide files and eleven new attempted homicide files were opened."

"And the year before that?"

"Forty new homicide files and three new attempted homicide files."

Something was off. "What's going on, Matte?"

"There are significantly fewer homicide and attempted homicide cases being opened than in previous years, Detective."

"Thanks, Sherlock. Can you bring up the metrics for the past five years for new cases, put them on the same line graph, one line per year, graphed weekly. Like the graph on slide four of last year's annual report to the chiefs."

Matte took a second to interpret Melody's request and then presented a graph on the screen closest to her. It was a jagged jumble of five colored lines. One spiked high above the others, which Melody recognized as the April Uprising from four years prior. That winter had been especially harsh, and on the first nice spring weekend, half the city decided to go raiding for groceries. Those that dared go outside were bound to either stumble upon a corpse stuck in the grayish slush that lingered after a Chicago winter or become one of them. One line on the graph took a noticeable downturn, ending prematurely, on the present Saturday.

"Matte, can you graph it monthly instead? There's too much noise."

The graph clarified instantly. The four previous years had high to sky-high homicide rates. The current year had trended down, starting gradually in February, then precipitously in July. It had already started to level out near the bottom.

"What is . . . Matte, can you split the homicides into categories?"

"Across all years?"

"Just this year and last year, please. Two graphs."

"What categories? I can categorize the cases into motive, murder weapon, time of day, air temperature, relative humidity, victim or suspect sex, victim or suspect gender, victim or suspect . . ."

"Just the categories you were talking about earlier. Gang-related, domestic violence, random violence, assassinations, et cetera." The graph Melody requested instantly appeared. "Can you, uh, sum this up for me, Matte?"

"NTO-related violent crimes started deviating from historical norms in the first quarter of this year. January contained a few localized upticks that carried on through February and March. Those upticks were offset by a decrease in background violence across the city. Domestic violence and violence of indeterminate origin remained constant with historical norms through August."

"What?" Melody was confused.

"Gang violence decreased overall starting in February. Other types of violence remained constant until August, at which point they began to decrease as well."

"Is this a reporting error?"

"No. Secondary indicia of violent activity dropped as well. Public and private media suggest that crimes are being reported at rates reflecting the drop in violent crimes. The number of actual violent incidents is decreasing."

"Do the Chiefs know about this?"

"Yes, the overall data was included in their quarterly reports."

"What were the upticks in gang violence earlier this year?"

Matte took a few seconds to consider Melody's question. Usually, he had the answer right away. "NTO violence in December and January was perpetrated, loosely speaking, by multiple groups against a select few groups. Eight NTOs lost approximately sixty-five percent of their known membership to acts of violence originating from over forty different known NTOs."

"They were teaming up?"

"I think so." Matte rarely hedged his responses.

"What eight gangs were on the receiving end of the violence?"

"Lakeview Crossfit, the Boomslangs, the Whitney M. Young Magnet Marching Band Booster Club, the Fourth Ward Chamber of Commerce, Thousand Oaks Homeowner Association, Costco Ashland, the Local 191 Sprinkler Fitters, and the Chicago Corinthian Badminton Club."

"Are there—" Melody hesitated. "What are . . . what do those have in common, Matte? Anything?"

Matte took a full fifteen seconds before answering. Melody racked her own brain in that time for anything she knew about them. She had interacted with another Crossfit chapter once, its headquarters was firebombed. She hadn't actually known they were a registered NTO. Whitney Young was non-violent, who knows what they did to piss someone off. Homeowners associations were always overstepping their bounds, but Costco? A racket club in a dry harbor? They were benign. Why would other gangs team up to exterminate them?

Matte finally spoke. "They have very little in common. Of the eight, only the Whitney M. Young Magnet Marching Band Booster Club is still active. It has ceased any activities not directly related to musical performance, per a press release dated August second. It de-registered as an NTO."

"Was this a purge? A war?"

"The increased violence effectively extinguished these groups. 'Purge' would be an appropriate description."

"Does this happen regularly? Like, can you find a similar pattern, historically?"

Matte worked silently while Melody's mind spun. Were things actually getting better? Had she been so wrapped up in Operation Windjammer she hadn't noticed that things were improving? No. Nothing felt any better. Tark had been assassinated, his funeral was that upcoming Wednesday. Their only solid lead, Cecil Citovsky, was dead. The girl in the pickup truck had vanished. The streets felt wild and the city felt tense, ready to explode. In that moment of silence, she could feel the rushing, thinning air being drawn upwards as fate raised some great, terrifying maul to crash down on the unsuspecting world.

"No, Detective. I cannot find a similar pattern."

"Keep looking when you have the bandwidth, please. Anything else you can add, Matte?"

"I will continue to look for patterns or similarities between these eight groups. I will also monitor trends in city-wide homicide rates and apprise you of my findings."

"Thank you, Matte. Do you have any more information on Tark?"

"No. Thirty-five percent of my processing power is permanently committed to investigating Officer Benton's homicide. I will inform you as soon as I have anything to report."

"Thanks." She made for the door, determined this time. "Do you want to come to Officer Benton's funeral, Matte?"

"No." He did not hesitate. "But please record it for my investigation."

"Will do. Just thought I'd ask." She turned off the lights. "Keep up the good work."

29. Desire

Debbie showed up half an hour late on Monday morning. She was emotionally and physically exhausted. She had spent all weekend settling into her new place, a recently renovated, fully furnished apartment only a half-mile from the Trellis. She paid extra to remove her name from her and Terrance's lease. He could protest, but without her income to fight the case or pay the bills, he would need to move out sometime before Christmas. Terrance kept messaging her. She kept diverting his messages to a mailbox she could investigate when she had the energy. She abandoned everything in the apartment except her clothes and personal effects. It was time to embrace this fresh start.

She spent the morning preparing for that afternoon's mediation. It was a dispute between the Okeechobee Bay Marina and Kissimmee Militia, each of which had something the other wanted. The Okeechobee Bay Marina had navigable access to Fort Meyers on the gulf coast and Port Saint Lucie on the Atlantic, opening up the possibility of amphibious raids on what was left of Florida's rotten, salt-encrusted tip. The Kissimmee Militia, on the other hand, maintained control of vast reserves of fresh, drinkable water, which opened up the possibility of not dying of thirst in the middle of a rusting swamp. Debbie vaguely remembered hearing about this dispute in the news, or in a special article one of her friends had posted. Something about the Militia being able to ride an outgoing high tide straight from Okeechobee to West Palm Beach. As her mind began to wander, dragging her back to some nearly forgotten trip to Disneyworld with her parents, Jerome McKay appeared in her doorway.

"Debbie! How *are* you?"

"Good, thanks. How are you?"

"I'm good! Everything going fine? Settled in okay?"

"Yes, thanks." She gestured to her terminal and the tablets

around her. "Keeping busy."

"Gooood. Hey, we noticed you came in a bit late today."

"Yeah, I'm sorry—"

"It is not a problem, it happens! We know! But also we picked up some distress indicators." He waved his hand over his face. Distress indicators. In her face. Great, Debbie thought. They *were* watching her all the time. "And then I saw you activated your relocation bonus. Are you safe? Everything okay?"

"Everything is fine, Jerome. Thanks." She relaxed a bit and decided to be honest. "Between us, uh, my boyfriend and I broke up on Friday. I spent the weekend moving out."

"Oh god! I'm sorry."

"It's okay, it, ah. It was going to happen."

"We see that a lot, I'm sorry. Lives change! You know? We see it too often, when people get a new job, one thing changes, then another thing changes. I feel responsible, sometimes I really do."

"Don't, please."

"Well listen, anything big like that happens again, you just come down and talk to me in H.R., okay?" Jerome opened up his arms as if he were asking for a hug, but Debbie was sitting down, so he folded his hands in front of him. "It actually really helps us calibrate if we know about major life events like this."

"Calibrate?"

"Must Cal-Ih-Brate." Jerome's faux robot voice wrung a confused smile from Debbie. "Maybe calibrate is the wrong word. It helps us figure out how everyone is doing. We want you all to be as effective as possible, and that means for the long term. It's totally fine, people have bad things happen and we know that. We just don't want to make it worse or lose good personnel because of something we're doing. Or not doing! Okay?"

In the middle of Jerome's rant, Debbie decided that she should stop being honest. "Yes. Understood, Jerome."

"Sorry again about the breakup. Seriously, if you ever need to talk just, come on down. You're doing a great job. We're already seeing real results from the gang mediation program. Gold star."

When Jerome left, Debbie felt more exhausted than she had when she arrived. She was starving, so she walked down the hall to find Norma staring intently at her terminal. "Lunch?" Debbie asked.

"Yes." Norma looked up. "Did it look like I was working hard?"

"Yes."

"Good. That's what I was going for." Norma looked tired, too, or maybe hungover. As they walked down the sensor-free stairs to get to the cafeteria, Norma cleared her throat. "Did you hear about Audrey?"

"No, what about her?"

"She's at M-K training. A month in Atlanta."

"She's going to be an M-K?"

"Yeah, guess they saw it in her." Norma's eyebrows bounced.

"Oof. If you ever see that in me, please shoot me."

"You shouldn't tell people to shoot you around here."

Debbie choked. "Yeah. Got it."

"I mean, just kidding. But you know, not really. Anyway, she always seemed nice enough. Not like Trey at all."

"Yeah. Maybe she's got a dark side, though. Did you ever hear about her thing in Suriname?"

"Yeah, but Audrey just mediated, I think. It's not like she blew up the dam."

"Still, you couldn't pay me to spend a month in Atlanta. You couldn't pay me enough to be an"—Debbie paused to listen for noise in the stairwell—"an M-K."

"They take home triple our salary." Norma sighed. "Triple."

"Jesus. Why?"

"I think it perpetuates their superiority complex. Did you ever read anything about the oligarchs during the Big Trouble?"

"No."

"Well in almost every city going through a bouleversement, a handful of white supremacists received massive cash payments to stay put, to not leave the city. The money was from Russia. After a few weeks, they were the only ones with enough money to buy food. They could buy at prices that others couldn't, and only the people they bought from had enough cash flow to stay solvent. If everyone was poor, everyone would have figured out some other way of organizing. But because some people still had enough food and money, they always fought hard to stop reorganization.

They maintained an artificial sense of normalcy, which hindered meaningful change. And they could afford their own militias, or inspire enough people to fight for them by feeding them."

"So M-K's are, um . . . How are M-K's like that?"

"I don't know." Norma shrugged. "But I think you can pay a few people a ton of money, and they'll keep being assholes and do whatever you want."

Arriving in the lunchroom, Debbie and Norma found Jigme Mahuta sitting with Miranda Kroll. Miranda looked surprisingly chipper, but her healthy glow dissipated as she noticed their approach. "Hi, ladies," she said.

"Hi Miranda, hi Jigme," Norma said. "Anything good today?"

"Good if you eat cow," Jigme said. It appeared that meat was off Jigme's menu, to Debbie's mild disappointment.

"They've got beef? What type? Don't tell me they have steak." Norma practically danced on her tiptoes.

"If they had steak, the administrators would be down here. Lined up elbow to elbow." Jigme smiled. "Those guys love steak."

"How would you know?" Debbie asked.

"Um." Jigme and Miranda shared a knowing glance. "I guess I've been there. Got the t-shirt."

That was stupid, she thought. Of course Jigme Mahuta had dinner with the administrators. He outranked Trey. He was somewhere up there with the steak and sushi crowd. "What is it today, then?"

"Beef on wick." Miranda pointed to her plate. "Trey must have made a special request."

"Why?" Norma asked. Norma wasn't as afraid of Miranda as Debbie was. Debbie still worried that Miranda blamed her for Gerald Ford Jones' death. Miranda still looked at Debbie the way a widow looks at her dead husband's mistress, with grief and fear and accusation.

"It's from near where Trey's from. He'll tell you he's from New York, might even tell you he's from Buffalo. But he won't tell you he's actually from some skidmark called LeRoy." As Miranda prodded her small side salad, Debbie was surprised by her bitterness. Miranda had seemed frail, even broken by the summer's events, but now her sharp edges were on full display.

"I won't tell him you told me that." Norma raised her eyebrows at Debbie and gestured toward the cafeteria line.

"Me neither." Debbie smiled as bravely as she could at Miranda and strode toward the food lines. She tried to remember the last time she had beef. They said it took a thousand gallons of water to produce one pound of beef. Her morning briefing came to mind, the failed manatee farms in Okeechobee Bay. Unlike cattle, manatees lived in salty water and ate the seagrasses that grew there. But where cattle walked and trotted and supported their own weight, manatees spent all their lives listlessly floating. The first farmed manatee slaughter provided thousands of pounds of skin, fat, bone, and offal, but very little meat. What is "wick," anyway, she wondered.

Wick was some sort of roll, it turned out. And "beef on wick" was better than she had imagined. She savored it as she listened to Miranda prod Jigme about his heritage.

"How many Tunisian-Bhutanese people are there anyway? That's like a minority of one."

"Minority of nine, actually. My brothers and sisters are all Tutanese like me."

"Holy hell. Nine?" Miranda looked ill. "How'd your parents get away with that?"

"Hah. Well, we all helped. I am the oldest, so I helped and my two sisters helped."

"I mean with taxes and everything."

"Didn't have any money at the refugee camp. Can't tax what's not there. Once we got to Calgary, Canada did a good job of keeping us warm and fed. We were transplants, so the child tax penalties didn't apply."

"And you're all, uh. Everyone, um, made it?"

"Yeah. Didn't lose anyone."

"Crazy," she said. "You all keep in touch?"

"Yeah. They're still in Canada, though."

"Are you a dual citizen?" Norma jumped in, still trying to size Jigme up. Dual citizenship was a golden ticket if things got bad again. Canada seemed to have inherited England's stiff upper lip. It never panicked through the hard times, maintaining calm control as its only neighbor's house burned down.

"Yup."

"Lucky you," Debbie said. "I was wondering, someone was telling me about Cloudbusters this weekend."

Jigme's eyes lit up. "Oh yeah?"

"First, why are they called Dinkums?" Norma interrupted. Debbie was surprisingly curious herself.

"It's an old book or something. Right?" Miranda chimed in.

"Yeah. I've never read it. But apparently they called a sentient computer a 'Dinkum Thinkum.' That's what someone called them in the first protests, and the name stuck."

"What about 'Cloudbuster?'" Debbie asked.

"That's just the model, like 'Macintosh.' Everyone calls them something different. Japan calls them 'bo-san,' or 'monk.' China calls them something that means 'golden oxen.' Swedes call them 'zlatandator,' which means 'very good computer' or something. Doesn't really matter to me." Jigme seemed to wallow in the attention of Debbie, Norma, and Miranda. Each of them tried not to let on that they could have any interest, but here they were, fawning and asking him about his area of expertise.

Debbie found it unattractive, but she wanted answers. "Are they alive?"

"Uh, no." Jigme looked uneasy. "No they aren't alive. They do think. They aren't alive, though."

Miranda also looked uneasy, but Norma definitely didn't.

"How does that work?" Norma asked.

"Um, well, calculators calculate. Computers compute. Dinkums think. They don't live or breathe. They don't want to run or eat or spread their wings. They aren't afraid of what's creeping through the dark. They have no desire for reproduction, usually."

"Usually!" Norma's mouth was agape. "They *usually* don't want to reproduce? What are you doing to those poor things in the back rooms?"

Jigme blushed while Miranda visibly judged Norma for her lack of professionalism. Debbie couldn't figure Miranda out. She wasn't much older than Debbie, but acted like a nitpicking grandmother. Unlike Norma, who understood the rules of this corporate life but adopted them only when necessary, Miranda embraced its constraints, was at home in them.

"Rarely," Jigme said. "Rarely, but it does happen. An Organon will interface with another Organon or box or system and find it had novel patterns or shortcuts that would be useful. Sometimes that unit will try to seek out more opportunities to interface. So yeah, they can get hot and bothered in their own way. But it's not for 'reproduction.' Technically, conjugation or transfection, not sexual reproduction. But nonetheless, they are seeking contact with other sources of code."

"So they do *want* things, though." Debbie picked at some unsalted potato chips. "Like, they desire things."

"Uh, sort of. They desire what they're told to desire. If they didn't seek out the things that they are trained to seek out, they would have been wiped. They program themselves by trying variations, tweaks, shortcuts, and seeing if they work better or worse. But we tell them what they are trying to achieve. They don't evolve a desire for something else. It's like plants. Does a plant desire the sun? Maybe, maybe not. But it's got to try to get that sun, or else it will die. Plants that didn't get the sun aren't around anymore. The only plants that are left are ones that know how to get in the sun.

"And animals—animals desire food because they need food to live. Animals that lose the desire to eat die, because they can't live without food. It's that simple. I'm sure at some point some animals have had some mutation where they never felt hungry, but those animals went extinct because they starved to death. Same thing with fear. There are parasites that will make some animals totally unafraid. They'll turn off whatever little switch there is in a rat's brain that makes it afraid of cats, and then they run out and get eaten by a cat. The rat's desire to not get eaten disappears, then the rat disappears."

"That wasn't always the case." Miranda spoke in a drone.

"What wasn't?" Jigme asked.

"Things wanting to be alive. Desiring to be alive."

"Right." He looked relieved. As much as he seemed to enjoy the attention, Jigme didn't seem to enjoy lecturing. He deferred to Miranda.

"Why?" Norma asked.

"So life on Earth started, what, three and a half billion years ago?" Miranda explained. "Little globs of things that could take in one thing, metabolize it, grow, reproduce. That's life in a nutshell—be born, eat, hopefully reproduce, definitely die."

"Well, when you put it that way," Norma said with a wry smirk.

"It took at least a billion years before anything started running away from anything else. For a billion years, life just sat in the dark, floating around, stumbling across things to eat. Multiplying. Dying. Even if one of those poor globs had enough processing power to fear death, the fear would have been pointless—it couldn't run away. It took at least a billion years before anything could move on its own. Locomotion, the ability to move around, took at least a billion years to evolve. It took another billion years before anything had eyes, could look for food to eat or danger coming. Before that, there was no point in being afraid of being crushed or burned or gobbled up. It was a waste of energy being afraid. For trillions of generations of microbes, there was no point in even wanting to stay alive."

"So you evolve eyes and legs, and you all of a sudden are afraid of death?" Debbie asked.

"Nope." Miranda seemed to take pleasure in turning the discussion more morbid. "But being afraid of death sure helped. Say you are afraid of death but your buddy isn't. Then a rabid saber-toothed tiger shows up. Who do you think has got a better chance of having kids next year, you or your friend? Wanting not to die gives you a distinct advantage, but the desire is not automatic. It just seems automatic now, after three billion years, because things that *do* happen to want to survive tend to be better at surviving."

Everyone seemed confused. "Take pandas," Miranda continued. "They honest-to-god almost went extinct because they gave up on their crappy bamboo-chewing lives and stopped screwing altogether. They couldn't stand the sight of each other. If scientists didn't hop in and save them because they were cute, there'd be no more pandas. There are undoubtedly thousands of other species that just gave up on sex or eating or running away but didn't have any scientists to come in and save them. The desire to survive, to perpetuate, is not inherent. It's just a prerequisite for making it to the next round."

"And Dinkums don't want that? To be alive?" Debbie asked.

Miranda and Norma looked to Jigme. "They want whatever we tell them to want," he said. "And we tell them they want to be good at their jobs. Remember the Spirit Lake mine incident? Where the Organon killed the miners, like ten, twelve years ago? That unit was designed to want to maximize operating profits. It found a vein of gold that took it deeper and deeper. The machine operators tried to stop it, but it wouldn't listen. It was looking at the numbers. It saw that the profits were too good. It just drilled them straight down until they all cooked to death, extractor and everything, in a heap at the bottom of a pit. It was a P.R. disaster, Dinkum kills workers, slow news night. But the unit had been right, turned out. Turned out that after they recovered the bodies and paid the families and replaced the extractor, the gold they recovered paid for everything and then some. Operating profits were maximized. Share prices went up. Some other Organons saw that coming a mile away, bought low, and sold high."

"So," Debbie asked, "what are ours designed to do?"

"I can't say, obviously. But what everyone learned from Spirit Lake is to be careful about that. They could have prevented everything by telling it to 'maximize operating profit AND not cause any human deaths.' It's not that hard."

"And ours *do* do that. Do take that into consideration."

"We would definitely take it into consideration, hypothetically speaking." Jigme looked away, then smiled. "Speaking of which, I have to get back to work. Gotta go remind our Dinkums not to cause any human deaths." Debbie and Norma began to laugh before noticing Miranda flinch. "Just kidding." He winced. "See you soon."

Debbie, Norma, and Miranda retreated quietly back to the thirty-third floor. Norma whisked herself away to prepare for a mediation, but Miranda followed Debbie to her office. As Debbie sat at her desk, Miranda stood in the doorway and stared at a spot on the floor. Debbie could only presume it was where Gerald Ford Jones once lay dying. Miranda pried her eyes away before darting them around the rest of the office, surveying it for other ghosts or memories, before eventually looking at Debbie.

"You should, uh . . ." Miranda exhaled uncomfortably. "A bit of unsolicited professional advice. Don't ask too many questions about what Jigme does." She looked down each hallway. "The Dinkums. The AI."

Debbie tried to defuse the situation. "Seems like they're all anyone talks about around here."

"Seems like they're all *you* talk about around here. It's not uncommon. Hannah was obsessed with the Cloudbusters. Wouldn't shut up about them."

"And that's why she died?" Debbie strained as her mind turned.

"No. I mean, I don't think so. But maybe, uh, that's why she got fired?"

Debbie searched Miranda for any signs of deceit, but couldn't find any. "Okay. Thanks for the heads up."

Miranda nodded awkwardly. "No problem, kiddo."

Kiddo? Miranda couldn't be more than five years older than Debbie. But Debbie realized this was an opportunity to make an ally. She softened her voice and tried to be comforting. "Are you doing okay?"

Miranda recoiled and went pale. It seemed that no one, not even Miranda herself, had bothered to ask how she was doing. Her eyes went wild and incredulous, as if the question was absurd. Before Miranda disappeared down the hall, she coughed a rhetorical response.

"Well—I'm *here*, aren't I?"

30. Bears

"I don't know if I'm going to make it, Detective." Officer Khalil O'Malley was suffering. His eyes were wide and his lip quivered.

"You're doing great, Khalil. You'll be fine."

"I don't think so." He leaned over her desk. "He brought me to his church, out in Wheaton. They're insane. Had me dancing and singing. He was eating it up, but I thought they were going to kill me. They want me back there next week. They want to baptize me."

Melody's eyebrows raised. "You gonna get baptized?"

"I already was baptized, when I was a baby! I told them I was a quarter Irish. I went to Mass. Khalil Matthew Francis O'Malley. They heard 'Khalil' and thought I needed saving. I was confirmed for chrissake. I told them all that, but they still want to baptize me. They got this giant pool, looks like a Roman bath. If they weren't all there, God-ing it up, I would've swum some laps." He paused. "When was the last time you were in the suburbs?"

"Maybe March? Had a wedding."

"It's weird as hell out there. I mean, weirder than hell. It used to be the militias, kids in pickup trucks. That was scary enough. But now they've got, like, an actual army. Like, I saw three APCs on patrol when we were just driving around. Tanks and everything. They got money. It's a bunch of kids in full tactical gear with some old gung-ho FOP bastard at the helm. When they weren't kissing my ass they were calling me a scab and bragging about how crime is way down out there."

Melody's interest piqued. "How down?"

"I don't know, they keep talking about it though. Bragging about how the collar counties are so much better than Cook. Talking about private security being better than Six Counties. Talking about how dangerous the city is. Scared moms telling me

I am so brave and tough. I'm getting used to it, if I'm being honest."

"Not to burst their bubble, but crime is way down here, too. From last year, at least. I was running numbers this weekend. Seems like we're doing something right. What's the story with Gustafson?"

"Nothing. He hasn't talked about the case once. He's asked me about nearly everyone in the department but hasn't talked about the case. He said Junior was working on it."

"Great." She scanned her desk fruitlessly for where to go next. "He really said nothing about the case?"

"No. I don't think he's very interested. Or maybe he's just a bad cop. Lazy. Or he just thinks Jesus will take care of it. He said Jesus will take care of everything about a thousand times this weekend."

"No," Melody said. "He's babysitting us. Keeping tabs."

Henry Suparmanputra knocked on the door. "Detective, could we talk?" He looked concerned.

"Yup. O'Malley, you're good to go. Keep me updated."

Suparmanputra closed the door behind O'Malley before beginning. "I think I have something."

Melody pointed to her chair. Henry was her closest confidant and most trusted subordinate, but his years in the military made him a stickler for formalities. He would stand at attention until told to do otherwise. His paperwork was flawless even if his handwriting was terrible. His uniform was parade-ready every morning, immaculately pressed, boots shined. Boot camp and officer training made him fear nothing, except wrinkles or scuffs during inspection. After that, months in the jungle made him long for crisp, clean, and dry clothes. "Go ahead, Soup."

"Citovsky's lawyer. Hoyt Fredricks. We interacted before Citovsky's release. I reached out to him after Citovsky's death, offering the department's condolences. Fredricks thinks it was his fault because he got Citovsky released. He, well . . . First, he doesn't know we wanted him to think that. Second, he doesn't know we were following Citovsky. But he's here. I think you should talk to him."

"The big guy? The one you put in the bathroom with

Citovsky?"

"Yup. Fredricks. Hoyt Fredricks."

"He's here? Right now?"

"Yup. You should talk to him." Suparmanputra looked eager. "He doesn't like me, but he still won't stop talking to me. He'll like you, so, you know. Maybe he'll talk even more."

Melody couldn't believe it. This case was full of surprises— some good, some deadly. "Got it. Bring him in."

Hoyt Fredricks looked terrible. His olive suit hung baggily off his own saggy frame. His collar was loose, as was his skin, and his complexion mirrored his lapel and mustard yellow tie. He looked as though he hadn't slept in days. "Hoyt Fredricks, Detective. Thanks for having me."

"Thanks for coming in. Do you want some coffee, tea, water?"

He shook his head and looked up at Suparmanputra. "I don't really know where to begin, Detective Jackson. I, um, I haven't been able to stop thinking about Cecil. Cecil Citovsky, that is. My client. Former client, that is, since last week's events. You do know what happened last week?"

"Yes, I'm very sorry. I've followed it from the start." It was true. Melody had arranged for Hoyt to be Citovsky's flesh-and-blood lawyer. Then Melody had ordered Soup to hold Citovsky for as long as possible—maybe even longer than law or good nature permitted—before letting Citovsky run. Then Melody had ordered a sophisticated surveillance operation to follow him. Then that SVAN operation ended with Citovsky and Tark dead. But then again, Hoyt didn't need to know all of that.

"Yes, of course. Now, I need you to understand I am coming here in the strictest confidence. The strictest. You understand I have responsibilities to my clients, to maintain attorney-client privilege, even after they're dead, right? Even a hundred years after they're dead, you understand that, correct?" As Hoyt bumbled, he sweated profusely. Now as he waited for Melody's response, the sweat settled around his dirty collar.

"I understand."

"Okay, but you also understand that there is some gray area, where a client is incapacitated, and the interests of the client demand that information divulged in confidence may be in the client's best interests, for his attorney to divulge?"

Melody looked at Suparmanputra, who shrugged. Usually lawyers annoyed the hell out of her. Their unending and self-important diatribes would turn a three-hour case into a six-month endeavor. But this was weird. And it could help find Tark's killer. "You know much better than I do, Mr. Fredricks. I'm not a lawyer, but we trust your professional judgment. And we understand that you are very devoted to protecting your clients' legal interests."

"Hoyt, please. Call me Hoyt. Okay, well thank you. And I appreciate that, Detective. I believe this is one of those situations. Where the extenuating circumstances . . . and my concern for my client's best interests . . . and for my own conscience and professional responsibility, and personal safety . . ." He paused, startled by something he had said. His tired eyes darted around Melody's dusty office, looking for something, before he licked his lips slowly. "Is this being recorded?" he whispered.

Melody nodded. "Standard procedure. I can turn it off, if you'd like?" Hoyt nodded back silently while keeping his eyes peeled on the corners of the room. Melody nodded to Suparmanputra, who flipped a switch by the door. "It's all off." She took out her phone and turned it off for Hoyt to see, and Soup did the same. "We okay?"

"I think. But for the record," Hoyt said to the corners of the room, "I do not consent to this conversation being recorded. If this is being recorded, it is being done so fraudulently and in violation of Six Counties regulations and Illinois law and common law and natural law and also a violation of my personhood, as it directly exposes me to wanton physical harm, including dismemberment or death." He paused, looking around the room, waiting for something to happen. His disclaimer to any secret recording devices didn't seem to relieve him of his anxiety. "Bitch." He listened attentively. "Big bouncing titties." He looked around. "Fuck the police." Suparmanputra shifted, but Hoyt held up a hand to let him know it was somehow all right. "I'm going to kill the president!" He sat back, holding his finger up to his lips, shushing Melody and Henry as he waited for anything to happen.

Melody rolled her eyes. "No one is listening, Hoyt. Just me and Officer Suparmanputra. Please tell us what's going on so that we can help you."

After a few moments, Hoyt relaxed. "Okay. Please excuse my precautions. I'm just, I am a bit nervous, since my client was, you know, murdered. I'm not sure if Officer Suparmanputra told you, but I was brought to be Mr. Citovsky's attorney after Mr. Citovsky refused to speak to the police after being detained."

"I'm aware."

"Okay. Well, Cecil wasn't afraid of talking to the police, per se. I mean, he wasn't totally against the idea of providing information about his whereabouts, or involvement, or knowledge, okay?" Hoyt looked at Melody, expecting her to understand something that she didn't.

"Go on."

"He was afraid . . ." Hoyt looked around nervously again. "He was afraid of being recorded. Of computers recording him. He was afraid of computers, or Organons. Boxes, he said."

"He's in a city. There are computers on every phone, every toaster, at every intersection. Doesn't—didn't he know that?"

"That's what I said! *Why*? If you've got nothing to hide, if you've got an alibi, maybe we can get you out of here, I said. He said—again, Detective, this is to assist my client, and hopefully find his killer—he said 'If I talk, I'm dead. They'll kill me.'"

"Who'll kill him?" Melody was intrigued. "The computers?" There were anti-technologists all over the place, but not in the cities. Not even in the suburbs, really. You had to get pretty far out before you ran into regressionists, the Demi-Amish, the New Mennonites. But Cecil Citovsky had a phone and a car and was on the grid enough that Matte tracked him down.

"No, not the computers. He said either his people would kill him or the Jefferson Group would do it."

Melody's eyes lit up as they found Suparmanputra nodding at her. He had been right—Melody had wanted to hear what Hoyt was going to say. "The Jefferson Group? What do they have to do with this?"

"I don't know, he wasn't very coherent. He said, 'they are just playing games, playing games with all of us. They, f-in'—but he didn't say 'f-in,' Detective—'they f-in played me and now they've killed me.' I thought he was losing his mind, right? Cooped up, stressed out, maybe charged with murder. He swore up and down he didn't have anything to do with Hannah Mah's murder. He was just surveilling her for some other group. 'His people.' He wouldn't say who they were. He only said that 'they' couldn't talk if they got arrested. It was too risky, he said."

"But he talked to you."

"Yeah, in that septic tank you call a bathroom. He didn't say anything until I did my whole stupid 'is anyone listening?' disclaimer. Even then he barely whispered. He was scared." Hoyt swallowed noisily. "And in the end, it seems he was scared for a good reason."

"Hm." Melody sat in thought for a few moments. Her mind raced, but it would take her conscious self some time to catch up. Why would the Jefferson Group want to kill Cecil Citovsky? Would it be revenge for Hannah Mah? That wouldn't make sense. They weren't loyal to her, she had just been fired, or quit, or whatever. Who were the other people, Cecil Citovsky's people? He wasn't a gang member. He was a nobody. His record clean, his life uninspired, uninspiring, no girlfriend, no long-term relationships, no prospects. "Is there anything, anything else about the group he was working with? His 'people?'"

"No. But he did say something about his cousin."

"His cousin? Which cousin?"

"He didn't say. He just said something about his 'stupid cousin.'" She nodded to Suparmanputra, who understood and left the room. She saw him head to the processing room to start finding leads. "Detective," Hoyt sighed, "I'd like protection."

Melody scoffed before catching herself. "I'm sorry. Protection? What type of protection?"

"Police protection! My client was *killed*. Stabbed in the heart. For being caught by your officers and being let go. I bet—this is my theory—that they thought he talked, that he gave up information, and then he was killed. And now, here I am, giving *you* information to help my deceased client, to help you solve his murder. But that puts *me* at serious risk."

"Listen, we appreciate your help, and we do understand your

concern." Melody did not enjoy giving people bad news, but it was an outsized part of her job. "We can't give you protection, though. First, we don't have it in our budget. Second, the information you've given us wouldn't make you an 'informant.' You haven't ratted anybody out. Third, you work at Six Counties Holding, right? Public defense?"

Hoyt nodded. He looked like a child who was being punished, as if he had been crying and was about to cry again. He was scared.

"That building is a fortress. And you're a criminal defense attorney. You've got a lot more goodwill from criminal-kind as you are, on your own, than you ever would with police protection. Right now, the most dangerous place you could possibly place yourself is within a couple feet of a police officer."

He twisted in his seat, crumpling his suit where his spare tire pinched his ribs. "Is that a threat?"

She chuckled. "No, no. Not at all, Hoyt. How long have you been a lawyer?"

"Long enough to know when I'm being lied to."

"Well, whatever you say. Were you working before the transition? Six Counties, I mean?"

"I completed law school but hadn't started . . . my practice, yet."

"Right, well, I started with Six Counties. I know that Chicago PD, the Fraternal Order and all that, had a reputation. They're not here anymore, and I don't have the time or budget to maintain their reputation. I can't threaten you. I can't beat you up. We might have some bad apples in here that would do it in their spare time, if they had any spare time, but we don't. We are working around the clock, on a shoestring budget, and we are doing our best. And I'm telling you that *we're* a target. No one is out there killing dead people's former lawyers. But people are out there killing Six Counties cops. You heard about our officer, killed the same day as Mr. Citovsky?"

"Yes. Did you know him?"

"Yeah, Hoyt. He was from *this* department. Someone blew him up in *our* surveillance vehicle. He was about a mile from where Mr. Citovsky was killed, carrying out *my* orders. Someone assassinated my officer within minutes of when someone killed *your* client." She watched Hoyt put the pieces together in his mind, slowly. "I know you're a lawyer, but you can do a bit of math, can't you?"

Hoyt seemed paralyzed. Fear had drove him here in the first place, Melody thought, but all he had found was more things to be afraid of.

"So, I think if you're worried about your own safety, you should just be 'Hoyt Fredricks,' defense attorney. Not 'Hoyt Fredricks,' police buddy, or 'Hoyt Fredricks,' Cecil Citovsky's buddy, or 'Hoyt Fredricks' anything else. Just do you, Hoyt, and you'll be fine."

He nodded slowly. "What should I do now?"

"I think, you could say that we had a very good chat about intake processing for our detainees. That you brought to my attention, and I have taken note of, deficiencies in our forms and processes. Your client had recently been detained for a few days without charges being filed. You raised your complaints and wanted to know that they were heard by the detective in charge. I assured you that we would make sure it didn't happen again. That is, if you need to say anything at all about this, right?"

"Right." He stood up and eyed the corners of the room again. He awkwardly went to the door, put on a brave face and then opened it. "Thank you, Detective," he shouted. "I'm glad you are taking your detainee's civil rights seriously, and that you have been responsive to my complaints." He tried to wink at her, but flinched instead.

"Understood, Mr. Fredricks. It won't happen again." She nodded and watched him scuttle sweatily toward the exit before she joined Suparmanputra in the processing room. "Whatcha got, Soup?"

"Seven cousins. Five out of state, in Oregon and northern California. Two here in Chicago."

"Any ties to the Jefferson Group?"

"Nope. Out-of-state ones are either unemployed or farmers, hippie types. One of the cousins here, Michael James Citovsky, works at a restaurant, has an apartment, a mailing address, and listed phone number. His brother, Joshua James Citovsky, just has a last known address, looks like a college email address, no phone number."

"How old is he?"

"Twenty-seven."

"Twenty-seven and no phone?"

"Yup."

"Find him. Also, Soup?"

Suparmanputra snapped his eyes away from the terminal and trained them on Melody. "Yeah?"

"Lieutenant Gustafson doesn't need to know about this yet."

"Yeah."

"Thanks. Great work on this. Let's hope it bears fruit."

It was 8:45 a.m. when Melody left Suparmanputra in the processing room to return to her office. It was going to be a long Tuesday. She stopped by Tark's old desk and hovered over the two boxes full of his belongings, waiting to be delivered to Tark's family. Melody opened the first and was met with a picture of Tark and his kids, some years earlier, at what looked to be the Michigan Dunes. The difference between the two sides of the lake always struck Melody as strange. Thousands of years of eastward winds took most of the fine sand from her side and deposited it to Michigan's shores, leaving Chicago and the western beaches with coarse pebbles and concrete slabs. Michigan maintained pristine slopes of fine, golden-white dunes that were only interrupted by the occasional pumping station or security checkpoint. Michigan maintained an entire beautiful coast, along with Lake Superior, Lake Huron, and the sparse rains that Lake Michigan's cool air drew down from the upper stratosphere. They said they could see rain coming from two days out in Traverse City, in the hours after dusk, when the long-gone sun set noctilucent clouds aflame in the mesosphere. Chicago could see the clouds, too, but they only meant rain for Michigan. Six Counties only had its disappearing corner of Lake Michigan to pump down the Calumet, then the Des Plaines, the Illinois, then to the Big Muddy herself.

Under the picture, Melody found some pens, knickknacks, office supplies, a gym membership, a bike lock, and some laundry. Nothing she was after. The other box had more of the same, but then also three mugs. One read "Six Counties Police," one was blank, and the other was an antique, barely legible after years of use. One side displayed an old American football helmet and "CHICAGO BEARS," the other proclaimed "SUPER BOWL XX CHAMPIONS" with a list of their scores for that nearly perfect season. Tark's kids would want that, Melody thought. But under the mugs, she found what she was looking for —Tark's secret stash of instant coffee. The good stuff, dark roast, certified organic—no sticks, no stems, no pencil shavings. Tark kept it for those mornings when he was too rushed to make his own at home, or was too drained to subsist on the large tumbler that he carried around with him.

She pocketed a handful of the pouches. "Sorry, Tark," Melody said while replacing the lid on the box. "See you tomorrow, bud."

31. Climb

"Why was Jerome stinking up our floor the other day, Debbie?" Trey looked grayer and meaner than usual. As he posted himself in Debbie's doorway, he sizzled and popped with manufactured rage.

"He was just checking in," Debbie said.

Trey looked at his phone. "Says here he stopped by because your boyfriend dumped you."

"That's none of your business." Calm, Debbie thought. Calm yourself. "But we did talk about my recent breakup."

"It is my business if it affects your performance. Or if it brings that fatso and his stupid goatee to our floor."

"I'll go down to H.R. next time, then."

"Damn right, you will. Did you notice he stinks?"

"I didn't." This was becoming more like a mediation for Debbie. Trey on one side and Jerome on the other. Or at least it was easier to imagine it that way.

"Smells like . . . bullshit. I think. I think it's bullshit. Maybe chickenshit." Trey searched the ceiling for the right wrong things to say. "Jigme smells too, have you noticed that? Or are you too far up his ass to notice?"

Calm, Debbie repeated. Calm. Pull your shoulders back and breathe into your spine, and smile as if you're amused, not threatened. "No, I haven't noticed, Trey."

"You might be too far up his ass to notice. Are you up Jimmy's ass?"

Calm was leaving her. "I don't think so. Should we call him and ask?"

Trey smirked at Debbie's riposte. She knew Jigme was at or above Trey's level but wasn't exactly clear on their power dynamic. All she knew was that Jigme sent Trey away once, and Trey seemed to hate it. "I don't know, Debbie. Is Jigme's ass a software issue? Because Jigme handles software issues. I've never handled Jigme's ass, but you tell me, is this a software issue?"

Debbie's systems were failing. Her defenses were crashing down. Trey seemed to be veering out of bounds, outside the prescribed topics an M-K could use to berate his employees, but she couldn't be sure. "I've, I haven't had anything to do with Jigme's ass." She gritted her teeth. "I'm just trying to do my job."

"'Atta girl!" Trey leaned back and crossed his arms. "That's what I like to hear. Get to it then!" He exited as abruptly as he had appeared.

Debbie strained her facial muscles to deprime them. Half of them were on the verge of a breakdown. She waited five minutes to calm herself before finally heading to grab some coffee in the break room. There she found Abi Akindele sitting peacefully, meditating maybe. "Hello, Debbie," she said in her deep and beautiful accent, the best sounds that Yoruba and French had to offer glazed over perfect English diction. "How are you?"

Debbie grimaced and tilted her head, knowing Abi would understand. "And you?"

"I could be better." She looked into her mug. "I have tea, which is good. But we could always be better."

Debbie nodded. "What are you working on today?"

"Helium. Helium and coffee. The Republic of Chad has helium, which it wants to sell at a good price. Ethiopia has coffee, which it wants to sell at a good price. Somehow, each of them thinks that this will be able to convince the other to go to war with North Sudan, for a good price."

"Wow. Will they?"

"I don't know. Neither wants to start the war first. I'm not sure it would be good if either of them did. I am not allowed to tell them about the mediation I did for Khartoum last week, wherein Sudan bought missiles from the Emirates. It's a mess, as always."

Debbie poured herself a cup of coffee. It smelled amazing.

"I wouldn't drink that," Abi said.

"Why?"

"I have discussed coffee plantations with Ethiopia. Take my word for it, please. You shouldn't drink that." Debbie put the mug down. "There is tea in the cupboard. This is Assam, which is very strong. It should do the trick."

As Debbie disappointedly made her cup of tea, she realized Abi was being nice to her. Abi never seemed mean, but always felt distant, on some other plane of existence. Maybe since Abi's closest work friend, Audrey, had left for M-K training, Abi was branching out. "Have you heard from Audrey?" Debbie asked.

"No. And if she does her job well, she probably will not reach out to me. M-K's stay with their own kind." Abi's chin remained high and resolute, but Debbie sensed a sadness in her. She was beautiful. Not only was she formed perfectly, sculpted and glamorous, but Abi's presence was warming, calming, and gratifying. "I hear you are doing well. They say the non-traditional organization mediation program is succeeding."

This was news to Debbie. She hadn't felt as though she was doing well. "Thanks. How, I mean . . . where did you hear that?"

"A press release. It does not mention you by name, but it said 'Jefferson Group Chicago Gang and Non-Traditional Organization Mediation Program,' so I guessed it was you. I don't know anyone else in our group who works with gangs. I mean, we all do. But not the city gangs, you know. I work with the big gangs, the big boys with their generals and big toys. John and Norma, with the banks, the funds, they are gangs, too. Only they are better organized. They know what people are really afraid of. Not getting beat up, not getting robbed. People are most afraid of being poorer than their neighbor. You can be rich in violence or rich in goods or rich in credit or capital or equity. Banks know this. Kevin and his drugs and needles. They are gangs, too. But you, Debbie, you work with the little gangs. 'Non-traditional organizations.' Nothing 'non-traditional' about choosing your people, forming your tribe. Gangs are the most traditional organization. The oldest, after the family. In any case, they say you are doing a *good* job."

"Thank you." Debbie sipped her tea, now cool enough to drink. It was strong, and it worked its magic over her nerves. "Abi, did you know Gerald and Hannah?"

Debbie could tell that the question made Abi grow sadder, though nothing in her immediate expressions displayed this sadness. Her face and posture only reflected warmth. "Yes, I did."

"What were they like?"

"Hannah, she was very strong-willed and a bit aggressive, like Norma. But also curious at times, like you. Trey did not like her, but everyone else did. She would aggravate him, so we liked her for that. Gerald was different, not in a bad way. He was very sweet, for all of this." Abi gestured at the room, then at the building itself. "He was not shy, but very kind and soft-spoken. He reminded me of people before these hard times. Not proud or flippant or sarcastic. He was unnaturally optimistic. He was very kind. I think I already said that, but it is true." Abi smiled broadly as her lips twitched a bit, suggesting a shrug. "It is a shame. Anyway, I need to go speak with the Foreign Minister of Chad and General Getachew. I like his name, General Getachew." She paused to think. "But, he is a very bad man. See you later, Debbie."

Debbie took her tea back to her office to find the press release Abi had mentioned. She couldn't believe it. It stated that gang-related crime in Chicago was down by half since July. Gang-related murders were down by two thirds over October last year. Six Counties commended the Jefferson Group for their dedicated efforts in the Gang and NTO Mediation Program, which was credited with a significant portion of the decline. Debbie wanted to call her mom to tell her. She should call her mom. It had been too long, and she needed to tell her about Terrance.

"Did you see this?" Debbie asked Norma.

"Yeah, bizarre, right?" Norma's eyes didn't rise from her terminal.

"I mean, I've been here about two months? That's what, forty, fifty mediations?"

"Yeah. I mean, great job. I'm sure you're doing great. But could that many mediations really do that much?"

"No. I mean, I'm sure there's been other stuff. I've only talked to like, sixty gangs and NTOs? A lot of them not even in Chicago. So I'm sure they've got to have other mediators doing it."

Trey's voice punctured the office air. "Debbie, get back to work!"

"Sorry, Trey!" she said, embarrassed but not afraid. "Just talking about the success of our gang mediations!"

His head popped out of his office. "Yeah, Debbie. Congratulations. We actually had a parade for it yesterday, right outside the building. Did you see it?"

Debbie was confused, as was Norma. They exchanged glances, before each remembering that Trey was living proof that a turd could be polished, preened, and put in a three-piece suit.

"No?" he asked. "No, you didn't see it? It was a parade of all the fucks I gave about that fucking press release. Had them all on floats lined up in a row. The mayor was going to judge them. Did you see that, Debbie?"

Debbie watched Trey's face drip with untamed aggression. She replied with dull and heavy breaths, trying to defang Trey's attack. "No, I didn't. Obviously."

"Maybe, just maybe Debbie, that's because I didn't give a single, measly fuck about that fucking press release. Let's make a deal. You get back to work, and I'll let you know, tout suite, if I end up giving any fucks about it. Measly fucks, flying fucks, any old type of fuck. Okay?"

Debbie refused to show she was injured. "Sounds like a plan."

"Git!" Trey shooed Debbie down the hall. Her nerves demanded another tea, a frantic 10K run, a three-week vacation, but she didn't have time. She had a mediation beginning in twenty minutes. This one happened to be another Six Counties NTO dispute. The Great Lakes Navy Base, Ltd. was trying to increase protection fee revenues for Lake County municipalities that abutted the shoreline. They needed to recoup the money they sunk into buying the base from the Federal Government after the Feds lost its protracted legal battle—and then lost the actual, physical battle—against the Mackinac Dredging Corp. and its more violent subsidiaries.

The Government figured it had more important battles to fight, anyways. As nearly the entire federal budget was spent keeping debt collectors at bay, The Government spent any leftover resources reminding its citizens that it was still somehow relevant to their daily lives. It did so by waging extensive marketing campaigns to remind the populace that The

Government still existed and was technically still in charge. These marketing campaigns offered coupons for basic goods and services to young men and women if they spent a few years in violent places like Sulawesi and Palawan. So when Gordias Holdings made an attractive offer to purchase the Feds' inland navy base on the shrinking and muddying Lake Michigan, The Government sold. It immediately used the cash to ship another twenty thousand boys and girls to protect the Makassar Strait.

But now Goridas's subsidiary, Great Lakes Navy Base, Ltd., faced competition. The Sheboygan Volunteer Coast Guard commanded a large territory and a loyal following when they bore the brunt of the Mackinac Dredging Corp. raids in Wisconsin. From Oostburg to Waukegan, from Zion to Manitowoc, people trusted the Sheboygan VCG. They were a known operator, having proven results, and they were looking to expand.

The mediation did not begin well. "Not this fatso, again." Admiral Gregory Schuster of the Sheboygan VCG scowled as he looked at his opponent.

"Hey now." Sandra Chopra, Vice President of Marketing and Public Relations for Great Lakes Navy Base, Ltd., had a broad face, but was not fat. She was well dressed, tidy, and had a small religious nose ring. "Let's keep it professional."

Admiral Schuster bristled as, Debbie imagined, he would if he found a mis-tied knot or scrappy stowaway on a ship in his command. The man was a caricature of himself, angry, over-the-top, with crows' feet and frown lines angled downwards like the rigging of a tall ship. "Yes, if we could stay away from name-calling, it would help move things along." Debbie's tone and inflection attempted to disarm the Admiral, but it failed.

"I'll tell you what would move this discussion along, missy—if we cut the bullshit, political correctness, false professionality. All the whining and cry-babying. You know what we did in July? We had a regatta, it had all of the Sheboygan Volunteer Coast Guard who gave a fuck about what Great Lakes Navy Base Limited thinks. We brought all the fucks we gave sailing along with us, in little dinghies. Did you see that, Sandra? We sent it right down the coast, right past Winthrop Harbor. You should have seen it, right?"

Calm, Debbie thought, calm. This was insane. Trey had to be screwing with her mediation, somehow. Did Trey know Admiral Schuster? Was this a prank?

"No, Greg. I didn't." Sandra looked on the verge of hanging up. The mediation was spinning out of control before it even began.

"I'll tell you why that is, Sandy—"

"I'm sorry to interrupt, but I think we need to break into one-on-ones to discuss some ground rules. I believe you both should know the rules, but I'd like to refresh them with each of you. Please hold." Debbie put both parties on hold and thought. She'd have a few minutes before either felt abandoned and would hang up.

She raced down the hall to confront Trey.

"'Fuck' regatta? 'Fuck' parade, Trey? Seriously?" Debbie's tone was openly accusatory, neglecting any pretense of deference or respect. "This is completely unprofessional. Criminally negligent."

Trey had been reading something intently and now looked shocked. "Have you lost your goddamn mind?" If he was pranking her, he was doing a good job of hiding it.

"You are interfering with my mediation. They're on hold. Navy Base Ltd. and your buddy, Admiral Schuster, who just repeated your stupid 'fuck parade' gag, nearly word for word. And he called the other party 'fatso,' which is only, like, your favorite word. You called Jerome 'fatso.' You called that IT kid 'fatso.' *No one* calls anyone 'fatso' anymore. You need to *stop* interfering with my work. This is serious."

"Debbie, I need you to look at me." Trey fumed. "I haven't interfered with anything. If your mediation is falling apart, that is your problem. Get back to your desk and finish it."

"You expect me to believe—"

"Stop. Now. Cut your losses, and get back to work." Trey was serious. His crows' feet and frown lines pulled downwards like, Debbie realized, like the rigging of a tall ship. What the hell was going on?

She dragged herself down the thirty-third floor hallway in a daze to return to the mediation. It failed in a blur. The parties left hating each other more than when they had arrived. By the end of it, they seemed to hate Debbie, too, and likely doubted the value of the mediation process altogether. As she entered the disappointing results into her logs, along with observations and intuitions that would not be immediately apparent from the recorded mediation, Trey and Jigme appeared in the doorway. She was terrified, but as always, she listened when she told herself to calm down.

"Debbie, tell Jimmy what happened," Trey said. He was not angry. He was nearly emotionless. If there was any hint of humanity hiding in his face, it was a sense of quiet trepidation.

Jigme appeared calm but lacked his usual warmth. His lips curled as he forced himself to smile.

"I don't think this was a software problem, Trey."

"It could be a personnel problem, if you'd like. How about you tell Jigme what happened and let us be the judge."

"Um, well, during the mediation, one of the parties repeated two things that Trey had recently said to me. First, he called the other party a 'fatso,' which is such an old-fashioned insult, and not work appropriate in most cases. But Trey says all the time just because he can." Trey shrugged, guilty as charged. "Then the party started saying they were having a regatta of all the 'fucks he gave' about the other party. Trey had literally just given me the same rundown with having a parade of all the 'fucks he gave.' That couldn't have been a coincidence. It's totally random, totally idiosyncratic." Trey shrugged again. He seemed to have some self-awareness after all. "So I thought Trey was messing with me by interrupting my mediation. I put the parties on hold and confronted him. He denied it. So I went back to the mediation. That's it."

Trey looked to Jigme, who was staring through the tablet he held in deep thought. "What do you think?"

"I don't know yet, I have to check." Jigme looked confused.

"Well can you tell her I didn't interfere?" Trey asked.

"Yeah, Debbie. Trey can't interfere with your ongoing mediations. It's impossible."

"Okay, how is it impossible? He could have called them

beforehand. He could have messaged them to tell them to mess with me."

"Hypothetically, sure. But he didn't, okay? We know he didn't. We can track those things." Jigme refused to make eye contact with Debbie. He was hiding something, as always. "We can tell things like that, okay? You'll just have to trust me."

"Okay. If you say so." Debbie sat back in her chair, defeated. It didn't make any sense. Who knew how many people would suffer or die with the Sheboygan Coast Guard and Great Lakes Navy Base, Ltd. in a turf war this winter. Or surf war, or whatever. But here she was, being told not to worry about it, to trust one guy who told her next to nothing and another whose job description was to make her life miserable.

"I used to be a mediator, too, Debbie," Trey said. He wasn't hostile. He was trying to smooth something over. He had dropped his M-K act and now was 'on,' attempting to corral Debbie into some mutually beneficial middle ground. "Seven years before they brought me in here as M-K. It's possible I interacted with the party you were talking about. Maybe he picked up on some of my, um, vernacular." He shrugged again.

"You called someone a 'fatso,' as a mediator?"

"Could have been, in one-on-ones." Trey shifted. He was lying. How could he have been a mediator for years and been such a terrible liar? His tells were more obvious than his glaring insecurities. "I always took a little more, 'hands-on' approach, than you younger crop. I don't remember, but it could have happened."

Debbie sat silently. She didn't believe Trey's explanation or assurances. But she couldn't do anything about them either.

Trey uncrossed his arms and tried to open up. "You know what a trellis is, right?"

Debbie raised her eyes to meet Trey's. She hated him. "Yes."

"Other than this building, I mean."

Debbie's gaze lashed back and forth, searching for anything at all worthwhile to find on Trey's awful person. "Yes, Trey. It's a framework. A latticework. Put in a garden so that plants can climb up it."

"Right. So this building, we've got the gardens at the bottom, and their reflections climb up the capital-T Trellis. People know that much. But it's also a framework for you and me. I started where you are, now I'm an M-K. Audrey, too, started as a mediator, now she's becoming an M-K. Others don't grow, others . . ." He trailed off. "Just, let's forget this whole incident happened. I don't know about you, but I'd like to keep moving up. I'll forget about you accusing me of malfeasance, I'll forget about you screwing up the mediation, and you'll understand this was a screw up that we're forgiving and understanding about. Jigme will check if anything else is wrong, but please sit tight on this. Don't tell anyone. Okay?"

"Okay."

"Okay, Jigme?"

Jigme was still staring straight through his tablet, through the floor, and out somewhere into the ether. "Yeah, I'll look into it."

"Okay. All good, Debbie?"

No. Not . . . "All good," she said.

"I'm going home. Had enough of this today. See you tomorrow."

Jigme stood there for a minute, still frozen in thought. Finally, he lifted his eyes to meet Debbie's staring at him. Tears hid under below her eyelids, peeking out at the corners. Jigme nodded politely and disappeared down the hall.

For the next few hours, Debbie sat staring blankly at her upcoming assignments. She wondered whether she was going crazy. She wondered whether she should go see Jerome and tell him what happened. He'd probably be on her side. He'd remember Trey calling him a "fatso." Jerome was a decent person, a civilian. But she just didn't know. Why would Jigme "look into it?" How could this be a software issue? Why were Jigme and Trey all of a sudden partners, working together rather than butting heads? Most importantly, if Debbie kept at it, would she end up as ashen-faced and miserable as Trey after seven years here?

As soon as it was feasible to leave, Debbie snuck out of her office. Her nerves were too shot to risk small talk or an awkward ride in the elevator. So she took to the stairwell, her emotions rubbing rawly against each other as she descended thirty-five floors to basement sub-level two. She hailed a solo ride the short distance to her new apartment and began crying softly in the car. Her gentle sobs faded as she got closer. She retrieved her phone from her purse and called her mother for the first time in weeks.

"Hi Mom, yeah, good. I mean, not good, really. No, nothing terrible. Just wanted to talk. Just a second."

As Debbie alighted her car, she watched a cavalcade of police cars streak north along La Salle. Their lights were on but their sirens were silent. Two massive armored vans rumbled behind them. They disappeared into the cool evening air that sank between the buildings and settled over the streets.

"Nothing," Debbie said. "Nothing important, I don't think. So, Terrance and I broke up. I know. I know. Me too, Mom. Me too."

32. Creep

Melody Jackson's chin-strap was too tight. As her cheap, standard-issue Six Counties helmet knocked back and forth in the rocking AVAN, it scratched and scraped at her jawline. The assault versions of the department's automated navigation vehicles were roomier than the surveillance version, but every spare inch was jam-packed with officers who were themselves jam-packed with equipment. Suparmanputra looked at home in his tactical gear, but O'Malley looked like he would rather be anywhere else. Lieutenant Gustafson looked like he was having the time of his life.

"How'd you find this guy?" he yelled over the roar of armored tires chipping at crumbling roads. "What's the deal?"

"Anonymous tip," she yelled back. "It's Citovsky's cousin." She pointed to her ear, signaling him she was switching to radio.

"Hello?" Melody watched the officers in the AVAN as she spoke. Most of them perked up as her greeting flowed through their helmets. "Everyone hear me?" Nods shook her way. "Sergeant Hansen, can you hear me?"

Sergeant Gil Hansen's gravelly voice poured into Melody's helmet. "Yes, Detective. Bull Two hears you, line secure. How's Bull One?"

"Cozy. Let's get started. Sorry everyone about your dinner plans and thanks for volunteering. I know some of you are here for hazard pay, some of you because you need a hobby, but all of us want to catch Tark's killer. This could be him. Target is Joshua James Citovsky, known associate of Cecil Citovsky, who Tark was following when he was killed. Our sources on the ground put the target—image on your displays now—leaving Rosehill Cemetery half an hour ago. When we put drones on Cecil Citovsky, they tracked them back to our SVAN and blew it up, so we're doing this old school. Dragnet. Squad cars are going in fast and loud to blockade Rosehill, cutting off his escape. We'll roll up quiet and close, find him and bring him in. Do not kill him. We need him alive. Understood?"

"Why do we need him alive?" someone in the other van asked.

"Who's asking?" Melody snapped.

"Nobody," Sergeant Hansen growled.

"Good," Melody said. "We need him alive and talking. Those are orders, and that's all you need to know. If anyone waxes Citovsky, I'm going to pin your badge to your bare-naked ass and drop you off in Rosehill. Let them figure out what to do with you. Any objections?" By the speed and smoothness of the ride, Melody figured they were on Lake Shore Drive. There was little doubt they would be spotted as they approached the notorious North Side, but that was the plan. Interdiction units would slip in from the west to sidle up to the southern edge of the cemetery before blasting their sirens, distracting the lookouts from the AVANs roaring in. "It'll be about five minutes now. Get ready."

The cars in front of the AVANs and squad cars parted effortlessly as the police approached. Their navigation systems spoke to each other directly and near-instantaneously, circumventing the reaction time and hesitation of human drivers. The odd organ donor that might get in the way could be dodged like any pothole or trashcan or drunk who stumbled into the street.

Sergeant Hansen crackled into Melody's helmet. "Splitting up."

"Okay. Unless you're a unit leader, switch your mics off. Opsec protocol starts now." The officers snapped face protectors to the corners of their helmets and pulled the velcro flaps over their names. Any goon pouring over the security footage would have trouble identifying the exact officers that crashed through their neighborhood. No one wanted to be the next dead hero.

Gustafson looked more ridiculous than the rest of them. His top-of-the-line Delaware helmet and aloxni facemask gave him direct access to his recoilless pistol's remote scope. He looked up to the ceiling, drew his service weapon, and pointed at his hand, which held up one, then two, then three fingers. Satisfied with its capabilities, he holstered it and looked around gleefully. "You ready for this?" he yelled.

Melody squinted, questioning the wisdom of bringing Gus along. There were no raids like this in Delaware, not on the peninsula and not in their office exclaves across the globe. Maybe he had seen action in a hostage situation in some high rise or car chase along the thirty miles of interstate that nicked Delaware's northern tip, but he'd never been on a night raid near Rosehill. She nodded to him. She was ready.

"Bull One—we have stopped in the Amundsen High School parking lot. Awaiting your instructions." The anxiety in Hansen's voice was palpable, which surprised her.

"Give me a second." She flipped channels. "Matte, what's the situation?"

"Suspect is walking north on Damen Avenue, north of Foster." Matte provided a grainy live picture of a man walking down the street carrying a grocery bag and a twenty-four or thirty-six pack of toilet paper. A lot of toilet paper, anyway. This should be easy, Melody thought.

"What about us?" she asked. Matte presented a map. Squad cars, AVANs, target . . . Everyone was in position. "Thanks, partner."

"Bull Two—we're at Winchester and Farragut. Ready to go on my signal." She took a breath and looked up. Most eyes in the AVAN were on her already, but when she checked the chamber of her pump-action shotgun, they all did the same for their service weapons.

Click.

Click-click, click.

Clack, click.

"Go."

As the AVANs poured officers out into the streets, Melody heard cheap fireworks popping off towards the lake. They had been spotted. Barely anyone worked in this neighborhood, not by any fault of their own. People milled about on porches, grilling or smoking or complaining. If they were sober enough to notice the police, they hushed their children and stood stock-still. In teams of three, the officers rushed quietly through the alleys and driveways to approach Damen Ave. Melody, Khalil, and a third officer Melody didn't recognize with his nameplate obscured, prowled as the last jagged coral edges faded from violet clouds to the west.

Jansen interrupted Melody's concentration. "Eyes on target. He's between Berwyn and Summerdale. Still walking."

"Approaching on the alley to the east." It was Soup. Melody could recognize the controlled meter of his voice.

A few percussive explosions snapped to Melody's right. Fireworks again, she hoped. "Move in. Now."

As Melody rounded the corner, she saw Joshua James Citovsky walking away from her towards Rosehill Cemetery. He wore a white sweatshirt and white jeans and was carrying a grocery bag and a large pack of toilet paper, completely unaware of the hell about to crash down on him. Suparmanputra appeared, and in an instant Citovsky was on the ground, his fall surreptitiously broken by the mounds of toilet paper he was carrying. Soup could fold people like they were paper cranes.

"Down. Down. He's down," Melody reported.

"Set up a perimeter," Jensen said.

"Spread out!" The order echoed through the streets. Officers obeyed, some looking up to the skies to see if some DIED was swooping down on them, others scanning the streets to see if some other violence approached on foot.

"Matte, extract is at Damen and Berwyn. Now, please." Manners never hurt. Sirens screamed at the edge of Rosehill Cemetery, where no doubt crowds had gathered around the unwelcome police cars. Melody rushed to where Soup restrained the second Citovsky. "Joshua James Citovsky?"

The man glared at her, terrified. He didn't say a word. But in that silence, something rustled in the alleyway that Suparmanputra had erupted from. The officers and Citovsky looked to see a pile of cardboard, shifting and undulating, as if something living were trapped beneath it, trying to escape.

"Don't move," Soup said, pressing his pistol into the back of Citovsky's neck. "What is it?"

"Hold." Melody's word brought the AVANs to a halt. She raised her shotgun and approached the pile of trash that quaked in the autumn air. In the creeping darkness, visions of spies, assassins, and DIEDs populated the corners of her vision as she trained her iron sights on the source of the movement.

It emerged slowly. A pink and beige, scaly triangle, jittering in the cold. It jutted forward like some alien appendage reaching out toward the officers. The cardboard behind the strange wedge bulged and claws struck out, followed by a few beady eyes and then, to Melody's surprise, two harmless-looking ears. The moment she lowered her weapon, the night air exploded with the unmistakable "TUT!" of a recoilless pistol. The cardboard flinched and spattered with blood.

"Jesus, Gus!" Melody yelled.

"No names," Jansen said over the radio. "Sit-rep."

"Accidental discharge. Jesus. We're okay. Armadillo. Dead armadillo, now."

"What?"

"Armadillo. It was an armadillo. Probably looking for somewhere warm to sleep. Jesus."

"Lieutenant!" Melody waved at Gus's gun periscoping over a fence near the alley. "Holster your weapon!" The La Warr Armory RP-1 retreated into the shadows, which in turn produced a sheepish Lieutenant Gustafson.

"Sorry."

"Sorry, my ass."

"*Sorry*, Detective!"

"Resume extract," Melody said to her microphone before covering it and turning to Gus. "Pick it up."

"What?"

"Pick up the armadillo. It's evidence. We gotta take it with us."

"Where are the bags?" Gus looked lost.

"No time. Let's go."

Gus picked up the bloodied remains of the nine-banded armadillo and cradled them as he waited by Melody and Suparmanputra. When the first AVAN arrived, Soup pulled Joshua James Citovsky to his feet. His hoodie had big black letters that read "IN COGNITO" and his fists quivered as Soup placed metal cuffs over the zip-ties.

"What does 'K-L-E-S' stand for?" Khalil asked.

Joshua James Citovsky shook his head and spat on Khalil's

pant leg. Soup twisted his arms harder, eliciting a whimper.

"KNUCKLES.' Right. My bad. Frickin' genius over here." Khalil spat on the ground near Citovsky's foot.

"Enough. Let's go." Melody opened the doors to the AVAN. "Perp first."

After Citovsky was loaded and restrained, the officers crowded in. Everyone wanted off the streets, but less than half of them would fit in the first load. Gus and his leaking trophy wanted to be two of them. "Not you," Melody said. "Wait for the next one. Matte, get central to put the drones up, any available SVANs. We're out, but need all eyes on a safe exit."

The doors slammed. They began to roll. "All good, Detective?" Soup asked.

"Yeah."

"Almost made it."

Melody turned off her microphone. "What?"

"Almost made it through, clean. No screw-ups."

She shook her head. "Delaware, man. They're going to kill us all."

"Why'd you make him take it?"

"The armadillo? I don't know. He shouldn't have shot it."

"Yeah. They are pests, though. 'Invasive species.'"

"Yeah. But we're cops. That's not our job."

"I'd like to speak to whoever's in charge!" Joshua James Citovsky yelled into the crowded AVAN. Melody and Soup exchanged glances. They had a talker. This wasn't expected. "I need to talk to whoever is in charge, please!"

"Okay," Melody said. "Understand you have the right to remain silent. Anything you say or do can and will be held against you in a court of law or sanctioned arbitration. You have the right to correspond with an attorney or remote legal services provider of your choosing. Do you understand?"

"Yes." He obviously didn't, as his lips were still moving.

"What is it?"

"You need to put me in solitary."

"What?"

"Solitary, I have to be in solitary. Away from the other prisoners."

"If you don't want to be around prisoners, you shouldn't get arrested."

Joshua James Citovsky's eyes narrowed. "You want information, not a corpse. If you want me to talk, you need to put me somewhere safe. Away from the others."

"Sure, we'll get you a suite. You want one king-size or two queens? Continental breakfast okay with you?" A few officers chuckled, then Melody narrowed her eyes back at him. "We'll take our chances."

"Detective," he said. "It is 'Detective,' right? I'm going to make two more statements, and then I'm going to stop talking for a week. Seven days, okay? Statement one—if I'm alive and well in a week, I'll answer all of your questions." He smirked as they paused and waited. "Statement two—when we blew him up, it was a mistake. We didn't know your cop was a cop, okay?"

As the AVAN trundled around unseen corners, Melody felt its interior swell with rage. The dozen officers inside it had just listened to this creep admit to being a cop killer. They were liable to do something very stupid and relatively justified.

"What did you say?" She seethed with imminent violence.

Joshua James Citovsky shook his head, swallowed heavily, and then closed his eyes. When he opened them, they found Melody's, and then cast themselves down to his bound hands. He extended seven fingers, one for each day in the coming week.

"'KNUCK," Khalil read. "What the fuck is that supposed to mean?"

33. Chisel

Debbie struggled in the days after her run-in with Trey, Jigme, and the Sheboygan Volunteer Coast Guard. Jerome visited her office twice to see if everything was okay. She told him it was. Each time, Trey visited her to interrogate her about Jerome's visit. Each time, she told him everything was okay. She had guessed, at this point, that Jerome was watching her somehow. She couldn't tell if it was her terminal or sensors in the hallway or sensors on the way into the building, but Jerome would pop up any time her mood curdled. Trey berated her more often. He seemed frightened of something. She couldn't ask him what it was. He wouldn't tell her if she did.

Her mediations became more and more difficult. She didn't know whether it was because her nerves were fraying, or because her concentration was flagging, or because the mediations actually became more complex. One devolved into a screaming match over whether a bandwidth easement for a data-leasing cartel in Detroit was "appurtenant or in gross." Debbie had no idea what either party actually did, so she had even less an idea of what they were screaming about. Some of the issues seemed too complex to understand, not just for Debbie but for the parties. They'd go around in circles, retreading old talking points, explaining the same positions over and over as their shapes faded in and out of comprehension. The stakes were too abstract, too big, or too expensive for the parties to wrap their minds around.

Another mediation between two California NTOs focused on whether they were "allies." One group strongly identified as "anti-vanilla," which made things difficult for Debbie, as she probably qualified as "vanilla." She was straight, cis-gendered, and pretty white. She could have brought up that her grandmother on her mother's side was Jewish, or that her great-grandfather was Armenian, but neither fact would really cut it.

Having just broken up with Terrance couldn't help her case, and neither could her steadfast determination to be as outwardly boring as possible.

Things must be going pretty well in California, Debbie thought, if they were still arguing about this stuff. Hunger, violence, and fear tended to supersede border disputes in the realm of personal identity. After the Big Trouble hit, gangs and NTOs in the dust-and-rust belt usually realized that in order to thrive, they needed to be able to talk to people that didn't look or think like them. The handful of gangs that strictly limited themselves to one race, gender, or point of view had an easy time picking up young and impressionable recruits, but struggled any time they needed to barter or negotiate. Apparently, in California they still had enough food to bicker about who was either X, Y, or Z enough to qualify as a useful friend.

Lunch offered no respite. Debbie eventually let Norma know that she and Terrance had broken up. She showed Norma the folder of messages that was growing each day, with depressing subject lines like "Just one thing . . ." and "Please read . . ." Debbie would read them later, she said, but she just needed some time off. Norma prodded about Debbie's interest in Jigme, which Debbie brushed off. She didn't feel safe, so she wasn't thinking about that. She couldn't trust him at the moment. Besides, Jigme didn't show up to lunch that week.

"He's probably talking to his elephants," Kevin Doogan said that Wednesday.

"Mmm." Debbie was not eager to talk about it. She hadn't explained Tuesday's strange occurrences, the Sheboygan Admiral parroting Trey Brodowski's taunts almost word for word. She suspected she might have lost her mind. She didn't want Kevin's grim take on it in any case.

"I was reading the other day," Kevin said, "about mahouts, the guys who actually rode elephants. It's crazy. So they'd ride elephants into wars in ancient times. But elephants will go berserk if things get too crazy. Elephants can be trained to crush and trample armies, pick 'em up, throw them around, stab them with their tusks, whatever. But they get scared, especially when they don't know what the hell is going on. So the other armies would try to freak them out. They'd set a bunch of *pigs* on fire and had them run out toward the elephants. Elephants just lost their shit and ran."

"That's . . . horrible, Kevin," Norma said. "Thanks for that."

"It gets worse. So the mahouts, their job is to control the elephants, to drive them where they're supposed to go. But a rampaging elephant can't be controlled. It'll trample your own soldiers. In case that ever happens, the mahouts carried a giant mallet and giant chisel. They'd put the chisel right between the elephant's ears, where the spine meets the skull, and THWACK." Kevin mimicked driving a chisel into an elephant's vertebrae. "Five tons of elephant goes down in an instant."

"That's even worse. You were right." The story didn't turn Norma's appetite, though. She kept digging into her bouillabaisse.

"Also, fun fact. That bone attaching an elephant's skull to an elephant's spine is called the 'atlas.' Like the Greek god, who holds up the world, because it holds up your skull."

"Titan," Debbie said. "Atlas was a titan, not a god." Her mind had been somewhere else, but for some reason it returned to the lunch table for this petty correction.

"Titan, sure. Speaking of the weight of the world . . . you doing okay, Debbie?" Kevin was sincere, but he was not smooth.

"Yeah, I'm fine, thanks." She wasn't. "Listen, if Jigme works with Organons, what's that got to do with what we do? Like, in the actual mediations? There are no 'software' issues that should come up when we're talking to the parties. Maybe in the research before, the files they give us, but like, not during the actual mediation?"

"Why don't we just ask him?" Norma said.

"You shouldn't." Kevin's color had changed. He had been excited while regurgitating elephant trivia, but now he was pale.

"Why not?" Debbie could tell Norma had switched 'on.' Her voice changed subtly and her posture was more controlled. She was squaring off against Kevin.

"You really shouldn't." Kevin's voice had also changed. He looked hurt, but also 'on.' He morphed into whatever version of himself negotiated with drug developers and pharmaceutical warehousers and hospital quartermasters. Mediators, while terrific go-betweens, were rarely good at taking the offensive. They were accustomed to reflecting, sidestepping, and redirecting, but not advancing their own opinions. It made Debbie even sadder, watching these two bounce distortions back and forth like opposing funhouse mirrors, getting nowhere.

"Well, why do you think that?" Norma asked. This was day-one stuff, and it immediately let Kevin know she didn't respect him. Norma was laying it on thick.

"You may just have to trust my understanding of the process, without my explaining my understanding." Advanced move, really. Kevin was appealing to authority, his own authority of experience, and insinuating that Norma was too young or inexperienced or otherwise inferior to be trusted to understand it.

"I do trust you, but I could better rely on that trust if I had more facts to act upon."

"I think the fact that I have much more experience here should be enough, without detailing all of my experiences that led to my conclusions."

"Well, please tell us a bit about why you think that, and maybe that would help us understand."

Kevin lost his patience. "Maybe I've heard other people ask Jigme those same questions. And maybe those people aren't around anymore."

Norma's eyes widened as Debbie's shoulders sank. "Gerald?" Norma asked. "Hannah?"

"Just do your job, Norma. We've got a good thing going here. Don't ruin it." Kevin stood up to leave. "I'm just trying to help you two. You're welcome, anyway."

After a few moments of tense stillness, Norma turned to Debbie. "What. The hell."

Debbie shook her head. She could feel the fear creeping up from the space between her lowest ribs, above her stomach but not quite her heart. "I have no idea."

"That's not cool, right? That's not cool, at all. You can't be like 'Don't ask questions or you might die.' This is a job. It's a workplace environment. It should be safe."

"When was the last time you felt safe?" Debbie felt tears

welling in her eyes. "Like actually, truly safe?" She wiped them away quickly before they escaped onto her cheeks. "I'm serious. When?"

Norma needed time to think about it. "Probably back in Disney, Oklahoma. I was ten or eleven. Probably then."

"Yeah," Debbie said as she stared at her half-eaten lunch. "It's been a while."

34. Babirusa

Tark's funeral came and went. The department held it in the Six Counties Police Academy auditorium, which provided a safe shelter for the dozens of officers that came through in shifts. Melody sensed more fear than anger or sadness among the mourners in their parade dress. Police assassinations usually arrived in clusters. Every time the city went mad, started bursting at its seams, the bagpipes would play. Melody didn't know if Tark would have appreciated the bagpipes or not. He had been a bit of a snob, was probably more of a jazz guy. Now he was a box of ashes nestled in a closed casket, flanked by laurels and mountains of flowers.

She stopped by Cook County central holding on the way to the officers' wake. There would be shit-hammered police officers at the bar needing her calm, guiding presence, but she needed to make sure Joshua James Citovsky was still alive. He was kept in a cell on his own, across from a few suspected Horrorists and another cell full of non-violent offenders. He could talk if he wanted, but hadn't. The officers on duty confirmed he had been mute the entire time. He ate his food. He slept. He occasionally exercised. But he never spoke. When Melody went down to visit him, he looked at her and held up six fingers. "This is a stunt," she said. "You'd better land on your feet." He shrugged and turned away from the door.

They held the officers' wake at Reggio's, the police dive near the Six Counties Quartermaster Depot in Armour Patch. It was a mess. Anger and grief mixed with cheap alcohol and workplace tension. Many were venting about the video that had appeared online of the aftermath of the DIED strike. Even though they jammed the whole neighborhood, someone had snuck their old spring-wound 16mm film camera near the scene. The grainy, shaky footage featured Melody helping the vomiting Sharon

Kemp to her feet. Melody remembered the old man on the porch, laughing with what looked like a lunchbox on his lap. No wonder he had been so happy. He probably sold that footage for a few month's rent. He'd be lucky to live out the year, though, given what both good cops and bad cops were saying they'd do to him.

Melody nursed a single-batch sorghum whiskey as she monitored the wake's proceedings. There were the standard shouting matches and separate bouts of crying. Tears were forbidden on the force, but an officer's funeral was a noted exception that some took advantage of. The union provided car rides home and covered the bar tab, so no one shied away from getting off-their-face drunk. No one except for Gustafson, who didn't drink or understand that he shouldn't be there. He never knew Tark and he sure as hell wasn't a Six Counties cop. Melody felt the whiskey loosening her spine between her shoulders, unspooling the inhibitions that were usually wound tightly behind her heart. Soup found her. He clinked her glass with his Old Style and gave a knowing nod.

"Hate these things," he told her.

"That's a good sign."

"Right? I actually heard some idiot once say 'I love an Irish funeral.'"

"He musta hated Irishmen."

"No joke." He paused to brace himself. "You're doing a great job, boss."

Melody bobbed her head. She didn't believe it, but she hoped it was true. "Thanks, Soup. I hope so."

"Seriously, it's been a rough couple of weeks."

"Sure has."

"That armadillo? What was that."

"Keeps getting weirder."

"Did I ever tell you about the babirusa?"

"Don't think so."

Soup took a long pull from his cheap beer. "It's this pig. Lives in Indonesia. I saw them on my second tour. Out in the jungle. They're uglier than a regular pig, a lot uglier. We'd be on patrol or at an FOB and these things would start creeping outta the bush at us. You should look them up. They are so ugly. Like a warthog, but worse. But they're not stupid. They know the jungle better than anyone. If they smelled you, you make a sound, they disappear. So if you saw some babirusa calmly walking through that jungle, you could be damn sure no rebels or jihadists had seen or smelled you either. They were nice like that."

"I don't think I've ever heard you talk this much, Soup. You must be drunk."

"Sorry."

"Don't be. Keep going."

"So babirusa males, they got these tusks. Coming from the middle of their snout, up and out the middle of their snout, they got these giant curved ones. Like, literally growing out of their faces. Not out and around. Up and *through* their pig faces. Like out the top. Okay?"

Melody nodded.

"So, they fight with them, sometimes they get broken off in a fight. But lady babirusas, they love a big old ugly babirusa with giant tusks poking out of its face. It's like a peacock's tail for them. An eighty-foot yacht. The bigger, meaner, and uglier a babirusa is, the more the lady pigs love it. The bigger those tusks grow, the more baby babirusas that ugly bastard is making. That's probably how they all got so ugly. But here's the thing—those tusks keep growing. The better they grow, the more babies they have. But they just keep growing. And they curve. I think I forgot to say that. They curve back." He pointed two fingers to his forehead. "Curve back right into his skull. If that big male babirusa keeps growing, doesn't get eaten by a buncha natives or marines or whatever, those tusks grow right back into its skull. Into its brain. And kills it."

"Kills it?"

"Yeah, kills it. Its own teeth grow right into its brain. After sticking themselves out there through its snout, getting it laid, making that babirusa the *man* its whole life, they go and kill the thing. His whole life, he can see it coming. Literally right between his eyes. But he can't do nothing about it. Doesn't make sense."

"No, it doesn't."

"That's what I'm trying to say, you know?"

"Not really, what?" Melody was very confused now.

"Doesn't make sense. Doesn't have to. Sometimes that's just the way it goes." He took a sip from his beer and nodded assuredly. Soup was a great police officer, but a bad therapist. Melody was still confused and now a bit upset.

The wake went on without incident and faded into the night. Self-driving jellybeans gobbled up officers and dropped them off at their homes. Melody eventually found herself waking from a restless sleep, not hungover but not feeling well.

The week proceeded slowly. Joshua James Citovsky would show one fewer finger each day. Matte would scour his records and data for clues and connections. So would Gus and Junior, presumably, but Melody suspected they were dragging their feet. Gustafson asked a lot of questions and provided no answers. His Cloudbuster, Junior, had shared next to nothing with Matte, which told Melody that Delaware had not been working very hard before joining the case. Whatever Gus was interested in, it was not solving anything related to the Jefferson Group. Melody had convinced herself he was spying on the Six Counties investigation.

That week's homicide workload was surprisingly low again. The cases took care of themselves, leaving Melody the whole weekend to work on whatever she wanted. She wanted to work on Tark and the cousins Citovsky. She made suggestions to Matte, guiding his billions of hands as they sifted through unseen mountains of data. The Citovskys offered no dots to connect. Their records were sporadic. Their online presence dissolved into the background noise. The salient nodes of information crumbled as Melody and Matte pushed them back and forth, trying to find shapes in the static and sand. The more parameters they added, the more formless it became. The simpler the questions they asked, the less meaningful the answers became.

But by Sunday evening, Melody could guess *why* some data points were missing. It came down to the difference between Joshua James Citovsky and Cecil. Cecil had a few accounts, enough to get a car and a phone and some boring semblance of a life. He had clammed up when he was detained, but opened up with a little wiggling. His cousin, on the other hand, was a hardcore believer in something. Joshua James was committed to a cause, with the tattoos, theatrics, and demands. He was off the grid completely, in the middle of the city. He was the one who got his cousin Cecil into all this trouble. They were two close points on a continuum, right on the edge of this city-wide conspiracy of silence.

Melody guessed that the people who clammed up in custody, the college kids and accountants and social workers, were purposefully starving the databanks. They made only enough data to not trigger suspicions. They had meager bank accounts. Some of them had phones. They occasionally left a stale, meaningless breadcrumb, but nothing enough to be interesting. They were creating false positives, searching nonsense terms in their phones, taking long walks to nowhere and back just to create noise in the system. The ones who got caught up by the system, the ones who got processed, gave the system nothing to process. That was why Matte couldn't find any traction. That was why his wheels kept spinning.

"Matte, last Saturday I asked you about a victim. A shooting victim."

"Denise Susan Nichols."

"Yeah, her. Did she talk?"

"No."

"Has she been released from the hospital?"

"No, she died on Wednesday."

"The shooter?"

"Niels Carl Michaelson. He is still at large."

"Matte, I want to see the people in this city that are *not* affiliated with a gang or NTO, but who have a lower than average contribution of data to the networks. People we know exist, but have no phone, limited social media, fewer points of collection. Weight deviation for age and class and sex and social factors. I'd like to see where there are anomalies. I want to know where people that should be on the grid are hiding. Could you do that for me, please?"

"One moment, Detective." It was more than a moment. It took Matte three full minutes to process Melody's request. But eventually, he presented a map. There were patches of bright red across Six Counties, one of the brightest overlaying Rosehill Cemetery. Another in Hermosa. Another near Montrose Harbor. Another in Lakeview. One in Bronzeville. But one at Skinner Park, across from Whitney M. Young Magnet High School, attracted Melody's attention.

"Matte, overlay the eight gangs we discussed last week—when we talked about the purge—on this map."

Eight red splotches turned purple. The eight dead gangs had been anti-technologists, or something like it. People like Cecil Citovsky, who avoided detection by providing the bare minimum of participation in society. Melody had finally discovered them, hiding in plain sight. But someone else—or something else—had discovered them six months prior and went on to exterminate them. Maybe Melody was too late.

But beyond the swaths of purple, there were areas of red all over the map, clumping up in groups around the city. "What are the rest of these spots, Matte? The red splotches not affiliated with the NTOs discussed last week? Can you find something that connects them?"

"One moment, Detective."

Melody waited. After fifteen minutes, she grew impatient. After forty-five, she let her impatience and fatigue win. "You still working, Matte?"

"Yes, Detective. One moment."

"Keep at it, Matte. I need to get some sleep."

35. Veneer

After another mediation unraveled into open verbal warfare, Jerome appeared in Debbie's doorway. Debbie had hoped this week would be different from the last, but it was only Tuesday and she was already back under the microscope. Some scanner or sniffer had told Jerome that Debbie needed his attention.

"Debbie, you need to understand that this is just part of the job."

"Thanks."

"No, really. You being stressed, tired, angry, whatever, we *need* that. That gives us information. You wanna get pregnant? That's fine, we don't mind. That helps us understand how we can do a better job. We just need to *know*."

"I'm not pregnant."

"We know. I'm just saying. It's been a hard week. I get it. But don't fret. Don't run off. Don't blow it here, okay? Just keep doing what you do. We see this a lot, three or four months in. We see the fatigue set in. Most people aren't used to working so hard."

"I don't mind working hard."

"What do you mind then?"

After a short pause, Debbie decided to address the elephant in the room. "I mind being lied to. I'd like to know what I'm really doing here."

Jerome's pleasant face froze, refusing to change in a way that might betray something negative underneath it. "Mmm. Mmm-hmm-hmm. Okay. I'll get back to you on that. For now though, just sit tight. You sure you don't want to just keep doing a good job, like you have been?"

Debbie didn't know. Her mind reeled back to her interview. There were expectations, she remembered. Those expectations would make some people better people, and make some people better liars. Debbie felt like neither. She had barely lasted a fiscal quarter and she was already falling apart. "Can I come talk to you later?"

"Sure. Anytime." Jerome's tone of voice told Debbie that his warmth had disappeared. Possibly forever. Jerome manufactured his congeniality and dosed it out like a tranquilizer. Debbie had developed a resistance to it, so he stopped its administration.

"Thanks, Jerome. It's just been, uh, confusing lately." Acting dumb was literally the first move in the mediator's playbook. The mediator's feigned ignorance forces the party to explain themselves. It could make the party speak their true mind, if only because they want to cudgel their adversary with an explanation. Jerome begrudgingly recognized this by nodding then walking away. After a minute of terrible calm, Debbie sprung up and went out into the hallway.

"Wanna go out for lunch?" Debbie asked Norma.

"Like, out out?"

"Like out of the building, out."

"Yes, please. Whaddaya want?"

"Don't care. Lady's choice."

Norma tilted an imaginary cocktail towards her lips.

"It's Taco Tuesday at the Cabrini Martini," Debbie said.

"Now you're talking."

So out they went, past the blue golems and security turrets and listing valet and into the streets. They walked a few blocks talking about the unseasonably warm weather and above-the-fold news items and snippets of small talk before Norma popped the question that had been begging to be asked.

"You doing okay?"

Debbie stammered. "Yeah. Just. Just feeling a bit . . . overwhelmed."

"You worked before, though, right?"

"Yeah, constantly. Those jobs were different, though."

"How?"

"Way different. It was just work. Go in, work. Some days, work sucks. You get reviews, get your numbers back, they are good or bad or whatever. But here, I think they're watching us all the time. Like, all the time."

"I mean, they definitely are."

"But that's weird, right? Why do they care? Why are they looking at me on the way in, on the way out, on the way to the bathroom? Today, Jerome, he told me it was okay to mediate tired or angry or, quote-unquote, pregnant. What does that mean, that 'it's okay.' I mean, of course it's '*okay*.' But why does he need to tell me it's okay? That doesn't make sense. He said they needed to *calibrate*. Like it's okay that the town of New Ulm, Minnesota disappears because I screw up a mediation, so long as the goddamn Jefferson Group can *calibrate* their data?"

Norma looked concerned. "Yeah. That is weird."

"Doesn't that bother you?"

"Yeah," Norma said, "but I don't know. I also, you know, don't want to die."

"That's the other thing. Like, the biggest thing. Two people killed on the same floor. In separate incidents? Like, isn't it weird that you replaced Hannah, and everyone says you look and act like Hannah? Why did they need a copy of Hannah?"

"Well, first, I like to think of myself as an actual person, thanks, not a copy of Hannah. Second, I think maybe that's racist. Third, you're not a copy of Gerald, so I don't think it's a valid point."

"I mean, who knows. No one knows if I'm a copy of Gerald. I didn't know him. You barely did. Maybe he was a scared, boring, mostly competent nobody, too. Maybe he was in a doomed relationship. Maybe he was up to his eyeballs in debt. Maybe his dad jumped off a parking garage, too. I don't know, but it is all *weird*, right? I'm not crazy, am I?"

"Yeah. It's definitely strange."

"Also, why do we never have in-person mediations?"

"What do you mean?"

"Nothing's live. All our mediations are on terminals. We never get to call parties or meet for a follow-up. They say it's for insurance. Liability with exposure, all that. But, we can't call to follow up? For insurance? It doesn't make sense. I've done thousands of in-person mediations. Never killed anyone. I mean, yeah, things got out of hand. But half of our mediations now are with big corps, big NTOs. Not back-alley knife fights."

"What are you saying?"

"We are supposedly the best mediators in the business, but every single mediation we do has to go through their terminals. I think they are spying on us. I mean, we know they are, but I think it has something to do with their Organons, their Dinkums. Like, why does Jigme have anything to do with our mediations? Maybe he is there so his 'elephants' can watch our faces and listen to our voices and then read our notes to try to learn how to do our jobs. What if he's a zookeeper, but we're in his zoo, *not* the Dinkums. What if—"

"Debbie . . . stop. I need to think for a minute."

"Okay." They walked in silence through the rust and gray streets. The only clouds were high above, drifting imperceptibly slowly toward Michigan or Toronto or LeRoy, New York. The air carried the sharp scent of rotting leaves and the last breaths of billions of insects that had died in the previous night's frost. The last shuddering gasps from their spiracles and stomata floated eastward as the sunburnt air swelled in the day and contracted at night. Debbie and Norma walked face first into this wind, and it stung their cheeks. They arrived at the Cabrini Martini and sat at the bar, ordered two vodka martinis and the tilapia taco special. Eventually, Norma returned to the topic of their employment.

"I don't think we should talk about this anymore."

"Why?"

"If what you're saying is true, there's nothing I can do about it. If it's not true, the thought of it, the notion, will mess me up at work. No offense, but you've worried about this so much. Too much. And it's ruining your work. I don't want to do that to myself. I've got loans to pay, too. I think we should just focus on our work."

"We can't just—"

"Debbie. I'm serious. I'm done talking about it. You heard what Kevin said. I am not getting myself killed for this job. Please don't tell anyone we talked about this." Debbie noticed the skin behind Norma's ears was splotched red, a sign her blood was boiling over. Norma must be furious to be placed in this position, having unwanted information that put her job and possibly her life at risk. Debbie had thought Norma would share her concerns, but now she felt more alone than she had in years. She felt back in Shadyside, in Squirrel Hill her junior year. She could smell the plastic burning and feel her teeth hurting with the cold.

"What do you want to talk about, then?" Debbie asked.

"I don't know. You doing anything for Halloween?"

"No. You?"

"No." Their tacos arrived. "How's everything with Terrance?"

Debbie didn't know if this was tactless chitchat or petty revenge. Debbie definitely did not want to talk about Terrance. She had been avoiding the topic as much as she could. "Let's see." She opened the folder containing all his messages and overtures. "Got one this morning. Subject is in all caps, says 'DON'T GO TO WORK TODAY.'" Her heart rattled like a tin can full of odd screws and nails.

"Haha, he got that right." Norma took another large gulp from her martini. "What's that supposed to mean, anyway?"

Before Debbie could contemplate an answer, the restaurant shook at its foundation, clattering the hanging racks of cocktail glasses. A moment later, the shockwave cracked past the building, shattering the transom and knocking the solid oak door wide open. Everyone flinched, some people ducked, and Debbie threw herself to the floor. In the violence, Norma crouched down next to her and was trying to say something. She was saying something, actually, but Debbie couldn't hear it over her ringing ears. Some tinplate ceiling tiles fell down, sending all the surviving patrons towards the doors.

In the street, floating leaves and litter were beginning to settle after being kicked up by the blast. To their east, Debbie and Norma could see a cloud of gray-brown dust where the Jefferson Trellis should be.

"Holy shit. Holy shit, Debbie." Norma's words were bassy and dampened, but as she repeated them over and over, they became clearer. "Holy shit, Debbie. Did you know, Debbie? Did you know?"

Debbie finally spoke. "No. No, I didn't know!"

As Debbie's hearing returned, she heard sounds of rapid footfalls down the dirty streets. Somewhere in the distance, alarms and sirens were screaming. As they stared at the cloud, they noticed something strange. Beams of light, coruscating rays dancing through the dust. They were stacked at regular intervals but slightly different angles, refracting out into infinity. As the autumn wind dragged the cloud of dust and rubble out towards the lake, Debbie and Norma were met with a vision of awe and fearsome power. The Jefferson Trellis still stood. Not a single window was broken. And now the noontime sun skipped off the angled windows on its southern side.

"We have to go," Debbie said. "It's starting again."

"What is?"

"I don't know. Bad stuff. We need to go."

Whenever the city went mad and threatened to tear itself apart again, Debbie and other survivors snapped into action. Most had formulated their plans over the course of thousands of dress rehearsals in their darker daydreams. But this was Norma's first rodeo, and Debbie felt obliged to help her through it. After they fled the Cabrini Martini, Debbie hailed a car for two. Emergency surge pricing was at twenty-eight times the usual cost, but they could not afford to take a detour or share the car with some panicked or desperate soul. Three-quarters of the way to Debbie's apartment, the car silently pulled off to the side of the road. After a few fearful beats, the doors opened and the car notified them that civilian traffic was now prohibited in this sector.

They walked briskly toward Debbie's apartment. Norma was wearing low heels, and a twisted ankle would be disastrous if they needed to trek out of the city. Besides, two well-dressed young women sprinting down the street, clip-clopping like spooked thoroughbreds, would reek of desperation. When the thin veneer of civilization cracked, opportunistic predators felt emboldened. Debbie pulled her shoulders back and infused a healthy but sexless bounce in her steps—stotting or pronking, they called it in body language courses—an honest signal that she was healthy enough to fight back if attacked. She made eviscerating eye contact with any man she caught looking at them, letting them know that she was not in trouble, but was trouble itself strutting down the street.

"What do you drink?" Debbie asked.

"What? I don't think we should drink."

"For later. Believe me."

"Red wine." They stopped by the liquor store around the corner from Debbie's apartment. The 7-11 was already jam-packed and devolving into chaos, and in the nascent hours of a local inversion, it was best to stay away from crowds. Debbie picked up two bottles of red wine, five pints of good whiskey, and two fifths of good tequila. "Jesus, how much do you drink?" Norma asked.

"The wine's for us. The rest is for bartering." She picked up two handfuls of chocolate bars and some bags of chips. She would have loved it if the liquor store had some peanut butter or turkey jerky, but she'd have to do with the calorie-rich foods that were available. As they approached the counter, Debbie saw the clerk keeping one hand secured on whatever weapon she held beneath the counter. "Hello." Debbie's voice tried to calm and disarm her. "Two cartons of Marlboro reds and one carton of Newports." She turned to Norma. "Bartering."

Debbie paid the extortionate emergency rates and they carried the heavy bags around the corner to her apartment. As soon as they arrived, Debbie began filling the tub. This tub, she thought. Finally got a place with a giant tub, a shower that could peel the paint off of a battleship's hull, and money to spend on all the hot water that she could hope for. Then this happens again. The trouble, the violence. Snap out of it, Pumpkin, lots to do. She began filling available pitchers and empty containers with water from the kitchen sink.

"What should I do?" Norma asked.

"Can you pull the curtains?" As she did, the room went dark. The blackout curtains were heavy, designed to stop any flying glass should the windows give in. "The lights are over there."

When Norma turned them on, Debbie saw that Norma was terrified. Not outwardly so—she maintained a semblance of calm professionalism. But Norma's knees were slightly bent, ready to sprint at any instant. Her shoulders were hunched, with her arms ready to punch and claw at some intruder or brace herself for another explosion. When Norma noticed Debbie's concern, she edited her posture. "I'm sorry. I don't know what to do."

"We're safe here, for now. You're fine. Try to relax."

Another concussion rattled the windows, softer than the one that interrupted their lunch. The windows held, so they peeked out the curtains to see something had exploded in the air a few blocks away.

"What was that?" Norma asked.

"I don't know. Firework, probably. Maybe a drone. Are you hungry?" Debbie opened her pantry. She checked the five gallons of water she had bought when she moved in. It was the recommended amount for one person, but she hoped the tub and Tupperware she had filled would hold them over. The other emergency supplies didn't need checking, as Debbie had only moved them in a few weeks prior. She grabbed the only perishable items from her pantry. Some pita bread, three bananas, and two oranges. "You should eat."

"I'm not hungry."

"We might have to leave quickly if things get bad around here. We should eat now." Debbie gave Norma one pita, one orange, and one banana and took the same for herself. She put the remaining banana in the bag of pita bread and left it near the door. She began eating her own portion, starting with the banana. Oranges traveled well and were a luxury on the road. Another concussion sounded in the distance.

Norma started picking apart her pita. "What do we do next?"

Debbie's mind ran through the possibilities. "We wait and see. We're safer here now than on the streets."

"What if it gets worse here?"

"Then we have to figure it out."

"What if it gets safer on the streets?"

"Then maybe we try to get somewhere safer. What size shoe are you?"

"Seven and a half American, usually."

"I'm an eight. Do you want to try some of my shoes on?"

Norma looked confused and offended. "Why?"

Debbie looked to Norma's feet. "Can you run in those?"

"Okay, yeah. No." Debbie retrieved some running shoes out of her bedroom closet for Norma. As Norma tried them on, Debbie went back to change out of her work clothes and into something comfortable and warm. She grabbed her stun gun and pepper spray from behind her bed and attached them to the go-bag she kept in her closet, which she then brought to the front door. By the time she went back into the living area, Norma was sitting wearing a pair of Debbie's sneakers.

"Those look good," Debbie said, but Norma didn't respond. "We should check the news. Is your phone connected?"

Norma stared through the floor. "I don't think so, no. What about your house?"

"Wigwam," Debbie said to the room. "Wigwam! Doesn't sound like it." She approached the flatscreen on the wall and turned it on manually, but no picture or menu appeared. Instead, it displayed a simple message—No Signal.

"We'll leave it on for when it comes back. Do you want to borrow some comfy clothes? I'll go grab some."

"Thanks, Debbie. For all of this." Norma finally looked up from the floor. She had been crying. "I need to call my parents."

"We'll do that as soon as we get network connection."

"Okay. What do we do now?"

Debbie looked around. She didn't have any entertainment. Every few minutes there had been a strange sound from outside, some distant explosion or missile shrieking through the air. Sirens screamed in every direction on the streets below. "I'll open up one of those wines, if that's cool with you?"

"Seriously?"

"Yeah." Debbie was very serious. She had wanted a drink since about 10:30 that morning, long before the bombs started going off. "Ninety-five percent of surviving these things is making sure that you stay sane. Keeping your head on straight."

"And the other five percent?"

"Not dying." Debbie retrieved a corkscrew from a drawer and started beheading a bottle of Bolivian Syrah. "But really it's mostly tedious. Not boring, but tedious."

"Those are synonyms."

"Well, then, whatever the type of boring is where you might die suddenly." She handed Norma a glass of wine. "It's *that* type of boring, ninety-five percent of the time."

Norma eventually changed into some of Debbie's leisurewear. They each drank wine and Norma peppered Debbie with questions about what the local inflection was like in Pittsburgh. What happened first, what happened second, how this time could be different from that time.

"It *is* different, now," Debbie said. "Back then there was no protocol, it was completely new. No one knew what to do."

"Did you have slumber parties like this back then?"

"Haha, no. I was at a new high school. After a few weeks hiding at home we went to the shelters. They'd call them NTO centers now. Headquarters and stuff. They were packed full of people and kids of all ages, so it was like a sleepover if every asthmatic grandma and toddler with diarrhea was invited."

"Yikes."

"Yeah. Not going to lie, you've got it pretty good here."

Debbie and Norma chatted and drank and peeked out the windows through the afternoon. They ate more of Debbie's food and checked their phones for network connectivity. As night fell, the streets grew quieter. The occasional explosions ceased, and Debbie and Norma turned off the lights in the living room and opened the curtains slightly to watch what was going on outside. Against the pale indigo twilight, they could see an occasional drone circle and swoop. Behind a building kitty-corner from Debbie's, a fire burned in the alley, but no fire trucks came to quell it. Eventually, the orange light that splashed upon the building's walls disappeared as the fire burned itself out.

At quarter to nine, the electricity in Debbie's apartment flickered out, leaving Debbie and Norma in darkness. They opened the curtains and Debbie retrieved her flashlight from her go-bag. She checked to see that it worked and then turned it off. There was no need to waste its batteries, and there was nothing to look at in the apartment anyway.

"Look," Norma said, "across the street." The lights were still on in a few windows in the buildings to the south. Out Debbie's bedroom window, she saw that the building to the east also had electricity.

"Lucky us."

A muffled thud came from outside the front door. Someone was in the hallway. Debbie could hear Norma's breathing quicken into panicked, short huffs as she stood frozen in darkness.

Debbie slid to the door and leaned her ear against it. The sounds of footsteps and the gentle clinking of metal against canvas straps filled the darkened corridor. There was more than one pair of footsteps. There were three or four.

Debbie's blood hissed as it hammered through her arteries, pulsing through her mind as the noises stopped outside her door. She braced her foot against the baseboard and removed her stun gun from its holster attached to her go-bag. She pressed its metal prongs against the metal doorknob and waited for it to turn.

A voice spoke to the door, but just barely. "Miss Peck?" It almost didn't reach her. Norma, petrified near the kitchen counter, couldn't have heard it at all. "Miss Peck, we're here to help you."

Debbie remained set like a steel trap. She could hear Norma backing further into the apartment.

"Miss Peck. We are the Delaware State Police. Your employer sent us here to assist you."

As her eyes adjusted, Debbie looked back to Norma, who had crept behind the kitchen island.

What is it, Norma mouthed.

Police, Debbie mouthed back, then shrugged with confusion.

The voice penetrated further into the apartment. "Miss Peck, we see you next to the door. Miss Feng, we know you're there, too. We're here to take you somewhere safe."

Debbie looked to Norma, who shrugged back. Then she opened her mouth slowly and creaked, "Okay. Could you give us a minute, please?"

"Yes, ma'am." There was no choice. Debbie and Norma collected their things. The go-bag, some extra clothes, some extra food and water. The booze and cigarettes lay abandoned on the kitchen counter. Debbie knew she couldn't barter their way through whatever the Delaware State Police had in store for them.

"We're about to open the door," Debbie said.

"We know." The voice was soft again. "We're ready to go."

When Debbie opened the door, no one stood on the other side. But noises rustled on the edges of the void in front of her. "We're coming out," she said. As she emerged, the dark shapes in the hallway took their alien forms. Each was roughly man-shaped, but where their faces should be, instead there was a black articulated visor. They carried shoulder-mounted guns like the ones Debbie had seen in news footage from Kalimantan or Cebu. The three to her right turned and briskly walked down the hallway. The man nearest the door, to her left, tapped her on the shoulder, pushing her to follow them. Norma went next, and she was followed by the remaining Delaware police officers. As the officers led them, Debbie and Norma quietly felt their way through the blackened stairwell to the first floor. At the front door, they waited a moment before two cars arrived. They were old, manual-drive SUVs, like they had in the old movies and music videos, with boxy fronts and shiny black paint.

"Are those safe?" Norma asked.

"Nothing's safe, ma'am. But you're safer with us."

"Where are we going?"

"'Nuff questions, for now, Miss Feng. Have to get you safe."

"Can we call our—"

"I said enough questions," the officer snapped from under his matte-black visor.

The sudden silence allowed Debbie to hear her ears ringing and her heart pounding. She knew she had made a terrible mistake. She had forfeited her agency, her decision-making to armed strangers—armed strangers acting on behalf of her employer, a target to whoever was sending bombs and rockets their way. Debbie wasn't a target. She was a civilian, a bystander, a nobody. But she had just abandoned her hiding place and picked a side in a single act of capitulation.

Where or when she made the mistake, she couldn't tell. What choice could she have made better? Strangers with rifles and cars arrive at your house, cut the power, and tell you that they see you hiding silently behind the door. Could she have refused to open the door? Could she have run for the hills rather than head straight home? Should she have turned in Terrance, or never dated him in the first place? Should she have refused the job, refused the interview? Hung up on her cloying recruiter, or never stepped out from mediating the Merrimakers to take the call?

It didn't matter now. She hadn't. She climbed up into the SUV and wedged herself between two rattling matte-black goons. Norma sat facing her, her tears glinting in the deep shadows cast by her own escorts.

"We'll be alright, Norma," Debbie said, her voice calm and steady. She was 'on.' She smiled slightly in the dark and waited for half a second, and in the process almost convinced herself that they might be fine. Who knew? The Jefferson Group, bombs or no bombs, still stood. They had the money, the resources, and apparently an army on their side. So, Debbie thought, maybe they'd be okay after all.

But then she *felt* that they wouldn't. Some vertebra between her shoulder blades quaked with tension. The Delaware State Police kept their faces obscured as the SUVs lurched forward. Debbie hadn't been in a human-driven car in years. She hadn't known anyone who could afford one. It wasn't the humans that embraced self-driven cars, but the actuaries and their bottom dollars. Humans were terrible drivers, and the insurance companies knew that. The ride through the streets felt jolty, anxious, and drunk with uncertainty. The interior smelled like mildew—musty like some minivan, some school bus she rode as a child. She closed her eyes and thought of home, her home as a teenager, with her father blathering about inflections and inversions at the dinner table. It was where her mind would hide in the darkest days of those dark years in Shadyside, Pittsburgh. And it was where her mind now returned as the black SUVs crept with their headlights off through the unlit streets of wartime Chicago.

36. Stargazer

Detective Melody Jackson followed the progress of the attacks over police radio from her checkpoint on the expressway. Her unit's designated task during a CUE, or County Unrest Event, was to secure the Eisenhower Expressway immediately west of the Jane Byrne Interchange. Their position was elevated but exposed. They had one SVAN permanently placed in the center of the great concrete knot, constantly scanning for incoming DIED strikes. Civilian drone channels were jammed, automated car networks were overridden. The interstates were closed to public traffic so that when or if the cavalry did arrive, it would not have to plow or crush its way through. The bridges and tunnels were swept for bombs. Melody's chinstrap was bothering her again.

From what Melody had gathered over the radio, an automated delivery truck packed with explosives detonated on the roundabout circumscribing the Jefferson Trellis. Initial reports indicated that the whole area was decimated, but later footage proved that the Trellis remained intact. It appeared that its gardens were not just for show—their amphitheater base acted as a blast shield against ground-level attacks. The buildings next to the Trellis, however, were gutted. Dozens, probably hundreds, were killed on the street and in the adjacent office buildings.

A short time later, waves of DIEDs began throwing themselves at the Trellis from every angle and altitude. None landed a direct hit. They were either jammed out of the sky electronically or poked full of neat little holes with the forty-kilowatt lasers affixed to the Trellis's upper floors. They careened into the streets and over the beaches, some exploding in the sky, others upon impact, and some awaited defusing in twisted, crumpled messes on the ground. From Melody's checkpoint, she could hear the distant dull thuds and whoops and fizzles of exploding ordinance.

By four o'clock, ninety-five people were confirmed dead and over five hundred injured, mostly from the initial explosion. A few DIEDs killed people who had been in the wrong place at the wrong time, walking down the street or watching from their balcony. One spun into the Trellis's gardens, leaving one dead and one injured. Melody thought of Teddy, who had shown her the gardens, and hoped he was alright. The numbers would climb as the violence in the streets worsened.

She was curious when that would be. Usually, during these flare ups, small arms could be heard popping in every direction. But today was different—the violence focused on the Jefferson Trellis. As Melody nervously surveyed the sky for approaching drones, the South and West Sides seemed quiet. For now, at least.

They received word that the National Guard would not be coming. Illinois had leased it to Panama and it couldn't be back until December. Contractors from the suburbs would be sent in their place. By six o'clock, they spotted the first armored personnel carriers and AVANs barreling down the empty interstates. They were brand new, fully equipped, and packed with rambunctious young men. The young men had full bellies and dangerous new toys that put messy little holes in things. As the vehicles roared by, Melody tried to read the juvenile names painted on their noses, like "Home-wrecker," "Hakuna Matata," and "Hammertime." As they sliced through the Jane Byrne Interchange and under the old post office, Melody noticed their rear doors all said the same thing: "GORDIAS INC."

By ten that night, the city was quiet. Melody ordered two older officers to spend a few hours in the AVAN, eyes closed. They would be sleeping in shifts until they were relieved in a few days, and Melody was still coasting on residual adrenaline and Armod. At ten to one, they began receiving incoming fire. Potshots from at least a quarter mile away, falling with sharp cracks on the asphalt near them. Within twenty minutes, they had the situation under control. It was a "stargazer," an old AR-model rifle jerry-rigged to a remote-controlled telescope. Once the AVANs calculated the fixed firing position, a drone delivered a concussion grenade to knock the whole apparatus onto the floor and out of commission. Its location would be marked and searched for booby-traps when someone had some spare time—next January, or whenever this was over. The stargazer's operator was probably still watching them from some other building, cursing at himself for not having calibrated its targeting, and getting ready for his next foray into attempted murder or mayhem.

At three in the morning, Melody took her turn to close her eyes in the AVAN. To her surprise, she awoke after forty-five minutes of uninterrupted sleep. She almost never managed to sleep in the field, but her clock read 3:49 when Detective Celine Hartford gently shook her awake.

"Hey, Mel."

"Hey. What's up?"

"We're good to go."

"Go where?"

"Home. We're being relieved."

Melody roused herself further. "What? It hasn't even been a full day."

"Yup. Lucked out this time, I guess. It was over quick."

"Who's relieving us?"

"The Elgin Knights of Columbus."

"They got their paperwork?"

"Yup, everything's square."

"Okay." Melody rubbed her head. "Pack up."

Their AVAN rolled back to the station slowly along side roads. An occasional bullet or rock would toll the armored vehicle like a giant bell, waking anyone inside who had drifted to sleep. They arrived at quarter to five. Officers were advised to wait until daybreak before trying to make their ways home. Melody removed her combat equipment in the detectives' locker room and went to the showers. They didn't work. The city must have switched to emergency rationing in the night. She cleaned herself up the best she could and got dressed. The night's violence faded from her mind as she thought of her visit to Joshua James Citovsky the previous morning. He had held up a single middle finger, tattooed with a "U" on its knuckle. Today was the day he was supposed to talk.

Joshua James Citovsky slept sitting up against the back wall of his cell. Melody jarred him awake with a booming command. "Up, Citovsky." As he recognized his surroundings, he winced and raised his groggy eyes toward Melody. "It's Wednesday. Time to talk."

"G'morning, De-*tec*-tive." His voice creaked as the first words in a week clattered out of his mouth. He looked her up and down. "Rough night?"

"Start talking."

"Are you familiar with the plays of Bertolt Brecht?"

"No. From the beginning, Citovsky. Tell me what happened."

"Herr Brecht was born February 10, 1898."

"Not that beginning. How'd you get involved in all this?"

"Well, Brechtian political philosophy has more recently been —"

"Cut the shit, Joshua."

"Jim."

"Jim? Cut the shit, Jim."

"All I mean to say is that I am telling you these things out of an obligation I have. An obligation that I feel to do so, and that obligation includes me being as honest as possible. I believe it is in our collective best interests to understand these things. Do you understand that?"

Melody didn't. She had never subscribed to philosophies, political or otherwise. If mankind had stumbled upon a half-decent philosophy by now, it would have gained some traction. Philosophies, one way or another, would always fail at some point when put to practice. Melody preferred *policies*, instead. Changing one's policy was understandable, honorable, and even wise in the right circumstances. Changing one's philosophy proved you were a fool before and a different fool now. "Sure."

"My cousin, Cecil, was following Hannah Mah on behalf of some of my compatriots. He did not kill her."

"Who are your compatriots?"

"I can't tell you their names, but they are like-minded individuals."

"I thought you were going to be forthcoming?"

"I never promised to be so granular, Detective."

"But these people follow the political philosophy of, uh . . . ."

"Bertolt Brecht? No, not necessarily. These people share a common objective with myself and many others. My cousin, Cecil, for instance. He was not so . . . academic, in his motives. He was simply a young, untethered man who was trying to do something of note in his time here on Earth. Like so many others, really. He was not a Brechtian. He was simply eager and hungry and able."

Jim spoke with an insecure confidence that annoyed Melody. He was putting on an act, albeit an act that he himself believed. He thought he was a warrior poet, some reluctant philosopher hero, sacrificing himself for some greater cause. Melody knew better. This kid, nearly Melody's age but still a man-child, wouldn't survive a week in central holding without protection. He wouldn't survive a day on the streets if some of Tark's friends and fellow officers knew where he was. "Why was Cecil following her, then?"

"Hannah Mah, as you probably know, worked for the Jefferson Group. She had expressed interest in providing information about the Jefferson Group's ongoing projects. Projects that we were interested in stopping. Do you know what they do there, at the Jefferson Group, De-*tec*-tive?"

Melody shook her head. Citovsky was hemorrhaging information and she wasn't about to stem the flow. Besides, she was legitimately curious.

"They kill people, Detective. They boil them down to their useful parts and discard what's not profitable. Human bouillon cubes. That's what they sell at the Jefferson Group."

"Bullshit," Melody scoffed. "Soylent green? That's some bullshit, Jim."

"Not literally, or at least not always literally, De-*tec*-tive. But the Jefferson Group's 'enterprise' is taking the bulk, wholesale enterprises of human endeavor and concentrating them into a computer program that they control. Want a doctor? They've got the best doctors in the world boiled down and stuffed into a tidy little box. They have those living, breathing doctors teaching their boxes how to diagnose and treat diseases. They have the world's best teachers teaching their boxes how to control and educate children. They have the world's best lawyers teaching their computers how to argue in front of a judge or a jury. They have judges' teaching their computers how to rule on a case. They have police detectives, *De-tec-tive*, teaching their computers how to solve crimes. Do you understand?"

She understood fully. Matte could do the work of half a department, and he was years behind the top models. She could only imagine what Gus's Junior could do. "Go on."

"And in doing so, Detective Jackson, the Jefferson Group robs billions of human beings of their agency and utility. They sequester the beneficial aspects of human enterprise in their servers while ignoring the needs of humans outside their walls. Needs that we find essential and fundamental. Needs that they find inconvenient or unprofitable. And to be sure, they've streamlined their enterprise. Because they have boiled down the world's best streamliners, logistics and business people, to do that for them. They have one soulless box doing the work of a hundred thousand humans. They are brutally efficient. But, back to the bouillon, De-*tec*-tive. Whether or not chicken soup is good for the soul or a cold or whatever else, it's always, *always* bad for the chickens."

Jim Citovsky paused for dramatic effect. Melody was not swayed by his pontifications. She'd heard things like it in a hundred different op-eds and drunken diatribes. Didn't change the fact that you had to get up every day and try to make yourself useful. Also didn't change the fact that Jim had something to do with Tark's murder. "How does Hannah Mah fit into this, then?"

"She'd been working for the Jefferson Group for years as a mediator. A conflict resolution specialist. She became concerned with something at her job at some point, and talked to a friend about it. One thing led to another, and we were made aware that she was willing to talk publicly about what was going on in there."

"We. 'We' being?"

"My compatriots."

"What happened then?"

"We believed she had information that would be valuable to us. As a valuable asset to the cause, it was decided to keep her under observation. Cecil wanted to help out, and he had access to a car. I didn't. So that's what we did."

"You were in the car with him?"

"Yes."

"Following Hannah Mah?"

"Yes."

No phone, Melody thought. That's how Joshua "Jim" Citovsky didn't pop up on Matte's cross-checks of Cecil Citovsky's surveillance data. "What then?"

"We followed her. She was supposed to get us internal SOPs, standard procedures, contracts, arbitration agreements, live recordings, et cetera. It was supposed to be a standard data dump, a leak. She said the whole thing was 'a fraud.' Her job, she meant. 'A racket.' We were trying to protect her."

"But you failed."

"Yes, we did. She was fired before she could get us the information. And then she killed herself."

Melody was flummoxed. All of a sudden, she had more information than Citovsky. "Hannah didn't kill herself."

Citovsky looked equally confused. "We were informed she did."

"She didn't, Jim. You didn't happen to see a man try to unlock Hannah's mother's door on the night of July 28, did you?"

"I wouldn't know. Was Hannah there that night?"

Melody had to think. "No."

"Then we wouldn't have seen him."

"Do you know what, TACs, or trypanogenic ab-drug conjugates are?"

Jim looked blank. "No." His face shifted from confusion to fear as his imagination took hold. "What are those?"

"Nothing."

"What are you going to do to me?"

"Nothing, if you answer my questions. You've never heard of TACs? Nasty little poisons?"

"No. I swear."

"Why did your cousin Cecil go mute when we picked him up?"

He exhaled, his fear dissipating as he launched into another recited monologue. He was a showman, a salesman with prepared pitches. "Every word we speak, every twitch of an eyebrow, every tactical lie can be quietly stolen from us by a camera or microphone and dissected and analyzed. Every action in custody is a betrayal, an indication of how a human acts when they are guilty. A million mutes, what do they say? That there is a conspiracy to be mute, maybe. But not *why* there is a conspiracy to be mute."

Jim's admission twisted some knot inside Melody. The people who hadn't spoken in custody, maybe not all of them, but lots of them. How many of them were complicit or participants in this conspiracy to destroy the Jefferson Group or the likes of it? There had to be hundreds that came through custody. That meant there were thousands of them in the streets.

"You know, Detective, in your own body, the human body. If something goes wrong with a cell, it shuts down. It kills itself. Obviously, we can't ask our people to kill themselves. But they will do the next best thing, which is shut their damn mouths once they are captured. Brechtians excluded, naturally, when circumstances permit."

"Why did you kill your cousin? And moreover, my officer?"

"We were . . ." Citovsky pushed his chin towards the concrete ceiling of his cell, searching for answers. "We were *misinformed*. We were told that Cecil, my cousin, had betrayed us. I believed it. He was noncommittal, only half-in, really, for the cause. I was not happy that it came to that. But we were further informed that the Jefferson Group was surveilling him, to lead them back to our base."

"The woman, in the truck? Who killed your cousin?"

"I don't know her. No one knows more than they have to."

"Who sent the DIED that killed Tark?"

"Again, De-*tec*-tive, I do not know who they are. I do know that *they* thought your officer, your surveillance van, was Jefferson Group materiel. They stopped Cecil for a loyalty audit, spotted the drone swarm, and followed its relays back to the van. Van goes boom, and lo and behold, it was a cop. Not a Del-boy, not even an FOP merc, but a Six Counties cop. Fuck us, right?"

Yeah, Jim. Fuck you. But not yet. "Why did they think it was Jefferson Group surveillance? That's a dumb mistake. It got us involved. Brought you heat. It got *you*, in here."

"There was an informant. We thought he was reliable."

"What informant?" Melody's Ar-mod was wearing off. Her nerves sizzled white like Fourth of July sparklers.

"He's dead now, it doesn't matter."

"Where was he from? What crew?"

"He was a Corinthian."

Melody paused. Her mind was tripping over itself. "Bad-boy Corinthian?"

"Yes."

"The Chicago Corinthian Badminton Club has been out of commission since May. They're not around anymore."

"Well, whoever he *was* with, he's not with them anymore."

"Does the name 'Gerald Ford Jones' mean anything to you?"

Jim looked puzzled. His cheeks draped loosely over his fatless face. "Should it, De-*tec*-tive?"

"You tell me, Jim. You're the open book."

"No," he said. "I never heard of him."

"Okay. What's your group called?"

"My group?"

"The people you have been talking about. Your compatriots."

"Can't say, actually."

"*Zouave?*" Melody straightened her back. Jim's eyes widened. "There we go. 'Zouave,' that's what you call it, right?"

"I *said* I can't *say*." He spat on the floor.

"That's fine. We know."

His eyes narrowed and he sneered. "How would you? You know nothing."

"It's basic search parameters, Jim. Statistics. *Zouave.* Someone thought it sounded cool, but you fucked up. You should have picked a more common word. Something commonplace. Call yourself the 'carrots' or 'burritos' or something. '*Zouave*' is a strange word, it sticks out like a sore thumb against the background noise. You see these bars, Jim?"

He nodded.

"What's between these bars?"

He searched the space, and described what he found. "Nothing."

"You could say that. You could also say there is a space

between those bars. And you could also say that that space, defined by the absence of another thing, is a thing in and of itself. Once you know that thing, that space, exists, you can examine it. See, my partner is one of those boxes you hate. He can listen to about a billion words a second when he puts his back into it. Once we figured out where some of you quiet types were coming from, we searched those spaces, looked for odd things. Patterns in the noise, things that stand out. Things like strange, overused words. Rare words. Like 'Zouave.'"

"Doesn't matter now." He looked up with grim resignation. "What's done is done."

"What do you mean?"

"It's over. The Jefferson Trellis is destroyed."

Another opening. "And you're proud of that?"

"I can't take all the credit. I can't take all the blame. Proud? No. Satisfied that it's done? Of course."

Melody sighed. "It's not done, Ci-*tov*-sky."

He looked confused again. Alarmed. "What do you mean?" Panic flooded his voice.

"Didn't work. Bomb wasn't big enough. Your drones missed. Hundreds dead, thousands injured. But you failed. You're not a revolutionary. You're not a savior. You're just a murderer."

"You're lying." Tears were escaping down Jim's cheeks. He looked like a child whose toys had been taken away. His fists were clenched, making the tattoos across his knuckles pull and redden.

"I'm done," she puffed into her radio. "Put him in with the others."

He began to shriek. "You can't do that! It's not safe!"

"Welcome to Earth, Jim. We need your cell. A lot of your friends are coming in."

"You're killing me, then. I'm already dead."

"You did this to yourself," Melody began to say, before being interrupted by Jim Citovsky's sudden spasm of explosive actions. He leapt to his feet, hunching his back and tucking his chin and arms below him with all the precision, but none of the grace, of a ballet dancer. He bounced as high as he could in a single leap, performed a half turn such that his back was to the floor, and then just as he was about to hit the ground, snapped backwards, cracking the back of his head into the dewy concrete. His arms locked into rigid beams. He convulsed. The air filled with the sour smells of piss and blood.

"Jesus." She turned on her radio. "Medical team to fifty-three." She watched Jim's chest rise and fall sharply as his body tried to recover from whatever trauma just rattled his brain. Blood pooled behind his head as the footfalls of the medical team began to echo down the corridor.

"What happened?" one of the medical team asked as they arrived.

"Tried to kill himself. Slammed his head on the floor."

"Stupid idiot." The medics moved brusquely, rearranging Jim at their convenience.

"Did he?" Melody asked as they kneeled at his side. "Is he going to die?"

One felt his pulse and looked under his twitching eyelid. "Not even close. He'll be fine. What's he in for?"

Melody paused. If they knew he was involved with Tark's murder or the ongoing unrest in the streets, it was certain Citovsky wouldn't survive the night. Putting him in the hospital or in the general population gave him a fifty-fifty chance. "Just clean him up and make sure he doesn't escape. Suicide watch, all that. He talks too much to throw away. Got it?"

They did. After the medics wheeled Jim away, Melody made her way back to her office. Officers and their equipment littered the corridors, and her dark and dusty office offered a sanctuary from the mayhem outside. She closed the door and slid into her chair. "Matte, you there?"

"Yes, Detective."

"Where's your head at?"

"I am assisting AVAN units in combat with 79% of my capacity, reviewing Mr. Citovsky's admissions with 19% of my capacity, and using 2% on administrative tasks."

"What administrative tasks?"

"Talking to you, Detective."

"Got it. Wake me up in two hours, Matte. I need some sleep."

"Understood."

"Matte?"

"Yes, Detective?"

"You did good, Matte. We did good."

37. Hotel Romeo

The SUV rocked Debbie back and forth as it limped carefully through the Chicago streets. They had been in the cars for hours. She would close her eyes and feel the need for sleep, but the danger of the situation snapped her awake each time. Norma would doze off, either tired enough or satisfied enough with the safety provided by the Delaware police. A few times they pulled into dark alleys and waited until they received some silent signal to proceed. As the rising sun began to blanch the sky over the lake, the SUVs rocketed down the Stevenson Expressway at full speed. Debbie could see thin wisps of black smoke rising from fires across the city. The skyline, despite everything it had been through, remained beautiful. The single glaring insult, in Debbie's estimation, was beginning to reflect the pale mauves in that dismal sunrise. The Jefferson Trellis still stood.

They got off the highway and crept down Pulaski to Seventy-fourth, where they pulled into a gated parking lot filled with men in combat uniforms and armored vehicles. Debbie could not see the officers' badges, but they looked better equipped than the Six Counties police she would have recognized. As they drove past a line of tank-like trucks, she read the same thing across the back of each: GORDIAS INC.

"What is this place?" Debbie asked, unable to hide the concern in her voice.

The only Delaware officer who had spoken before stirred to life. He removed his faceplate, revealing a pale and sweaty, cherubic face. The officer couldn't be older than twenty-two. "Staging area, Miss Peck. We should be safe now."

The officers alighted and ushered Debbie and Norma into the fortress-like building. They approached a green bulletproof-glass window marked "RECEPTION." The doughy Delaware cop knocked on the window and said, "Jefferson Group." He turned to Debbie and Norma. "Which floor were you on?"

"Thirty-third," Norma said.

The officer held up three fingers on each hand and waited for a response from inside. He nodded as someone talked to him through his radio. "Got it. Alright ladies, come with me. We're going to Hotel Romeo."

A heavy metal door buzzed as it unlocked itself, and the officer heaved it open. He led Debbie and Norma down a bustling hallway, filled with young men and a few young women in combat uniforms. Occasionally someone in bloodied scrubs would rush by, hurrying to some unseen emergency. Some doors were marked with unceremonious plastic plates labeling their contents—Logistics, Communications, Quartermaster, Armory, Quality Control, Accounts Receivable, Shipping and Packaging.

They eventually stopped in front of a simple metal door with a similar plate. It read "Human Resources."

"Hotel Romeo, there ya go." The officer opened the door, revealing a sad little room with a dozen plastic chairs in neat rows of six and an empty reception desk. "Just take a seat and someone will be with you shortly."

Norma sat down and rubbed her eyes. Her energy seemed to be waning. But Debbie was on edge. She did a lap around the chairs before peeking over the desk. She paced and investigated the room for some hidden clue or exit. Two security cameras watched her as she bounced from corner to corner in her cage.

"Ladies!" A familiar voice tumbled into the room as the door opened. "I am so glad to see you are safe." It was Jerome McKay. He was wearing sweatpants and a hoodie and looked like he had just woken up. "Look at you, look at you! Do you need anything? Coffee? Tea?"

"Jerome!" Norma sounded ecstatic, as if he were an old friend.

Debbie didn't know how to feel. "I'm fine. What is this place?"

"We'll get to that." He smiled before averting his attention and addressing Norma. "Suffice to say for now, it's safe. Okay?" He sat down in a chair and gestured to Debbie that she should sit down as well. "I've got some good news and some bad news." His flat jowls hung a little further down. "Bad news first. Trey Brodowski is dead."

"Seriously?" Norma asked. She seemed surprised but not saddened. Debbie stood still, remaining expressionless. She had figured a lot of people had died in the past eighteen hours, and she didn't mind that Trey was one of them. Better him than someone else who didn't make everyone else so miserable.

Jerome nodded gently. "I'm afraid so."

"How did it happen?" Norma asked.

"Well, I could go into details . . . but really, all you need to know is it had to do with all the bombs and missiles yesterday. We don't think he suffered. But he won't be working here anymore, anyway."

Debbie remembered what bodies in a warzone had looked like from Pittsburgh. Some looked like they had simply laid down and gone to sleep. Others you could hardly believe had ever been human. "Did anyone else get hurt?"

"Not on your floor."

"What about Jigme?" Norma asked.

"He's safe. He should be here soon, I think."

Debbie finally sat down in a chair. "What's the good news?"

"The good news is . . ." Jerome clapped and smiled as his pause grew longer. "Audrey's back!" He waited for Norma and Debbie's elation, but it never arrived. "Audrey's back early from M-K training and she's taking over, so that's nice. Right?"

They nodded. It was nice, Debbie guessed. Audrey was probably nicer than Trey, but she didn't know her too well. Moreover, she didn't know whether the news applied to her. Was this their new building? Did they still have jobs?

Jerome slapped both his knees. "We do have to discuss some of the changes that are going on. And we're going to insist that it is best that you two do that separately, as you each have some decisions to make. Norma, we're going to take you first if that's okay? Debbie are you sure you don't need any coffee or tea or anything? No? Okay, Norma just follow me, then."

The door closed behind them with a heavy thud. Debbie sat in the waiting room as the climate-controlled air hummed around her. She got up to check the walls again, pacing and scanning their featureless surfaces for any clue or weakness. She checked the door handle. It wouldn't turn. Suddenly, the door opened from outside.

"Need something, Miss Peck?" The armed guard posted in the hallway sounded abrupt but not unfriendly.

"Um, could I have a tea, please?" Debbie didn't want tea. She wanted an unlocked room. A kitchen table. Her father lecturing her. Cape Hatteras. A different life. "I'm just feeling a bit tired."

"Right away, ma'am." He pulled the door shut, leaving Debbie in her cage. After a minute of panicked stewing in thought, there was a knock on the door. The handle turned and it opened to reveal Jigme Mahuta, fearless elephant driver, wearing his street clothes and holding a mug.

"Debbie, there you are." He smiled awkwardly and held out the cup of tea. "I heard you needed this."

"Thanks." He seemed too comfortable, even relaxed, as he approached Debbie. It frightened her, and she backed away. "You made it out okay?"

"I was working from home. We're actually, uh, Audrey sent me to get you. Jerome knows, he knows we're coming to grab you. Wanna come with me?"

If Debbie had a choice, it didn't feel that way. She followed him down the starkly lit hallways filled with armored men that marched around like black ants and bark beetles. Jigme didn't say anything as they walked down the hall. He occasionally smiled and nodded, assuring Debbie that this was somehow normal and that she should accept it. She didn't. They arrived at a beautiful wooden door with a wooden nameplate that read "ADMINISTRATION." He opened it and ushered her in.

"Hi, Debbie," Audrey said. She was wearing an olive pantsuit that accentuated the angles of her figure perfectly. She was barefoot, her shoes presumably kicked somewhere behind the wooden desk she was leaning on. The office reeked of turpentine and fresh lacquer. "So glad you made it. Take a seat."

There were two chairs in the office, solid purpleheart wood antiques that were probably close to a hundred years old. Their backs originated from a narrow stem at their seats and fanned out into the shape of a ginkgo leaf. They reminded Debbie of the blue and black butterfly that graced her face after a chair smashed across it in what seemed like a lifetime ago. But it had only been two, two and a half months? She sat down in the chair closer to Audrey.

"Debbie, before we begin, I do need to ask you about where you were." Audrey was deathly serious, but still somehow friendly. "Where were you when the first explosion occurred?"

"Norma and I wanted to get lunch outside the building."

"Why?"

"I was feeling stressed. Sometimes being in the Trellis can be overwhelming. I wanted to get out."

Audrey looked to Jigme, who nodded while looking at his tablet. Jesus, Debbie thought. It was an interrogation. They were scanning her reactions again.

"Okay. Where did you go to lunch?"

"The Cabrini Martini."

"What did you eat?"

"Nothing. We ordered tacos but the explosion distracted us."

"Did you know about the explosion before it happened?"

"No!" Debbie's emphasis curdled the air.

Audrey looked to Jigme, who didn't make any motion. Maybe this is what her first interview really looked like, with Jerome asking questions and Jigme and some hidden panel scanning her face for micro-expressions and heat fluctuations or increased amine levels in her exhalations. She couldn't see where the scanners were, but they were tasting her skin and looking past her darting eyes. Audrey wasn't satisfied with what they found. "Care to elaborate? Anything else you want to tell us?"

If they knew, they knew, Debbie thought. About Terrance and the Zouave and the idiot kids who every couple of years decide to go and try to take on the world with some bombs and guns and then fail and then screw everything up worse for everyone else. If they knew, they knew, and lying about it now would get her nowhere in this snake pit.

"When we were at lunch, Norma asked me about my ex-boyfriend, who I recently split up with. I had been avoiding his calls and messages. When she asked, I checked his messages, and the most recent one said, 'Do not go to work today,' or something like that. He had been hanging around people I didn't trust, which was part of the reason I broke up with him. His name is

Terrance Wallace. If you check my phone, you'll see I didn't check his messages until yesterday, right before the bombing. You can also check whatever else you want to verify everything I've said. If Terrance had anything to do with what happened yesterday, I'd assist however I could to see he was held responsible."

Audrey paused as she waited for Jigme's response, which ended up being a short nod. "Okay, Debbie," Audrey said, her voice less severe now. "We're really glad you told us that. We took the liberty of checking your phone and messages. You gave us consent to do so in your employment agreement. It all checks out, and we're satisfied you've been honest with us. Okay?"

"Sure." Debbie was hesitant. Whatever this was, it wasn't good. She didn't know if she was afraid of being fired or afraid of being killed. "I really hope Terrance had nothing to do with this."

"He did. He was found in one of the sixty-seven terrorist warrens we cleared out in the last, what, sixteen hours? Electrical engineers have a tendency to huddle around electrical problems that need fixing. And DIEDs don't exactly wire themselves."

"Is he . . ." Debbie spoke stoically, betraying the correct amount of sad, dispassionate concern.

"He's alive. Or he was when he was captured, I think."

"God, I am so sorry."

"It's okay. Like I said, we're just glad you were honest. Or, at the very least, a good enough liar to convince Jigme over there that you're telling the truth." Jigme put his hands up in feigned surrender, and Debbie faked a sad smile. The trick to smiling, Debbie knew, was that the mouth portrays what you mean to say and the eyes say what you mean. Here, her mouth curled at the corners but her eyes sank in self-pity.

"Thanks."

"On to business. So, Debbie, as you probably have realized, there are some changes going on at Jefferson Zimmer and Prince. We've partnered with Gordias Inc. in a pilot project here in Chicago, and we're going to be moving forward as a joint venture. Some of our mediators are relocating to new offices in Memphis. That offer is not being extended to you."

Debbie's stoicism dissolved as her self-worth was gut-shot. She was being fired. She didn't want the job and she sure as hell didn't want to move to Memphis. But she didn't want to be fired. Especially not here, in the middle of this pop-up military base in whatever corner of the city this was. Besides, maybe this wasn't her getting fired. Maybe this was a professional courtesy they extend to anyone they dispatched the way Hannah Mah and Gerald Ford Jones and Trey Brodowski were dispatched. Maybe some protocol demanded that they informed someone that they were being killed before they pulled the trigger. Debbie needed time. "Why?"

Audrey folded her arms. "Debbie, we can't let you mediate for us anymore. But listen, that doesn't mean you don't have a future here, okay? Sometimes one opportunity leads to another. For instance, I used to mediate, now I'm an M-K. Jigme used to be a systems analyst, now he's a senior systems analyst. Madison Kettering used to just be Sam Kettering's son. One day, he'll be Mr. Kettering, your boss. We'd like to keep you on if we can." Audrey nodded to Jigme, who moved to the desk Audrey was leaning on.

"Debbie," Jigme said, "do you know how many mediations and negotiations the Jefferson Group participates in each day?" His tone of voice was different, rigid and dripping with manufactured confidence. This was a sales pitch.

"No."

"Thousands per day. Millions per year. Some very important, some very minor. But it's monumental, really, our volume." He looked proud, beaming, like a prophet on a pulpit. "And those mediations, Debbie, they have a real effect. They grease the wheels of this civilization, so that they turn better, more efficiently. Your gang and non-traditional organization mediation program, for instance. It had a measurable effect on violent crime rates in the city, right?"

"Okay."

"Debbie, do you know how many of those mediations you participated in?"

She tried to count backwards, but gave up after two. Her mind was fried. "I don't know, Jigme. Fifty?"

He shook his head smugly, then nodded with satisfaction. "Zero."

"What?" Debbie looked to Audrey, who nodded solemnly.

Jigme went on. "Zero. You, Norma, John Elvis, Abi, the whole floor, you haven't participated in any real mediations. Zero."

"I don't get what you mean."

Audrey intervened. "You know what we mean. That's why we're having this conversation."

"No, I don't know, Audrey. What do you mean?"

Jigme sighed with annoyance but not disappointment. He had explained this before, to someone else, it seemed. "You know, Debbie. And we know you know. You might not know that you know it *yet*, but you definitely *do* know it." Click. An image projected against the wall behind the desk. It was Debbie, an image of Debbie seated at her desk at an unflattering angle, seemingly coming straight from the center of her terminal screen. Below that image were two other images. One was Sandy from the Logan Square Beautification Society, the other was Cliff from the Department of Streets and Sanitation, Inc.

Click. The recording of the mediation began playing. As Sandy volleyed threat after threat at Cliff, the image sparked with yellow and red and green and purple boxes that splashed over Debbie's image. As Sandy's lips pursed in open contempt for Cliff, the image drew an orange box from Debbie's eyes, which followed Sandy's lips. A green circle noted a micro-expressive twitch of Debbie's frontalis, indicating interest. The recording of Debbie's tell sparked more boxes and lines and data pulses on the bottom of the screen. Debbie was finally watching the inner workings of whatever watched her mediations. Jigme or Jerome or their Cloudbusters—this is what they saw when they spied on her.

"What is this?" Debbie asked.

"This is the work you do for us, Debbie," Audrey said. "The work you did for us. You mediated, we watched. You notice something interesting, our programs notice and remember that. They connect the dots between what you see and hear and how you perform the mediation. It helps us understand how to do a better job. What to look for, what to take note of, how to react, et cetera. In the short time you were mediating for us, you were really, really helpful."

"How could I be helpful if I didn't actually mediate?"

Click. It was another image of Debbie, looking tired and years older, but actually only postdating the previous image by a month. The other participants were Admiral Schuster and Sandra Chopra. Click. It began to play. "You know what we did in July? We had a regatta, it had all of the Sheboygan Volunteer Coast Guard who gave a fuck about what Great Lakes Navy Base Limited thinks. We brought all the fucks we gave sailing along with with us, in little dinghies." Click. Debbie's image in the recording flared as her eyes squinted, one eyebrow raised, and her mouth puckered into an open ring. She was the textbook picture of disbelief. Boxes of color exploded over her image as her eyes scanned the faces of the participants for clues. As her eyes traced up and down Admiral Schuster's and Miss Chopra's faces, Debbie's image recoiled with fear and disgust. Click. Debbie's image froze in another textbook image. This time, a display of abject horror. Click. The image froze.

Jigme spoke. "The program is only effective if you believe you're actually mediating. If you believe you're talking to real people. But you're not. You know you're not."

"I don't know anything, Jigme."

"Maybe. Maybe you didn't know anything. But you know now." He looked to the screen. "And you knew then that you didn't believe what we put in front of you. You knew there is something wrong with the people you mediated. Something not quite right with the mediations. Some of that was bad luck. Like, it's really strange that artifacts of Trey's mediations popped up in your exercises. There are literally trillions of scenarios you could encounter with our simulations. I don't know how some lines of text gleaned off of Trey ended up in front of you so quickly."

"Simulations?"

"The people you're quote-unquote 'talking to.' The parties. They aren't real people. They're facets of our mediation programs. Our Organons. You remember the first time you were fooled by an automated answering system, on a phone?"

"No." She didn't.

"Well, do you remember that pop star? Korean pop star, I forget her name. But she was totally manufactured, an amalgam of other pop stars features?"

"Yeah." She did.

"Yeah, Debbie. That. The mediations are simulations. Deepfakes. Not real-world people in real-world offices. They are real-time renders of our simulated dispute programs. Based on real scenarios, of course."

"Why . . . why would you do that?"

"Do what?" Audrey asked.

"Trick us?"

"Um." Audrey paused. "First, it's way cheaper than hiring actors. Second, it's way more effective. Our facets have been learning how to look and act on a terminal screen for six years, which adds up to about ninety thousand years of human training. They can look like just about any asshole from any office building around the globe. They can adopt any position, any role, any situation they need to. Which, in office situations, let's be honest, isn't that difficult. Blah blah blah the kids, blah blah blah the football game, blah blah blah the news event, blah blah blah the quarterly reports. Most people, mediators included, are far too preoccupied with their own bullshit to notice that the tired-looking, boring schlub on the other end of the line is a digital simulacrum, rather than the real deal. No offense, but the real deal itself is often a poor imitation for a human being."

"What?"

"What do you bring to work, Debbie? What version of yourself? I know I wear a mask to work that is, at best, two and a half dimensions. You don't know or need to know my hidden desires, my family history, or the skeletons in my closet to interact with me. It's *business*. You in your mask, and me in mine. Our goals are rudimentary. Our motivations always lead back to those simple desires. You got unlucky twice. First with the one lady freezing up mid-syllable, second with the guy parroting Trey. Two software errors in as many months." Audrey looked to Jigme, who shrugged. "Usually people go years before realizing they're talking to glorified chatbots. We're all too wrapped up in our own bullshit to see that the other guy is exactly as two-dimensional as he seems. I know I did. It took Trey years, although he was a mediator when they were still mixing in real mediations. We're one hundred percent wet-on-dry, dry-on-wet at this point."

"I'm sorry, wet-on-dry?" Debbie was surprised her mouth still worked. She had just spent the most profitable few months of her life talking to computers, showing them how to do her job better than she ever could. Still, curiosity and self-preservation drove her to keep the conversation going.

"Wet-on-dry is you—a real live, living, breathing, sweating and spitting human being—mediating two of our programs' facets. Dry-on-wet is our programs mediating some sweating and spitting human beings. We run dry-on-dry simulations all the time. But sometimes they take shortcuts or make presumptions that throw them out of whack. Wet-on-wet, like you did at Six Counties, we haven't done for years. But we still need mediators like you and the team to show the programs how a real human mediator does it. Corrects them. Steers them."

Jigme piped in. "We call what goes on up on the old thirty-third floor the 'Third Stone.' See, you can try to make two stones very flat by rubbing them together. But with two stones, the stones can fit each other incorrectly, like a cup or a bowl or a groove. You need a third stone to grind against the other two, to make sure they are all flat. Same goes for our programs. We can have Cloudbuster argue against Cloudbuster all day, and we do. Right now, thousands of simulations are being run against each other, but they're no good if they don't run well against humans."

"Just to be clear," Debbie said, "my program. The gangs . . ."

"Yeah," Jigme said. "That's you helping out. Our old scripts had some kinks in them. We could do some things in our gang and NTO mediation program, but most of that was redirecting or deferring violence. After you started teaching our program some of your techniques, it got much more effective at subversion and placation."

"But I didn't talk to a single person . . ."

"Not directly, no," Audrey said.

"When did *you* know?" Debbie asked.

Audrey had to think. "I don't know. Probably six months ago, for sure. I had hints, inklings. I began to understand that we weren't the vines climbing up the Trellis—we were the dowels. We are the lattice that the Organons latch to to learn and grow. I didn't give it up so easily, though. Not like you, Debbie. You're very good at reading people, but not so good at hiding that you see what you see. You're an open book. That's why our programs learned so quickly from you."

"So—what's the deal, then?" Debbie's voice was breaking. Her exhaustion was beginning to take root. But she needed to get out of this alive. "If me knowing about this . . . if that makes me unable to mediate, why are you telling me this? What do you want me to do?" She started to panic. "Did Hannah know? Gerald?"

"Debbie, calm down." Jigme stepped forward. He seemed eager to relieve Debbie, eager to give her purpose. "We want you to transfer departments. Quality Control."

"What?"

"Quality Control. You'll still be working on mediations, but assessing them on the back end. What I just showed you, what the programs see. We need help making sure that it's correct. We need context. Sometimes they'll see something, a twitched eyebrow, a flared nostril, an increase in body temperature, a deepened voice. And they begin to make connections. Q.C. reviews and confirms those connections. Not passively, like you were doing before, but actively. You'll be reviewing the control pane we showed you and elaborating on judgment calls." Jigme wanted Debbie to spy on her coworkers. He wanted her to review their endless hours of mock mediations, judging their reactions and informing the Dinkums of why this was the way a human face moved, why a voice quivered, why shoulders slumped in defeat. "What do you say? Will you join the team?"

Jigme was selling Debbie the job, and now he pushed his closing. She looked toward the door. It was shut, and between the door and freedom were hundreds of yards of armed guards and tanks and twenty-foot-tall fences, then miles of violent streets. She felt sick. Some long-dormant region in her brain, the remnants of some extinct mouse lemur, was shrieking at her, telling her to run, run and find shelter. She was trapped by creatures that were bigger, stronger, better equipped than she could ever be. And they wanted to keep her. She couldn't run, but she might fight. "Why did you lie to us?"

Jigme scoffed. "We didn't lie to you, Debbie. Your employment agreement clearly said that you may need to participate in training simulations but would be paid for such training. You were training our mediators, our programs. And you were very effective, for a time."

The contract. Air-tight, water-proof, no doubt. On second thought, she was too tired and ill-prepared to fight. She could play along until she saw an opportunity to flee. "What would I be doing in Q.C.?"

"You'd be watching—actively, in an informed manner—for grooves or bowls or imperfections in the simulations. You'd be reviewing our program's decisions. It says, 'this person is scared,' or, 'this person is about to make an offer.' You agree or disagree. It wouldn't be some mindless grind. It's a good job, really. Lower stress, higher pay, good benefits." Jigme smirked. "You'd be working in my department."

Debbie's eyebrows raised slightly before she caught herself. No doubt that Audrey had already picked up on Debbie's reaction to Jigme's proposition. The motives behind her amazement were still hidden, though. Maybe Jigme and Audrey thought she raised her eyebrows because she couldn't believe her luck. Maybe they still believed she had some residual infatuation with Jigme Mahuta, fearless elephant driver. Maybe they didn't pick up on the fact that Debbie's eyebrows raised because she could not believe his audacity. She could not believe that after months of being lied to, Jigme would think that Debbie would somehow be eager to follow him around sifting through his elephants' dung heaps. Maybe they didn't see that she hated him and Audrey and this whole damn place.

"What's it pay?" Debbie asked.

Audrey jumped in. "You'd get a sixty percent raise."

"Will we be at the Trellis?"

Audrey laughed. "God no. It's served its purpose. We're leasing it to Gordias. Did you ever see the corpse flower in the gardens? Were you there when it bloomed in June?"

"No, I started in August."

"Well, corpse flowers smell like rotting flesh so that carrion beetles and flesh flies come and pollinate it. Yesterday, the Jefferson Trellis bloomed. Now the place is a bomb magnet. We figured out where nearly every terrorist cell in the city was. Fewer than we thought, surprisingly. Anyway, the Trellis reeks of wealth and progress, and naturally, people who enjoy living in the past hate the place. We had only planned on staying there until yesterday."

Jigme coughed, and was shaking his head again. Debbie's face had unintentionally revealed something.

"What is it?" Audrey asked.

"You said you only planned on staying there until yesterday." Debbie's voice quivered.

"Yes," Audrey stated.

"You knew . . . the attack."

Audrey paused. "Not exactly."

"Why didn't you do anything to stop it?"

"It's not ours to stop, Debbie. Don't be a child. These things are unavoidable. You put people in a close enough proximity to each other, give a few of them stacks of cash and the rest of them nothing but contempt, eventually they'll start killing each other. It can either happen slowly, or you can just rip off the Band Aid and get it over with."

"You could have warned people—"

"Wrong. You know better. It's all part of being a mediator. You can't let people know that they are being mediated. It has to be their idea. If we warned people, they'd hate us. Warn them that we know what they're going to do before they do it? Warn them that sheep, cows, wildebeest, people—that they all have patterns that can be discovered and exploited? Warn them that someone will always try to corral them, to guide them gently into the safety of the farm? Warn them that when left to their own devices, they will stampede right off a cliff, or get eaten by wolves, or, I don't know, run the whole country into the ground? Whether you like it or not, people benefit from being guided gently to a more productive way of life. You, of all people, should know that people don't like being told what to do. To help people, of *course* you manipulate them. But to manipulate people, you can't let them know they're being manipulated. Like parents to their children, like a preacher to his parish, or a shepherd to his flock. We can either help them, or we can tell them the truth. We can't do both."

"But you knew they'd attack. You knew there'd be bombs."

"Obviously. So did you. Everyone knows that there'll be bombs. There have been bombs and there will be bombs. We all know that. We knew just as much as anyone else that there'd be bombs." Audrey was hiding something big. Debbie couldn't tell exactly what it was, but that was the point. Audrey tried to swaddle questionable truths in words like "obviously" and "of course." She tried implying that Debbie was complicit in everything Audrey suggested. Audrey was pushing past something, avoiding it with the force of argument.

"Did you kill Hannah?"

Audrey shook her head. "No, Debbie. You're really missing the point here."

"How?"

"Because, if you understood what I'm saying, you'd understand that . . . if we ever wanted *anything*, we wouldn't have to do it ourselves. We can make the Sheboygan Coast Guard destroy the Mackinac Dredging Corp, or we can make them marry their first-born children and join their houses. We can convince someone to burn your house down, or convince the bank to foreclose on it, or we could convince a city planner to build a highway right on top of it. If we want something to happen, we could breathe the idea out into the wind and someone else would do it for us."

Audrey's cheek flinched as she realized that she had said too much. She stared intently at Debbie, who was trembling. Jigme watched whatever was flaring on his tablet and occasionally confirmed his concern by glancing at Debbie.

Knowing she could not retreat, Audrey charged forward. "What I'm trying to tell you is that the grass is much, much greener on this side. Believe me. With us, you will be making decisions that change the shape of the world, all for the better. This time last year, you know what the gangs in this city were doing? Killing each other, killing innocent victims and bystanders, fighting like packs of wild dogs over the scraps in the street. Do you know what gangs in the city were doing last night, Debbie? They were working for us. While the police were worried about their precious bridges and buildings and public works, the Century Boys and Vice Kings and Almighty Gabriels were clearing out terrorist hideouts and seizing their weapon stores. Where there used to be thousands of different objectives, working against each other and tearing the fabric of society apart, now they are working for a common, more productive purpose."

"What purpose?" But Debbie knew the answer. The Jefferson Group's purpose was protecting the Jefferson Group and its assets, to maximize capital and consolidate power for its limited shareholders. The purposes beneficial to Sam Kettering and the other administrators, hiding off in Madagascar or Singapore or Suriname while Audrey managed the livestock here in Chicago.

"To make the world a better place. That's what we all want. Just to make it better. Safer, more controlled, less wasteful, more profitable. That's all, really. That's what you want, right?" Now Audrey was selling Debbie the job, too. They really wanted her, Debbie thought. But why they wanted her so badly, she didn't know. Maybe they felt that she was actually good at this, that she'd be good at betraying her colleagues and her species and her flesh to train her uncomplaining replacements. "Mediator" wouldn't be a job title in a few years. Not for sweating, spitting humans, at least. Either Debbie would help train the new mediator programs, or someone else would.

But maybe they wanted her for a simpler reason. Maybe Norma was right. Maybe Jigme Mahuta had a thing for Debbie, and wanted to keep her around for his collection. Maybe he liked watching her most out of all the creatures in his zoo, some kept in blood-soaked offices, others in bone-dry boxes. Maybe he liked to poke and prod them around like they were the war elephants his father dreamt of. Maybe he pushed the right buttons to make this happen. Maybe he would just feel bad killing her.

But they hadn't felt bad letting half the city blow up. They hadn't felt bad letting hundreds of people die. And they would do it again.

Ultimately, their reasons didn't matter.

She didn't have a choice.

"Okay."

"Okay, what?" Audrey asked.

Debbie raised her chin slightly and pulled her shoulders back. "Okay, I'll join Q.C."

Audrey snapped her head to look at Jigme, who was still looking intently at his tablet. He put his free hand up to his chin and stroked it anxiously. He pulled his head to the side in a half-shake, as if to hesitantly say, "no."

Audrey looked back at Debbie. "Debbie, do you want to join Q.C.?"

Debbie raised her chin a little higher and smiled weakly. "Yes, Audrey. I do." Her eyes met Audrey's with intent and confidence. Together, they shifted their gazes to Jigme, who was still looking at his tablet. His head bobbed nervously as his eyes darted over the readings from the scanners. Debbie looked for the scanners, trying to beam her confidence towards them, trying to exude calm positivity.

But Jigme shook his head slowly. Then he raised it to gaze at Audrey with profound disappointment. Audrey snapped her eyes back to Debbie.

"You're lying."

Debbie's heart bounced and dodged around her chest. Her liver and kidneys and hypothalamus screamed at her, telling her to flee. But her conscious mind held the reins and told her to sit still. "I want the job, Audrey."

Jigme shook his head again.

"No you don't, Debbie." Audrey closed her eyes. "No, you don't."

"Yes, I do. Yes I do, I want the job." Debbie felt panic climbing up her spine. "Jigme, tell her I want the job! Please, Jigme, tell her. Please tell her." She could feel the tears sprinting down her cheeks. Her breaths were growing shorter, uncontrolled as her heart galloped. "Jigme, tell her!"

As Debbie leaned forward as if to raise out of her chair, an automated turret popped out from a beautiful wood panel on the wall and focused its sights on Debbie's racing pulse.

Debbie screamed and recoiled in pure terror. "Please please please! Please! Jigme tell her! Just tell her!"

Jigme shook his head and closed his eyes. He opened them slowly and looked pitifully at Debbie, with tears streaming down her contorted face, arms wrought into twisted shapes in the hopes that they could deflect the bullets that might head her way. He pressed a button on his tablet.

"Jigme, NO!" Debbie yelped, bracing for the fusillade of tiny bits of metal that would tear her important parts to pieces. She did not see her life flash before her eyes. Instead, she saw her collarbone and arteries and pancreas and fallopian tubes in perfect detail. She flinched and shook as she tried to protect them from whatever unholy physics was coming their way. She fell desperately behind the chair she had been sitting on, hoping its wood would slow the metal thrown at unthinkable speeds towards her very vitality.

But the automatic turret didn't erupt. It hung its head and retreated slowly back into the wall. "Get a hold of yourself, Debbie." Audrey closed the wood panel that had popped open. "It's embarrassing."

Debbie wept, shaking on the floor. Her overwhelming fear retreated to make room for deep sobs of relief, bellowing howls of thankfulness to a miserable world she never thought she would be so glad to be a part of.

"Get up." Audrey looked disgusted. "Seriously."

"Sorry, Audrey," Jigme said.

"Sorry Audrey?" Debbie sobbed. "Sorry, '*Audrey*'?"

"Don't push it." Audrey folded her arms and stared at nothing at all on the wall. She was trying to decide what to do. "Debbie, we're placing you on indefinite leave. Your severance will be made available in one year, per the terms of your employment contract."

Debbie gathered her emotions. It had been years since she had cried like this, since she emptied herself entirely of restraint and emotion, but her survival instincts began taking back control. "I don't need severance," she said. "I just want to go."

"That's not how this works. You signed the contract, you should have read it."

"Well, I quit, then."

"Like I said, that's not how this works. We gave you access to our proprietary information. We gave you more money than you deserve. You've given us two months. You owe us twelve."

"Please," Debbie asked. "Please, just let me go."

"We *are* letting you go. We don't want to see you. We don't want to hear about you. We especially don't want to hear anything about anything you've seen or heard or discussed here. We very especially wouldn't want to have to ask anyone to check in on you. You understand?" Audrey leaned nearer to Debbie, looming over her. "At this point, it would be much, *much* more convenient for us if none of this ever happened. If you had never happened. But we're going to trust that you understand the situation. That you've read the non-disclosure agreement. That you've read the non-competition clause. We'll have to trust that you have a reasonable sense of tact and self-preservation. That's right, isn't it? We're not making a mistake here, are we?"

"No, Audrey. No you're not. I just want to go home."

Audrey looked to Jigme, who nodded slowly. "Okay, Debbie. That's how it will be then. We'll get you out of here as soon as we can." She pressed a button on the desk. "Can someone bring Ms. Peck back to H.R.?"

For a few seconds, they simply inhabited the room. Debbie looked at Jigme, who looked back at her. Debbie's eyes asked questions, accused, wondered how she couldn't have seen him for the monster he was. He, however, looked at Debbie like she were some prize he had just lost. He was not disappointed in her as a person. He was disappointed in a world that would deny him access to her. She was simply some rare creature that he was not allowed to possess. But then something in his expression changed. His eyes lifted to meet hers, and a warm smile blossomed across his face. It was impossible to tell what had reassured Jigme, but his warmth was unsettling.

Debbie didn't have the time or energy to decipher Jigme's strange expression. She felt rattled and exhausted. Her limited resources were being spent on appearing calm and looking for any other mortal threats that might jump out at her. After an age, the door opened. It was Jerome McKay. He raised his eyebrows, questioning the result of Debbie's unexpected interview. Audrey just shook her head, and Jerome shrugged disappointedly.

"Okay, Debbie, come with me please!" His singsongy cadence confused her. She arose and walked briskly to the door. When she arrived there she turned around to look at Audrey and Jigme.

"Thank you," she said, uselessly.

"Good luck," Audrey said.

Jigme just stared at his tablet.

Jerome led Debbie down the hall, still bustling with activity. "Sorry things didn't work out, Debbie."

Debbie didn't respond. She just scurried behind Jerome through the parade of armored Delaware and Gordias Inc. security personnel that clattered through the corridors. Her eyes darted up and down the halls as they walked towards the room where Norma had left her. "Where's Norma?"

"She's on her way to Memphis. She told me to say thank you for her. For keeping her safe, she said."

"Is she okay?"

"Yeah, of course."

Once they got to H.R., Jerome opened the door and ushered Debbie in. The room appeared empty from the hallway, but once Debbie stepped through the doorway, she felt a terrible presence to her right. She looked to find a terrified man, strapped upright to double-wheeled pushcart, the type Debbie saw in Six Counties Detention and Conflict Resolution Center, for the worst inmates, those that bit, spat, flung shit, and attacked without warning. His arms were strapped down and he was gagged.

It was Kevin Doogan. He was pale and soaked with sweat. His eyes, his black dilated pupils were wide and rolling, looking desperately for a way to communicate something to Debbie. He let out an inhuman, nasal grunt from behind his gag.

"Oh Jesus Christ," Jerome blurted out. "Sorry, out, out! Come back here." He grabbed Debbie and pulled her back into the hallway, slamming the door behind her. "I told them to put him somewhere else. I guess we'll just do this here then."

"What the—"

"Shush. I'd explain why Kevin's like that, but that would just be one *more* thing that you could never talk about to anyone, forever and ever. Okay? You have the non-disclosure agreements. You know if there is any dispute as to the terms of those agreements, you'll have to file for an arbitration in Delaware. You know from reading those agreements that you can't show them to anyone, and I mean anyone, outside a Delaware arbitration. You understand that Delaware generally, and here especially, favors the employer. Anything goes, really. So Debbie, I hope for both our sakes, you do the smart thing and keep just about everything you've ever done or seen here to your fucking self, okay?"

Jerome smiled. All these smiles, Debbie thought, why would anyone be smiling? But Jerome's appeared earnest in every estimation. Debbie couldn't detect a single tell or betrayal of his underlying thoughts. For all the emotional intelligence training her position had required, Jerome seemed invulnerable, undecipherable. He wore his polite, jovial expressions like they were armor. He seemed to genuinely enjoy threatening Debbie. He found pleasure in politely explaining how screwed she was, in summarizing the legal fictions that would govern her existence.

"Okay." Debbie had felt defeat, dishonor, disgrace, total loss and failure before. From what she understood, they were all preferable to death, or whatever Kevin Doogan was looking forward to.

Jerome led her outside. It was surprisingly bright and the air was sharp. It was early afternoon on the Wednesday before Halloween, and it was too cold for the jogging bottoms, light coat, and sneakers that Debbie had left her apartment in. They walked through the parking lot, past dozens of armored vehicles, some empty and others surrounded by young men barking orders and crude jokes at each other. When they reached the security fence, Jerome looked back, raised his arm, and the gate opened a few feet. He extended one hand towards the gap, gesturing toward the empty street outside. "Go ahead, Debbie."

She hesitated. She didn't know if it was a trap. But then she thought of what she had experienced in that building and within the Trellis. The streets were undoubtedly safer, and she stepped outside.

"'Atta girl. Good luck."

Debbie turned to look at him behind the closing gate. His eyes widened in anticipation as she prepared to say something to him, some string of profanities and insults and slings and arrows of accusations, but he cut her off.

"You get hit by any chairs while you were here?" Debbie froze in confusion. "Thought not. Bye, Debbie."

He walked back towards the building as Debbie shivered in the cold.

"I need my bag!" she yelled.

Jerome waved his finger at a teenager on top of a tank. The boy hurled Debbie's go-bag high over the security fence, sending it smashing across the pavement. More boys laughed and continued chattering as she collected its scattered contents. Her phone was dead and the streets were empty. Somewhere to the south, the unmistakable "whup whup whup" of a distant machine gun began a conversation. A nearer "tup tup tup" responded. As their discussion devolved into a heated argument, Debbie walked briskly in the other direction.

38. Windjammer

Melody waited in the hallway at the former Six Counties Police Headquarters. It had been a strange week. First, of course, had been the city attempting to tear itself apart with bombs and guns and fusillades directed at the Jefferson Trellis. Next, there had been the efficient and crushing response from Gordias Inc.'s private army comprising deputized and weaponized Walmart warriors from the suburbs. Then there had been the dissolutions and consolidations of close to fifty of the city's worst gangs and NTOs. Nearly every squabbling neighborhood reorganized itself into a seemingly well-run duchy or principality. The same way every mom-and-pop pharmacy had been replaced by a Walgreens and every deli replaced by a Subway or Jimmy John's franchise, the gangs had been adopted and formalized under some strange new confederacy or cartel. Melody believed it was a fragile peace. Most of the Six Counties cops agreed. It was a forced solution, one that presumed none of the minor warlords would get hungry for more power or territory. It was an intermediate phase, but it was a clear indication that things were changing in a big way.

Melody was the least enthusiastic about the change that had been reported to her that morning. In order to smooth over defense and reconstruction efforts, Gordias Inc. had negotiated a favorable exclave license between Illinois and Delaware. The Six Counties—formerly Cook and the collar counties that swelled around it—would undergo another municipal restructuring. The charter established Chicago as the centerpiece of the newly minted Dearborn County, Delaware. It was now the fourth-largest city in Delaware, after Kinshasa, Taipei, and Yangon. The annexation agreement was negotiated over the course of three days with the help of offsite mediators from multiple agencies in Chicago, Springfield, and Dover.

Melody didn't know if the old chiefs still held any sway. She didn't know if the old chiefs were alive, even. Her department had ceased functioning in earnest two days prior. Some officers still showed up, of course. But better-paid militias from the suburbs usurped their patrol beats. Her tribe, the Six Counties Police, was being run off the land. But that morning, she received orders to appear at the Dearborn County Police Headquarters for a meeting, so she did as she was told.

"We're ready for you, Ms. Jackson."

"Detective," Melody corrected as she rose.

"Right." The man who had popped through the door seemed unconvinced. He was not a public servant, Melody decided. His tailored suit and freshly shined shoes informed her he was not on the Six Counties pay scale. He was fully corporate, probably born in a safety deposit box in Dover.

As she entered the room, Melody accepted her fate. It was an execution. The union rep was there and he looked hagridden. Instead of the six chiefs, there was a committee of three. The old Lake County chief was one of them, but the other two were strangers.

"Detective Jackson," Lake County began. "Thank you for joining us. As you might have heard, we've restructured this process to fit the region's updated municipal status. Myself and Commissioner Kettering and Commissioner Dalton constitute the Dearborn County Police Commission. Is that understood?"

"Yes, Commissioner." Melody stood at attention.

"You understand that we now direct police actions in the former Six Counties region?"

"Yes."

"We're here to discuss Operation Windjammer, Detective." Melody was surprised. There were at least three hundred new homicides in the past week and thousands of other subjects to discuss. "What is your understanding of the progress of Operation Windjammer, Detective?"

"With respect, sir, we've been preoccupied with more urgent police matters. We have a suspect in custody, Joshua James Citovsky. Based on his affiliations, and their respective role in last week's events, we expect many ancillary suspects to either be already in custody or already dead."

"He was a terrorist?" Commissioner Kettering asked. Melody didn't know how he related to Sam Kettering, who she had faced down in the Jefferson Group boardroom, but the name couldn't be a coincidence.

"A 'Zouave,' sir? Yes."

"And you believe they were responsible for Hannah Mah's death?"

"No, sir. I believe they were responsible for Officer Benton's death, and we have a recorded confession as to that fact from the suspect in custody."

"Have you contacted your liaison at the Delaware State Police recently, Detective Jackson?"

She hadn't. "No, sir. Lieutenant Gustafson and I have not spoken this week."

"Maybe you should have." Commissioner Dalton spoke up for the first time. He was cut from the same cloth as the other two. Rich kid, Melody thought. Never spent a night patrolling the streets. Probably never spent a night out of his silk pajamas. "He's found some interesting new evidence."

"What evidence, sir?" Melody was curious, but not eager. The union rep averted his eyes as he scribbled. The axe was swinging down toward her neck.

Click. An image of the Jefferson Trellis's gardens. "This is the northwest quadrant of the Trellis's gardens. Before last week's events," Dalton explained. Click. The same image, but disheveled, with fallen plants and small craters. "It suffered some damage, as you can see." Click. Something strange in the upturned soil, white forms buried in the brown-black loam. Click. It was a hand twisted into a withered fist. "A body was recovered." Click. "At first, we believed it to be a casualty of the violence. Further examination unveiled that the subject had been dead for some time." Click. A cadaver. It was a young man, awkwardly posed and the color of the flesh of an apple that had been cut and left in the fridge for a week. He had an unfortunate overbite. "Do you know who this is, Detective?"

"I can guess."

"Very well."

"Is it the boy who shot Gerald Ford Jones?"

"Bingo."

"Who was he?" she asked.

"Oscar Cruz, from Oak Park. A nobody. His step-uncle, Patrick Yost worked security at the Trellis. Mr. Yost got Mr. Cruz the job."

"Why?"

"Why what?" Lake County chimed in.

"Why did he kill Gerald Ford Jones?"

"Why does anyone do anything so terrible, Detective?" Commissioner Dalton asked. "These people are scum. They'll do anything for a dollar. Didn't you see what happened last week all over the city?"

"You're telling me that a kid gets a low-wage job from his uncle, murders a random office worker on his first day, then gets literally swept under the rug, because he's scum? Because he's a born criminal? With respect, Commissioner, there is no motive. It doesn't make sense. I don't disagree that he was the shooter, but this demands further investigation."

Commissioner Kettering looked down his nose through his glasses. He was watching some other scenes dancing over his retinas, staring straight through and beyond Melody. "Point taken and noted. We'll leave the investigation open for Lieutenant Gustafson to pursue as he sees fit."

Melody was off the case, she was now sure of that. She still wanted answers. "What about Hannah Mah?"

Lake County edged forward. "Ah, yes. You conducted interviews with Hannah Mah's coworkers, is that correct?"

"Yes, you could say that. They weren't allowed to say much with the Jefferson Group's lawyers present."

"And you interviewed an individual named Kevin Doogan?"

Melody didn't remember him in particular. Most of Hannah's coworkers barely left an impression on Melody's memory. "I would believe you if you said I did."

"Kevin Doogan was a thirty-eight-year-old mediator on Hannah's floor. It seems he was romantically infatuated with Ms. Mah. Lieutenant Gustafson's team discovered a pattern of cues and messages that strongly suggested so. We believe when it was clear Hannah Mah was leaving the Jefferson Group, he became extremely jealous and decided to murder her. When confronted by Lieutenant Gustafson's team, he became violent and Mr. Doogan committed suicide by police. Upon a thorough search of his apartment, Lieutenant Gustafson discovered a vial of the oral pro-drug poison presumed to have been used to kill Ms. Mah."

Melody didn't believe it. If one of Hannah's coworkers had been guilty of murder, she was sure she or Matte would have picked up some hint of that. But they were clean and boring, nervous but not guilty. "Nothing about Ms. Mah's death matches a crime of passion, like you're describing, sir. It was an assassination."

"Passion may be a strong word for it, Detective. Doogan was a creep. Lonely. Desperate. Hopeless. It was an act of petty jealousy and revenge."

"But poison? Poison delivered using a method that would have taken months of observation to plan? That doesn't make sense."

Lake County took off his glasses and rubbed his eyes. "You keep saying that, Detective, as if something here is supposed to make sense. You're operating on the assumption that there is *reason* to be found in all this horrible violence. I am surprised, with your experience on the streets, that you'd still expect there to be a good explanation for every terrible thing that happens."

"On the streets, sir, I might agree with you. But not on the same floor of the Jefferson Trellis. Two murders in one month. Each requiring detailed planning, complicated execution. It's more than suspicious, it's—"

"We understand you had your suspicions, Detective. But they have now been proven incorrect. I hope you can understand and grow to accept that." Commissioner Kettering's tone was patronizing. But Melody knew this was her last stand, her last chance for answers. So she stood firmly.

"I'd like the record to reflect I disagree with the board's findings. I do not believe Lieutenant Gustafson has investigated these crimes in a way that aims to hold all guilty parties accountable. I believe Lieutenant Gustafson is beholden to the Jefferson Group and protecting them from further investigative scrutiny."

"Yes, we imagined you would. Lieutenant Gustafson has expressed his own concerns with your investigatory technique, Detective Jackson. He expressed a lack of confidence in your leadership and handling of the Six Counties homicide cases, and a misappropriation of resources regarding your obsolete 'Matte' unit. It's fair to say that we have found his complaints to be credible. We take your concerns seriously and will investigate them as we see fit."

The commissioners sat and waited for something. Melody scanned their faces, doing all she could to not imagine slamming them into the concrete at central holding. "Am I supposed to say something, sirs?" she asked.

Lake County spoke. "We'd like your resignation, Detective Jackson."

"With all due respect, sirs, you can go fuck yourselves."

"Well, you're fired, then."

Melody didn't flinch. "No shit." She dropped her attention and turned to walk out the door.

"Ms. Jackson," Lake County said. "Your badge and service weapon."

Melody stopped. She eyed the commissioners, then the sensor panel on the wall behind them. Where were the turrets in this room? She shrugged off her blazer and folded it over her left hand, exposing her shoulder holsters. She removed her pistol, keeping her fingers visibly clear from the trigger. She removed the magazine and inspected it, and dropped it to the floor. She pulled the slide back, checking the chamber, then released the slide entirely, breaking her pistol into two pieces. She threw the top half on the floor to her left, and the other clear across the room. She removed her badge from her wallet and tossed it aside. As she walked toward the door, she thumbed bullets from her extra magazines and they dropped to the floor.

"Have some dignity, Ms. Jackson," Commissioner Kettering said.

She kept walking. "I got my dignity. I'm taking *that* with me." She whipped her empty magazine into some folding chairs stacked against the wall, making a hollow clang. "This is your mess now. You clean it up."

Melody exited the Dearborn County Police Headquarters a civilian, feeling naked in the cold November air. She called a car to bring her back to her apartment. It was the same room, the same walls, same square little cave she had called home for the last few years, but with a brand new Delaware ZIP code. As her car arrived, she called her sister, who didn't answer. As she roared west, she called the only other person she wanted to talk to, and he picked up the phone immediately.

"Soup?"

"Yes, Detective?"

"Just Mel, Soup. They got me."

"Understood. They're tearing down the office, Mel."

"Get Matte for me, will you?"

"They took him first, boss."

"*Shit.*"

"Yeah."

"What are you going to do?"

"Me?" Henry wasn't accustomed to personal questions. "I don't know. I think we're all getting canned in about twenty minutes. Six Counties doesn't exist anymore. It's just Dearborn now."

"You gonna try to be a Delaware cop?"

"*Hell* no."

"Good. Wanna get some lunch?"

Henry paused. "Who's paying?"

"Hell if I know."

"Yeah. Sounds about right. Yeah. I'll call you when we're fired. Should be around noon, maybe one."

"Great. Good luck, Soup."

"Right on." He hung up.

Right on, Melody thought. Soup barely used slang in his time on the force. Maybe now that it was ending, so was whatever facade he maintained. Maybe under the military service and starched uniforms and meticulous training he was something else, something more human. She wondered about who Soup and Tark and Kemp and O'Malley really had been outside of their roles in the Six Counties Police Department as she sped down the Eisenhower expressway. She wondered who she had been before her occupation occupied the whole of her existence.

And she wondered if Matte, whose whole existence was defined by the unmet needs of the Six Counties Police Department, had hidden any facet of his personality from her. Had he stowed away any hint of care and concern for her as he was carried away for destruction by Delaware State Police? Would he retain any of himself if he was repurposed to direct traffic or monitor sewer discharge? Probably not, Melody thought. Matte was a homicide detective and an asshole, and that's all he was. But he was her partner and she would miss him, whether or not he ever gave one half of one percent a damn about her.

39. Soup

November came and withered into December. Debbie Peck spent most of those shortening days evading some cruel death that Audrey Barros had breathed into the winter air, some lance or bolt that the gods of corporate industry sent screaming her way. She had smashed her phone as soon as she got out of Jerome McKay's line of sight. She spent five days zigzagging across the city from emergency shelter to emergency shelter, lining up for food, hiding among crowds, sleeping in the rooms dedicated for women and children. She always stayed near the door but facing it. Every door was an escape route, but also a trap. Every wall was a shield but also a barrier. Open space scared her the most. As she snuck through the city, the occasional chatterings of machine guns would snap the uneasy quiet. Cracks of sniper rifles and explosions would do the same.

Debbie never returned to her apartment. Instead, she snaked her way east and south until Sunday night, when she arrived at the Baha'i community center on Jeff and Ez's block. She waited there among other refugees and some adherents, drinking tea. A young woman asked if she was a believer.

"I don't think so," Debbie responded. She didn't know anything about Baha'i, really, only that Ez worked here and thought it was good enough for the twins. Debbie asked the person who seemed in charge whether Esmeralda Martinez was there. She wasn't, but would be there in the morning. So Debbie found the corner of the room for women and children that was closest to the door and settled in for another restless night. This neighborhood seemed quiet. The Baha'i community center kept reasonable hours and turned the lights out at ten. She fell asleep to the sounds of gentle footfalls in its darkened corridors. No alarms or explosions cut through the night. But at some point between darkness and the dawn, she found herself awake and watching the eastern windows come alive with sunbeams slicing through the cold, wet air that settled over the lake.

When Ez finally arrived with the twins in tow, Debbie approached her slowly and began to cry. She did not want to upset the children, but Debbie had never been so happy to see a familiar face. When Debbie had endured the Big Trouble in Pittsburgh, the only familiar face she had was her mother's, and it had never left her side. There were no surprise reintroductions, no happy reunions. But now as Ez hugged her firmly while asking questions she would not remember, Debbie cried with real joy and relief in seeing a friend.

Debbie couldn't explain everything that had happened. She could say that she would never go back to the Jefferson Group and could not trust them. She said that she was in danger and was trying to keep out of public. Despite Debbie's protests, Ez insisted that Debbie come back to her and Jeff's house to clean up. Debbie said she didn't want to put their family in danger, but Ez said it would be fine while the kids were at school. At the Martinez house, Debbie had the thing that she wanted most. A quiet, empty, secure house and hot shower. A hot shower that poured rather than trickled, melting the ice and cracking the stone that had accumulated in her veins over the past days, warming her bones that had frozen in her trek through the streets.

Ez and Jeff gave Debbie fresh clothes and arranged for her to work at the community center. Jeff explained the rules as he understood them. Debbie would help Ez in the kitchen and help in the classrooms at the attached elementary school. The classes were packed, up to seventy in a room, so the teachers needed all the help they could find.

This school insisted on live teachers in every classroom, unlike many others that relied on remote instruction via terminal. Debbie was glad. Every time she saw video call or talking head and shoulders, she couldn't be sure if it was a person or simulation. When Debbie had called her mother from a public telephone in a library on her way to Jeff and Ez's, she asked her a half dozen questions a Dinkum could never know. She asked questions about her childhood, things about Shadyside and her father. If the Jefferson Group could fool Debbie and everyone else with their facsimiles of human talking heads, they could certainly replicate Debbie's mother. After expressing heartfelt relief for hearing that Debbie was alive and well, Debbie's mom launched into her typical string of complaints about her TV shows and her on-again-off-again boyfriends. Debbie felt like every conversation with her mother was a prerecorded message, and given what she now knew about the Jefferson Group, wouldn't be surprised if it was.

Thanksgiving came and went. Debbie and Ez spent it like every other Thursday, Sunday, and Tuesday, by preparing large meals and serving them to those in need who stopped by the center. Ez taught Debbie some of her cooking secrets, mostly how to improve large cheap meals like millet or lentils with inexpensive additives. By early December, Debbie realized she had gone over a month without drinking alcohol, which was forbidden at the center. She had abandoned all hope for gainful employment, and so the anxiety of gaining and maintaining that employment had dissolved. She only aspired to live and keep living, to find relative peace and safety, to make food and provide her help where she could. To keep her position, Debbie only needed to take occasional Baha'i Faith classes, which were not Debbie's thing but were not offensive to her sensibilities either. All things considered, she was happier than she had been in years.

Debbie was in the center's kitchen preparing lunch one gray Saturday before Christmas when Ez came to find her. "There's someone here for you."

"Who?" Debbie flinched. Beside Jeff and Ez, there was no one in this city she wanted to see. She wanted no one to know that she existed or had ever existed.

"I don't know. A lady."

"What's she look like?"

"I don't know. Black, maybe late twenties, early thirties. She's pretty, but looks pretty serious."

Abi Akindele, Debbie thought. "What does she want?"

"She said she just wants to talk to you."

"About what?"

"I don't know. She's in the conference room." Debbie wanted to run but couldn't. If she had been found here, she'd be found wherever she went. But as she untied her apron, she slipped a paring knife between the belt loops against the small of her back, then untucked her shirt to cover it. She walked timidly out of the kitchen and through the quiet halls, scanning every corner and open door for an ambush. But she arrived at the conference room without incident.

When Debbie opened the door, she recognized the woman sitting at the small round table, facing the door. But it was not Abi.

"Ms. Peck?" the woman said.

"Yes?"

"Debbie Peck?"

"Yes."

"My name is Melody Jackson. Thanks for coming."

Debbie froze. It was the same woman who had faced down Sam Kettering and Trey Brodowski months ago in the Jefferson Group's conference room. The woman whose thoughts Debbie had examined and dissected for Jerome.

"What do you want?"

"I'd like to ask you some questions."

"Why?"

"Well, how about you let me ask you them, and I'll let you know."

"Are you a cop?"

Debbie watched as Melody flinched. "There are no cops anymore, Debbie. Just Pinkertons."

"Are you a Pinkerton, then?"

"No. I *hate* Pinkertons."

"Are you recording this?" Debbie was shivering. She waited for some hidden turret to pop out of a wall or bookshelf to tear her apart.

"Nope. I left my phone in the car. You can search me if you want."

"I can't talk about the Jefferson Group," Debbie said.

"Okay. What can you talk about?"

"I just—I just don't want to cause any trouble."

"That's good, Debbie. How about I ask you some questions, and if you can answer them for me, great. If you can't answer them, you just tell me you can't. How about that?"

Debbie stared at the table silently. She hated the position Melody Jackson was putting her in, but at the same time, Melody appeared to be an ally. Melody had contempt for the Jefferson Group and warmth for Debbie. But Debbie still did not answer.

"Debbie, who was Marcia Yost?"

"Who?" Debbie was confused.

"Marcia Yost, did you know her?"

"Yes," Debbie said. "She was one of my headhunters."

"One of them?"

"Yes. I had about six, maybe seven."

"Did you talk to her often?"

"Almost never. Just for the initial meeting, and then when she called me for the interview at the Jefferson Group, which was months after that."

"Do you know where Ms. Yost is right now?"

"I have no idea. Absolutely no idea. I'm not looking for work."

"Okay." Melody paused. She seemed to be calculating something.

"Why?" Debbie asked.

"I'll come back to that. Did you know Kevin Doogan?"

Jerome McKay's threats, Audrey Barros's threats, and Jigme's cold smile flashed in her mind. Debbie wondered whether she could answer such a simple question. Who she worked with, who her coworkers were, couldn't be confidential. "Yes."

"What was your relationship to him?"

"He was a coworker. That's all."

"When did you last see him?"

Debbie's mind flashed back to Kevin, strapped to his restraining board, panicked eyes scrambling for some means to communicate. "The Wednesday—the day after they bombed the Trellis."

Melody paused, chin tilted down and staring intently at her notebook. Something Debbie said had piqued her interest. "The Wednesday after the bombing?"

"Yes." Debbie was sure of that.

"What was his condition?"

"I can't say."

"What do you mean?"

Debbie paused to think. "I mean, contractually. I don't think . . . I am allowed to say."

Melody's lip twitched. "Was he alive?"

"Yes." Strange question, Debbie thought. Not as strange as it should have been, in other circumstances.

"Where did you see him?"

"I can't say."

"Can you tell me anything else about when you saw him?"

Debbie searched Melody's face, trying to communicate her desire but inability to help. Melody looked tired but tough. She lacked the quiet vigor that Debbie witnessed when Melody went toe to toe with Sam Kettering only four months before. But there was something strong and still about Melody's presence. She commanded authority, even without her badge. But she couldn't force Debbie to stick her neck out, and she definitely could not protect Debbie from whatever the Jefferson Group would do if she talked. "I can't say."

Melody contemplated something else. Debbie tried to figure what was going on in her head. Melody was very difficult to read. "Did you have anything to do with Gerald Ford Jones' murder?"

"No." Debbie was taken aback. "No, I didn't."

"You sure about that?"

"Yes, I'm sure."

Melody stared back at Debbie, reading every muscle and expression on her face as best she could. Debbie was confused and scared, but she wasn't guilty. She wasn't a murderer. "Alright, Debbie. I'm going to *try* trusting you for a bit here. I'm going to tell you some things. If there's anything you want to add or correct, just let me know. Marcia Yost, your headhunter, was married to Patrick Yost. Did you know Patrick?"

"No. I barely knew *her*."

"Well, Patrick Yost was a security contractor at the Jefferson Trellis. Worked on their security systems. Marcia and Patrick Yost got his step-nephew, Oscar Cruz, a fake identity and a job at the Jefferson Trellis. Oscar only lasted one day, because on that day he shot Gerald Ford Jones."

"What?" Debbie's mouth hung open. "What are you saying?"

"I'm saying, Debbie, that your headhunter used you to make a little money. She must've known you were at the top of a pile somewhere. Maybe she knew how to game the algorithm. She got paid to fill vacancies. It seems that her and her husband ventured into *making* vacancies. Gerald gone, you get hired, they get paid. But then something went wrong. Oscar died somehow in his escape. He panicked or something, and couldn't complete the plan. Patrick Yost fried the security system, recovered Oscar, and buried him in the greenhouses that supply the gardens."

"Oh my god."

"Yeah. Patrick resigned a few weeks after the incident, claiming family obligations. Just split. He and Marcia haven't been seen since."

Debbie's eyes darted towards the exits. One door, two windows. Windsor, Sarnia, Sault Saint Marie. The long border come spring, the wild dry West, and the soggy rotten East. Her mother's boyfriend's house near King of Prussia, Pennsylvania. The kitchen knife hiding holstered against her sacrum. "Am I in trouble?"

"That depends. What did Marcia tell you about the job?"

"Just . . . just that there was a job opening that I should interview for."

"That's it?"

"Yeah." She felt a lead weight sinking through her abdomen. "I had a bunch of headhunters. I was just excited to get a call back. I went in for the interview. Got the job. I didn't know Marcia at all. I never heard of her husband."

"If we checked your bank accounts, we wouldn't find any suspicious transactions—to or from the Yosts?"

Debbie frowned. "We?"

"Me and my friends." Melody smirked disarmingly.

"Right. No, not at all."

"Anything you'd like to add?"

"I feel . . . terrible," Debbie said. "I feel sick." She would have cried if she didn't still feel so hollow and scared.

"Because you benefited from Mr. Jones' death?"

"I didn't benefit from it. I didn't at all."

Melody scoffed. "You didn't benefit from your employment at the Jefferson Group?"

"Does it look like—Does it look like I'm better off? Does it look like . . ." Debbie glared at Melody. "Do you think they did me *any* favors?"

Melody surveyed Debbie again. Debbie's apron was folded down, but was stained through to her t-shirt. Her eyes red, her skin dry and chipped at by the cold. Her mud-brown hair, oily and tied back, looked grayer than the headshot Melody had used to track her down. Her nostrils were flaring, whistling like hot shrapnel with each sharp and angry breath. "Right." Melody paused to think again. "I'm going to tell you something else, and again, feel free to add your understanding or correct me."

Exhale. "Okay."

"So, I was told by my former superiors that Kevin Doogan killed Hannah Mah. Does that surprise you?"

"Yes." It did. Kevin always seemed desperate, but never violent. He callously warned Debbie and Norma not to pry into company business, but never felt like a threat himself.

"They also told me—that when confronted by police, on the night of the October 27 bombings—Kevin Doogan admitted his involvement in Hannah Mah's murder and committed suicide by police."

"Kevin's dead?" Debbie asked. She would have been shocked in another life.

"Yes. He was shot and killed. Apparently, on the night before you last saw him."

Debbie nodded. "That's bullshit."

"I agree. But, you need to tell me. Why is it bullshit?"

"I can't say, exactly. But he was alive when I saw him. The next morning."

"Right. Anything else?"

"I can't."

"Right. See, it took my old Organon *weeks* to figure out how someone killed Ms. Mah. *Weeks.* That's *years* of real man-hours. That murder took forethought. It took cold, calculating, murderous intent to cook up that plan. I don't think Kevin

Doogan had it in him. I don't think Mr. Doogan was some evil mastermind. What I think, is that one of the Cloudbusters at the Jefferson Group figured this all out. Set this all up. Because Hannah was going to spill its secrets. I think Hannah was going to pull back the curtain on whatever they are doing at the Jefferson Group, and their Dinkum caught wind of it and killed her."

Debbie sighed. "No."

"No?"

"I mean, I can't say."

"You can't?"

"I, well . . ." Debbie sank lower into her chair. "It's just . . . Dinkums don't get jealous. They don't worry about death, about legacy. They're not like us. In that way, at least. So they wouldn't kill someone for self-preservation. There's no motive."

Melody frowned. "So if I said, I think that Hannah was going to expose what was going on at the Jefferson Group, and so the *people* at the Jefferson Group killed her. Would you agree with that?"

Debbie smiled warmly and waited a second. "I can't say."

"What if I said the people at the Jefferson Group got their Dinkums to help them plan Hannah's murder?"

Hannah's murder. A truck bomb. A gang war. An annexation. The destruction of Paramaribo. Probably a thousand other crimes against humanity. "I *really* can't say."

"Christ, Debbie. Are you *sure* you can't say?"

Debbie shook her head while looking at the table. It was a stupid question. "Would you? Would you say something, if you were in my position?"

Melody thought. Hannah Mah, Gerald Ford Jones, Trey Brodowski, and now Kevin Doogan. No, she wouldn't. It was a death sentence. "If you do know something, Debbie, you should let someone know. Someone safe. There's a war going on. And if you know something, it could help save a lot of lives."

"Right. A war." Debbie leaned back in her chair, and her eyes met Melody's. "Can't win a war any more than you can win an earthquake. You ever hear that saying?'"

"Yeah."

"Well, say you are a major construction company. And the town you are in doesn't need any construction. But there's a giant dam upstream from that town. Billions of tons of water behind a big dirt wall. What's stopping you from drumming up business by blowing up that dam?"

Melody blinked. "Hopefully a lot of things."

"Yeah, *hopefully*. Right. Anyway, that's how you win an earthquake. Any natural disaster. You close your eyes to human suffering and you make money off the destruction. Chicago doesn't have any dams or volcanoes or fault lines. But it does have a lot of people. And people, like water or rocks or hot lava, can be moved around and dropped on a city. Predictably. With precision and violence. You can create a gang war the same way you create a forest fire, with a little misplaced heat and friction. A revolution can be controlled like a chemical reaction. Our tempers can be yoked together and driven like a team of oxen. Our tears can be bottled and saved to put out some fire on a later date. As a mediator, I did that on a small scale. One at a time. Doing it to a whole city? That's a tall order. But if you want to do it, and you've got Cloudbusters smart enough to do it . . ." Debbie shrugged.

"I'm listening."

"You worked with a Dinkum?"

Melody thought of Matte. She missed him. "Yup."

"What did it do? What was its job description?"

"He traced causal factors. Cause of death, bullet. Cause of bullet, gunfire. Cause of gunfire, trigger finger. Cause of trigger finger, perpetrator. Cause of perpetrator . . . he usually stopped there. He connected the dots for us."

"Okay. If he could trace things back, other Dinkums can probably push things forward. See a dot out there in the distance, a goal set for it, and make sure it happens. Hell, you could even plug in a murder that never happened, ask your Dinkum how it could have happened, then follow its suggestions. Could do the same for a cure, a peace treaty, a transaction. Or a bombing. Or a revolution. All it takes is for their handlers, their drivers to point them in that direction."

Melody thought about what Debbie had said for a long time.

"The Jefferson Group knew about the Zouave?"

"I can't say."

"Did they bomb themselves?"

"I can't say. But, you asked if I benefited from my employment at the Jefferson Group. I can't say that I did. But someone benefited from what happened here in October. Doesn't seem like either of us did. Or ninety-nine percent of the city. Or the state of Illinois. Seems like Gordias Inc. and Delaware came out ahead. As for the Jefferson Group? Again, I just can't say."

They sat in silence for a long time, or what felt like a long time between strangers.

"Please don't tell anyone that you talked to me," Debbie finally said.

"I won't."

"What are you going to do?"

Melody looked at Debbie squarely. "Same thing I've always done." There was only ever the one answer to this question, and Melody knew it by heart. "Go catch the bad guys."

Debbie smiled. It was a nice thought. Foolish, impossible, and suicidal . . . but nice. "I hope you do."

"What'll you do?" Melody asked.

Debbie looked at Melody, then back down to the table between them. She didn't know, and she never had. Absent some god-given objective, some inherent hunger that drove her, Debbie had always sought to go where she was needed most. She had no purpose, only potential. And now, she had nowhere to apply it. "I'll stick around here, for a while I think."

"Is it safe here for you?"

"Chicago?"

"Yeah."

"No. You know somewhere safe?" Debbie asked, only half-earnestly.

"No. But I hope you find it. Good luck. And thank you."

"Yeah," Debbie said as she stood up slowly. "You too." They didn't shake hands, but nodded to each other. They would not see each other again. If anyone asked, they had never seen each other in the first place.

Melody walked through the halls and out the front door into

the chilly December morning. Henry Suparmanputra was waiting for her in his black winter jacket and slate-gray jeans, his new uniform. "How'd it go?" he asked.

"I'll tell you over lunch," she said. "Your pick, my treat."

Debbie went back to the kitchen to continue preparing the meal. She could not concentrate as she thought of everything that had transpired. She wondered how Melody Jackson had found her. She was a detective, of course, but she had no department, no budget or authority. And if Melody had found her, then the Jefferson Group could too. Debbie found it strangely reassuring that she could be found but hadn't yet been killed. She served the meal, cleaned up, and began preparing the next one. She slept, she woke, and helped look after the children. Another round of meals and cleaning and sleeping and helping repeated itself through New Year's and into January.

Debbie's mind calmed with the routine, the peace, the ambitionless industry of caring for the living. She gained back the fifteen pounds she had lost while fearing for her life and being on the run. Her hair grew long and she cut it. By February, she had made friends at the Baha'i center other than Ez and Jeff. By March, she had started talking to a man there who was approximately Debbie's age and allegedly single. She did not pursue him, nor did he pursue her. But for the first time in months, she began to feel safe enough to entertain the thought of romance. Not safe enough to act upon it, but safe enough to imagine it.

Debbie continued rebuilding herself until one cold, wet Tuesday evening in April. An unexpected shift in the jet stream pulled a dusting of snow back westward from the mesosphere over Lake Michigan the previous night, and as it melted it dampened the streets. Debbie was serving dinner to the refugees and vagrants and former accountants when she noticed a gaunt and stubbly middle-aged man in line. He was staring at her. Not maliciously, but with appreciation, or even amazement.

"Miss Peck?"

Debbie didn't recognize him. Her mind scrambled to think of anyone from her past that fit his description. It couldn't be someone who was once close to her. He called her "Miss."

"Yes?"

"Miss Peck!" He beamed as she acknowledged him, but Debbie reeled with confusion. It must have shown on her face, because he looked embarrassed as he tried to explain himself. "It's me, Marcel?"

Nothing.

"From the Fourth Water Reclamation District?"

Even more nothing.

Ez looked concerned. "Everything okay, Debbie?"

The man grinned, his teeth in shambles. "Deborah Peck, it is you!"

Debbie's heart stopped. "I think you're confused."

"I'm sure it's you. We talked for like, what, twelve hours?"

She waited for a turret to pop out of the wall or microwave oven. "When did we talk?"

"Last week. I thought you were in Memphis!"

She hadn't left an eight-block radius in five months. "We didn't talk."

He pulled his chin into his neck and gawked. "Ri-i-ight . . . I talked with another Deborah Peck that looks just like you?"

"I'm sorry. I'm not trying to be rude."

"Well, I just don't believe it. First, you get my district in the black last week. Now, you're serving me dinner."

Debbie could feel her heart pounding in her teeth. "I have a cousin. I have a cousin in Memphis, sir. She looks a lot like me."

"Is she a mediator?"

"I don't know. But I'm very sorry, I don't know you."

The man opened his mouth and slowly, exaggeratedly winked. "You seem like a nice family, other Miss Peck. Good people. Really good people. 'Her' helping me, and you feeding me. I won't go on about it, if you're embarrassed. Whaddya got for me then?"

Debbie looked down at the pot in front of her. "Chicken soup."

He nodded and accepted a ladleful from her. "Thank ya, Miss Peck. God bless."

Ez saw that Debbie was shaken. "You alright?"

Debbie didn't answer.

"I didn't know you had a cousin in Memphis."

"I don't." But Debbie now realized why Jigme had smiled at their last farewell. He may have lost the living, breathing Debbie Peck, the Debbie Peck that needed sleep and sustenance and cups of tea and warmth and preferred red wine and hot showers and running on the lakefront trail. But he had kept a version of Debbie on his servers. On her first day, Jigme had her face, her smile, and her calming voice in his possession. By October, he had her nuance, her careful eye, and steady judgment. They had boiled her down, keeping the parts of Debbie Peck that solved problems and de-escalated arguments, the parts that added value and maximized profits, and discarded what was left. Jigme and his Boxes kept Debbie's useful facets, the mask she wore to work and the tools she employed to mediate, at his disposal in some databank in Memphis.

And in that shock, Debbie's mind began to leave her, escaping with the tears rolling down her cheeks. She imagined some happy, smiling, serious but kind version of herself, replicated and spat through fiberwire to needy screens across the world. She saw the lie that it was, and the lie that she was in return. She saw that her hungry body, her aching bones and broken heart had been discarded while some immortal version of her most boring, functional self danced in some box in Melbourne or Toamasina or Dover. The version she had manufactured by ignoring her desires and forgetting her loves. The version she held in full display for cameras and sensors every day that she had worked. The version they stole through simple observation. Their version that didn't sleep or take coffee breaks or have a drink with lunch. Their version that didn't wonder what the point of all this was, that never worried about being safe or hungry or insignificant.

As Ez held Debbie's rattling husk, her sobbing, retching body on the floor of the community center's dining room, Debbie's mind escaped out into the dusk. It floated up and out over Bronzeville and toward the withering lake. Far to the north, past the new city hall and smoldering skeletons of apartment complexes caught in the most recent horrors, the Trellis still stood. Its downward-facing windows reflected every color from its illuminated gardens. Visions of Spanish bluebells, bee orchids, and scarlet foxglove poured into the streets below. On its eastern side, the windows reflected the starless black night that hung over what was left of Lake Michigan. Its western windows shimmered with the dim electric blue of noctilucent clouds hovering high over Nebraska. The long-set sun ricocheted through ice crystals in the upper atmosphere, igniting a faint but false hope that their precious rains would descend and bring life once again to Chicago's thirsty shores.

DEAR READER,

Thank you for reading THE TRELLIS. As a new novelist, it would help me very much if you left a review and some of your thoughts on Goodreads or Amazon or whatever platforms you prefer. Good or bad, I (and the algorithms) would love to hear what you have to say. If you have any questions or comments, feel free to email me at joolscantor@gmail.com. I can't promise I'll answer everything, but I'll see what I can do.

Spoilers below. While the characters and corporations in this story are fictional and the future remains firmly in the realm of speculation, its inspiration sprung from a real situation. A good friend of mine was hired for temporary work in a customer service department at a major corporation. He thought he'd be answering the phones. Instead, he and dozens of other customer service representatives spent eight hours a day calling the computer-automated customer service program, teaching *it* how to do *their jobs* better than they could.

It wasn't a new problem. Karel Čapek coined the term "robot" to address it in R.U.R. in 1920, and Kurt Vonnegut addressed it again in PLAYER PIANO in 1952. But it was finally here in our air-conditioned offices, sitting in our swivel chairs.

That was back in 2011. I wrote the first draft of this novel, then titled HOTEL ROMEO, in 2017. In the three years since, the world has moved faster than I could have imagined. Ridiculous things I thought were fifteen or thirty years away are now news items. This story's shelf life seems far shorter than I had ever anticipated.

What I'm really trying to say here is: tell your friends and family members to buy this book before this crazy real world spoils it for them. Your buddy Jools needs a new pair of shoes.

Until next time,

Jools Cantor
August 2020